somehow still you

REVERIE BOYS
BOOK ONE

SAMANTHA ANNE

Copyright © 2025 by Samantha Anne

All rights reserved.

No part of this book may be reproduced in any form or by any electronic or mechanical means, including information storage and retrieval systems, without written permission from the author, except for the use of brief quotations in a book review.

Without in any way limiting the author's exclusive rights under copyright, any use of this publication to "train" generative artificial intelligence (AI) technologies to generate text is expressly prohibited.

This is a work of fiction. Any names, characters, places or incidents are products of the author's imagination and used in a fictitious matter. Parts of this story draws inspiration from real healthcare settings, all scenarios, institutions, and characters are entirely fictional. Any resemblance to actual people, trusts, places, or events is purely coincidental or fictional.

Cover design by Megan Jayne (@meganjayne.designs)

Interior design and illustrations by Samantha Anne.

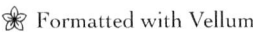 Formatted with Vellum

content warning

Thank you so much for picking up Somehow Still You 💌

You should be aware that this book forms the first half of a duet within the Reverie Boys series. Ellie and Kieran's story might not end in a neatly tied bow, and their story will continue in a second book.

This book is intended for an 18+ audience: it explores themes of emotional resilience, healing, and love after trauma. Please note that this novel contains depictions of emotional abuse, gaslighting, gambling addiction, infidelity, emotionally complex sex scenes, physical intimidation, panic attacks, and the aftermath of domestic violence. The story also includes references to teenage pregnancy, financial abuse, parental rejection, and grief following the death of a parent. There are on-page sex scenes grounded in complex emotions, emotional intimacy, as well as casual alcohol use and strong language.

Reader discretion is advised. Your well-being always comes first.

♥

*for those who learned to leave
who dared to believe they deserved more
had the courage to rewrite their story*

this one is for them

♥

contents

Prologue	1
1. The Same Apology	7
Ellie	
2. Fame Feels Hollow	19
Kieran	
3. The Name on the File	27
Ellie	
4. Off Beat	39
Kieran	
5. The Foundry	49
Ellie	
6. Something Bent the Rules	61
Kieran	
7. Smoke and Mirrors	73
Ellie	
8. Not Done With You Yet	83
Kieran	
9. Blurred Lines	95
Ellie	
10. No Pressure, Just Us	109
Kieran	
11. The Space Between	121
Ellie	
12. When the Music Stops	135
Kieran	
13. When Worlds Collide	145
Ellie	
14. Tides of Tension	159
Kieran	
15. Where it Ends	171
Ellie	
16. Home Again	183
Kieran	
17. It Isn't Black and White	193
Ellie	
18. Between Beams and Silence	207
Kieran	

19. The Dam Breaks *Ellie*	217
20. Somewhere Safe *Kieran*	229
21. A Place to Land *Ellie*	241
22. String Lights and Sunsets *Kieran*	251
23. Barefoot on the Grass *Ellie*	259
24. Almost *Kieran*	271
25. Catching Me Softly *Ellie*	279
26. Four Rooms and a Bean Bag *Kieran*	293
27. When the Mask Slipped *Ellie*	303
28. Now That I Found Her *Kieran*	317
29. A Line in the Sand *Ellie*	327
30. Frostbite and Freedom *Kieran*	339
31. The Family I Chose *Ellie*	349
32. Fuck It *Kieran*	359
33. Spoil Sport *Ellie*	375
34. Under My Skin *Kieran*	385
35. The Ones Who Show Up *Ellie*	395
36. It's Always Been Her *Kieran*	407
37. Everything and then Nothing *Ellie*	421
Acknowledgments	435
About the Author	437

Songs that inspired my writing process and became the soundtrack to Ellie and Kieran's story—capturing the highs, the lows, and the heartache.

Zombie - YUNGBLUD
Tattoo - Loreen
Somebody Else - The 1975
The Archer - Taylor Swift
Outnumbered - Dermot Kennedy
Never Let Me Go - Florence + The Machine
Happier Than Ever - Billie Eilish
Take Me Home - Jess Glynne
Daylight - Taylor Swift
Beyond - Leon Bridges
All I Want - Kodaline
Invisible String - Taylor Swift
Look After You - The Fray
Love Me Back - Max McNown
Jar of Hearts - Christina Perri
Care About Me - JESSIA
Now That I Found Her - GIO DARA
The Night We Met - Lord Huron
Before You - Benson Boone
Constellations - Jade LeMac
Sweet Disposition - The Temper Trap
Stargazing - Myles Smith
Hands Down - Dashboard Confessional
Your're The One That I Want - Alex & Sierra
Flashlight - Jessie J
Somebody To Someone - Natalie Jane
feelslikeimfallinginlove - Coldplay
Ordinary - Alex Warren
Still Falling For You - Ellie Goulding
She's Been Through the Fire - Brian Rhea
Brown Eyes, Brown Hair - Caleb Hearn

prologue

THE FIRST TIME I SAW Kieran Hayes, everything was bathed in gold. Festival lights shimmered through the rain-soaked air, thick with the scent of damp grass, greasy burger vans, and the sharp bite of cheap cider. Music pulsed through the night and vibrated straight through my chest. A rhythm I could feel deep in my bones. The crowd surged around me—all tangled limbs and breathless laughter pressed close by youth, recklessness, and just enough alcohol to make it all feel like magic.

At that moment, you could be anyone and do anything, even if it was just the cider talking, and the world was too loud to make you second-guess it. Maybe you'd pay for it later—with silence, or shame, or the sting of wanting something you couldn't keep. But right then, amidst the chaos, it felt like freedom.

A version of yourself you could almost believe in.

I was twenty-five, still learning how to exist beyond the weight of a thousand and one responsibilities. For eight years, nothing had been mine. Every decision and sleepless night had belonged to my daughter—Mia. The unexpected result of a high school romance that burned too bright and too fast.

But having Mia meant carrying the constant pressure to prove I wasn't a walking failure just because I fell pregnant at seventeen, juggled shifts to make rent, and crammed study sessions between play-dates, school runs, and scraped knees.

My parents weren't the warm and supportive type, and maybe that's why I clung to the idea of a future that looked good on paper. Because their love came with conditions that were measured in milestones and respectability.

They never understood why I kept Mia. Thought I'd fucked up any chance of success the second I missed a sixth-form revision session in favour of giving birth. They've met every decision since with the same tight-lipped concern, like they were watching me assemble flat-pack furniture without the instructions. Perfectly horrified, but not enough to help.

I spent years proving I hadn't thrown my future away. That I was still someone worth being proud of. That I could make something of myself, even if I'd taken the scenic route. But it felt like I was trying to win a game they decided I'd lost a long time ago.

I clawed my way back into education after torching it all in high school, dragging myself through lectures and coursework. While everyone else sprinted ahead, I found myself moving in the opposite direction, buried under textbooks and chasing half a shot at university like it was the only way out.

When exam season finally wrapped up and Naomi—my best friend and the sister I never had—burst in, waving tickets to Sound Busters Festival. I didn't hesitate.

It had been our tradition since we were nineteen. Mia had her own version, too: a week with her dad back when she was little enough to be thrilled by blanket forts, extra bedtime stories, and being allowed ice cream for breakfast (although she never quite kicked that habit). He spoiled her in the way dads often do when they only see their kids part-time and she always came back sticky, overtired, and grinning ear-to-ear.

But that year, the festival wasn't on the cards. Rent was due, college was eating me alive, and Mia had somehow outgrown every item of clothing she owned overnight. I'd already made my peace with missing out.

Until Naomi charged in like a glitter-covered fairy godmother

SOMEHOW STILL YOU 3

and handed me back a piece of myself I hadn't realised I was losing. An entire week of music, food, and an irresponsible amount of alcohol was exactly what I needed. One chance to let my hair down and remember how it felt not carrying the weight of everything and everyone.

That brings me to Kieran—some bloke with a guitar and a grin bright enough to power the entire festival. Loud, magnetic, and impossible to ignore. The type of person who pulled you in without even trying. A fleeting moment wrapped in sound, sweat, and starlight. The kind you never got to keep but remember anyway—usually around 2am, when you were slightly drunk and pretending not to Google his band.

Not that I've ever done that. *Obviously.*

We met by chance. One of those blink-and-you'll-miss-it moments that seems like nothing at the time, but then burrows under your skin like it's paying rent.

He was fresh off stage, sweat clinging to the collar of his faded T-shirt, the fabric stretched and sticking in places, outlining the lean muscle beneath. A bottle of beer dangled from one hand, the other raking through his wild, dark hair. He wasn't much taller than me. Six-two, to my five-eight, maybe? Just enough that I had to tilt my chin when he looked my way.

I wasn't looking for anything back then, just a fleeting distraction. A bit of fun. Something that didn't need explaining or apologising for.

But then he looked at me, with those ice-grey eyes that scanned me like I was something worth knowing. He had this gravitational pull that I never stood a chance against. And just like that, I was caught in a web of something I couldn't control.

We spent the week in our own world, tucked into the edges of a festival that never seemed to slow down. Music thrumming through the air, laughter spilling from crowded food stalls, the scent of smoke and sweat clinging to everything.

But when the lights faded and reality came crashing back, I walked away. Left before hope could take root. Before I dared to believe it could've been something more. Something worth holding on to.

Only a few months after the festival, I met David. Or rather, the powers that be—meaning my parents—guided him toward me. He was four years older than me, safe and steady—the *right* choice. The man my parents nodded at with quiet approval.

After years of disapproving glances and passive-aggressive remarks, David felt like a ceasefire. A man with a plan. He offered stability I could cling to. The kind I told myself I needed, that *Mia* needed.

As time passed, the idea of Kieran slipped further and further away with every practical adult choice I made. Until he was nothing more than a bittersweet memory. Softened at the edges and tucked beneath a life built on routine and appearances. A life that, from the outside, almost passed as perfect.

Until the night Kieran walked into A&E four years later, with blood on his hands and that same infuriating smirk. I was halfway through a night shift wearing scrubs that hadn't felt clean since I put them on, and still a few months shy of being a qualified nurse.

And when those eyes landed on mine, they dragged back everything I'd forced myself to forget. The festival lights. The music. *The almost.* It all hit me at once, like stepping into a song you haven't heard in years but still know word for word.

My pulse stumbled, the air turned thin, and for a second I was twenty-five again, standing on the edge of something I'd never let myself fall into.

I should've just kept my distance. Patched him up, offered a polite smile, and sent him on his way. Professional, detached, and uncomplicated.

But fate, those invisible threads I never quite believed in, had already started stitching us back together.

Before Kieran appeared, I told myself I had everything under control. A quiet life. Something neat and expected. The illusion of calm held together with to-do lists and blind optimism.

But the God's honest truth? The cracks had been there long

before Kieran ever walked through those hospital doors. I just hadn't let myself look closely enough to see them.

Now, looking back, I think that night under the festival lights was when everything truly began.

Not just with Kieran. But with me.

With the version of myself I was before all the compromises.

Because when he walked back into my life, something shifted. Something I couldn't ignore, no matter how tightly I clung to the life I'd convinced myself was enough.

And maybe I'd been waiting all along. For someone to remind me who I used to be.

I just didn't know I'd already started leaving the life I thought I was trying to save.

CHAPTER 1

the same apology

ELLIE

I CAN'T REMEMBER THE LAST time I had a decent night's sleep — where you wake up and actually feel human again.

I'm in the last official year I can claim to be in my twenties, and somehow this wasn't quite how I pictured my life turning out. Less living and laughing, more caffeine-fuelled survival.

It's already too warm for this early in the day, the July heat wrapping itself around my neck like a damp scarf as I dash across the car park, bag thumping against one shoulder, eyelids staging a quiet rebellion. By the time I haul myself into the car, it's less vehicle, more convection oven. I crank the window, blast the fan, and grip the wheel like a woman clinging to the last shred of her dignity. I just need to make it home. Ideally, without swerving into a bush, or having a meltdown on the A27.

People talk about burnout like it's a phase. Something you bounce back from with a long weekend and a bubble bath. But this? This is the tiredness that seeps into everything — my limbs, my thoughts, even my patience.

Still, I'm not about to fall at the last hurdle.

Three long, soul-crushing years are finally coming to an end, and I can almost see the finish line. Two more months, and I'll officially call myself *Staff Nurse Carter*. And then, maybe it'll all be worth it.

I built this life, so I guess I can't complain, right? That's the line I feed myself on loop: *you're lucky*, and maybe I am.

I've got stability, somewhere to call home, a family, and a job that keeps me moving. Or rather, another gruelling placement — standard fifty-hour weeks with all the responsibility, none of the salary, and the joy of being mistaken for someone who *actually* knows what they're doing.

By the time I pull into drive, the sky's painted a pale gold, and Windrush Hollow is beginning to stir. There's a low hum of birdsong in the hedgerows, the distant whine of a lawnmower starting up, and Mr Henderson's terrier is yapping frantically from number seventeen like he owns the damn street.

It's a coastal town, tucked just outside the city of South Havens. A quiet patch in the south of England where the sea air clings to your washing and people think *nipping to the shop* is a social event.

I grew up in the city, and for a while after having Mia, I stayed at home with my parents. Figured it'd help, or maybe it would make the whole single-mum thing less of a tightrope act — didn't take long to realise I'd *severely* miscalculated. It was like parenting under a microscope and somehow, I was always the dodgy specimen. I needed space, something quieter, something slower. Somewhere I could learn to do this on my own, without an audience or a running commentary from the sidelines.

So, I moved here. It's a place you can breathe without the traffic roaring through your window at 2am and where the neighbours nod at you from across the road. Mia and I have been here nearly eleven years now, and honestly, I can't imagine living anywhere else.

Every house on this street is a variation on the same theme — decent-sized, detached, lawns trimmed within an inch of their lives, and hanging baskets so pristine they could have their own feature in the *Royal Horticultural Society* magazine.

Our roses gave up after Mia punted a football into the bushes last summer, and the front gate's been shedding paint since January. There's a metaphor lurking in all that decay, but honestly? I'm too knackered to care.

For a second, I just sit here, engine ticking, hands gripping the steering wheel like it's the only thing keeping me upright. My head throbs, my back's staging its own protest, and my eyes are dry from too many hours under fluorescent lights.

I've just spent thirteen hours in the fiery depths of hell. South Havens A&E. Code blues, drunk teenagers attempting parkour off pub roofs, a stag-do casualty who refused to remove his inflatable T-Rex costume, and a regular who turns up every Friday with a nosebleed. Never a dull moment.

I exhale, peel myself out of the car, and shuffle up the path—keys jangling in my hand. As soon as I open the door, the scent of David's aftershave hits me—sharp and woodsy, with a hint of spice. It's warm, familiar, and oddly comforting.

The hallway is dim, thick with that early-morning quiet. No creak of floorboards from upstairs, no hint of movement. The clock on the wall blinks 7:47 a.m.

Steadying myself with a hand on the wall, I kick off my shoes.

I climb the stairs slowly, the weight of the night shift still clinging to my limbs like wet fabric. The landing is silent. No sign of life. No cartoons humming from the Mia's bedroom.

I cross the hall and nudge the bedroom door open. The curtains are drawn tight, and the room is steeped in that heavy, post-sleep stillness. David's sprawled across the duvet, one arm hanging off the edge, phone resting on his chest like it gave up long before he did.

"David," I whisper, nudging his shoulder gently.

Nothing.

I try again, a little louder this time. "David."

A groan, then a rustle of duvet. He blinks up at me, bleary-eyed, hair flattened on one side. "What?" he mumbles, voice thick with sleep.

"It's nearly eight."

He squints at the clock. "Shit," he mutters, scrubbing a hand down his face. "I must've slept through the alarm."

"David, I thought we agreed—" I start, quiet but tired.

He exhales sharply, dragging his palms down his face. "Babe, come on. It's *one* morning. Can we not do this?"

"It's not... this keeps happening." I say quickly, my stomach already knotting.

"Right, because I'm completely useless." He's up now, pushing his hair back. "One mistake, and you act like it's the end of the world."

That's not what I'm doing. That's not what I meant. But still, the guilt creeps in, sharp and fast.

"I didn't mean it like that. I just—" I murmur, voice shrinking.

"Well, it's what it sounded like, Ellie." His tone lands heavier than before.

My throat tightens. The more I try to explain, the worse it feels.

"You always get yourself worked up over nothing," he mutters, shaking his head. "It's not that fucking deep."

I open my mouth to speak—but he's already turning away. Done. Like the moment never deserved more than that.

A second later, I hear the en-suite shower burst to life, hot water hissing against the tiles.

I stand there for a beat too long, still trying to piece together what the fuck just happened and whether I'm the one who turned it into something it didn't need to be.

I take a long breath, roll my neck, and cross the landing to Mia's bedroom—just another morning.

"Mia?" I call out softly.

"Mum?" Her voice is muffled, thick with sleep, floating out from behind her half-closed door.

I lean against the frame for a second and let my head rest there. "C'mon, sweetie," I mutter. "You need to get up."

There's a groan, followed by the familiar rustle of sheets.

"I was having an amazing dream," she called after me. "You ruined it, by the way!"

Ten minutes later, Mia trudges into the kitchen with her bag half-zipped and one sock already retreating from her ankle. Business as usual. Her ponytail is a chaotic afterthought, and her skirt is hitched high enough to start a uniform violation. I raise an eyebrow. She rolls her eyes like I've just ruined her life.

"David didn't wake me." She mutters, plonking her bag on the worktop.

Without a word, I grab her bag and start looking for her lunchbox. My silence louder than it needs to be. I peel back the lid, nose wrinkling at the smell of warm yoghurt and something squashed beyond recognition.

"I know, bug. But, you're almost thirteen now," I say, discarding the leftovers. "You really do need to start setting an alarm. Just in case David isn't up on time."

She nods, still half-asleep, but there's a flicker of something behind the yawn. Understanding, maybe.

"Now come on, get some breakfast. I'll make your lunch, and we'll make it work, okay? We always do."

I turn to the fridge and pull out whatever's edible. Something that'll pass whatever absurd, sugar-free rule the school's decided on this week — cheese sandwiches it is, practical and uninspiring. I throw in some carrot sticks, an apple, and a yoghurt to make it look like I tried.

"Thanks, Mum," Mia says, grabbing her lunch and dropping her cereal bowl into the sink.

"Are you leaving your hair like that?"

The glare she gives me could flatten a city.

"Okay, okay, I'm sorry," I say, raising my hands in surrender. "Get your shoes on, and we can go."

We head out to the car and the sun is climbing now, casting long shadows across the drive. The air smells like freshly cut grass, and someone is blasting the radio from an open window. It's too early for '80s synth-pop — but here we are.

Mia slides into the passenger seat, earbuds in, thumb scrolling. The door shuts, and she's gone. Mentally elsewhere, physically two feet away. I glance at her as I start the engine, but she doesn't look up.

She's growing up so fast I can't keep up. All eye rolls and sarcasm, with a sudden need for independence. I still catch glimpses of the little girl she used to be, though. The way she tucks her hair behind her ear, or the way she bites her lip when she's nervous. But those moments are getting rarer by the day.

When we pull up outside the school gates, Mia's already halfway out of her seat before I've even stopped the car.

"Bye, bug," I say, blowing her a kiss.

She turns just enough to throw a half-hearted wave over her shoulder. "Bye, Mum."

And then she's gone, swallowed up by a sea of uniforms and laughter.

I pause for a moment, shift the car into gear, and pull away. There's a hot mug of coffee waiting for me at my favourite little spot down by the beach.

A sleepy row of shops sits above the pebbled shoreline, with Brenda's Café nestled between the pharmacy and the DIY shop. Far enough from the tourist traps to stay quiet, but close enough to the sea that the windows fog with salt in winter.

It always smells like melted butter and warm sugar, and there's usually a stack of handwritten specials on the notice board by the door. It's nothing fancy, but Brenda's a saint who knows my order before I sit down.

She's been here for as long as I can remember. Gave me my first job when I was eighteen, a sleep-deprived mum trying to keep my head above water.

On the days my parents couldn't help—and there were plenty—Mia would nap in her pram, tucked beside the café counter, bundled in blankets, no matter the season. Her dad wasn't around much in the early days, and I learned pretty quickly that I couldn't rely on him.

So I brought her with me. Because I had to.

Brenda would fuss over Mia like she was her own. Rocking the pram with one hand and flipping pancakes with the other, somehow managing to do both without ever burning anything.

I don't think she ever meant to become family. But somewhere between the crumpled baby wipes, and too many pots of coffee—she just did.

Naomi's already at our usual table by the window, stirring her coffee like she's in the opening scene of a perfume advert. She wears her sunglasses indoors, and she's piled her dark curls—rich against her deep brown skin—into a messy bun. She's chaos and charisma wrapped in gym clothes and last night's eyeliner.

We've been inseparable since high school. The kind of friendship that survives bad haircuts, worse boyfriends, and the general horror of being a teenage girl. While I was doing bottle feeds and nappy changes, Naomi was off chasing her dream of being the next big soap star—a dream that lasted as long as her patience. Then, while I was resitting my A-levels, she bounced through a bunch of odd jobs before landing beside me in the first lecture of nursing school. Like the universe had planned it that way all along.

Some people find their soulmates in romantic partners. I found mine in the girl who punched a boy in the ribs for calling me a *milk machine* during lunch break.

"Hello, eye bags," she says as I sink into the chair opposite her.

"If I fall asleep mid-conversation, just roll me into the recovery position and throw a croissant in my bag."

She grins and slides one across the table. "Already sorted. Salted caramel lattes on the way, too. You're welcome."

She sips her coffee and watches me over the rim. "Tonight, right?"

"Same time, same place."

Naomi lets out a low laugh. "God, we are living the *dream*, girl."

"If the dream is running on fumes, then yeah. We've definitely peaked."

She cocks her head and narrows her eyes at me in the way she always does when shit's about to get serious. "You okay?"

"Same shit, different day." I shrug, tearing off a piece of croissant.

She doesn't even blink. "David wasn't up?"

"How'd you guess?"

"How many times have we had the exact same conversation?"

There's a pause. Just long enough to be heavier than it should be. But she's right.

"You need to say something," she says, voice low but steady.

Stirring my just-arrived latte, I sigh as if it might offer a solution. "If I push, it turns into an argument. And honestly, I don't have the energy for that on top of everything else."

Naomi frowns. "It's not about an argument. It's about being fair. You're working double shifts, raising Mia, studying, and he's what?"

"He's not a bad person, Nay." I snap, more than I mean to.

"I didn't say he was, Ellie" she replies.

I look down at the croissant in my hands, suddenly less hungry than I was five minutes ago. "I'm just tired. That's all. And he's always working, too. It's just a lot right now—for both of us."

Naomi watches me for a long moment, eyes steady. "When was the last time you felt *held* though, Ellie? Properly held. *Supported*. You keep doing everything on your own like that's how it's supposed to be. But where's the person who's meant to meet you halfway?"

"That's not fair," I confide, suddenly aware of the sting behind my eyes.

"Maybe. Or maybe it's easier to pretend you don't need more than you've got."

I glance down at the torn pieces of croissant on my plate. She doesn't push. Just reaches over and taps the back of my hand. Her voice softer now.

"I'm just saying. You deserve someone who looks after *you*, too."

I nod, and then we fall quiet. Not the awkward kind, but the kind that exists between people who've known each other long enough to not have to fill the silence. Naomi never rushes me, she just places the truth gently in my lap with no pressure to pick it up until I'm ready.

The café hums around us now. Cups clinking, the hiss of steaming milk, bursts of laughter by the counter—but Naomi's words land and lodge deep. When *was* the last time I felt held? I rake through my memory, looking for something, anything.

Blank.

Maybe that's the answer right there. I take a sip of my latte—it's already gone cold, but I drink it anyway.

The drive home is a blur. Hands on the wheel, brain somewhere else entirely.

A few minutes in to the drive, I flick the radio on—more out of habit than anything else. Static fuzzes for a beat before a voice breaks through, warm and easy. Some local host chatting about weather fronts and village fêtes. I let it play in the background, winding through the lanes with the windows cracked just enough for the breeze to stir my hair.

Then: "Next up, a brand new track from Midnight Reverie— these lads have been making waves on the indie circuit, and if you haven't heard this one yet, you're in for a treat."

I freeze, fingers tightening instinctively on the steering wheel.

And then I hear it. That opening riff. A slow build. And his voice.

Kieran.

Smooth, low, unmistakable.

It catches something in my chest and suddenly, I'm not in the car anymore.

I was twenty-five again, standing in a field of strangers, soaked to the skin. Rain poured in sheets, thunder rolling somewhere beyond the hills—but we were laughing, wild and breathless and full of something that felt too big for the moment.

He'd grabbed my hand without hesitation, weaving us through the pulsing crowd, slipping and sliding in the mud.

We'd bundled into my tent, dripping and flushed, steam rising from our clothes as we sat cross-legged on crumpled sleeping bags, talking for hours. About nothing. About everything.

There was one moment where he looked at me like he saw straight through my armour. I'd never felt so known. So... seen.

I blink, the present snapping back around me like elastic.

The lane ahead narrows, trees crowding close.

"What the *fuck* was that?" I hiss to myself.

I don't even know the last time I let myself think about Kieran Hayes.

And I'm not about to start now.

I crank the volume down and shove the memory back where it belongs. Lodged deep. Out of reach.

I get a sense of déjà vu as I step back into the house and kick off my shoes—the tile cool beneath my feet. The silence slams into me, and even my breathing feels intrusive, every inhale echoing louder than it should.

I move on autopilot—keys in the bowl, bag on the hallway table, and climb the stairs. I step over the laundry basket that's officially graduated from *to-do* to permanent hallway fixture and give it a resigned nod on the way past.

Shadows stretch across the bedroom, curtains still pulled tight, holding the daylight at bay. You know those blackout ones that shut everything out? Best fifty quid I've ever spent.

The duvet on David's side is crumpled and shoved halfway down. His phone charger's still plugged in, tangled around the empty pillow like he'd left in a rush. But there's no sign of him now.

I sit on the edge of the bed and run a hand over my face. My body is screaming for sleep, but my brain won't get the memo. It's still ticking over. Mia's tired eyes, Naomi's voice ringing in my head, the song on the radio, that half-finished assignment, and the pharmacology exam I should really start revising for.

Then my phone buzzes.

> DAVID
>
> Sorry about earlier babe. I love you, you know that? x

I stare at it for a long moment as I twist my engagement ring around my finger, the metal cool against my skin. I don't doubt that he loves me. But sometimes it needs more than just words—love is in the *doing*. In the remembering. In the boring, everyday things.

Love gets Mia out of bed in the morning. It makes sure there's milk in the fridge, toothpaste in the drawer, and enough energy left over to ask how my shift went. Even if the answer is just, *I don't want to talk about it.*

I don't need grand gestures. I don't need fireworks, candlelit dinners, or a trail of rose petals leading to the fucking dishwasher. I just want closeness. The kind that wraps around you and *stays*. I want to be known fully, gently, without condition. I want a love that feels like breathing, not suffocating. A partnership, not a performance.

I used to think we were building that. That it would grow in the in-between moments. Tired laughs, brushed shoulders, shared glances across messy rooms.

But now it just feels like I'm clinging to a version of us that only ever lived in my head. I don't know when things shifted, or when the warmth dulled into habit. When I stopped expecting to be held and started feeling selfish for even wanting it.

Still. I don't want a fight. Not today.

> Don't worry. I love you too ♥

It's automatic, a reply I've sent a hundred times before. Short, soft, and non-confrontational. I know what he needs to hear, and I'm too tired to serve up anything else.

I tuck my phone under the pillow, crawl beneath the sheets, and let the quiet press around me.

My eyes close, but sleep doesn't follow. I lie there, staring up at the familiar outline of the ceiling, and wonder if this is what love is supposed to feel like.

Because if it is… when did it start to feel so lonely?

CHAPTER 2
fame feels hollow

KIERAN

THE TOUR BUS IS MOVING, but nothing else is.

I'm slouched on the sofa, one arm flung over my eyes like it might block out more than the harsh glare of the overhead bulbs. My ears are still ringing, my shirt's still damp, and the adrenaline is long gone.

Outside, streaks of orange and black blur through the tinted windows—just another motorway driving us to a new city, where we'll do it all over again.

We're halfway through the UK run. Six months of promoting the hell out of our music, trying to prove to the label that we're worth the gamble. It's kind of a trial run to see if the hype holds, to see if we're more than noise and novelty.

It's been years of grinding. Late nights, cheap gigs, vans that have seen better days. Now, for the first time, it actually feels like we're getting somewhere. We're playing in bigger venues, the crowds are getting louder, and the fans sing lyrics back at us like they mean it.

Still, I feel like I'm five minutes from falling apart. Because with the momentum comes the pressure—the label breathing down our necks, the deadlines stacking up, the spotlight that never blinks.

And beneath it all, there's this constant, low hum of fear. That I'll mess it up. That I'll be the one to crack under it and take everything down with me.

My phone's a blur of notifications, all bleeding into each other—texts from near-strangers, a few names I half-recognise, a missed call I'm pretty sure is PR.

I ignore it all. Open Instagram. Close it. Open it again two seconds later, like maybe this time it'll show me something that matters. Something that feels real, instead of just more noise.

It doesn't.

There's a tagged photo. Someone in the crowd caught me mid-song, jaw clenched, head thrown back under the lights. Hair a mess, sweat curling at my temples. The caption calls me a *legend*, but all I see is someone trying too hard to make it look like he know's what he's doing.

The door at the back of the bus creeps open, and my attention shifts as Luca strolls in, dragging his guitar case behind him. His dirty blond hair sticking up in every direction, like he's just rolled off a beach instead of a stage. He's the only one who manages to treat this life like a damn holiday—so laid-back, he's horizontal.

Luca tosses me a beer and drops onto the sofa next to me, cracking his open like this is just another Tuesday night. "You look like shit, mate."

I grunt. "Cheers."

He laughs and leans back, taking a long swig. "Didn't think you'd survive that last encore, thought we were gonna have to drag you off stage like a passed-out toddler."

I smirk. "I'm fine. Getting pretty good at making it look like I have it all together."

"Sure you are." He eyes me over the rim of his bottle. "Thing is, you've been doing it for a while now, Kieran."

Meeting his gaze, I think about saying something real—that I *still* love the music, that being on stage feels like the only time I can breathe, but it's everything that comes with it that's eating me alive.

I swallow it down and let the moment pass. "Tell that to the crowd."

Luca shrugs, but he doesn't push it. He just finishes his drink and

SOMEHOW STILL YOU 21

stands, stretching his arms up with a groan. "Get some sleep, bro," he says, heading toward the bunks. "You're starting to look like your own before photo."

I stay where I am, beer still sweating in my hand. My phone's back in my grip, the screen lighting up my face in the dark. My thumb shifts to the photo gallery. I open it—not even sure why.

The screen floods with memories. Old photos of us back in the dive bar days, high on hope and instant noodles. Ryder pulling faces, Luca half-naked in the background of nearly every shot, Theo passed out in a drum case. I'm smiling in most of them. Genuine smiles.

I swipe to the next photo. And *fuck*.

Her face hits like a sucker punch to the ribs. Long brown hair tangled from dancing, cheeks dusted with glitter, that wide, sun-swallowing grin. She isn't looking at the camera, just off to the side, her half-lidded eyes fixed on something else, lost completely to the music.

And just like that, it's all back. The heat, the noise, the blur of that entire week. But mostly, just her. The girl in all the colours. The one who made the entire world slow down just long enough for me to notice.

She looked like freedom. *God*, I just wanted to know her.

Four Years Ago

It's the end of our set on the first day. We're playing one of the smaller stages, but it feels massive to us. My pulse is still hammering from the final chorus, chest thudding like it hasn't decided if we're flying or free-falling.

Then I see her.

She's leaning against the barricade, plastic cup in one hand, the other resting on the metal rail behind her like she owns it. She's not screaming or filming like half the crowd—she's just watching. Locked in. As if the music's under her skin and she's letting it move through her.

She's wearing this glittery dress that catches the light every time she shifts, legs for days, curves that make it impossible not to stare, and these mismatched earrings that somehow pull it all together. Glitter dusts her cheeks. Her long brown hair hangs in loose, heat-softened waves, like it's been kissed by summer.

She's not trying to stand out. She just does.

And she's smiling. Not the polite kind. Not the kind you give a stranger. This one's real.

Before I've even decided to move, I'm already jumping off the stage. I grab a beer from the side and head straight for her, heart thudding harder than it did mid-set.

She sees me coming. Smirks. Doesn't move an inch.

"Hey, you," I say, flashing a grin.

Her lips curl. "Hey," she says casually, like I'm not dripping with sweat and nerves. "You're Kieran, right?"

I raise a brow. "That obvious, huh?"

Her head tilts, just slightly. She gives me a slow once-over that feels less like a glance and more like an X-ray. "I think it's the hair." She reaches into her bag, pulls out a flyer, and waves it at me. "Also, this says so."

"Ah. Solid detective work."

"I'm Ellie."

"Ellie." I let it settle in my mouth.

"Eleanor, technically. But I only hear that when I'm in trouble."

I grin. "Trouble, huh? Good to know."

She raises an eyebrow. "Why? Planning to cause some?"

I lean in a little, just enough to test the air between us. "I'll let you know."

Her smile curves sideways, a little mischievous now.

"Beer?" I ask, holding out the bottle.

She eyes it, then me. "You always this charming, or is this just a post-set ego trip?"

"I'm a very charming man."

"Hmm." She takes the bottle and lifts it in a mock salute. "Alright then, rockstar. You've got five minutes. I've got a hotdog on the way."

I laugh. "I'm competing with meat in a bun?"

"Not just any meat," she says seriously. "Naomi's been talking about them like they're the best thing since sliced bread."

"Big competition, then." I say. "But I've got charm, half a beer, and the confidence of a man who just wore leather trousers in thirty-degree heat."

She gives me a long once-over. "The trousers were—a choice."

"That sounds dangerously close to an insult."

"More of an observation."

God, she's quick. Everything I throw, she volleys back like it's nothing. No fawning. No wide-eyed awe. Just standing there, arms loose, eyes bright, like she's waiting to see if I'll drop the act or double down.

Fuck, if she doesn't intrigue the hell out of me.

I lean against the barrier beside her—close, but not too close. "Who's Naomi? Your wing woman?"

"She's my best friend," Ellie says, taking a sip of beer. "We've been coming here since we were nineteen."

"You two tear it up every year?"

"We used to. These days, it's two nights of chaos followed by the rest of the week on our backs, drinking coffee in the acoustic tent."

I chuckle. "Rock and roll."

"Exactly." She bumps her shoulder against mine, light but lingering.

I glance sideways. "So, Ellie. What's a guy gotta do to earn extra time?"

She looks at me, long and steady. "Be real."

I nod. "Yeah? I think I can manage that."

She smiles—soft, but guarded. "Then maybe you'll get it."

"I think we're about to have the best week ever." I grin.

Her eyes flick to mine. "What makes you so sure?"

I shrug. "I'm standing here, aren't I?"

She smirks. "Bit full of yourself."

"Occupational hazard."

She tilts her head, voice dipping just a little. "What makes you think I'd be interested in spending the week with you?"

I lean in close enough to feel the warmth rolling off her. Close enough to see the freckles dusting her nose, the tiny heart-shaped mole just beneath her left cheekbone.

"Because I'm not just some rockstar, Ells," I say low. "I'm the guy who *spotted you in the crowd—the girl in all the colours—who couldn't stop grinning once the music started."*

Her lips twitch. A faint blush rises in her cheeks.

"And if I don't usually go for the whole lead singer thing?"

"You'd be missing out," I say, with a wink. "But I'm persistent."

She stepped back a little, her smile widening. "We'll see about that."

A jolt from the bus brings me back. I blink at the ceiling like I've just surfaced from underwater. I glance at the photo of Ellie that's still lit up on my screen, her frozen smile shining back at me. My thumb hovers over it, as if I might delete it.

I don't. I just lock the screen and toss the phone onto the cushion beside me.

Christ.

I hadn't let myself think about her in, I don't even know how long. Not in a way that makes something shift behind my ribs.

When she left with no explanation and no way to reach her—it cracked something open in me and left this unfinished corner in the back of my mind I never quite knew what to do with.

I told myself it was just a week. A blip. A bit of fun wrapped in glitter, loud music, and cider buzz.

Still—there was something there. Some spark of *what if* that never had the chance to burn into anything real.

I tried to let it go. And mostly, I did. Buried it under work, noise, late nights, louder crowds. Threw myself into the blur of it all. There were women, too. A string of them, if I'm honest. Some stayed a while. Most didn't. None of them ever really stuck.

They liked the version of me that lived on stage. The noise, the swagger, the stories. They wanted the idea of me, not the quiet parts. Not the mornings after or the soft-spoken bits. But Ellie—she never wanted the façade. She saw right through it.

She made me feel… seen. Not watched, not admired—*seen*. And no one's ever made me feel like that since. She left a mark. Not the kind that fades, not really. Just settles somewhere low and steady, like a chord still vibrating long after the song ends.

Maybe it was never meant to last. Maybe we were just two people who caught each other at the right moment—just not the right time. I don't know. I gave up trying to make sense of it a long time ago.

It's too late for all that, anyway. She's gone, and I'm still here.

But there's this gnawing in my gut I can't shake. Like something's shifting. Like the ground's about to move beneath me, whether I'm ready or not.

I close my eyes. Try to sleep. Try to push it down like I always do.

But it lingers.

Won't let go.

Not tonight.

CHAPTER 3

the name on the file

ELLIE

THE FLUORESCENT LIGHTS AT South Havens Trauma Hospital buzz overhead, flickering with a stubborn defiance that makes me want to climb up there and hand-deliver them to maintenance as a personal favour. The hum burrows into my skull, a constant, low-level static that never quits. Pretty sure they're engineering my slow descent into madness, one flicker at a time.

The waiting room isn't just full—it's bursting at the seams. The air's thick with stale heat, cheap hand sanitiser, and that unmistakable mix of blood and burnt toast. In the corner, the air con wheezes as it tries to keep up, but like everything else in this place, it's barely holding on.

Patients spill into every corner. There's a guy cradling his wrist like it might detach at any moment, two teenagers bickering over whose turn it is, and someone snoring in the far corner, loud enough to rattle the vending machine.

Just another night in A&E.

Beyond the chaos of the waiting area, the department pulses with motion. A blur of scrubs, rushing feet, and half-shouted orders. Monitors beep in uneven rhythms, gurneys rattle down the hall, and a paramedic barrels past, shouting out vitals like he's narrating a Formula One race.

I lean on the edge of the reception desk, trying to roll out a tight knot between my shoulder blades. Naomi nudges me gently, sliding a paper cup into my hand. "You look like you need this more than I do right now."

"You're an actual angel sent from heaven." I take a sip and immediately grimace. "I take that back. What in the devil's name is this?"

"Drink," she says. "It's basically poison, but it's caffeine."

"It's a human rights violation."

She grins. "Welcome to the NHS."

The intercom crackles to life, a garbled voice calling for a trauma consult. No one even flinches. We're all too far gone to register anything but our own to-do lists.

"Ellie, you're up in bay three." Linda appears at the desk, clipboard in hand, blonde ponytail slightly lopsided. Her eyes are tired, but she still moves like someone running on pure instinct. She's the nurse in charge tonight and also my mentor—which sounds formal, but mostly means she trusts me not to cock things up too badly.

Lately, that trust has been showing. Each shift, I feel a little steadier. A little surer of my hands, my instincts, my place in the pandemonium. The doubt's still there, but quieter now. Drowned out by the rhythm of doing.

"Laceration to the hand," Linda says. "Looks straightforward. Patch him up and send him on his way."

"Got it," I reply, stepping forward to take the file. I scan the top with automatic precision, my brain already shifting into clinical mode.

Male. Age thirty. Left hand. Minor laceration.

And then I freeze.

Name: Kieran Hayes.

My heart stumbles in my chest, skipping like a scratched CD.

No.

The name stares up at me, black ink on white paper. I grip the clipboard tighter, the edges biting into my palm.

It can't be him. Surely not. Kieran Hayes isn't that uncommon. *Right?* But the second I see it, I'm already gone.

I can't sleep.

I've tried—twice. First lying flat. Then curled on my side, pillow over my head like I could muffle the thoughts and the laughter echoing from a nearby tent. But the air's too warm, the ground too lumpy, and my brain won't shut the hell up.

Then I hear it.

A guitar strumming faintly and unpolished, as if only for themselves.

I sit up, heart already tugging me toward it. I yank on my hoodie and wellies, unzip the tent as quietly as I can—careful not to wake Naomi—and step out into the night.

It's calmer out here.

The anarchy of the day has faded into a low hum. Tents glowing, whispered conversations bleeding into the open air. The Ferris wheel in the distance is still lit, slowly spinning, casting streaks of pink and gold into the night sky.

I follow the sound.

Kieran's sitting on a log near the edge of the lake, his back to me, guitar balanced on his knee. He's hunched slightly, plucking at the strings like they're helping him think.

I pause for a moment, just watching him—lit by moonlight and the occasional flicker of the wheel's glow. He looks peaceful.

"Couldn't sleep?" I breathe.

He glances over his shoulder and smiles—God, that smile—then he shifts sideways, patting the log beside him.

We sit for a while. Saying nothing. Letting the moment settle around us like a blanket.

Kieran keeps strumming, aimless but soft, like the guitar's an extension of his thoughts. I stare out at the lake, watching the water catch the distant lights in ripples. Now and then, laughter echoes from the tents behind us, but it feels far away. Like we're in a pocket of something untouched.

It's just easy *with him.*

The silence drifts into conversation—not deep, not heavy. Just little things. As natural as breathing.

He plucks at a quiet chord and lets it ring out into the air between us. "Where do you see yourself in five years?"

I don't answer straight away. I watch the Ferris wheel turning in the distance, slow and dreamlike.

It's such a simple question, but my brain scrambles under it. I think of my *parents and the pressure they pile on me. I think of deadlines and exhausted nights at the library, of lectures that blur together.*

Mostly, I think of Mia. Of how everything I do is for her. But at this moment... I don't want to tell him about her. Not yet.

Right now, I'm not a struggling single mum buried in coursework and bills. I'm just a girl under the stars beside a boy who makes the world go quiet.

I swallow. "Honestly?" *I say, turning to look at him.* "I have no idea."

Kieran laughs softly, not mocking—just like he gets it. "Fair."

"I mean, my parents want me to do something sensible—secure—you know? Whatever that means. Uni, job, house, stability—tick all the boxes so they can say they raised me right."

He hums. "And what do you want?"

I shrug, eyes still on the water, because no-one has ever really asked me that before. "I don't know. I've always thought about being a nurse."

I pause, tugging at the frayed edge of my sleeve. "It's not some noble thing. I just... I like helping people. Showing up when someone needs it most. Just being there when they are at their most vulnerable."

Kieran says nothing. He just listens, and it makes the words come easier.

"I've spent so much of my life feeling like I'm floating. But when I think about nursing, it feels... real. Like I could actually make a difference."

I glance at him, a self-conscious laugh slipping out. "That probably sounds stupid."

He shakes his head. "Far from it."

"Yeah, well... I doubt it will ever happen."

He shifts beside me, then places his guitar on the ground, turning so we're facing each other. His voice softens.

"You can be anything you wanna be, Ellie. You just have to believe it."

The words land heavier than they should. Not cheesy. Not thrown away. Just... honest.

My heart squeezes.

I clear my throat. "Alright, wise one. What about you? Where do you see yourself in five years?"

He leans back slightly, eyes flicking up to the stars. "Still playing, hopefully. Touring. Writing. Just... making music, I guess. Making my dad proud."

There's a pause.

He doesn't mention his mum.

And I notice.

The silence hums for a beat too long. I don't ask—but something in my face must shift, some unspoken question rising to the surface—because he sees it.

His eyes flick to mine. "She died when I was eleven. Breast cancer."

The words are plain. Undramatic. But they land like a stone in my chest. I shift closer, our knees brushing again. A slight movement, instinctive. "Kieran…"

"It's alright." He says it like a reflex, but his voice catches just slightly on the end. "I don't really talk about it much. My dad's solid. He raised me. Did the best he could. But yeah… it's just been us for a long time."

There's something in his voice that sounds like strength held together by worn threads. And I suddenly want to touch him. Not for comfort. Not for sympathy. Just so he knows, I'm here with him.

I reach for his hand. Thread my fingers through his.

"That must have been so hard," I say, my voice low, almost afraid to disturb the space between us.

He swallows, nods. "It was just as I was starting Year Seven. New school, new everything. Everyone else was busy figuring out who they were, and I was just… trying to get through the day without falling apart."

His thumb brushes over mine, slow and deliberate.

"I didn't handle it well," he says after a moment. "Not for a long time. I was angry. Quiet. I couldn't focus on anything. I felt like there was this… weight inside me that no one else could see."

He draws a breath, voice softening. "Then I met Theo, our drummer. He was all chaos and bad decisions. Just showed up one day and decided I needed shaking loose. Dragged me into this music project he was doing. Said I looked like the kind of kid who needed a power chord more than a maths grade."

A quiet laugh escapes him, and it curls right into my ribs.

"He wasn't wrong," Kieran murmurs. "That's when everything changed. Music gave me something else. Something louder than the grief. Bigger than the silence."

I say nothing. I just hold his hand a little tighter. Let the story breathe between us.

He looks down at our hands. "I don't know why I told you all that."

"I'm glad you did," I whisper.

I rest my head against his shoulder, and he exhales slowly, pressing his cheek into my hair as his arm slips around my waist.

We sit like that—two people made of jagged edges and quiet resilience.

The music in the distance fades. Tents glow softer behind us, shadows lengthening as the night deepens around the edges.

And somehow, in the middle of all this mess—grief and dreams and uncertainty curling into the dark—I feel it. That strange, settling quiet in my chest.

Like maybe I'm exactly where I'm supposed to be.

"Earth to Ellie?" Naomi's voice cuts through my spiral. "You look like you've seen a ghost, babe."

I blink hard, eyes glued to the file. "Sorry. Just… spaced out a bit. Sleep deprivation."

She narrows her eyes, clearly doesn't buy it, but lets it slide.

I glance down again at the clipboard, mouth dry. This is a joke, it *has* to be, some cosmic piss-take. Out of all the hospitals in the country, out of all the shifts I could be working, he walks into this one. Now.

I stare toward the bay, pulse roaring in my ears.

I stop outside the curtain, gripping the file, heart thudding like it's trying to claw its way out of my chest. My fingers hover. Hesitate. The rational part of me scrambles for a loophole. Maybe it's not him, maybe it's just some harmless, weird coincidence. I take a breath. One of those steady, clinical ones we're trained to walk patients through. In through the nose, out through the mouth.

It barely scratches the surface.

My stomach flips as my mind sprints ahead, conjuring every version of who could be behind this curtain.

I pull it back. And there he is.

Kieran Hayes.

Slouched on the gurney like it's his natural habitat, scrolling on his phone with his good hand. Older now. Sharper. More stubble along his jaw, hair shorter but still defiant, messy in that way that always looked deliberate. He's in ripped jeans and a faded band tee, effortless, like he's just wandered off a stage and into triage. But it's the eyes that get me. And when they meet mine, the air thickens.

Recognition moves across his face, soft and sure, like sunlight spilling into a locked room. His mouth tilts into that smile. The one that used to undo me in a single look.

"Hey, you," he says. Voice low and rough. Familiar. Like no time has passed.

And just like that, the floor tilts beneath me. My mouth opens. Closes. For a second, I forget what the English language is.

Then instinct kicks in. I straighten my spine, snap back into nurse mode, and grip professionalism like a shield. Because if I let it slip for even a second, I'll shatter.

"Mr. Hayes," I say, the words tasting wrong in my mouth. "I'm Ellie, and I'll be your nurse today. Is it alright if I remove this bandage to examine the wound?"

He raises an eyebrow. "Mr. Hayes, huh?" His lips twitch as if he's trying not to laugh. "Kinda formal. I think I like it." Then, softer, less amused now: "This how we're doing this, then? *Ells*?"

The nickname hits like a slap and a whisper all at once.

God.

I freeze. Just for a second. Long enough for him to catch the flicker in my expression, the heat rushing to my skin. That name has passed no one's lips but his. It belongs to him. It belonged to the girl I was when I was with him.

I clear my throat, holding his gaze just long enough to make it neutral. "Unless you'd prefer another nurse, I'll be the one treating you tonight."

He leans back against the pillow, phone forgotten, eyes locked on mine. "Oh, I think I'd rather have you."

I say nothing. Just focus on the bandage. My fingers are shaking more than I'd like, but I move with the same careful precision I've practiced a hundred times, like muscle memory might hold me together if nothing else.

I keep my eyes on the wound and can feel him watching me as I wipe blood with a sterile cloth. My hands are steady. My mind? Anything but.

The skin around the cut is red and a little inflamed. Superficial but messy. "How did this happen?" My voice remains clinical and detached.

He shrugs. "Had an altercation with a beer bottle."

A small smile tugs at the corner of my mouth before I can stop it. I dab on antiseptic, checking for any glass. Focusing on the task.

"So, you did it huh?" he says, voice soft.

I place two Steri-Strips over the wound. "Still a student. I qualify in two months." My voice comes out clipped. Automatic.

He nods slowly, lips curving. "Looks good on you. The scrubs. Total cliché, but… it works."

I glance up just long enough to catch the spark in his eyes.

He leans back again like he owns the room.

"You smell the same," he says.

The words crawl under my skin. He shouldn't remember that. He shouldn't notice. It's been *four* years.

"Careful," I say, defaulting to a grin. "Might start thinking you missed me."

His smile deepens. "Wouldn't want that getting out."

"Still a smart-ass, I see."

"Only around you."

The old rhythm slips into place like it never left. Witty, warm, and stupidly effortless. It takes me off guard how easy it is to fall back into being that girl. The one who joked. Who flirted without overthinking.

And just as quickly, the guilt sweeps in.

I straighten slightly, tone shifting. "You're bleeding and in hospital," I say, trying (and failing) to sound stern. "This isn't the time to flirt."

He shrugs. Unbothered. "I'd argue it's the perfect time. Life's short, Ellie. And you were always fun to flirt with."

I roll my eyes, clearing the trolley with hands that don't quite behave. The silence that follows stretches taut.

Then I drop a gauze. It slips from my fingers and flutters to the floor. I mutter something under my breath, bend down at the same time he does, and we both reach for it.

Our hands brush. And just like that, I'm frozen. His fingers close

SOMEHOW STILL YOU 35

over my hand, but he doesn't let go. Doesn't move. His eyes find mine, steadier than I expect, searching. And for a second, the rest of the room disappears.

"Where did you go, Ellie?" The question isn't sharp. It's quiet. Careful, even. But it hits like a thunderclap.

I swallow against the heat rising in my throat. "It was a long time ago, Kieran."

His gaze doesn't shift. "Doesn't mean it didn't matter."

I clear my throat, step back, and give us both the space we suddenly need. "Sometimes a moment's all you get," I whisper. "You can't ask for more than it's willing to give."

The silence stretches again, full of everything neither of us is saying.

"You made walking away look easy." His voice is soft now. No edge. No smirk. Just the weight of something real.

I almost laugh. *Easy?* If only he knew.

But what's the point in revisiting any of it now? The why, the when, the mess of it all. In a few minutes, I'll be gone, just like I was before.

Another shift. Another patient. Another version of him I'll file away. I take a step back, reset my shoulders, and rebuild the distance.

"You're all set, Mr. Hayes," I say, voice neutral. "Keep the Steri-Stips on, keep the area clean and dry."

I pause, just for a breath. "My mentor will be over shortly to double check everything, so sit tight." No warmth, no room for interpretation. Just the mask, the boundary. The need to get out *now*.

He watches me. Says nothing at first. Then, simply: "Thank you, Ellie." The words are soft. Weighted.

I nod and turn to go. Fingers curling slightly at my sides.

But then…

"Tell the girl in all the colours," he says behind me, his voice lower now. "The one who used to dance like no one was watching…"

A pause. Long enough to make my breath hitch.

The words dig into something soft inside me—the girl he's talking about doesn't feel real anymore. She's all but vanished beneath sleep deprivation, and the type of existence that doesn't leave room for dancing.

But he *saw* her.

Even back then, when I didn't think anyone was really looking.

My throat goes tight.

I don't turn around.

Then, softly, he continues. "I'm still here. If she ever wants to finish what we started."

I stop. The words crashing over me.

But I don't look back. I can't. I step into the corridor, breath snagged in my chest like a trap, and the second the curtain falls behind me, everything feels too bright. Like someone turned the sun up a few notches and forgot to dial it back down.

The lights are still buzzing overhead, stuttering like they're short-circuiting just to spite me. The sound scrapes along my skin, worms its way into my skull, louder now, relentless. "*Seriously,*" I snap at no one in particular. "Can we please get maintenance to fix these bloody lights?"

A few heads turn. I don't realise how fast I'm moving until I nearly take out a trolley. A junior doctor glances up, startled. I mutter a half-hearted *sorry* and keep walking.

My name echoes behind me, Naomi probably, but it doesn't register properly. Everything sounds like it's underwater. Muffled and distant.

I can't breathe.

My chest tightens like someone's winding rope around my ribs and pulling, inch by inch.

My pulse thuds in my ears, and the hallway tilts slightly, narrowing around me.

Get it together.

I make it to the back room where they dump bedpans and store half-empty bottles of cleaning fluids. I push the door open harder than I mean to and lean against the cold tile wall. The smell of disinfectant hits like a slap, but the air in here is cooler.

Breathe.

But the air won't come right. My chest lifts in shallow bursts, like I'm sucking oxygen through a straw.

Not now.

Not here.

My hands tremble. Fingers twitching with that warning burn. That familiar flicker that says I'm about to lose it.

He was here. Not just a name on a file. He was here. Flesh and blood. Grin and memory. Four years gone in an instant. And it's like no time has passed at all.

What the hell is wrong with me?

The walls feel like they're pressing in. My knees threaten to fold. My vision blurs at the edges, dark spots swimming.

"Ellie?" A voice cuts through the static.

I flinch and turn my head slightly. Naomi. She smells like jasmine and sugar. Her perfume slices through the bleach and panic. She's beside me in an instant. One hand on my shoulder. The other brushing my hair back from my damp forehead.

"Hey. Look at me." Her voice is soft but anchored. Steady. "I've got you, alright?"

I try to nod. I Can't.

"You're okay," she murmurs, gently guiding me down onto the closed lid of a bin. She kneels in front of me, fingers warm and sure as they wrap around mine. "I've got you, Ellie. I've got you."

And finally.

I breathe.

CHAPTER 4

off beat

KIERAN

I*t's been a few days* since Ellie patched me up, and I feel like I'm walking around with a ghost stitched into my skin. I fumbled like an idiot and let her slip through my fingers—*again*.

I can't shake it. Not her. Not the way she looked at me, like she didn't know whether to hug me or bolt to the nearest exit. Not the way my name sounded coming from her lips, like the chorus of a song I forgot I knew by heart.

Now here I am, pretending to be fine. Trying to act like I'm not quietly coming undone in the middle of a band rehearsal that's supposed to prep us for the biggest gig we've played yet. The Foundry. No pressure.

The studio we've rented for the week isn't much. Exposed brick, concrete floors, and a sofa that looks like it's witnessed at least three breakups and a low-budget music video. It smells like stale beer, takeaway grease, and something vaguely floral. Like someone tried to Febreze it and immediately gave up.

The walls are covered in posters. Gritty, sun-bleached, half-peeled flyers from bands that came before us. Some made it. Some didn't. Some probably stood right where I'm standing now, chasing something that felt just out of reach.

It's wild to think how long we've been at this. Me and Theo, anyway.

We were the start. Two teenage misfits, stuck at the back of a classroom we didn't care about, bonding over a shared hatred of science. He used to drum on the underside of the desks until the teachers snapped. Never could sit still—still can't. I used to write song ideas in the margins of my homework and fail maths with elegance.

Luca joined a year later. Moved down from up north with this aura about him and an accent we pretended not to mimic. He was two years above us. Calmer. Played guitar like it was an extension of his arms. From the first time he plugged it in, it was obvious he wasn't just good—he was solid. And that's what we needed. Someone to keep us from burning out before we even got lit.

And then Ryder. We weren't even looking when he turned up. Some open mic night in a dive bar with sticky floors and three working lights. Kid sat down at the keys like it was nothing, played like it was everything. The room didn't even blink, but we did. It was one of those unspoken *this is it* moments. He was in the year below us, mouthy, too pretty to be that good, and full of a strange blend of chaos and ache. But he fit. Instantly.

From there, it was one heck of a grind. Rehearsing in my dad's garage with a mic we stole from the school studio, playing student nights for tips and broken speakers. We recorded our first EP in Theo's cousin's spare room, using mattress foam as soundproofing and hoping the dog wouldn't bark mid-take. It was messy. It was loud. But it was ours.

And somehow, against the odds, people started listening.

None of us thought we'd make it this far, not really. We were just four kids making noise and having fun doing it. Now it's stages, setlists, and cities I can't keep track of.

It's everything we wanted.

Regardless, there are days when it takes its toll. The pressure. The pace. How strange it all is.

I'm tired. Not unhappy. Just worn. Grateful—fuck yeah. But

there's a difference between wanting something and knowing what it takes to keep it.

I glance around the room, pulled back by the thrum of familiar chaos. The low hum of amps warming up. Cables snaking across the floor.

Theo's drumming on the back of a chair, restless and half-feral as always. His knee's bouncing like it's trying to start a mosh pit on its own. Intricate tattoos cover every inch of his exposed skin, shifting with each movement, the drumstick spinning between his fingers like it has a mind of its own. He's wired on the kind of energy you would want in a bar fight, or to wind up the sound guy on tour.

Ryder's draped across the sofa, keyboard balanced on his lap, baseball cap on backward. He's half-pretending to be laid back, but I can see it—the way his fingers test the chords, like he's translating something he hasn't found words for yet. That kid has genius-level talent, but he'll never admit it.

Then there's Luca. Sat opposite me with his guitar resting against his chest, like it's breathing with him. Hair a mess. Sleeves rolled. Arms crossed. Watching me with that quiet, big-brother patience that somehow doesn't feel patronising. He's already figured out what's wrong, I can tell by the way his gaze flicks between me and the notebook at my feet, but he's not saying anything. He never does, not until he needs to. Luca's the reason this band hasn't combusted. Our anchor. The only one of us who doesn't start fires on instinct.

And me? I'm slouched on a folding chair, fingers trailing over my guitar strings like they're barbed wire. I've been looping the same three chords for twenty minutes, hoping lightning might strike.

It won't.

Not with her still playing on repeat inside my head.

The notebook on the floor is a mess, the same one I've been scribbling in for years, the one my dad bought for me. Almost-lyrics, false starts, crossed-out verses, and broken lines clutter the pages. But nothing sticks. Everything feels thin, hollow, like I'm chasing a sound that slipped away before I even knew it was there.

Luca breaks the silence, fingers coaxing out a low, bluesy riff. It cuts through the fog in the room, but not deep enough to clear it.

Theo groans, tosses his sticks down with a clatter, and plants his feet on the table in front of him like he lives here. "Alright, alright. We've been at this for hours and the only thing we've managed to write is an aggressive riff that sounds like a pissed-off raccoon got hold of a distortion pedal."

Ryder doesn't even look up. "Facts."

"Two days," Theo mutters, scrubbing both hands down his face. "Nick wants a full song ready in *two fucking days*. What kind of crack is that guy smoking?"

Nick—our manager, part-time miracle worker, full-time ball-ache—looks like he walked straight out of a crime drama. All flannel shirts and dad jeans, with a greying moustache and a permanently unimpressed expression.

He means well. But he's got the emotional subtlety of a sledgehammer and the patience of a gnat. Deadlines are sacred to him. Sanity? Less so.

"The expensive kind," Ryder replies, deadpan, tapping out something vaguely melodic on his keys. "Or he's convinced we're actual wizards. Abracadabra, here's a banger!"

Theo swishes his drumstick, mimicking Nick's voice. "Conjure me a hit, boys! Save the music industry. Be the moment!"

Luca exhales through his nose, barely looking up as he adjusts the tuning peg on his guitar. "We've pulled off miracles before. But yeah, this one's a stretch."

Normally, I'd be right there with them, throwing jabs, leaning into the sarcasm, spinning some joke that lands just left of sincere. But today, it's all static.

I glance down at my guitar and strum the same chords I've been playing for an hour. Nothing lands. Nothing fits.

Ryder hears it and shifts his gaze. "Kieran, you've been stuck in that loop for ages, man. You good?"

"Fine," I lie, and it's immediate. Automatic.

But none of them buy it.

Luca leans forward, elbows on his knees, quiet with concern. "You've been off since we got to South Havens. More than usual."

"Uh-oh. Is this about a *girl*, Romeo?" Theo quips.

I shake my head, brushing it off. "It's nothing. Just, stuff."

"Don't *stuff* me, man," Luca says, calm but pointed. "You've got that look. Like someone nicked your favourite guitar pick."

Then, quieter than usual—gentler—he says, "Talk."

Christ.

That one word lands like a pin in the middle of the room.

Theo shifts. Not much, but enough. The easy slouch vanishes from his spine. He drags his feet off the table without a word and leans forward. Ryder straightens too, folding his arms like he's bracing himself—not for judgment, but to hold space.

No one asks what's wrong.

No one rolls their eyes or reaches for a joke to cut the tension.

They just wait.

It started years ago. One night in the garage, when Theo smashed a snare clean in half and no one knew what the hell to say. Luca just looked at him and said it: *Talk.* One word. No judgement. No demand. Just a door quietly opened.

Since then, it's been the same rule.

When one of us says *talk*, the rest of us shut the fuck up and listen.

And now, they're all looking at me.

Waiting.

"Come on. It's either girl trouble or a mid-life crisis. Or both. Odds are good." Theo says.

I blow out a slow breath, dragging a hand through my hair. "It's Ellie."

The name lands like a mic drop.

Theo whistles. "Shit. That's a name I haven't heard in a while."

"Four years," Luca says smoothly, like he's been keeping emotional data stored as trivia.

Ryder's head snaps toward me. "Wait. Ellie as in *festival* Ellie?"

I nod once. "The one and only."

And just like that, the mood shifts and the banter evaporates, replaced by something quieter.

I set my guitar down carefully, like the weight of it is suddenly too much, and lean back in the chair, eyes drifting up to the water-stained ceiling tiles.

Ryder perks up, eyes glinting. "Fuck. You ghosted us for like a week after that festival. Don't even try to deny it."

"I didn't *ghost* you," I grumble.

"You didn't talk," Luca says, not unkindly. "You played the saddest guitar I've ever heard, missed two rehearsals, and then punched that guy at The Rook when he made that crack about groupies."

"That guy was a prick," Theo chimes in, ever helpful. "But yeah, you were a bit of a wreck, mate."

Ryder leans forward, intrigued. "Come on. It was one week, wasn't it? She must've had magic powers or something. Who the hell leaves that deep a mark after seven days?"

I stare at my guitar, jaw tight, thumb brushing a dent in the fretboard. "I saw her again."

The room stills. Even Theo stops.

"What?" Luca's voice is lower now, that steady tone he gets when something matters.

"A few days ago," I nod, slow and deliberate. "South Havens A&E. Cut my hand. She was my nurse."

There's a beat of stunned silence.

"You're *joking*?" Ryder says, blinking.

"Nope."

"She treated you?" Theo's already halfway to grinning. "Like, patched-you-up treated you?"

"She did more damage than the beer bottle," I mutter, rubbing the back of my neck.

Luca's watching me now, head tilted, guitar quiet on his lap. "What was it like?"

I blow out a breath. "Like being punched in the chest. Same smile. Same eyes. Same voice. Except, I don't know. Different."

"She say anything?"

I nod. "Not really. She looked like she wanted to bolt the second she saw me."

Ryder cocks his head. "Did you ask her why she left?"

I hesitate. "Said it was just a moment. That we couldn't ask for more than it was willing to give."

Theo whistles. "Cold."

That ache rises in my chest again. I reach for my guitar case and flip open the side pocket I never touch. Not for gear. Not for picks.

The note's still there. Folded and creased, edges soft with time, but I know every word by heart. Even after all this time, I never threw it away.

My fingers hover over it before I lift it free, thumb smoothing the worn fold, once, then again. "She left me this. Last day of the festival."

No one speaks. No jokes. No jabs. Just quiet.

"We woke up together the morning of our last day. Sun burning a hole through that shit old tent of hers. She was still there. Warm. Real. I thought…"

I pause. Swallow. "Doesn't matter. We were packing up later. I opened my case and found it. Folded under my picks like she knew exactly where I'd look."

Another beat. My grip on the paper tightens. "I must've read it a hundred times that week. A thousand since."

Kieran,

I don't know how to say goodbye to you, so I won't. But I have to go.

This past week has been everything. More than I ever expected it to be, and I will never forget you.

You'll always be my rockstar. The guy with the music in his veins and the fire in his eyes. The one who made me believe, even if just for a little while, that the world could slow down.

Maybe one day, when the universe is feeling kind, our paths will cross again.

Until then... play something for me.

Yours for the week, Ells. x

I stare at the floor, the paper soft in my hands, edges worn from years of rereading. My throat goes tight.

"I didn't even get her last name," I groan. "She just… vanished."

Saying it out loud scrapes something raw. Like peeling back a layer I'd convinced myself had healed over.

Theo exhales, low and slow. "That's brutal."

"She wrecked me," I admit. "Not because of what we were, but because of what we never got to be."

Ryder leans forward, voice softer now. "And now she's back."

"Yeah."

"And you're still hung up on her."

I don't respond. I don't need to.

The silence that follows is thick enough to wade through. No jabs. No laughter. Just the hum of the studio and Theo's drumstick clattering off the edge of the table.

Luca finally speaks, voice level. "So? What are you gonna do about it?"

I rub a hand down my face. "I don't know."

Ryder groans, tipping his head back dramatically. "Seriously? The universe hands you a literal plot twist and you're just gonna mope?"

Theo adds, "You had one job. Get her number."

I shake my head. "It's not that simple."

Ryder throws his hands up. "It's never that simple with you."

"Because I don't want to fuck it up again," I say, sharper than I mean to. "Because if I do this wrong, I don't think I could handle her her walking away twice."

The room quiets, and I rest my elbows on my knees, pressing my palms together like I'm holding something fragile.

"She's in South Havens," Ryder says, tapping his lip. "You've got a name, a hospital… that's more than a breadcrumb. That's a trail."

Luca adds, "And we've got a set in the city at the weekend. Maybe it's more than coincidence."

I let out a shaky breath. "What am I supposed to do? Show up at her job like some lost puppy with a song in my back pocket?"

Theo shrugs. "Worked for you with that intern at Rebel Radio."

I glance at my guitar again, still resting against the chair. "What if she's not the same girl?"

"What if you're not the same guy?" Luca counters.

The conversation slowly drifts. Theo paces. Ryder's back to tapping keys. Luca tunes his strings like he's turning over a thought in his head.

Eventually, Ryder hits a sequence that makes Theo stop and nod. Just like that, they slip into it. A rhythm. A groove. Years of chemistry built in moments like these.

But I don't move.

My hands hover near the strings. My brain tries to summon words, but nothing comes. Because I'm still there. Still in that hospital room. Still watching her walk away in slow motion.

The pressure from the label, the looming gig, the fans waiting for something new. It all fades into background noise.

All I can think about is her.

CHAPTER 5
the foundry
ELLIE

THE COMFORTING AROMA OF BAKED cheese and rich tomato sauce curls through the kitchen, warm and familiar. The lasagne sits in the centre of the table, bubbling at the edges, the scent of fresh basil rising in lazy spirals. This isn't just dinner, it's tradition. Friday nights, my lasagne, the three of us around the table.

David takes a bite, chews thoughtfully, then sets his fork down with a sigh and rests a hand on mine. "You know, Ellie, I swear this gets better every time."

Across the table, Mia swings her legs, curls bouncing as she launches into a debrief of her math test. "So then, Mr Jacobs tried to catch us out with this stupid question, right? But I remembered what you said, David. Keep it simple. And boom! I finished first."

I reach over and squeeze her hand. "Knew you'd ace it, bug."

David nods along, still smiling—but I catch it. The slight delay. The fraction of a second where his eyes flick to his phone on the as it lights up on the table. The way his fingers tap the stem of his wineglass like they've got somewhere better to be.

"That's great, Mia." he says, turning his phone so the screen faces the table.

Mia doesn't notice. She's already diving into the next part of her story, hands flailing for emphasis. But I do. The tiny disconnections.

The subtle switches. The way presence can be offered, then withdrawn, without ever leaving the room.

Still, I tell myself it's nothing. He's had a long day. Stress. Meetings. The never-ending carousel of networking and numbers. His job pulls at him in a hundred directions at once. And sometimes, dinner —the one I make us sit down to every Friday—is just another thing to show up for.

"So," I say, keeping my smile in place, "anything trip you up?"

She frowns, thinking. "Well, there was this one question—"

"Speaking of good news," David cuts in, straightening in his seat, voice suddenly bright. "The firm got a couple of tickets to a gig at The Foundry tomorrow night."

He's animated now. Just like that. Like someone flipped a switch and plugged him back in.

David works in finance. Not the spreadsheets-and-numbers kind, but the polished, high-stakes side—*the firm*, as he calls it, deals in private equity, wealth portfolios, venture capital. I've never fully understood the details, but I know the language: opportunity, leverage, return. Deals struck over club dinners and quiet rounds of golf. It's less about money, more about *movement*. Who you know, what you can make happen, and how clean you can make it look on paper.

And David's good at it. He has that easy, inherited confidence. The kind that comes from growing up around handshakes that mean more than signatures. He doesn't just ask for things—he *secures* them. Knows which strings to pull, which favours to call in, and how to make you feel lucky he thought of you.

There's something magnetic about it.

"I managed to grab two," he adds, meeting my eyes. "Thought you and Naomi might want a night out."

I blink. "The Foundry?"

He nods. "Yeah. Some indie band, apparently. Everyone's talking about them. I figured it might be your thing." He smiles, and this time it lands—earnest and hopeful—like he wants it to be the right gesture.

"Thank you," I say, a little surprised. "That's... really thoughtful."

And it is. The gig, the timing, the offer to hold down the fort with Mia—he didn't have to. But he did.

Still, something in me twists and I don't know why. A quiet question with no obvious answer.

The line outside The Foundry snakes around the block, full of low chatter, laughter, and cigarette smoke. The bass from inside pulses underfoot like a second heartbeat, thudding through the warm air.

It's one of those classic British summer nights. The kind that clings to your skin, heavy with leftover heat from the day, a mix of humidity and energy that makes everything feel alive.

The sky's still holding onto its light, stained pink at the edges, and people linger in the street like no one's in a rush to go home. Everyone's dressed lightly in tank tops, crop tops, and linen shirts unbuttoned halfway down. Naomi's already fanning herself with the back of her phone, her curls frizzing slightly at the ends.

"I swear to God," she mutters. "If I don't get a drink in the next ten minutes, I'm going to melt into a puddle of glitter and sass. And I'm already losing circulation in my toes standing here."

"You'd lose circulation sitting still on a sun-bed. You're so dramatic."

"Rude." She pauses. "Accurate, but rude."

I glance down at my outfit, shifting on my feet. I opted for a simple sage green cami tucked into a denim mini skirt, paired with my favourite ankle boots and a light knit cardigan slung over my arm.

Naomi clocks it immediately. "You and that bloody emergency cardigan," she says, eyes dancing. "What are you preparing for? A sudden snowstorm? A surprise Arctic expedition?"

"It's called being *practical*," I respond, deadpan. "You'll be begging for it when you're cold later."

She snorts. "If I get cold, I'll flirt my way into someone's hoodie like a normal person."

I roll my eyes, but I'm smiling now. I've made an effort tonight. A nod to who I used to be, back when getting dressed up for a night out meant music, mischief, and that giddy thrill I haven't felt in years.

I take a breath and let it out slowly. Tonight is supposed to be fun. Just me, Naomi, and whatever bad cocktails they're serving inside.

"So," Naomi says, tone light but a little too deliberate, "David got the tickets?"

"Yeah. Someone from his office had extras, I think."

"Nice of him." She hums. Casual.

I feel the weight behind it—the pause, the unsaid—and something twists low in my stomach. But I smile anyway, brushing it off. "It's nothing shady. Probably just someone at work who owed him a favour. You know what his work's like."

Her eyes narrow, not unkind, just sharp. "And he just gave them to you?"

"It's not a trap, Nay." I huff. "He thought I could use a night out. That's all."

There's a pause. She knows it hasn't always been easy with him, and she's been my sounding board since the beginning. She's heard it all. The silent treatments. The sudden, too-late gestures. The way David could twist a situation until even I wasn't sure what had actually happened. She knows the patterns as well as I do. Held my hand through the fallout. Passed tissues through the bathroom door and poured me wine when I didn't want to talk.

"I just want to make sure you're okay. That's all."

"Look, he's been better lately. *Really*. He's trying."

"You always say that."

"I know."

A beat. "You still believe it?"

I pause, unsure whether to lie, deflect, or crumble entirely. "I have to, Naomi."

She doesn't press. Just gives my hand a small squeeze,

anchoring me the way she always does. Then she changes the subject, letting the moment drift off like steam. Because that's what best friends do when you're not quite ready to hear the things they already know.

"So, who's actually playing tonight?" she asks. "I didn't even check."

"Honestly? I have no idea. I didn't really come for the music."

Naomi grins. "You came for the cheeky Vimtos and questionable decisions."

"Exactly," I say, grinning. The kind we've been making since we were sixteen — when we were definitely too young to be out drinking, flirting our way to free shots, heels in hand by midnight, and no idea how we were getting home.

"I'll leave the car park snogging to you, though."

Naomi gasps, mock-offended. "Excuse you — I have standards."

I arch a brow. "Do you? Tell that to that scaffolder you climbed like a tree."

She snorts. "He was charming, actually. And built like a Greek god."

"With the personality of a houseplant."

"Details," she says breezily, linking her arm through mine as the queue shuffles forward.

Posters and gig flyers cover the walls, the type you usually half-glance at and forget, until one of them stops me cold.

Special Guests: Midnight Reverie

The words don't register at first. Like my brain's buffering. Then it hits. My lungs seize. My vision narrows.

"What the..." Naomi steps forward, squinting at the poster. Her voice drops. "Shut the *actual* front door."

It's his name. His band. That crooked smile, now ten feet tall and airbrushed.

And he's here.

My heart's pounding so hard I think I might spontaneously combust.

Naomi turns to me, slow as anything. "Wait a second... Kieran Hayes? *Your* Kieran Hayes? Festival guy?"

My throat closes. I nod once.

She stares at me. "Ellie. Is this... are you... what is HAPPENING?"

Then, quieter. "Mate, how long has it been?"

I try to dodge her gaze, but there's no escaping Naomi. Not when she smells romantic chaos.

The words crawl out of my mouth. "Less than a week."

Naomi blinks. "Pardon?"

"I saw him." A beat. "At the hospital."

"You *what*?"

"I thought it was just a coincidence," I whisper. "Same name. And then I pulled back the curtain and... there he was. In the fucking flesh."

Naomi actually screams. A full, unfiltered, guttural wail that makes at least four people in the queue whip around.

I shrink behind my cardigan like it might save me from public shame.

"NO. WAY. How the hell did you not tell me?!"

"I was processing."

"Processing?" She throws her hands in the air. "Processing what? That you ran into *the* Kieran Hayes, festival-god-Kieran, and just — what? Gave him a plaster and sent him on his way?"

"Steri-Strips," I correct.

"Oh my god, I'm going to scream again."

She does. Quieter this time, but still deeply dramatic.

"What happened?" she demands, grabbing my arm like she's about to stage a full interrogation. "Tell me *everything*."

I shake my head, breath catching. "It didn't go well. I froze. I was trying to stay professional, but he recognised me straight away."

Naomi's face shifts, a familiar softness creeping through.

"I nearly had a cardiac arrest on the spot. Full heart palpitations. I thought I was going to pass out and land face-first in his lap."

Naomi lets out a wheeze. "Please tell me you didn't."

"Sadly, no," I mutter. "Would've been a fun way to go, though."

Naomi snorts so hard she chokes on air. "And now you're about to walk into a sold-out venue," she says, "and watch him on stage. After all these years."

"Apparently so," I mutter. "Because the universe is determined to be that bitch."

She grins. "She really is."

"What am I going to do?" I whisper.

Naomi shrugs, but her grip tightens gently on my hand. "Don't know. But we're not leaving."

I nod. But my stomach is a blender on high. Because even now, even with panic twisting every nerve in my body, there's something else underneath it.

A flutter. Light and hopeful. Like possibility.

And I hate myself for feeling it.

For the first time in years, it feels like I'm standing at the edge of something. But I can't tell if it's a cliff or a bridge.

When we finally reach the doors, the bouncer gives us a once-over, barely glancing at our tickets before waving us inside. Naomi blows him a kiss just to be cheeky, and I can't help but laugh.

The moment we step through, the heat hits like a wall. It's thick and humid, steeped in sweat, smoke, and anticipation. It smells like sticky beer mats, hairspray, and the perfume that clings to your clothes for days.

The crowd pulses with warm energy, moving like one massive, swaying organism. Someone brushes against my arm, another shoulder bumps against mine, and I instinctively draw closer to Naomi.

Inside, the world blurs. Lights strobe and flicker across the sea of heads. All pinks, violets, and a sharp, electric blue slice through the haze. The bass thrums up through the floor, into my boots, and settles deep in my chest. My pulse catches it—syncs with it.

Naomi leans in, shouting over the music. "God, it hasn't changed at all, has it?"

She's right. The place still has that same rough-around-the-edges charm. All exposed brick and scaffolding, the bar lit up in pink neon, condensation streaking every surface. It's packed, but intimate in the way only a good venue can be. Like the walls themselves know they're holding something alive.

Naomi laughs, tugging me by the wrist toward the bar like a woman on a mission.

"First round's on me," I say, raising my voice over the noise.

The bar is hectic—sticky floors, plastic cups stacked in haphazard towers, and bartenders moving in sync with one another. Everything smells like citrus spirits and too many spilled Jägerbombs.

"Two cheeky Vimtos," Naomi says without missing a beat.

The bartender nods and starts pouring. I tap my card against the reader, expecting that satisfying beep.

Nothing.

He glances at the machine, frowns. "Could you try chip and PIN?"

With a polite smile, I insert my card and slowly punch in my PIN.

Declined.

I freeze for half a second, heat blooming in my cheeks.

Naomi clocks it.

"Don't tell me you've forgotten your pin," she says with a grin, nudging me like it's all a joke. Light. Casual.

"I haven't," I murmur. "It's just being weird. I think I've got my other card somewhere."

She doesn't wait. Just taps her card with a mock sigh. "Next one's yours."

The machine chirps its approval and the drinks are ours.

I slip my phone from my bag as Naomi disappears toward the toilets and open my banking app, frowning as the login screen flashes up. I enter my details.

Error.

Incorrect username or password.

I try again. Slower this time. Same result. My throat tightens. The screen blurs slightly under the pulsing red light of the bar.

I find David's name in my contacts and hit call.

The noise swells around me—glass clinking, someone shouting a lyric at the top of their lungs, the bartender slamming shots onto the counter. I press a finger to my free ear and slip toward the edge of the room, near a side wall where the crowd thins just enough to breathe.

He answers on the third ring, voice warm and low in my ear. "Hey, Ellie. Everything okay?"

"David, hey—sorry, I know it's late. I just—something weird happened. I'm at the bar and my card just got declined." I shift further into the shadowed alcove near the fire door.

There's a pause, then his voice, smooth and steady. "Declined? That's odd."

"Yeah. And now I can't log into the app either. Keeps saying my details are wrong, but I haven't changed anything."

He makes a thoughtful sound, the kind he always makes when he's halfway through solving something. "Ah, yeah. That'll be the tech stuff. I was on the phone to the bank this morning—total nightmare. They're having issues with the app again. System upgrades or maintenance, something boring like that."

I blink, watching a group of girls in glittery tops pose for a selfie near the toilets. "Right. I thought maybe—"

"Ellie, come on. Everything's fine. I checked it all earlier. Just one of those glitches. Happens all the time."

I exhale slowly, a little of the tension leaving my shoulders. "Okay."

"Don't need to stress yourself out over something stupid like this. You've got enough on your plate."

I nod, even though he can't see me. The music swells again, a bass drop shaking the walls.

"I promise, everything's fine babe. If it helps, maybe just uninstall the app for now? While they're sorting the bugs out. It's only going to keep stressing you out if you keep trying to log in."

I chew on the inside of my cheek. "Yeah… maybe."

"Do it for your own peace of mind, okay? I'll keep an eye on everything from my end."

My thumb hovers over the app. Still unsure. Still a little off-kilter.

"You trust me, don't you?"

"Of course I do, David."

"Then let me take care of it," he says, voice soft again. Reassuring.

"Okay," I murmur.

"I love you, Ellie. You know that, yeah?"

A beat catches in my throat. "I love you too."

"Go have fun."

The call ends with a soft click.

I stare at my phone a moment longer, the music from the bar washing back in. Lights flash. Laughter rises.

Naomi appears at my side, cheeks flushed from the heat, hair slightly mussed like she's already had words with a broken hand dryer.

"You alright?" she asks, not loudly—but I hear it.

"Yeah," I say, offering a quick smile. "Just cleared up the bank thing with David. Apparently it's technical issues. App's playing up."

She nods slowly, not quite convinced, but not about to push. "That's annoying. Everything sorted now?"

"Yeah. All good." I take a long sip of my drink. Too sweet. Too strong. Just what I need.

We drift away from the bar, plastic cups in hand, weaving through the crush of people until we find a spot near the back wall— just far enough from the stage to breathe, but close enough to feel the energy ripple through the room.

Naomi's already scanning the crowd, eyes bright. "Alright, then. Let's find someone beautiful for me to flirt with before I forget how."

I try to let the night pull me under. Let the music and the noise fill in the gaps. But it's like my body knows something I haven't said out loud.

He's here. Somewhere in this building. Breathing the same air.

The thought hits like static in my blood.

I close my eyes and tip my head back, letting the thrum of the bass settle under my skin. Around me, the room is all movement— glasses clinking, someone laughing too loudly, strobe lights painting the ceiling. It should be enough to drown it all out.

But it isn't.

I'm not thinking about the drink in my hand or the music filling the room. I'm thinking about a guy with wild hair and a voice that cracked something open in me once.

I shouldn't care. I shouldn't *want* to see him.

But I do.

It's like the universe is whispering. Nudging me in some direction I can't quite place.

And as Naomi leans in to tell me something about the guy from the queue who definitely winked at her, I already know—I'm not going to be able to look away when he steps on that stage.

Because a part of me is still listening for him.

And some foolish, buried part of me is already leaning in.

CHAPTER 6

something bent the rules

KIERAN

THE BUZZ OF THE CROWD outside The Foundry is nearly louder than the hum of our amps. It's always like this, those first few minutes on the edge. I'm already wired, the bass thrumming under my fingertips, sending sparks up my spine.

There's something in the air tonight. Something electric. And my gut says this one's going to be special.

The stage lights cast a hazy glow over the room. Luca's off to the side, noodling through some lazy melodies, looking cool as hell, but his tapping foot gives him away. Ryder's hunched over his keyboard, fingers flying like he's hacking some secret code. And Theo, he's going at the drums like he's summoning a thunderstorm, sweat already rolling down his neck, grinning like noise is his love language.

"All right, lads, focus!" Luca calls, flashing that easy smirk. "Let's not blow our eardrums before the gig starts, yeah?"

I exhale, only just realising I've been holding my breath, and I roll my shoulders back, stepping up to the mic as we dive into soundcheck.

The sound engineer's voice cuts through the monitors. "Kick drum, please!"

Theo practically bounces on his stool and starts hammering the kick like his life depends on it, sending vibrations through the stage.

"Snare!"

CRACK.

"Easy, Animal," I call, wincing. "We're checking levels, not starting a bar fight."

Theo just grins like a kid hyped on sugar.

"Lead guitar."

Luca sends a low, smooth riff through the system. Fingers sure and steady.

"Second guitar."

I adjust the strap across my shoulder, fingers gliding automatically over the strings. The minute I hit the first chord, the nerves rattling in my chest settle, just a scratch.

"Keys."

Without missing a beat, Ryder launches into the cheesiest pop riff he could find, something electronic and obscene.

"Full band!" the engineer calls.

We kick into something from the set list and play half a verse just to check the mix. As soon as Theo settles into the beat, Ryder's keys cut in. I layer my guitar over Luca's, and something in my chest unlocks. Even at half-speed, even for soundcheck, it feels good.

The song wraps, and the engineer gives us a thumbs-up from the back.

"We good?" I call out, voice carrying just enough edge to hide the nerves chewing at my insides.

"All good," he replies.

"Right, hydrate, then beers," Luca announces, rolling up his cable with military precision.

"Hydrate *with* beers," Theo counters, hopping off his kit.

Ryder drapes an arm around my shoulders as we head offstage. "You're feeling it tonight, Hayes. I can tell. You've got that sparkle in your eye."

"Just nerves, mate."

Backstage, the air hums with breathless anticipation. We're all crammed onto the battered old sofa in the green room, beers in hand, legs tangled, half our gear still scattered across the floor. Theo clinked the neck of his bottle against mine, a grin stretched wide across his face.

"Tonight's gonna be a good one, boys," he said, eyes bright and buzzing. "And I'm telling you now, if I fall off my stool mid-song, it's from adrenaline, not booze."

"Or both," Luca muttered, deadpan, though even he couldn't fight the grin tugging at his mouth.

"Cheers to chaos," Ryder said, tipping his bottle in a lazy salute, legs draped over the arm of the sofa like he had not a care in the world.

We're halfway through the world's worst toast when Nick barrels in, the door banging against the wall so hard it makes us all jump.

"Oi, rockstars!" Nick grins, arms flung wide, dark hair already shoved back like he's been pacing the venue all afternoon. "Thought I'd find you back here."

He drags a chair into the middle of the room, spins it backward, and drops onto it, all wired up with energy. "Sold out," he says, practically vibrating. "Did you hear me? Sold out. A thousand bodies lined up round the bloody street. Crowd's already going wild. Security's pushed 'em back from the doors twice."

Theo lets out a low whistle. "Nice."

"And the new song," Nick goes on, grinning like an idiot, "it's magic, lads. You know it, I know it. You just have to go out there and play it like you own the damn place. South Havens is about to put you on the map. This is it. This is the moment they'll talk about when they say they saw you *before you blew up*. So..." he points a finger at each of us, sharp as a shot. "Go out there, melt some faces, make 'em sweat, and for God's sake, Kieran, smile once in a while. It won't kill you."

I huff a laugh, tipping my head back against the sofa, eyes slipping shut for half a second. My heart hammers now, double-time. Part nerves, part anticipation crawling under my skin, tightening and coiling until I'm not sure whether I need to throw up.

This isn't just another gig. This is *the* gig.

"Anyone else suddenly need to pee?" Theo mutters, and the room cracks up.

Nick pushes to his feet, claps a hand on my shoulder. "You've got this, kid. All of you."

I look up, meet his eyes, and nod. That knot in my chest, the one that's been pulling tighter all day, loosens.

Ryder raises his bottle, grin lazy and sharp. "To wild crowds and impending stardom, boys."

We clink our bottles together, and the sound of our laughter bounces off the battered walls.

South Havens is waiting. And for the first time all day, I feel ready to meet them.

The hallway to the stage is narrow and dimly lit, the walls lined with battered old posters of bands who've passed through before us. My boots scuff against the concrete floor, each step rattling up my legs, and my heart hammers hard and fast, like it's trying to punch its way out of my chest.

The closer we get, the louder it gets—a low, rising roar, like the whole place is charging up. It's not just noise—it's a weight pressing against my skin, crawling up the back of my neck, sinking into my ribs until I can feel it deep in my bones.

Theo bounces at my side, drumsticks flipping between his fingers like some magician warming up for a trick. Ryder slides his sunglasses down and wiggles his eyebrows at me, all swagger and sharp edges, but even he can't hide the flush creeping high on his cheeks. Luca walks steadily at my side, jaw set, guitar slung across his back, cool as a cucumber. But I know him too well to miss the pulse ticking hard at his temple.

We hit the side of the stage, and the lights bleed through the curtains in shards of colour, the heat rolling in waves thick enough to choke on. I sneak a look, just once, and the crowd is there. Packed in tight, shoulder to shoulder. Faces tipped toward the stage, a sea of movement, sweat, and sound, ready to eat us alive.

Jesus. My throat goes dry. My fingers twitch around the neck of my guitar, and for half a second, I wonder if I'll remember how to play a single damn note.

Without a word, we move, slipping into our usual huddle just off-stage. Arms slung over shoulders, foreheads pressed close, the four of us wound tight in a circle we've formed a hundred times before. And just like that, the noise fades. Not because the crowd gets quieter, but because this, right here, is ours.

No words. We never need them. This is the quiet before the storm, the breath before the dive, the only moment that belongs to just us before we hand everything over to them.

I shut my eyes, feel Luca's arm heavy across my back, Theo's fingers tapping a restless rhythm against my shoulder, Ryder's low chuckle under his breath as he rocks on his heels. My heart slams so hard it rattles my ribs, and for a second, I wonder if they can feel it thundering through the huddle.

When we break apart, no one says *good luck*, or *we've got this*. We don't have to. We just nod, eyes locking—one, two, three, four—and then we're moving, stepping into the light as the house drops and the crowd explodes.

This is it. Our moment. The biggest crowd we've ever played to, packed into a venue known for launching the best in the indie scene. The Foundry doesn't just host gigs—it makes careers. And tonight, the label's in the room. Watching. Waiting.

No turning back now.

I drag in one sharp, electric breath and step onto the stage, and the noise swallows me whole.

By the halfway mark, I'm drenched, lungs burning, adrenaline on a knife-edge. The room's vibrating. Every chord, every lyric, echoes back louder, wilder.

Ryder steps forward, smooth as ever, mic in hand. "South Havens, you still with us?"

The crowd explodes. I rake a hand through my hair, laughing.

"Before we kick off the second half," Ryder says, "just gonna say… this?" He gestures at the crowd. "This means everything."

I step forward, glancing at the boys. My brothers in all but blood.

"I don't say this enough," I begin, voice steady, chest tight. "But, these guys? They're my life. This band, this music, you lot, it's what gets me out of bed in the morning. We've taken knocks. Got back up. But this…" I sweep my hand across the stage, the crowd, the moment wrapped around us like lightning. "This is why we keep going."

Luca claps my back, then pulls me in and plants a quick, exaggerated kiss on my forehead. "Proud of you, mate," he grins, easy and genuine. Ryder throws his arms wide, stoking the crowd, and Theo crashes a cymbal dramatically.

I scan the sea of faces in the crowd. And then—

Fuck.

Honey-brown eyes. A punch to the chest.

Ellie.

At first, I think I'm seeing things. But no, it's her. So undeniably her. Hair curled softly over her shoulders, glass in hand, eyes locked on mine.

Like a tidal wave, every memory slams into me at once.

Dancing in the rain outside the acoustic tent, shoes forgotten, mascara smudged, her laughter louder than the storm.

Sharing chips at midnight, salt on our fingers, her knee knocking into mine as we talked for hours.

Lying in the grass behind the food trucks, counting constellations neither of us could name.

Her head on my chest as the crowd thinned out, eyes closed, murmuring along to the last song of the night like she wanted to memorise it.

That early morning walk back to the tents, cider-sticky hands linked loosely, both of us tired and a little hungover, but not quite ready to say goodnight.

The way she looked at me like I wasn't just noise and chaos, but something steadier. Something worth keeping.

It all hits in a rush. A hundred moments, all crammed into a single week, that somehow mattered more than it should have.

And now she's standing there. And all I can think is: *how the hell could she just walk away? How did we never finish what we started?*

I half-step back and grin just enough to steady myself.

"So, uh..." I say, voice settling, "we've been working on something new." The crowd erupts. "You lot," I grin, "are gonna be the first to hear it. Right here. Right now."

"South Havens!" Ryder jumps in. "This one's for you."

But it isn't.

Not really.

Luca eases into the opening riff, slow and aching. Ryder's keys follow, threaded with nostalgia. Theo drops into a heartbeat rhythm, low and steady.

I step up to the mic, not the part of me that plays the frontman, but the part that remembers her.

The room dips into stillness, and my eyes flick over the crowd. But I don't see them.

I only see her.

And suddenly, none of it matters. Not the label, not the chaos, not the noise. Because this was always hers.

Maybe one day, when the universe is feeling kind, our paths will cross again.

Until then... play something for me.

Her note plays at the front of my mind as the music swells, lifting with me until the last note hangs in the air like a held breath. And for a second, everything stops.

Then the roar.

But I don't move. Don't smile. Don't soak it in.

I'm still watching her.

And all I need to know is: *Did she hear me? Did she feel it?*

Adrenaline thrums under my skin, my heart pounding like it hasn't got the memo that the set's over. Sweat clings to my neck, my chest, my collar. But I don't care. We did it. We gave the crowd everything, and they gave it right back.

Offstage, the venue is still buzzing with leftover energy. The music shifted into something louder and less important. The kind they pump through the speakers after the main act to keep the buzz alive.

I weave through the crowd, past fans and sound techs, and there she is. Standing by the bar, backlit by neon, laughing with Naomi, hair catching the light like the old festival days. My heart kicks hard.

There's no hesitation. My feet are moving before my brain catches up.

She watches me approach, eyes wide and unreadable. But she doesn't move. Doesn't look away.

I lean against the bar, close but not too close, forcing a confident grin. "Careful," I murmur. "Keep ordering drinks like that and you might need someone to carry you home."

She laughs, quiet and breathless. "Kieran."

The way she says my name. It lands under my ribs, soft and familiar, like it never left her mouth.

I lean in, grinning just enough to cover the sudden thump of nerves. "Oh, no more Mr. Hayes? That was quick. Thought I'd have to earn my way back to first name status."

She shakes her head, lips pulling into a small smile, but it's cautious. Like she's trying to figure out the rules of this.

Of us.

Of whatever this is.

I curl my fingers around the edge of the bar. Anchoring myself. "You gonna give a guy five minutes?" I ask, nodding toward the booths at the back of the bar where the lighting's low, the shadows are soft, and the music's dulled just enough that we won't have to shout.

Ellie blinks, just once—but I catch the flicker. The tiniest smirk at the corner of her mouth.

She remembers.

I shoot her a wink, just to be sure.

She hesitates slightly, eyes flicking to Naomi, who's already deep in conversation with Ryder. Hands animated, face lit up in full storyteller mode. Whatever she's saying, he's eating it up. "I'll just let her know," Ellie says.

I nod. "Okay."

We find a booth tucked in the corner, the kind that feels like its own little world. She fidgets, smoothing her skirt, brushing a finger through a ring of condensation on the table.

Between us, a candle flickers in a grimy glass jar, illuminating her face as her long lashes cast shadows down her cheeks. For a second, I forget how to breathe.

She's stunning. Not in some over-the-top way. But in a way that ruins you a little. The kind that makes time fold in on itself. And my heart? It doesn't stand a chance.

"You know. You've broken at least three hearts tonight," I grin.

She tilts her head, amused. "How'd you figure that?"

"Bartender's watching you like his whole playlist just turned into breakup songs."

Ellie laughs. And *God*, it undoes me. "You're ridiculous," she says, lifting her glass.

"Maybe. But you look good, Ellie. Meant what I said ya know. The nurse thing suits you."

She raises an eyebrow. "So you've got a thing for knackered women in scrubs?"

I shrug. "Just you."

That catches her, and she falters, cheeks flushing pink. And that's when I see it.

The ring.

My stomach drops. It's like slow motion. The glint, the realisation, the wave of gut-punching clarity that follows.

She's engaged.

For a second, it's like the air leaves the room. The noise of the bar — the laughter and the music — it all fades into a dull, hollow thrum.

"Nice ring," I manage, aiming for casual, though my throat feels tight. "Who's the lucky guy?"

"David," she breathes, twisting the ring around her finger.

David. The one who gets her. The one who gets the girl I lost.

I scrape together a smile, even as something sharp twists in my chest. "How'd you two meet?" I hear myself ask, voice light, and I don't even know why I'm asking.

Ellie gives a small shrug, fingers still restless against her glass. "Our parents are friends. It wasn't some big thing. No sparks, no drama. Just something that sort of... happened, I suppose."

"And the rest is history, huh?" The words slip out before I can stop them, a little too sharp around the edges.

"Something like that." She offers a smile, but it doesn't quite reach her eyes.

There's something in her voice—a pause, a softness that isn't quite conviction.

A crack she doesn't know she's showing.

"Well, while I'm laying all my cards on the table, I have a daughter too."

Jesus Christ. That stops me cold. "A *daughter*?"

Ellie nods, slower this time. "Her name's Mia. She's twelve."

I blink. Twelve. The number lodges in my brain, dragging the rest of the maths with it.

I think of that week we spent together. Everything we shared. Everything she let me see.

And yet—this never came up.

"You didn't mention her," I say, not accusing, just... stunned.

She shifts in her seat, fingers fidgeting with the cardigan in her lap, and lets out a soft, uneven laugh. "I know."

Then, after a beat—

"It's just... not something I always share straight away. Especially back then. I'd only just started figuring out who I was outside of being someone's mum."

She pauses, eyes flicking to mine. "I've had my fair share of judgement over the years."

I nod slowly, letting it land. Letting her words settle into all the space that suddenly feels like it was always waiting for them.

"I would never have judged you, Ellie."

She shifts in her seat and nods. "She was eight when David and I met. Callum—Mia's dad and I were... well, we were kids ourselves

SOMEHOW STILL YOU 71

when she came along. Total shock for both of us. By the time Mia was born, we figured we were better off as friends."

My brows lift slightly, a flicker of surprise that softens into something like admiration. "You know… that's actually kind of impressive."

Ellie shrugs, shaking her head. "Trust me, it hasn't always been smooth sailing. Kinda had to learn a lot on my own."

I tip my head, watching her carefully.

She hesitates, fingers circling the rim of her glass. "It's not the life I pictured, definitely not. Not at seventeen, not even at twenty-five. I was… young. Stupid, really. I beat myself up about it for a long time, the choices I made, the way things turned out."

She lets out a quiet breath, eyes dropping to her hands. "But I have Mia, and she's happy. And I wouldn't change it for the world."

"Hey," I murmur, voice gentler now, the grin softening at the corners. "For what it's worth… we're all young and stupid sometimes. It's not a bad thing. It's how we figure out what matters, yeah? It's how we grow."

She huffs a small laugh, shaking her head. "Yeah, maybe."

For a moment, it's just the weight of everything unsaid. The almosts, the maybes, the what ifs. Pulling the air tight between us.

Ellie shifts slightly, fingers brushing the edge of her glass. When she speaks, her voice is soft, almost hesitant, like she's stepping carefully into the quiet.

"That song," she murmurs, eyes lifting to meet mine as she swiftly changes the subject. "It was incredible, Kieran. I don't think I've ever heard you sing like that."

I hold her gaze, something loosening in my chest. "Some songs," I say, "aren't just written. They're felt."

Her breath catches.

"And you, Ellie?" My voice dips lower. "You were always meant to feel this one."

And there it is, that impossible hum that always charged the space between us, trembling on the edge.

But before anything can shift, a voice barrels through the haze of the venue.

"Ellie-Bellie! There you are!" Theo clambers through the crowd like a human Labrador, with Ryder and Luca on his heels. Naomi follows behind, double-fisting drinks and looking smug as sin.

And just like that, the storm rolls in.

"Oh my god, look at you. Come here!"

Theo reaches straight across the table and pulls Ellie to her feet, sweeping her into a dramatic hug, boots lifting clear off the floor.

"Theo! Put me down!" she yelps, somewhere between laughing and protesting.

I lean back and watch the way her fingers grip his jacket, the flush in her cheeks, the way her smile hits like a punch to the ribs.

As the booth fills with noise and laughter, her gaze finds mine again. And it stays. And whatever this is?

I want in.

Maybe it's madness. Maybe it's the universe playing games. But I have to believe it means something. That she wasn't just thrown back into my orbit for nothing.

Something bent the rules, shifted the stars, just long enough to bring her back into my life. And I'd rather burn than try to figure out why — or walk away wondering, what if?

CHAPTER 7

smoke and mirrors

ELLIE

Naomi's kitchen looks like a war zone. Textbooks, notebooks, and loose papers cover every available surface on the island. Our carefully curated plan for a productive study day long since gone to shit—derailed somewhere between the second glass of wine and the realisation that we're both too emotionally fried to care about academic success right now.

Naomi slides the wine bottle toward me with the seriousness of a professor delivering a lecture. "You know," she says, arching an eyebrow as she tops up my glass, "I'm almost certain this wasn't in the study plan."

She takes an exaggerated sip, swirling the liquid like a wine-taster judging a vintage. The fact we picked the bottle purely because it was under a tenner and had a vaguely romantic label is irrelevant.

I lean against the worktop, studying my glass and twirling it between my fingertips like the pro I'm not. "Who says studying and Thirsty Thursday can't coexist?" I gesture at the open textbook in front of me. "Besides, this is all nonsense. The hospital's where the real learning happens. Three years of this shit and I'm ready to throw the towel in."

Naomi lets out a theatrical sigh and flicks through a stack of papers with the same enthusiasm most people reserve for tax returns.

"Right? But at least I now have a deep and spiritual understanding that the mitochondria is the powerhouse of the cell. That's gonna be super fucking helpful when I'm elbows-deep in shit and ward rounds one day."

I snort-chuckle so hard I nearly aspirate my last sip of wine, which would be a tragic way to go. "Girl, preach." I raise my glass in mock solidarity, shooting the textbook another look of betrayal. It just sits there, taunting me with its perfectly highlighted margins and colour-coded tabs that no longer mean anything.

The truth is, my brain checked out over an hour ago.

Perceptive as always, Naomi leans back on her stool, stretching her arms behind her head. "Alright," she says, with that devilish glint in her eye, "spill. How are you really feeling about the gig on Saturday? Because from where I'm sitting, you've still got that post-concert glow."

She pauses for a beat, then grins. "Or…" she sing-songs, "is there something else keeping you all, what's the word, distracted?" She wiggles her eyebrows, looking far too pleased with herself.

I down the rest of my wine, staring into the empty glass like it might give me answers. "It's Kieran," I admit. "*Fuuuuck*, Nay. That man still does something to me. He did back then, and he still does now."

Just saying his name makes my chest tighten. His face, his voice, the way his eyes found mine in the crowd. It's all on a loop in my head, no matter how hard I try to shake it.

Naomi's grin widens like a cat who's just found the cream. "Ohhh, we're talking about the *moment*, huh? Eyes lock across the room, violins swell, angels sing, and all that?"

"Don't be so dramatic," I mutter.

"Come on, Ellie," she presses. "Admit it. He looked at you like the rest of the world didn't exist."

A quiet laugh escaped me as I shook my head. "It's embarrassing. The second he looked at me, I was just… gone. It was like I was sucked back into that summer all over again."

Naomi's smile softens. She swirls her glass lazily, watching me. "That's not embarrassing, Ellie. That's something most people would kill to feel. But let's not pretend it was just nostalgia. You don't look at someone like that unless the connection is still there."

With a sigh, I run a hand through my hair. "There is no connection. I've got Mia. And David is..." I pause, the words sticking. "He's trying."

Naomi lets out a sharp snort. "Babe, you say that like he's a puppy learning to sit. *He's trying.* That's how low your bar is now?"

I shoot her a look, but she doesn't flinch. That's the thing about Naomi, she never sugar-coats. Never lets me off the hook when I talk in circles.

"You know what I mean," I say, quieter now. "He's... present. For the most part. And I can't just throw that away because my heart did a pirouette the second Kieran showed up."

The words sit between us, raw and unfiltered. Naomi doesn't speak right away. She just sips her wine, tilts her head, and studies me.

"Okay," she says eventually. "No one's asking you to throw anything away. But maybe... just ask yourself the real question."

I glance at her warily. "Which is?"

She leans forward, elbows on the table. "Do you want Kieran in your life? Not in a sweeping, cue-the-dramatic-music kind of way. Just... as a friend. Do you want that?"

The question drops like a stone straight into my stomach. Because the answer's already there. Quiet. Certain.

Yes, of course, yes.

But reality has a way of raining on clarity, so instead, I sigh and drop my gaze to the half-read page in front of me.

"It's not that simple," I murmur.

Naomi snorts and gestures vaguely around us. "Ellie. Nothing in your life is simple. Simplicity left the chat a long time ago. So maybe just... choose what makes you feel good for once?"

I manage a weak smile, but the ache under it won't let go. My fingers trace the rim of my wine glass, stalling.

"It's just weird that after all these years he was just... there," I admit. "Like it's meant to mean something. But, I'm engaged. And Kieran and I -" I stop, swallowing down the weight in my throat. "We have a past. A beautiful, unfinished moment in time kind of past. But could we be friends?" I pause again. "I mean, *fuck*, he might not even want that."

I stare at my textbook again and pour myself another large glass of wine.

Naomi watches me carefully now, her voice softer. "You're allowed to want things, Ellie. You get to have people in your life that you choose to put there."

I huff out a laugh. "Yeah. Because going for what I want has worked so well for me in the past."

She clinks her glass against mine, all sass and affection. "There's a first time for everything, boo. Besides," she adds with a smirk, "if anyone deserves a win, it's you."

I sit on Naomi's words, swirling my wine and taking a long sip. But all I can see is Kieran, eyes locked with mine. That feeling hasn't faded. If anything, it's worse now. Because I remember what I walked away from.

That night, sleep refuses to come easily.

My mind's too full. Spinning with questions I don't know how to ask and answers I'm too afraid to name. Every time I close my eyes, I see him. That look. That voice. That pull. Like the universe has planted him back in my life just to fuck me over.

And I hate it. I hate how easily the memory of him slips in. How a part of me wants to feel it again, just for a second. And I feel guilty for it. For the way my thoughts keep drifting back to him, like I'm wired for it.

I think of David, of how he's been lately. Saying and doing all the right things. But still, it doesn't quiet the noise. It doesn't stop this... pull.

I shouldn't be thinking about Kieran. Not like this. Not when I belong to someone else. But the lines are blurry tonight. There's an ache I can't seem to shake. A low, gnawing feeling that something's been missing for a long time, and maybe I've just been too scared to admit it.

When I finally drift off, it's not into rest. It's into memory.

And there he is.

Leaning against the metal frame of the Ferris wheel like he owns the place. Arms folded. One boot crossed over the other. That smirk tugging at his mouth like he knows exactly the effect he has on me. His eyes catch mine, and for a beat—just one long, suspended beat—the world tilts. Everything else fades. It's just him.

He pushes off the frame and strolls toward me, slow and easy. Faded tee clinging just enough. Hair a mess. Boots scuffed to hell. The kind of beautiful that doesn't know it's beautiful, which only makes it worse.

My breath hitches before I can stop it.

"You've got this look," he murmurs, close enough that I feel the heat of him. *"Like you know exactly what you're doing to me."*

"It's the festival," I tease. *"It makes everything feel a little... brighter."*

Kieran leans in closer, the lights from the Ferris wheel catching along his jaw, casting golden fire across his skin. *"Nah,"* he says. *"Pretty sure it's just you."*

My pulse skips. There's a flutter, low in my stomach, sharp and sweet—the kind I haven't felt in years. Not like this.

"You always this charming?"

He grins. "Only when I'm trying to impress someone."

"Am I supposed to be impressed?"

He lifts a brow, all mock offence. "Are you?"

I pretend to think it over, dragging it out. "Kind of."

"Kind of?" he echoes, clutching his chest like I've stabbed him. "You wound me, Ellie."

I roll my eyes, but I'm smiling. I don't stop him when his hand brushes against mine. My breath catches, and the space between us folds in, as if it was always meant to be.

My breath catches, and the space between us folds in, like the universe is quietly nudging us closer. Like it wants this to happen.

He looks at me like I'm the only thing left in the world worth seeing. And for a moment, I want it. I want him. The closeness, the warmth, the pull of something I've been pretending I don't need.

His fingers skim up, barely grazing my jaw, a touch so feather-light it makes my skin hum. My lips part, a yes hovering, a heartbeat from breaking free. His breath mingles with mine, close enough to count the flecks of grey in his eyes. Could fall into them if I'm not careful.

Time stretches, tightens, holds its breath with us.

And I see it—just for a second.

His mouth brushing mine.

The soft hitch of breath.

A kiss I haven't tasted in four years, but somehow still know the shape of.

But then, something sharp slices through the glow.

A whisper.

The flicker of a ring.

Mia's laugh—distant but clear—like a song I'd forgotten was still playing in the background.

The guilt slams into me like a gut-punch.

I pull back.

Kieran's hand slips from mine. His face twists, not in confusion, but in something closer to heartbreak.

And then the world shatters.

The lights above explode into streaks. The music warps, distorting into static. The air grows too thick to breathe. I try to call his name, but no sound comes.

The ground gives out beneath me, and I fall. Wind screams past me. My body is weightless. Helpless. Hurtling downward like I shouldn't have landed in this moment.

And then I wake.

Heart thrashing. Drenched in sweat and shame. My body jolts upright in bed, breath caught somewhere between a gasp and a sob.

The room is still.

Quiet.

The darkness is thick, like it hasn't decided whether to hold me or smother me.

The dream clings to me. My skin buzzes. Every nerve lit up like it still remembers how I felt that night.

I glance at the clock. 2:27 a.m.

The other side of the bed is empty.

I push the covers back and slide out, my feet hitting the cold floor with a quiet thud. For a moment, I just stand there in the hallway, listening to the stillness.

Then I see it. The faint glow of light beneath the door at the end of the hallway. David's study.

I move before I can think better of it. Light steps. Bare feet. Hands loose at my sides.

The door creaks slightly as I ease it open. And there he is. Hunched over the desk. Back to me. Hands pressed to his temples like the weight of the world lives there. The screen's glow casts long shadows across the room, painting everything in pale, flickering blue.

I follow his gaze straight to the monitor.

That familiar layout. That sickening rhythm.

My chest tightens.

He promised. *Swore*, actually, after the last time. Said he was done. Said he was different now.

And here he is.

Again.

The morning light cuts through the curtains, sharp and cold, painting fractured lines across the floor like cracks. The house is silent, but not peacefully so. It's the quiet that hums with tension, like the air is waiting for something to snap. My chest feels tight. My stomach is hollow. Every breath I take feels like it has to sneak in.

When I get downstairs, David's already at the kitchen table. Head bowed over his phone, scrolling with that detached focus he always has when he's avoiding reality. He doesn't look up. But he doesn't need to. The tension hangs thick and sour in the air, twisting like a storm cloud waiting for the strike.

I sit across from him, fingers gripping my knees to stop the tremble. My pulse is loud in my ears, fast and uneven. I swallow, forcing my voice to steady. "David... can we talk?"

He glances up, briefly. A flicker of something, then gone. Replaced by that calm, careful expression I know too well. "Sure, babe. What's up?"

I open my mouth. Close it again. My fingers twitch in my lap. The words are there, coiled and ready, but I can't seem to push them out.

"Last night..." I begin. "I woke up and you weren't in bed. I saw the light in your study, I just..." I trail off.

He doesn't move. Doesn't blink. Just watches me. Quiet. Waiting.

"I couldn't sleep," I try again. "The light was on, and I..."

David sighs. Soft, but it lands like a slap. He sets his phone down slowly. Deliberately. Like I've already accused him. Like I crossed a line.

"Ellie," he says, voice low. "Why don't you just man the fuck up and say it?"

My heart drops.

He leans back in his chair, arms folding. His jaw clenches, and his eyes cut straight through me. "You think I was gambling."

The words land with a thud. He said it, not me. But it feels worse that way. Like I've confessed to something unforgivable without ever opening my mouth.

They scrape against something fragile inside me. Guilt. Or fear. Or that small, quiet voice that's been growing louder lately. The one that's wondering if I *do* know the difference. If maybe I'm not just being paranoid.

I want to defend myself. Say, *I didn't mean it like that*. But maybe I did.

"Why don't you *trust* me?"

Another blow. Not because he's right, but because he *sounds* right. Wounded. Reasonable.

"It's not that I don't trust you. I just. I saw..."

"You saw what?" His voice sharpens. "You wake up, see a light on, and that's your first thought? That I'm gambling again?" He laughs, dry and humourless, as he shakes his head. "Jesus, Ellie. Do you even hear yourself?"

I flinch. His tone is calm, but it's laced with something venomous. He looks at me like I've betrayed him. Like I've attacked him.

Maybe I have? When he puts it like that. Have I crossed a line?

"But—"

His hand slams down on the table—sharp, sudden, loud.

The sound cracks through the room like a gunshot, rattling the edge of my nerves.

I flinch, instinctively.

"I wasn't gambling!" he shouts. "I was *working*. Something urgent came up. You know my job doesn't just clock out at five, right? Half the time I'm pulling strings when you're fast asleep."

"I wasn't accusing you of anything," I say, too fast, trying to diffuse the situation. "I just... it felt like before, and I panicked. I thought I saw—"

He cuts me off. "Before. Right. Because none of it matters. Nothing I do now counts. Doesn't matter how long it's been, how hard I've worked. You still think I'm *that* guy."

My gut twists. I cross my arms around myself, holding tight. And just like that, the doubt slips in. Sharp-edged. Unwelcome. But familiar.

What if I'm wrong?

What if I just saw what I was expecting to see?

David exhales through his nose and rakes a hand through his hair, like *he's* the one who's hurt. Like I'm the one making this hard.

"I've done everything for this family," he says. "For you. For Mia. And I still have to defend myself every time you let your imagination run wild."

His eyes find mine. Cold. Frustrated. "Do you really think I want to be up late in that office instead of lying in bed next to you? You think I enjoy this, Ellie? Someone has to keep this life going. Someone has to provide. Especially since you're not exactly bringing much in right now."

There it is. Slipped in neat and quiet, like it's just a fact, not a jab. Like I'm the charity case in my own home.

And sure, technically, he's not wrong. I'm not earning, not really. Just a student nurse with a mountain of debt, scraping by on student loans that barely cover the mortgage and a box of tampons. But the way he says it? Like my ambition's a burden. Like I should be grateful he hasn't handed me a bloody invoice.

My breath catches then, and the guilt creeps in like smoke.

He has been better. Working more. And maybe I am the one who can't let it go. The one who keeps dragging us back into old patterns.

"I wasn't trying to start a fight," I whisper.

David leans back, sighing like he's made peace with a tantrum. "I know," he says, softer now. "But Ellie, you've got to trust me. We have a good thing. You, me, Mia. We're building something here. But every time you pull this shit? Every time you doubt me? That's what breaks it. Not me. *You.*"

The words sting. Sharp and heavy. My throat tightens, but I say nothing. Because maybe he's right. Maybe I *am* the problem.

He reaches across the table and takes my hand. His grip is firm. Steady. Like a lifeline. Like he's already forgiven me.

"I love you, Ellie. I love Mia. But you've got to stop making up problems that don't exist. Let me prove I'm not that guy anymore, without turning it into a war every time."

I nod, numb. "I know. I'm sorry. I'll… do better."

His lips curve into a small, satisfied smile. "That's all I ask, baby."

The tightness in my chest doesn't leave. It just sinks deeper and heavier.

Not because I believe him. But because, once again, I tell myself this is my fault. That I'm the one who's in the wrong.

Even if some small, aching part of me is finally wondering…

What if I'm not?

CHAPTER 8

not done with you yet

KIERAN

I HADN'T PLANNED ON STAYING in South Havens this long, none of us had, but the next leg of the tour doesn't start for another week, and I'm not exactly rushing to leave.

Something about this city has its grip on us. Like it wrapped its fingers around our wrists and whispered, *just stay a little longer.*

That's what I tell myself, anyway.

But the truth? I know exactly why I'm still here.

It's been just over a week since the gig. Since I saw her in the crowd, saw the ring, and heard about her daughter. And I still can't get her out of my head.

I know I've got no right to want anything from her. Not even her time. Call me selfish. But I do. I just want to know her again, even if it means biting my tongue and pushing back every instinct to reach for more than she's able to give.

Every morning, I escape to a beach I found on the edge of the city. This quiet stretch in Windrush Hollow, tucked away from everything.

I hit the sand and don't stop until my thoughts begin to unravel, blurred into the rhythm of my breath and the slap of my feet against the earth. I learned the hard way that running on dry sand is absolute hell. It's like nature's version of a treadmill—except it's laughing at you the whole time. So now I stick to the shore, where the sand's firm and wet, the water licking at my shoes with every stride.

The sea air slices clean through the fog in my head, cold and sharp, the kind that wakes you from the inside out. Waves drag themselves up the beach in a slow, steady rhythm. Dogs tear past in pure, feral joy, barking at the surf like they've got a shot in hell of catching a wave. A golden retriever is losing its mind over a stick.

I slow at an old stone wall overlooking the beach and drop onto it, chest heaving, muscles burning in that good, spent way. The retriever finally snags its prize, tail wagging like it's just won the bloody lottery.

I huff a laugh, scrubbing sweat from my face with the hem of my T-shirt.

This place is peaceful. It's quiet.

It feels like home.

Pulling out my phone, I scroll to Dad's name. Two rings, and he answers.

"Hey there, son." His voice is warm and familiar, laced with that quiet concern he always tries—and fails—to hide.

"Hey, old man. How you doing?"

"Oi, less of the old, *sprout*." He chuckles. "Still running laps around the lads at the club. They're convinced I cheat at dominos, though. Honestly. How can you even cheat at dominos?"

I grin, the nickname tugging something loose in my chest. *Sprout*. Mum started calling me that when I was a kid—short for *bean sprout*—because I shot up so fast and never quite grew into my limbs. Tall, gangly, all knees and elbows. It stuck.

"And Mrs. Patel?"

"Ah, still at it. Trying to marry me off to her cousin, bless her. Keeps sneaking round with curries and what not '*for the freezer.*' She thinks I don't notice."

"She'll wear you down eventually."

"Not bloody likely. Told her I'm too stubborn to be anyone's project. Besides, I like my peace and quiet."

There's a rustle on his end, the clink of a mug. "Got your mother's old mug here," he adds, voice softening a little. "Still makes the tea taste better, I swear."

I smile faintly, pulling my knees up. "You're a sentimental old sod."

"Someone's got to be." His laughter fades into a calm silence.

I already know what's coming next.

"So," he says, gentler now. "How's the road treating you?"

I exhale, watching the retriever flop into the sand like it had just fought a war and heroically surrendered. "Good. We're sticking around South Havens a bit longer. Next gig's not for a while."

"Unusual for you lot to stay put."

"We're trying something new," I offer. "Taking a breather."

He makes a noise like he's not buying it. "And are you taking a breather? Or are you just keeping busy in new ways?"

My jaw tightens. "I'm fine, Dad."

"Didn't say you weren't, kiddo." His voice softens. "Just… you push yourself too hard. Always have. I know the band means the world to you, but you don't have to break yourself to prove you've earned it."

The words land harder than I expect them to. I stare out at the horizon, heart thudding behind my ribs. "You think I should stop?"

"No," he says, firm. "I just think… you've made it. You're living the dream. Just slow down a bit, son. Let yourself feel it."

I swallow the lump rising in my throat and grip the phone tighter. He doesn't say things like this often, but when he does, they stick.

He's been in my corner since day one.

Saved for months to buy my first guitar. Sat through every off-key school concert without complaint. Never once told me to play it safe.

But he knows me. Knows how I chase the high like it's a badge of honour.

"I hear you," I mumble.

"I know you do. Just take care of yourself, alright?"

"Yeah."

"You too, old man."

He chuckles. "Talk soon."

I linger on the wall, roll my shoulders, and try to shake off my dad's words. He means well, he always does, but the thought of slowing down, of standing still long enough for everything to catch up to me makes my skin itch.

Because I don't really know who I am without the noise. The touring, the rehearsals, the chaos. It's not just what I do. It's who I am. Who I've been since I was a teenager and desperate to prove I could make something of myself. That it wasn't just a phase. That I could be someone.

For my dad. For me. For…I don't even know.

If I slow down now, if I stop for even a minute, I'm scared I'll look around and realise I've built my whole life around a version of myself that only works when everything's moving. And if I'm not chasing it anymore. Then what?

I push off the wall and stretch—muscles still humming from the run—and head back up the narrow, cobbled street that winds through the village.

The place has this rare charm that's untouched by modern conveniences. No high-rises or chain shops. Just crooked stone buildings and rusted iron brackets holding weathered signs.

I don't plan on stopping. But the smell of fresh coffee and warm pastry curls through the air and sucker-punches my willpower.

I slow outside a little café with paint peeling from the windowsills, flowers tumbling from hanging baskets like the place is trying too hard to stay charming, and pulling it off.

Before I can think better of it, my hand pushes open the door. The bell overhead jingles. A soft, familiar chime lands warm in my chest.

Inside, the place whirs. Mismatched tables, scratched-up chairs, yellowing walls plastered with crooked frames. It smells like espresso and sugar, and I breathe it in like oxygen.

At the counter, an older woman in a flour-dusted apron arranges croissants like they're fine art. Laugh lines etched deep into her cheeks. Her eyes look like they've seen every kind of heartbreak and reunion this village has ever had.

"You look like someone in desperate need of caffeine and something sweet," she says, looking up.

I grin. "That obvious?"

Brenda, according to her name tag, finally looks up, sizing me like she's trying to place me.

"You're that musician?" she asks, eyes narrowing slightly. "Had a group of girls in here the other day. Wouldn't stop talking about some band that played in the city. Kept showing me this lead singer. That you, then?"

I smirk. "Depends. Did they say he was devilishly handsome?"

She lets out a throaty laugh. "Bit of an ego on you, huh?"

"Occupational hazard."

Brenda slides an almond croissant toward me like a dare. "Go on, then. Tell me that's not the best thing you've had this side of the coast."

I take a bite. Warm, flaky, rich with marzipan and butter. Unreal. "Okay," I say, mouth full. "That's amazing."

She beams.

Then the door chimes. I don't look up. Just another customer. Another sleepy regular. But something shifts, something I feel before I see. I glance toward the door. And there she is.

Windblown hair. Some oversized t-shirt that is swallowing her whole. Tiny shorts. Legs for days. Soft in all the ways I remember, except now there's a tightness to her posture. Like she hadn't slept in a week, and her thoughts followed her in.

She hasn't seen me yet. And I can't move. Can't speak. Can't fucking breathe.

What is the universe doing to me?

The air shifts as I lean away from the counter, suddenly unsure how to play it.

There's this pull. This ache to know her again. To understand the girl I've been thinking about since the second I saw her in that damn hospital.

Ellie steps up to the counter like she's done it a hundred times, completely unaware I'm here, and Brenda greets her with a smile.

I watch, frozen, as she tucks a strand of hair behind her ear. And suddenly, the café feels way too small for my chest. I could leave. Slip out the door, pretend I was never here. But before I can think better of it, the words are already out of my mouth.

"Hey, you."

Her shoulders twitch, barely, but I see it. She turns, slow and uncertain. Our eyes lock, and for a second, we just stare at each other.

"...Kieran?" The way she says it. It's not just surprise. It means something. Still holds weight.

"In the flesh," I say, leaning against the counter like I'm not internally spiralling.

She lets out a soft laugh, and it makes my pulse spike. "I—what are you doing here?"

"Same as you, apparently. Coffee. Croissant." I smile. Keep it light. Pretend my heart's not trying to punch its way out of my chest.

She glances between me and Brenda, who gives her the most unsubtle *talk to him*, eyebrow raise I've ever seen.

Ellie smiles, despite herself. "I didn't expect to run into you here," she says, quieter now.

"Ditto." I let the smirk fade. "Wouldn't blame you if it's not a welcome surprise."

Her eyes drop, then lift again.

"It's... unexpected for sure." A beat. "Kind of funny how we keep ending up in the same places, huh?"

"Yeah." I nod toward the back of the café. "I'm happy to sit... if you are. No interruptions this time."

She hesitates, just for a second. I can practically see the wheels turning. But then she smiles.

And Jesus, it flips something in me.

"Sure," she says. "Why not?"

We weave past tables to a quiet corner at the back. The air feels different here, thicker. Charged. Like the room knows what's sitting between us.

She slips into the seat across from me, eyes flicking around like she's still catching up with the moment. Like part of her's already halfway out the door.

But when her gaze finds mine, something settles. Not entirely, but enough.

"So," I say, keeping my voice light. Steady. "What's your story, Ellie?"

She looks up, that cautious smile flickering at the corners of her mouth. "Busy. Mostly uni and shifts at the hospital. Mia's got a load of school stuff going on, so there's always something."

She pauses just for a second, as something softer crosses her face. "Nothing very exciting."

"Sounds like you're juggling a lot."

"Less juggling. More — barely hanging in there."

"Still sounds pretty impressive from where I'm sitting."

She glances down at her coffee, like it's easier to focus on the steam than take the compliment. "What about you? Figured you'd be off in some new city by now."

"Yeah, usually," I say, raking a hand through my hair. "But we've got a break before the next leg of the tour. Thought we'd hang back a bit, find some quieter spots. Soak up the calm."

"Right," she says, glancing toward Brenda, who's *definitely* pretending to mind her own business.

"You found the right place. I've been coming here since I was a teenager. Brenda's local royalty."

"She mentioned she's been here a while," I say with a smile. "And these croissants are something else."

"Yeah," Ellie says. "I've had one almost every morning since I started uni."

"How's it going?"

She huffs a soft laugh, eyes lowering to her cup. "It's been a long road, honestly. It hasn't been easy."

"I bet. You did it though, Ellie." I say, meaning it.

She glances up, a surprised smile tugging at her mouth. "Yeah. It took time. And a few — okay *a lot* — of nervous breakdowns."

I grin, but it fades into something softer as she looks at me again — really looks. There's something open in her eyes now, something unguarded.

"I nearly didn't try," she says, her thumb brushing the rim of her cup. "I used to lie awake some nights convinced I wasn't smart enough. That I'd missed the window, you know? Too old, too behind."

I don't speak. I just watch her. Hold her gaze and let her keep going.

She draws in a breath. "But that night—by the lake. Do you remember?"

"I remember everything, Ellie." And I mean every word.

She flushes, pink creeping up her cheeks.

"If it wasn't for you," I say quietly, "I don't think I ever would've gone for it."

My heart twists, something tender blooming in my chest. I shake my head gently, voice low. "You were always gonna do it, Ells. Give yourself more credit."

She looks down, a faint smile tugging at her lips, but I catch the way her eyes shine.

"You're the one who showed up. You put the work in. And it sounds like you earned every damn croissant."

"Brenda's been a constant through most of it. Always made space for me here. Even when I showed up with Mia in tow, crying over textbooks and deadlines."

I watch her just for a second, the way her face softens when she talks about it. About that version of herself, fighting to become something new.

"She kind of stepped in when I needed someone," she adds, quieter now.

Something shifts in her face. An opening. A tiny crack in the armour. So, I tread lightly. "And your parents?"

She doesn't answer right away. Just nods once, eyes on her t-shirt as she picks at the hem. "Oh, they're around in their own way. I'm still trying to tick their boxes." A pause. "Things were weird with them for a long time. Like somewhere along the way I stopped being the person they wanted me to be."

She gives a small shake of her head. "They were embarrassed, I think, when I got pregnant. More worried about what the neighbours would say than… about me."

I don't speak. Just listen. Let her have the space.

"It's better now, though." She blurts, like she needs me to know she turned it around. "Not perfect. But I think they like where I'm at these days."

That catches me. The way she's trying to make it sound okay. Like she has to defend her own past just to take up space in the present.

I nod, slower this time. "They should've liked you back then, too."

My voice comes out quiet, but sharper than I meant it. "You didn't deserve to feel you were anything less than amazing."

"It was what it was." She shrugs, but it doesn't land like peace.

"But what about you, anyway?" she asks then, steering the conversation away from herself with quiet precision. "How's life been treating you?"

She tilts her head, waiting.

"The last few years have been... mad, honestly. Like, every day's felt like a bit of a pinch-me moment. Bigger crowds, bigger venues—stuff we used to daydream about."

Ellie smiles, warm and proud in a way that makes something settle low in my chest.

"You lot deserve it. You've worked your arses off."

"Yeah, we have," I admit, not bothering to play it down. "It's all gone so fast, though. One minute we're stuffing gear into the back of Dad's car, and the next we're touring the UK. It still doesn't feel real half the time."

She leans back slightly. "How's the tour going?"

"It's been good. Wild, mostly. We're in the last stretch now—wraps up in September. After that, it's just... waiting, I guess."

"Waiting?"

I shrug. "To see if the label wants to sign us on for an album. They're hinting, but nothing confirmed yet."

She arches a brow. "That's exciting."

"Yeah. We're hopeful. If it goes through, we'll probably be back in the studio in the new year."

Her smile softens. "You deserve it, Kieran. All of it."

We let the silence stretch between us, and for once, it doesn't feel heavy. Just honest. But I couldn't help myself. There was still one thing I needed to know.

"Ellie…" I say, my voice low, almost a whisper. It pulls her attention back to me. "Why did you leave?"

I let the moment settle. I'm not trying to trap her in the past — I just need to understand.

"I think I just freaked out." She looks at me like she doesn't know whether to run, cry, or laugh. Maybe all three.

"I wish I could give you a more concrete reason. But… I had Mia," she says, voice soft but steady. "And I didn't know how to juggle everything."

She pauses, eyes drifting somewhere past me. "My parents didn't make it easy. Everything I did felt like it was under a microscope — like they were constantly waiting for me to fuck up."

There's a quiet beat before she speaks again, her voice lower now.

"I think that's why I made a lot of the choices I did. I stopped trusting my own instincts."

Her eyes flick up to meet mine, searching. "And then there was you." Her voice turns gentler. A truth slipping through.

"That week… it meant more than I can explain. You were this beautiful moment of calm in the middle of everything. And God it felt like being seen for the first time in years."

She glances up at me, then away.

"But that scared the shit out of me. Because the rest of my life didn't feel like that." She pauses. "You felt like something I wasn't allowed to have. My life was already so messy. And you…" her voice wavers, "you didn't deserve to get pulled into it."

She swallows hard. "So I left. Not because I didn't care. But because I did."

And just like that, the missing piece I've carried around for years falls into place.

"Ellie." I breathe.

I reach across the table, fingers brushing against hers softly. Like I'm afraid she'll pull away.

SOMEHOW STILL YOU

She doesn't.

"I spent so long thinking I did something wrong," I say, voice rough at the edges. "Replaying every moment. Trying to figure out where I screwed up. I thought I said something. Or pushed too hard. Or maybe I just… wasn't enough."

Her eyes soften. And then she reaches back, hand curling into mine. "You didn't do anything wrong, Kieran. Not one thing." Her voice is quiet, but there's no doubt in it. "It was all me. Just stuck in my head. You were the only thing that felt right that week. But by the time I realised how much that mattered, it was already too late."

And that truth cuts deeper than rejection ever could.

Something settles between us then. Not closure exactly. But *something*. A thread. A beginning, almost.

I let the silence breathe. Then I reach into my pocket and pull out my phone, placing it gently on the table. "I don't know if this is out of order," I say, nudging it toward her. "But, if you ever need anything, or just want to talk. You've got me. No pressure or expectations."

She stares at the phone like it's delicate. Like it might tip the balance. Then, slowly, with fingers steadier than I expected, she picks it up, types her number, and hands me her phone in return.

Our fingers brush again when I pass it back. A flicker of contact that says more than either of us has dared to say out loud.

She holds my gaze. "I never thought we'd end up here," she says, voice soft. "Talking like this. After all this time."

"Neither did I." My voice comes out rough and honest. "But I'm glad we did."

I save her contact and tuck my phone back into my pocket.

"I want to be in your life, Ellie," I say, barely above a whisper. "Whatever way you'll let me."

She doesn't answer straight away. Just looks at me. Really looks. Like she's trying to decide if letting me in is safe this time.

And then she smiles.

Not wide. Not easy.

But it's real.

And right now, that's everything.

We stay there longer than we probably should and Brenda keeps the coffee coming without asking. And for the first time in a long time, I don't feel like I'm performing. I'm just here. With her.

Eventually, she checks her phone and winces. "Shoot. I've gotta go. School pickup."

"Right," I say, trying not to sound disappointed. "Yeah, of course."

She grabs her bag and gives me a quick smile. "Bye, Kieran."

"Bye, Ellie."

She waves at Brenda on her way out, and then she's gone.

The café feels instantly quieter. I sink back into my chair and run a hand through my hair.

Then my phone buzzes.

> ELLS [14:38]
> Thanks for the coffee, rockstar ☆

I don't even try to hide the grin that takes over my whole damn face.

CHAPTER 9
blurred lines

ELLIE

THE LAST FEW WEEKS HAVE passed in a blur. Hospital shifts, dissertation edits I barely remember writing, and wine-soaked therapy sessions with Naomi that always start seriously and end with us snorting with laughter. Life's been full. Good. Maybe even normal.

And David?

He's been... different. Like nothing ever happened.

Like I didn't wake up to an empty bed, didn't see the glow of his monitor at 2am, and feel that cold sink into my chest. Like he didn't walk me back from my own memory the next morning like I'd imagined it all, like the facts were foggy and unreliable.

He's been sweet. Attentive. Bringing me coffee just the way I like it. Making Mia laugh at dinner. Remembering tiny, throwaway comments like he's trying to prove something.

And I want to believe it's all in my head. God, I want to.

Because if he's trying, then maybe this wasn't all for nothing. Maybe I didn't waste years. Maybe I wasn't wrong.

And I've been trying too. Smiling in the right places, laughing on cue, meeting him halfway like we're rebuilding something steady. Like I'm not still holding my breath. Like I'm not still waiting for the slip.

But history has a habit of slapping me in the face. Because the thing with David is—it's always a pendulum. One minute, he's present and polished, all warmth and thoughtful gestures. The next, he's distant. A constant blow of hot and cold.

It's giving me whiplash. And I never know which version of him I'm going to get.

But I keep hoping the good one sticks. The one I love.

Then there's Kieran.

That day in the café cracked something open in me. Something I'd boarded up a long time ago. We've kept in touch, like we said we would. A few messages here and there. Nothing too serious.

And it's nice. *More* than nice.

But I don't know what to do with it. I just know it's easy. As natural as breathing.

But today isn't about any of that. Because today is August 16th. *Mia's birthday.*

She's thirteen. A fucking teenager.

And just like that, the breath catches in my throat.

I don't know how we got here. How that tiny, wrinkled baby I brought home—red-faced with lungs of steel—now steals my shoes and argues about curfews. How the girl who once clung to my hand now insists on doing everything herself. How the years slipped through my fingers while I was too busy holding everything else together.

I'm not ready. I don't think I ever will be.

The kitchen smells like citrus and mint. The punch bowl sweats on the counter as I stir it slowly with a wooden spoon. Non-alcoholic. Mia's request. There's lime, raspberries, and sprigs of mint from the pot on the windowsill. Sweet and summery. Exactly how she wanted it.

"Smells lovely in here," Mum says, drifting in with sunglasses in one hand and her phone in the other. "Is that for the kids?"

I nod, letting out a quiet laugh. "Yep. Mia's big on mocktails now, apparently."

"You think that's suitable?" Her voice is breezy, but there's a thread of disapproval underneath.

"Called a mocktail for a reason, Mum."

She hums, lips pursed as she peeks into the jug. "Still. Seems a bit... grown up, doesn't it?"

I bite the inside of my cheek. "It's fruit juice, Mum. With mint."

"Mm. Can never be too careful, though. Don't want to set the wrong impression." She says vaguely.

My jaw tightens, but I smile anyway. "She's thirteen. Not feral."

"Well, you always did like to learn the hard way," she says with a small, pointed smile, like it's a joke. Like it's not another one of her tiny barbs dressed up as maternal concern.

I can feel her watching me, waiting for something. But I keep my eyes down and stir the punch.

"She looks lovely today," Mum diverts. "That green dress suits her." Then her gaze shifts. Slides over me. Lingers. "You're not wearing that out to the party, are you?"

I glance down. Jean shorts, cropped white vest, and flip-flops. It's thirty-two sodding degrees outside, and the least amount of clothing I can wear and still pass as remotely acceptable, the better. I feel good. Put together, even. Sun-kissed skin, hair up, a hint of mascara. It's the most like myself I've felt in weeks.

"It's boiling," I say, trying to keep it light. "And it's not like it's a black-tie gala. It's a garden party, Mum."

She hums, that familiar, soft criticism wrapped in a smile. "It's just, it's a bit casual, isn't it?" She raises an eyebrow. "There'll be photos, Eleanor."

I wince at the name. My mouth opens, then closes. I hesitate.

"There's a lovely linen dress in your wardrobe," she says, almost offhand. "The pale blue one I bought you. It brings out your eyes."

The door swings shut behind her with a soft click, and I'm left alone in the kitchen. The only sound is the fizz of soda in the punch bowl.

I wasn't going to change. But now all I can see is the look in her eyes. All I can hear is that edge in her voice. The one that's been with me my whole life.

And, as always, I fold. Smooth the corners and make it easier for everyone else. I don't even know when I started doing that. When I stopped defending my choices. When I decided it was simpler to just nod, smile, and slip into whatever version of myself made things run smoother.

I tell myself it's not a big deal. It's just an outfit. It's just a day. But deep down, I know what it is. It's a habit I don't know how to break.

Still, I wipe my hands on a tea towel and head upstairs.

At the back of my wardrobe, I find the pale blue dress she was talking about. Knee-length. Sweet. Safe. The dress you wear when you want people to say you look "*well*" but not ask any follow-up questions.

It's fine. Nice even.

I tilt my head. Try to see what she sees. Not the creased linen, or the faint tan lines, or the tired, sloping curve of my shoulders.

Just the version of me that looks like she's got it all together.

I don't recognise her. But I zip it up anyway.

Because today, I'll show up and I'll smile. Because whatever else is happening, this day is Mia's. And she deserves a mum who makes her feel like nothing else matters.

I square my shoulders, take a breath, and head back downstairs into the thick August air. Into laughter. Into the life I built for her.

The garden hums with late-summer energy. Smoke curls from the barbecue, carrying the scent of charred corn and sizzling burgers. String lights sway overhead, throwing soft halos across the uneven grass. Layered voices fill the air, rising and falling with the rhythm of familiarity.

Everything looks like joy.

My parents huddle near the patio table, chatting with David's mum and dad. They all look like they've stepped out of a country club brochure—pearls, expensive watches, pressed linen, wine glasses never empty.

"Mum!" Mia calls from across the garden, waving me over with a half-eaten cupcake in one hand. "If I have to hear one more person say how grown up I look, I'm moving to Antarctica."

I snort and make my way over, ruffling her hair as I pass. She ducks away with a groan. "Seriously?"

"Oh come on, you love the attention."

"I tolerate it," she says primly. "Big difference."

I grin and loop an arm around her shoulders before she can wriggle free. "Happy birthday, bug."

She sighs but leans in for a beat, just long enough for a squeeze. "Thanks, Mum."

I glance around, scanning the crowd that's mostly made up of neighbours, friends, a few stray relatives. Then I lower my voice, keeping it casual. "Did your dad stop by this morning?"

Mia nods, licking a bit of icing from her thumb. "Yeah. He dropped off a card."

"Did he stay long?"

"Nah, just a quick hello. He had work." She says it lightly, without bitterness. Just a fact.

I nod. "Did he give you anything nice?"

She shrugs, but there's a small smile tugging at her lips. "Cash. Classic move. But he wrote something sappy in the card."

I bump her shoulder gently. "You alright?"

"Yeah," she says, glancing up at me. "I'm glad he came. Even for a minute."

There's a flicker of something in her eyes. Fondness, maybe. That careful middle ground where love lives, even if closeness doesn't.

"Good," I whisper. "I'm glad too."

Then she's off again. She darts back to her friends surrounding the punch bowl, clinking plastic tumblers of pink fizz like it's champagne. I watch her go, this brilliant, growing girl who somehow carries grace wherever she goes.

And then I realise. I did this. Whatever else I've messed up. I gave her this. A life full of joy to live in.

Across the garden, David steps out of the kitchen, a tray of drinks balanced neatly in his hands. He moves with careful ease, like someone playing the part of a host in a scene he's already rehearsed. His face gives nothing away, just that same smooth, unreadable calm.

"Babe, can you give me a hand with the food?"

"Sure."

I follow him inside, the sound of laughter fading as the door swings shut behind us.

The kitchen is warm and slightly chaotic. Every surface taken hostage by trays and foil-covered bowls, the air dense with the mix of grilled meat and garlic butter. Somewhere beneath it all, there's a hint of overripe strawberries and something beginning to scorch. The birthday cake sits on the counter, pristine and over-decorated, like it knows its moment's coming.

David sets the tray down and turns to me, watching. "Everything okay?"

I nod. "Yeah. Why wouldn't it be?"

He shrugs, mouth twitching into a smile that doesn't quite make it to his eyes. "Just checking."

I reach for a plate, peeling back the foil on the grilled chicken like it demands my full attention. He hands me the still-warm garlic bread, the scent of herbs and butter rising between us.

"You've done good with her, you know," he says.

It catches me off guard. Lands somewhere soft. "We both have, David."

Something shifts in his eyes, but it's gone before I can name it. He steps in and kisses me softly, lingering for a few moments. "Let's get this outside before someone sends a search party," he says with a grin.

His hand trails low as he moves past me, giving my ass a squeeze. Then he pulls me in, just for a second, arm snug around my waist like it's instinct.

I roll my eyes, let out a low laugh, my hand finding his chest out of habit.

Then I grab the tray and follow him out.

The kitchen door swings open, the rush of summer air hits my skin like a reset, and the sound of laughter floods back in, bright and unbothered.

Back outside, Naomi has arrived. And, as always, she's already commanding the entire garden like it's her personal stage. "All right, where's my favourite teenager?!"

Mia's face lights up the second she hears her. She bounds across the grass—a grin stretched wide across her face and throws herself onto the bench beside Naomi. Her friends flanking her like loyal sidekicks.

Naomi pulls a small, perfectly wrapped box from her bag and hands it over to Mia, who wastes no time tearing through the wrapping paper like it's the last present she'll ever receive. There's a split second of silence. Then…

"SHUT. THE. FRONT. DOOR!"

Sweet mother of God. That child has spent *far* too much time around my best friend.

She holds up a box of LED strip lights—eyes wide, mouth hanging open. The exact lights all teenagers apparently need to achieve some kind of bedroom aesthetic.

Naomi grins. "Your room's about to look sick. I expect a full remodel by tomorrow."

"Oh my God. This is perfect."

Claire leans in, eyes wide. "Okay, but are you going full Pinterest aesthetic or more gamer-girl vibes?"

Claire's lived three doors down since she and Mia were in nappies, and they've been inseparable ever since—matching Halloween costumes, friendship bracelets, secret codes scribbled in glitter pens. Their bond is stitched together by a thousand sleepovers and more inside jokes than I can keep up with.

Mia arches a brow, cool and unbothered. "Why not both?"

Naomi snorts. "Smart kid."

From across the garden, I smile, heart catching in my chest. She's still mine. Still my little girl. But in moments like this, when she lights up completely without me… I see her becoming someone else.

And I love her for it. Even if it stings a little.

Naomi reaches into her bag again and pulls out a slim, flat package. "This one's a bit more sentimental," she says, voice lighter than her eyes.

Mia opens it carefully this time, peeling the paper back at the corners, unfolding it like it might break. She flips it over and freezes.

The print is simple. Elegant.

Bold black lettering that reads: *Don't dream it, be it.*

And below that, in delicate script, the lyrics to one of her favourite songs.

Mia's mouth opens like she wants to say something, but nothing comes out. She just stares at the print, fingers curled tightly around the frame like it might vanish if she lets go.

I glance at Naomi, who isn't smiling now. Her expression is soft. Grounded. She watches Mia the way only Naomi does, like every version of her matters.

"You made this?" Mia finally breathes.

Naomi nods once. "You told me it was your favourite. Figured it belonged on your wall, not just stuck in your head."

Mia clutches it to her chest. "I'm never taking this down."

Naomi just smiles and reaches into the bag for one last gift and hands it to Mia. She opens it slower this time, peeling back the layers like she's drawing it out on purpose.

Inside is a sleek neon sign, glowing softly in a rich violet, that says *Mia's Zone* in looping cursive script, which makes a bedroom feel like its own minor planet. Mia's jaw drops. "NO WAY."

Before anyone can blink, she's throwing her arms around Naomi, tight and fierce, like she means it. Naomi laughs, surprised, but hugs her back without hesitation. "Glad you like it, kiddo."

I stand back, watch them tangled up in each other's joy, and something inside me twists. Not painfully. Just enough to remind me how lucky we are.

Naomi doesn't have to show up the way she does. She doesn't have to know exactly what Mia loves. But she does, every single time.

I walk over. "You're kind of amazing," I say quietly, nudging her shoulder.

She smirks. "I know. I'm basically the best unofficial aunt that ever existed."

"You really are."

Naomi glances at me sideways, and something in her expression softens. "Hey, don't get all misty-eyed on me. You'll ruin your mascara."

I snort. "Waterproof."

"Prepared queen. Love that for you."

Mia pulls away, beaming, her eyes brighter than I've seen them in weeks. "THIS IS THE BEST BIRTHDAY EVER!"

A cheer goes up from the girls on the bench, and one of them starts a half-hearted chant of "Speech! Speech!" that dissolves into laughter.

David steps forward then, placing a hand gently on Mia's shoulder, his voice light. "All right, who's ready for cake?"

The girls erupt with a chorus of yeses and enthusiastic clapping.

And for just a moment, everything feels… good. Like, maybe for a few hours, we got it all to work.

The house is quiet now. The quiet that only settles after something good. Something loud and full and fleeting.

The scent of birthday cake still clings to the air, tangled with smoke and the faint sharpness of Prosecco. Crumpled wrapping paper spills out of bags near the back door. Plates crowd the sink. Empty glasses line the worktop where they've been abandoned. The place is a mess, but it's the best kind.

Proof that people were here. That something was celebrated.

I move through it slowly, barefoot, the hem of my dress brushing my knees as I gather plates, stack glasses, throw napkins into the bin without really seeing them.

There's a shift in the air, then. That instinctive prickle at the base of my neck, the kind that tells you someone's behind you before a single sound gives them away.

I don't turn. Just keep rinsing the plate in my hands, water running hot and steady, steam curling up into my face.

Then I glance over my shoulder.

David's in the doorway, one shoulder propped against the frame like he's been there a while. Shirt wrinkled, collar open, a strand of hair has fallen across his forehead, softening the usual sharpness.

Like he's shrugged off the polished host and let something real breathe through the cracks.

There's a smirk at the corner of his mouth, faint and unreadable. He says nothing.

"You left me to clean all this on my own?" I ask, aiming for playful.

He hums, stepping in. "Just giving you a head start."

The scent of whiskey follows him in, subtle but sharp enough to catch. It hangs between us like smoke.

Then he steps in behind me, his hands sliding around my waist like muscle memory.

"You were amazing today," he murmurs, lips brushing the shell of my ear. "Everything was perfect."

His hands drift lower, fingers slipping beneath the hem of my dress. They skim the backs of my thighs, light at first, then bolder, more certain. He palms the curve of my ass through the lace, and a low sound hums in his throat. Part appreciation, part possession.

I know this script. The nights soaked in whiskey and want.

"You looked incredible," he adds, his mouth grazing skin.

A chill prickles across my arms.

I grip the edge of the sink, grounding myself. My heart stutters against my ribs. "David…" My voice is thin, tight.

Before I can think, he moves and lifts me onto the worktop like it costs him nothing. The cool marble kisses the backs of my thighs, and my dress rides up around my waist, leaving only the lace of my thong between us.

He kisses below my ear, hand sliding to my thigh. The hem of my dress hikes higher under his fingers, and my pulse kicks, sharp and wrong.

"I need you," he breathes, lips ghosting over mine, and the words wrap around me like vines.

I should stop this.

Because when he's whiskey warm, and his eyes are a little darker —sex stops feeling like love. It's a transaction.

And I know how it ends. The heat, the high, the hollow ache that follows.

And still—I open my legs for him and lean into it. Searching for something that *feels* like closeness, even if it's only skin-deep. Because somewhere underneath it all, I miss how it used to feel when love wasn't something I had to reach for.

His fingers tangle in my hair, tugging my head back so his mouth can drag down the line of my throat, teeth grazing, tongue chasing the sting.

He groans low against my skin, hips pressing between mine, his arousal obvious even through the layers. "You feel that?" he mutters, voice thick. "This is what you do to me, Ellie. I've been waiting all fucking day."

Then his hand shifts, grazing further up my thigh—warm, certain, searching.

His eyes meet mine, and he pauses. And when he finds no hesitation, his fingers slip beneath the lace and press inside me. "Fuuuuck, Ellie."

A shudder rolls through me as his fingers curl, and my grip tightens on his shoulders, head falling back, breath catching in my throat.

"Oh my god. David…"

He silences me with a kiss, then his hands move fast and mechanical. The zip of my dress, the unclasp of my bra, the cool air kissing skin as the fabric slips away. He palms my breasts like he's starved, thumbs flicking over the peaks before he rolls one between his fingers, then pinches hard enough to make me gasp.

"You love this," he mutters, tongue flicking over my nipple before biting down sharply.

My breath stutters. Nails curling into his back as he presses harder—deeper.

He only pauses long enough to yank my thong down, the lace a brief afterthought before it hits the floor. Then the buckle of his belt, the low rasp of denim, the sound of foil tearing in the silence.

And I should tell him to slow down. To breathe. To see me. But I don't. Because right now, I want this too. I want to be wanted.

He strokes himself once, watching me, his gaze sharp and hungry. "You gonna take this?"

I nod, my thighs tense.

Then he grips my hips and thrusts into me in one unrelenting stroke.

I gasp, back arching, body stretching to take every inch of him.

"Fuck," he groans, fingers digging into my thighs as he moves, deep, fast, relentless. Like he's burning through something only I can extinguish.

I cling to his shoulders, nails digging into the fabric, searching for something solid to hold on to as he drives into me again and again. His body is feverish against mine, skin damp, hips snapping with brutal precision. The stretch is sharp, the friction rough.

David is everywhere, his breath hot and ragged against my cheek, his voice low and filthy in my ear, his hands dragging me closer, spreading me wider.

"You like this," he growls, fucking me harder. "You love it when I take you like this. When I fuck you like I *own* you."

A moan breaks loose from my throat, raw and involuntary, caught somewhere between want and shame.

And he's right. In this moment, I want to be his. I need this just as much as he does. To disappear beneath someone else's need.

Tonight, I *let* him take. And I *take back*. Touch for touch. Thrust for thrust.

We fall into a rhythm that's fast and filthy.

He groans into my skin, voice rough, almost desperate. We fuck like we're both trying to forget something.

My breath stutters, chest tight, skin prickling with heat. I shift, trying to find that one perfect angle, that friction I need. "Wait—David. Shit—I'm so close—"

He grunts, adjusting, but not enough. Not where it counts. Already chasing his own finish line.

I bite my lip and wrap my legs tighter, desperate to drag myself over the edge. My body is right there—coiled and trembling, screaming for release. That low, urgent pulse building, begging, clawing its way up my spine.

But it slips again.

Too fast. Too shallow. Too out of sync.

I grind against him, breath caught in my throat. "David—fuck. Just, hold it there."

He moans my name, hips stuttering as he comes.

Too late.

It's over.

He leans in. Presses a gentle kiss to my forehead, like a period at the end of a sentence.

He pulls out with a grunt, breath ragged. Straightens. Re-buttons.

And I sit there, dress bunched at my waist, skin cooling, letting the quiet settle into my bones.

CHAPTER 10

no pressure, just us

KIERAN

THE STUDIO'S HUMMING WITH THAT particular brand of chaos only a photoshoot can summon, fake calm layered over silent panic. Stylists dart between racks of clothes, someone's yelling about lighting, and the air's thick with hairspray and nerves. Overhead, the lights glare down like surgical lamps, hot and unforgiving. I'm pretty sure I'm a walking fire hazard. One spark near this fringe, and it's game over.

A stylist circles like a predator, clicking her tongue and adjusting Luca's outfit for the fourth—no, fifth time. He just stands there and takes it, scrolling on his phone like he's already too famous to care.

One, he's not. And two, I'm already over it.

I get why it matters. All the magazine spreads, socials, promo shots. It's part of the deal. But standing here, under lights that feel like they're trying to microwave my soul from the inside out, the whole thing feels fake. The forced poses, the plastic grins, the way you've got to act like someone you're not just to sell an image.

We're a band, not a brand. And this? This feels like a costume party where no one knows who they're dressed as.

Luca leans against a column like he's modelling for a designer ad he forgot to tell us about. Guitar slung over his shoulder, leather jacket worth more than my first car, hair somehow defying gravity and humidity with the same smug elegance.

"Come on, Kieran," he calls, eyes still on his phone. "Quit auditioning for *The Bachelor* and give us something usable."

I shoot him a look. "I'm just keeping it classy. You wouldn't recognise it if it bit you."

Ryder lifts his head from where he's sprawled on the floor like a moody rock god, sunglasses on indoors, fake cigar in hand. Kid doesn't even smoke. "Mate, you look like you're about to deliver a TED Talk," he says with a grin. "Give us some sex appeal."

"My entire existence is sex appeal. You're just not evolved enough to handle it." I joke.

"Not evolved?" he laughs. "I've seen toast with more heat than you."

"That's what your last date said when you took your shirt off."

Luca chokes on his drink. Theo cracks up from the corner. There's a pause, then Ryder snatches one of Theo's drumsticks and hurls it at my head. I duck, grinning as it bounces harmlessly off the white set wall.

"Oi!" Theo groans. "Respect the gear, you animal!"

The photographer waves from behind the lens. "Alright, lads. Band shots. Classic setup. Hands in pockets. Look relaxed. No statues. Natural energy."

Theo, still lurking off to the side like a bored assassin, rolls his neck with a dramatic crack and stretches like he's about to leap into combat. "Natural? Easy," he says with a wink.

Luca scoffs. "He said natural, not fossilised. I've seen houseplants move more than you."

I glance at Luca's reflection in the polished chrome of a lighting rig. He's fussing with his hair again, like he's not already 90% camera-ready. "How much product did you use this morning? Your hair's a global warming risk."

"Listen," Luca says, turning to the camera with a pout that could melt lenses, "some of us have standards. Am I giving tortured rockstar or high-end shampoo ad?"

Ryder snorts. Theo snickers. "You look like you're about to flog a 2-in-1 conditioner at Boots," he says, deadpan.

We crack up. The tension breaks. Just like that, it's not a photoshoot anymore. It's us. Chaotic and ridiculous. Then we shuffle into position, teasing each other between takes.

The lights flash.

The camera clicks.

The shoot finally wraps up, the photographer giving us a satisfied thumbs-up, like we've just passed some invisible test. Everyone's still bantering as we drift toward the changing room in loose formation. Theo imitating Luca's pout, Ryder humming some dramatic rock ballad off-key.

"Bus beers?" Luca calls, already herding the others toward the exit. "Picked up some of that weird IPA you like, Theo."

Theo perks up immediately. "The mango one that tastes like bin juice? Fuck yeah."

Ryder tosses me a look over his shoulder. "You coming?"

"Nah," I say, tugging my hoodie over my head. "Gonna walk for a bit before crashing."

Ryder raises a brow. "You alright?"

"Yeah, bro." I say. And I mean it.

Theo whistles low. "Bloody hell. Kieran Hayes voluntarily skipping beers. Who are you?"

Luca chuckles, shoving the door open. "Next you'll be telling us you made a salad on purpose."

"Go fuck yourselves," I mutter, laughing.

"Alright, man." Ryder says, clapping me on the shoulder as they head on to the bus. "Have a good one."

The door swings shut behind them with a dull metallic clunk, their voices fading into the distance. And just like that, it's quiet.

The boys are always happy to crash on the bus. It's all part of the grind, the freedom, the chaos of being on the road. And I love it. I really do. There's something addictive about the movement, the noise, the late-night writing sessions fuelled by takeaway chips and half-sober philosophy. It's what we've always dreamed of.

But when we're parked somewhere for more than a night or two, I book a room.

Nothing fancy. Just a quiet bed, a working lock, and four walls that don't move with the wind. There's nothing deep about it. Some nights I just need the stillness—to press pause. A door I can close. A night where I can just stretch out without someone snoring in the bunk across from me.

The sun dips low now, casting a golden haze over the town. It's one of those late afternoons where the heat loosens its grip, and the breeze slips in to take its place. I take a slow breath, letting it fill my chest.

This is one of my favourite things about being on the road. New places. New skies. The quiet magic of landing somewhere unfamiliar and letting it surprise you.

Even in the noise of tour life, there are these moments that feel still. Like the world's pressing pause just long enough for you to notice it.

I walk without purpose through the town square, dragging my feet a little from the day's chaos. Photoshoots, rehearsals, too many hours pretending to be cool when all I want is to collapse on a sofa.

But the town has other plans.

A food festival takes over the streets, a riot of colour and sound. Stalls overflowing with treats line both sides of the road, adorned with neon signs and paper lanterns. The air is thick with the scents of spice, sugar, and summer. I slow my steps, letting the hum of it all sink in.

The air is thick with life. Locals chatting, kids darting between legs, couples swaying lazily to an acoustic set drifting in from the next street. Music threads through the buzz like a heartbeat.

I blend in easily, just another face in the crowd.

I wander past a row of food stalls. Dumplings sizzling in woks, tacos stacked high with bright toppings, paella bubbling in wide, sun-scorched pans. The scent is everywhere. Rich, spiced, and mouthwatering.

But it's the sweetness that catches me. That stops me in my tracks.

SOMEHOW STILL YOU 113

A wisp of warm sugar curls past on the breeze—thick with cinnamon.

I glance sideways.

There's a bubblegum pink truck parked near the edge of the square, a string of fairy lights drapes lazily along the awning. A girl with space buns and gold hoops dusts fresh churros with sugar, then leans out to pass them to a waiting customer.

For a moment, I just stood there, frozen. The nostalgia hits me like a wave, and I'm transported back in time, the memory flooding in so quickly I almost lose my balance.

Because then I saw her. Clear as day.

Ellie moved as if the moment belonged to her. Chin lifted, hair bouncing with every step, eyes cutting through the crowd with sharp precision. No time for hesitation. No interest in subtlety. She didn't so much walk as glide, like the beat had crawled under her skin and decided to stay. Like joy was something she didn't just feel, but commanded.

She had my hand in hers, tugging me through the maze of food trucks like it was some kind of mission. Her laughter was loud, and her eyes sparkled with something wild and electric.

"We're close," she said, tugging my hand with renewed purpose.

"To what, exactly?"

"Salvation," she shot over her shoulder. "In the form of fried sugar."

I would've followed her anywhere, to be honest.

"There!" she gasped, skidding to a halt in front of a bubblegum pink truck.

"You dragged me through half a muddy field for this?" I teased, out of breath and entirely hers.

"I swear," she said, flashing a grin that made my chest ache. "These are life-altering. Melt-in-your-mouth, ruin-you-for-all-other-donuts level of good."

"Bit dramatic."

"It's called having standards, Hayes."

The vendor is an older guy, thick grey moustache, and a t-shirt that reads DONUT WORRY, BE HAPPY. He clearly recognised her. Gave her a warm nod, as though she were a regular.

"Two boxes," she said, then turned to me with mock-seriousness. "One for me, one for him."

She was all sun and fire, and sugar cravings. There was a rhythm to the way she moved, even when standing still. Like her body was always half a beat ahead of the world. She leaned her head against my shoulder, our fingers still laced together. The sun caught in her hair. The moment held, slow and easy.

As we waited, she started swaying to the music coming from a nearby stage. Something mellow and summery. Without thinking, I stepped in close and slid my hands to her waist, drawing her gently back into me. She didn't flinch. Just leaned in like it was the most natural thing in the world. I rested my chin on her shoulder, breathing her in as we swayed. Just the two of us, moving to a rhythm no one else could feel.

She tilted her head back to look at me, curls falling over her shoulder. "They're going to ruin you, you know," she breathed.

"You're already ruining me," I murmured.

Her smile faltered, just slightly. Enough to make my chest tighten. "That's not fair," she said, voice almost too quiet for the crowd around us.

"Neither are you."

She didn't answer, but the look she gave me. It could've stopped time.

The donuts arrived—steaming, golden, and sugar-dusted. She took one, bit into it, and actually moaned.

"Fucking heaven!" She mumbled through a mouthful, eyes fluttering shut in bliss.

I tried mine. Warm dough. Melted sugar. Ridiculous. "Alright, you win," I said, licking sugar from my thumb. "They're actually unreal. Happy?"

"Ecstatic." She reached over, brushing a smudge of sugar from the corner of my mouth with her thumb, slow and deliberate. Her fingers lingered. "You missed a spot."

My breath caught. "You're kind of dangerous, you know that?"

"And you're adorable when you're messy."

"Careful, Ells. I might just fall for you."

Her grin slipped into something softer. She didn't say it back. But she didn't let go of my hand, either.

Later, we sat on the grass with our backs to the sunset, shoulders touching, paper boxes empty at our feet. Her head tilted to rest against mine.

"Best week of my life," she whispered.

I said nothing at first. Just let that truth hang between us. "Mine too," I said eventually. And in that moment, I could've stayed there with her forever.

The memory fades, but the feeling lingers. Soft around the edges, like a dream that doesn't want to let go.

I blink, the sunlight sharp against the van's exterior. There's a line, but it moves fast. When it's my turn, I step forward and clear my throat. "Two, please."

The woman behind the window nods, already reaching for the tongs. "Still warm," she says with a smile.

I nod, as I take the paper box she hands over.

I walk a few steps, tearing a piece off the first one before I even sit down. The noise of the crowd hums around me, the buzz of summer still in the air. But all I can hear is her voice. All I can see is her smile.

I lean back against the bench, wiping my fingers on a napkin I don't remember grabbing, and watch the breeze dance through the bunting overhead.

I don't know what that memory means anymore. Whether it was the beginning of something or just a beautiful detour. Whether I was just lucky to have it, or stupid for ever thinking it could last.

But I know one thing.

She mattered.

And no matter what happens now... she still does.

The walk back to the hotel is slow and unhurried. I've got my hood up and my hands buried in my pockets. One of those unpredictable summer nights where the heat gives up all at once, and the air turns sharp around the edges.

The noise from the park fades behind me, swallowed by the low sweep of distant traffic and the occasional burst of laughter drifting from an open window. I pass shuttered cafés, their chairs stacked and signs flipped to closed, corner shops buzzing with neon, and takeaways spilling warm light onto the pavement. The entire street feels like it's holding its breath. Caught in that strange, in-between hour where the day hasn't ended, but it's already starting to exhale.

By the time I reach the hotel, the weight of the afternoon catches up with me. Not just the hours on my feet, the rehearsals, and the shoot, but everything else. The memory. That feeling I haven't quite named, sitting just behind my ribs.

The room is plain and functional. Crisp white sheets, blackout curtains, a desk no one uses. I flick on the bathroom light, peel off my shirt, and step under the shower. The heat loosens the knots in my back, steam curling around me until the glass fogs over.

Ten minutes later, I'm in sweatpants and a loose tee, beer in hand, sprawled across the hotel's stiff little sofa with the TV playing football highlights.

I'm mid-sip of beer when my phone buzzes, and Ellie's name lights up the screen.

ELLS [21:07]

Hey, you up?

I don't even hesitate.

Always. You okay?

The reply takes a moment. I sit forward, resting my elbows on my knees, phone loose in my hands.

ELLS [21:10]

Can I call?

Of course.

The ringtone barely gets through one full cycle before I answer.

"Hey, you," I say softly, leaning forward, the beer now forgotten on the coffee table.

There's a pause. Just long enough to make my heart knock a little harder in my chest. Then her voice filters through. Quiet, a bit worn, almost thin around the edges.

"Hey." She sounds tired.

"You okay?" I ask, my voice instinctively gentler. "You sound…"

"Shit?" she finishes with a soft, humourless laugh. "Yeah. Accurate."

I sit up straighter, elbows on my knees, phone pressed tight to my ear.

"I'm just… knackered." She continues. "The hospital was manic, then I did a shift at Brenda's, I've got three uni deadlines breathing down my neck, Mia's at her dad's, David's working away again, and the house is a shit hole."

She pauses, the silence stretching. "Sorry. Verbal diarrhoea. I should come with a warning label."

"It's okay, Ellie." I chuckle. "I'm glad you called. I'm always here, you know that, right?"

"I know," she murmurs. "It's just hard sometimes. I don't know where the line is between venting and over sharing anymore. I feel like I'm always 'too much' or not enough, and I…" She stops herself. Breathes.

"Hey. Don't do that. You're never too much."

There's a beat. Then she asks, "How was your day?"

I give her the short version. Rehearsals. Photoshoot. The usual chaos. She listens, quiet and steady, on the other end.

"I'm so happy for you all," she says after a moment. "Really. You've worked so hard. And it's… it's amazing, what you've achieved. I hope you know that."

I swallow, her words catching in my throat.

"Thank you," I say, quieter than I meant to.

I go quiet for a second, soaking that in. I don't know if she realises how much it means hearing that from her. But I don't push it. Just let it settle between us.

Then I feel her pulling back a little. That shift. The way her voice gets lighter, like she's building a wall out of casual words.

"Ellie," I breathe. "Are you okay?"

Another pause. This one longer. Then, softly, cracked at the edges: "I'm just… burnt out, I guess. It's like I'm spinning plates, and every single one's about to smash."

My heart aches at the sound of her unravelling. "And David?" I ask carefully.

"We're fine," she says. But something in the way she says it doesn't ring true. "His job has him working away more often these last few months, so I guess I'm just feeling it more with him being away almost every weekend."

Fine. That cursed, loaded word.

I want to reach through the phone and tell her she deserves way more than fine. More than exhaustion and silence, and feeling like she's carrying everything alone. But I hold my tongue.

"You're never alone, Ellie." I say instead. "You've got people around you. People who care. I'm one of them. Even when I'm at the other side of the country."

She doesn't answer right away, but I hear the shift in her breathing. She's letting something go. Just a little. "Thank you, Kieran," she says softly.

I nod, even though she can't see me. "Anytime, Ellie."

I sense the heaviness still clinging to her, so I shift gears. I want to give her something lighter. Something that might make her laugh. "Guess what I thought I saw today."

"What?"

"Remember that donut van you were obsessed with?"

She gasps, full and delighted. "No! Shut up."

"It wasn't the same one, but it got me for a minute."

"Please tell me you got one."

"Two. Obviously."

She laughs dramatically. "You're the worst."

That sound. *God*, I miss that sound. It's like a window cracking open on a stuffy day. Clean air. Sunshine. The smallest breath of something I don't want to name too soon.

The night wraps itself around us like a blanket. Her voice dips lower as she grows sleepier, more languid with each breath. I don't rush it. I don't push. We talk until the city quiets outside the window. Until the football highlights end. Until the clock blinks past midnight and neither of us wants to hang up.

We talk about the tour, Mia, and her dissertation stress. We circle old memories and tease at new ones. We don't define it.

It's just… us. And it's perfect.

Eventually, she murmurs, "I should go to sleep. Got an early shift in the morning."

"Alright," I say, though part of me doesn't want the call to end.

There's a pause, and then… "I'm glad I called."

"Me too."

"Night, Hayes."

My lips tug into a smile. "Night, Carter."

The line goes quiet. I don't move right away, just sit there in the dim hotel light, the phone still warm in my hand.

My heart does that stupid thing it always does after her. Soft around the edges, a little tangled, a little too hopeful for its own good.

Confused.

But reaching anyway.

CHAPTER 11
the space between

ELLIE

I WAKE UP FEELING LIGHTER.

It's unfamiliar, like stepping outside after a storm and realising the air is different. Cleaner somehow, easier to breathe. A weight I didn't even know I was carrying has lifted, just enough to notice.

My mind, usually thick with fog the moment I open my eyes, feels... clear. Not empty. Just quieter. Like someone's finally turned down the volume on the constant hum of worry I've learned to live with.

The kind that clings to your chest before you even get out of bed. That flicker of panic over everything and nothing all at once.

But right now, it's like the static has softened.

No spiralling thoughts, no mental checklists screaming for attention. Just a rare, fleeting stillness.

I don't trust it, not entirely—but I let myself breathe in it anyway.

Because these moments don't come often.

And when they do, I've learned to hold them like something fragile.

I stretch beneath the covers, muscles stiff but loose in a way that suggests I slept well for once.

And then, uninvited but not unwelcome, Kieran's voice floats through my thoughts. A warmth spreads through my chest before I can talk myself out of it. The memory of our late-night call wraps around me like a duvet.

I roll onto my side, watching the soft morning light spill through the curtains. The room is quiet, awash in gold and grey. A breeze skims my bare arms, light as a whisper.

I hadn't expected this friendship with Kieran to slip back into my life. But it has.

And I like it.

My world has never been big. My circle? Smaller still. Naomi's always been my constant, my person. The one who sees straight through me, calls me out when I pretend I'm fine, and loves me anyway.

But beyond her, it's always been me holding everything together, carrying the weight, fixing what no one else sees.

The house is still. Mia's still at her sleepover, and David won't be home until later this afternoon. I could stay curled in this moment, let myself soak in the rare calm of it all. But there's a buzz beneath my skin, a familiar itch for movement, for momentum, for anything but stillness. So, I lean into the one thing that never fails me.

Work.

Or, more specifically, powering through my last stretch of unpaid shifts before I qualify.

The pace of the emergency department. The rhythm, the clarity, the way it demands my full attention and gives me no room to think about anything else.

I check the time, swing my legs over the side of the bed, and plant my feet on the cold floor. A short Sunday morning shift, not much, but enough to make the day feel useful. Enough to keep the rest of my thoughts at bay.

The department thrums with its usual chaos. Shouts echoing down corridors, monitors beeping in staccato rhythms, footsteps scuffing against linoleum. The air crackles with urgency, the sharp tang of antiseptic woven into every breath. There's no mistaking where you are. Not for a second.

I move through it on instinct, clipboard in hand, Crocs squeaking against the floor. Nurses dart between bays like they're caught in a current, doctors fire instructions across the department, and in the waiting room, restless patients shift in plastic chairs, tense and tired.

I'm not qualified yet. Not officially. But some days, I forget that. So does the team.

They don't baby me. They don't hold my hand. They just hand over charts and cases like I already belong here. And I do. At least, that's how it feels on the good days.

Every shift stretches me. Sharpens me. Builds something in me I didn't know I had. And I'm close now, so close I can taste it.

The noise, the pressure, the chaos. It should be overwhelming, but today, it's exactly what I need. Because here, there's no room to overthink. No space to spiral. There's only the next patient. The next chart. The next moment I need to show up for.

A boy walks past me, maybe eight or nine, one hand clutching his mum's and the other pressed to a paper towel taped over a cut on his eyebrow. His eyes are glassy, tear tracks drying on his cheeks.

I crouch to his level, softening my voice. "That's a brave look you've got there."

He gives the tiniest nod, bottom lip trembling.

I reach into my pocket and pull out one of the *'warrior'* stickers I keep stashed for moments like this. "Here," I say, sticking it on his T-shirt. "You earned this."

His fingers graze over it like it's gold and his mum mouths a silent thank you as I stand again.

And just like that, I'm back in it.

Another nurse calls my name, and then I'm moving — pulse check, wound cleaning, pain scale, chart. Next.

Later that afternoon, everything slows. The shift ends, and with it, the noise recedes. I peel off my scrubs like armour, each layer a little lighter, and trade the hospital's harsh electric buzz for the soft, familiar comfort of home.

It's quieter here. Gentler. No one is asking for anything, except snacks. And even that feels manageable.

Dinner's a chaotic medley of use it before it poisons us. Oven chips, a sad handful of peas rescued from the bottom of the freezer drawer, and some questionable protein that might've once had a label but now lives purely on hope.

Mia talks non-stop about the weekend at her dad's. The new puppy they got (*"tiny, yappy, traumatised the cat"*), the film they watched, and a boy who might have a crush on her (*"but he's gross, obviously"*).

I nod. I laugh. I listen.

And somehow, without planning it, we end up tangled on the sofa. Blankets everywhere. A bowl of popcorn wedged between our knees. A rom-com already halfway through. I've missed the plot entirely, but I don't care.

This is the part that matters.

"I swear, Mum, if Peter Kavinsky looked at me like that, I'd do *literally* anything," Mia declares, jabbing a finger at the screen with an unfiltered intensity only teenage girls can pull off.

I snort, reaching into the bowl of popcorn and grabbing a generous handful. "Oh, for sure. That boy could convince me to take up extreme sports."

Mia gasps in mock horror. "*Please*. You almost fainted that one time we watched *Mission: Impossible*."

"In my defence," I argue, voice muffled through popcorn, "he was hanging off a literal glass building. With suction cups. My palms were sweating. I had a full-body stress response."

She lets out a dramatic laugh, flopping sideways into the cushions and nudging me with her shoulder. "You're so soft. It's adorable."

I raise an eyebrow at her. "I'm soft? You still cry at *The Lion King*."

"Wow. That's *so* different, Mum" she says, eyes glued to the screen. "That's traumatic."

I grin. It's just us, wrapped in layers of blankets on the sofa, the flicker of the TV washing warm light over the room. Popcorn everywhere. Her feet tucked under my legs in that familiar way that says *I still need you*, even if she won't say it out loud anymore.

These pockets of time? They're everything.

She feels so grown lately. But right now, with smudged mascara and her hair a little wild from lounging, she's still my little girl. I glance at her profile, at the curve of her cheek, the way her mouth quirks with every swoon-worthy line of dialogue.

I reach over and tuck a strand of hair behind her ear. She doesn't flinch or roll her eyes, just leans into the touch, soft and unthinking.

Then —

Bang.

The front door slams hard enough to rattle the frame on the wall. The moment shatters.

I jolt, pulse jumping.

Mia looks up at me instantly, eyes wide. She doesn't say anything — but I feel her watching. Reading the tension in my shoulders.

I force a smile and soften my voice. "It's okay, bug," I murmur, brushing her fringe off her forehead. "Why don't you go upstairs and see if you've got any homework to finish for tomorrow?"

She hesitates for a second, gaze flicking toward the hallway. Then she nods.

"Okay," she says quietly, slipping off the sofa.

There's no greeting from David. No, *"Hey, I'm home."* Just the creak of floorboards, the rustle of a coat being hung, and the distant clink of glass.

It's the silence that gets me. That familiar, calculated quiet. It slinks through the house, pulling something tight across my chest.

Because the last time he came home from a trip like this — I found out he'd been holed up in a casino for most of the weekend. Said it was *networking*. Said it was nothing. But a month's wages disappeared into the kind of place where time doesn't exist and daylight's a rumour.

Now, every slammed door—and the hollow silence that follows—feels less like an entrance and more like a warning shot.

I gather the empty popcorn bowl, take a breath, and follow the sound of ice clinking into glass.

David stands at the kitchen counter, his back turned. He opens the drawer, rummages for the bottle opener, then cracks the cap off a beer with a low hiss.

He doesn't move for a second—just stands there, one hand braced on the marble, fingers splayed like he needs the surface to keep him steady.

His shoulders are locked. Spine too straight. Like he's holding something in with sheer posture alone.

There's a weight to him tonight. Folded in. Quiet. Sealed shut.

"Hey," I whisper, not wanting to startle him. "Didn't hear you come in."

A lie—but it buys me a second to find my footing.

David doesn't look up. Just tosses the bottle cap onto the counter and lifts the bottle to his lips. "Long weekend," he mutters.

I nod, hovering in the doorway like a guest in my own kitchen. "How was the trip? Everything go okay?"

There's a pause. Too long to mean nothing. His jaw tightens. "Yeah. Fine. Stressful, but... fine."

He says it like a door closing. Full stop. End of discussion.

I cross the room slowly and set the popcorn bowl in the sink, trying to keep my tone light. "You were meant to be back hours ago. I thought maybe—"

"*Fuck, Ellie!*" His voice snaps like a wire pulled too tight. "I said I'm fine."

I flinch, blinking hard. "I was just asking," I say. "You don't have to snap."

He sighs, already turning away. "Jesus, can we not do this right now?" He reaches past me for the fridge door, still avoiding my eyes.

"Do what?" I press, the edge creeping in despite myself. "Talk? A normal conversation without it turning into—whatever the hell this is?"

Another sharp exhale through his nose, as if I'm exhausting. Like concern is a personal attack. "I don't need to be interrogated the second I walk through the door."

That word—*interrogated*—lands like a slap. Cold and dismissive. It freezes something inside of me.

I should walk away. Should let it go. But instead, I step forward, closing the space between us. My fingers finding the loosened knot of his tie.

"David," I murmur. "I missed you. That's all. It's been two days. You're always working away lately."

I tug the tie loose, undo the top button of his shirt, then the next. My fingertips brush against his skin. Warm. Familiar. But still, he feels miles away.

"You're tense," I whisper, leaning in to press a kiss to his neck.

His hands settle on my hips. Not pulling me closer. Just... resting there. Like habit.

I lift my face to his. Kiss the edge of his jaw, then trace my mouth toward his lips. Waiting. Hoping. His forehead presses gently to mine.

But then he exhales and steps back.

The cold hits instantly.

"Ellie," he says, voice frayed at the edges. "I'm shattered. This isn't the time."

I go still, my hands falling to the hem of his shirt. "For what?" I ask. "*Sex?* Is that all you think I want?"

My voice is too sharp. Too brittle. But I can't help it.

"I just want to be close to you," I say, softer now.

He exhales again, slower this time. Still won't look at me.

"I miss you," I admit. "Not your body—*you.*"

He doesn't speak. Doesn't move. The silence expands—thick with everything we aren't saying.

I let my hands fall away. The ache sets in fast.

He rolls his shoulders, like he's trying to shake off more than a long day. "I need a shower," he mutters. "And I've got stuff to catch up on."

Not work. Just... *stuff.*

He leans in automatically, pressing a kiss to my forehead. But it barely lands. A motion without meaning.

Then he turns and walks out. Up the stairs. Gone.

I stare at the space he leaves behind. The quiet rushes in like water.

And just like that, whatever I was hoping for—connection, warmth, anything—is gone.

As the evening gave way to the night, the house slipped into a heavy quiet.

The TV is off, the blankets Mia and I were wrapped in are folded neatly over the sofa's armrest, and the popcorn bowl is drying on the rack. The only sound now is the soft whirling of the dishwasher, and even that feels too loud in the stillness.

I move through it on autopilot, wiping counters that are already clean, straightening cushions, folding a tea towel over the oven handle. It's not about tidying. It's about making sense of something when nothing else does.

I pick up my phone from where I left it beside the sink. One new message.

> NAOMI [23:12]
> Girl! I just went on the BEST date ever. Junior doctor. Seriously – he's a 10!

A breath of laughter escapes me, barely a sound, more an exhale of disbelief. Of course she did. Leave it to Naomi to find a whole-ass rom-com subplot after every shift. She's magnetic like that.

I dry my hands and type out a reply.

> 😄 you always do find the best ones, don't you?

> NAOMI [23:13]
>
> Can't help it. Still grinning. He was hot. AND he paid. In full.

Her joy feels like it's coming from a different universe. One I remember living in once. Before the silence. Before the rejection. Before David became a stranger in a house we both still pretend feels like home.

And still — I stay.

Because sometimes, when the light hits just right, I get a glimmer of the man I fell in love with. The one who made me laugh without trying, who used to make me feel like I was the only thing in the room that mattered.

He's still in there, somewhere.

Or maybe I've just convinced myself he is.

Four years is a long time to give to someone. Long enough for memories to outweigh reality. Long enough that you stop noticing the shift until one day you're waking up next to someone who doesn't see you anymore.

But I want that feeling back.

I want *him* back.

And that hope — that ache — is sometimes louder than the voice in my head telling me it's already gone.

> I'm happy for you, Nay. You deserve that. Tell me everything tomorrow?

> NAOMI [23:15]
>
> Of course. But what about you? How was your night?

My fingers hover over the screen. I could lie. Say it was quiet. Say it was fine. But the truth pushes forward.

> David's home. But he was off. Snapped at me.

I stare at it. Then, I hit send. Her response is immediate.

> **NAOMI [23:19]**
> What an ass hat!! 😒

I let out a low laugh, the kind that stings a little on its way out.

> I just wanted to feel like we were still... us. I don't know. I reached for him. He pulled away 🥺

> **NAOMI [23:21]**
> That sucks, Ellie. You deserve someone who reaches back. Every time. Not just when it's easy.

I press the screen to my chest for a moment, like her words might sink in deeper if I hold them there.

> **NAOMI [23:22]**
> You're doing more than enough Ellie. Don't let him make you feel like you're the problem.

I blink against the sudden burn in my eyes, set the phone down on the worktop, and lean against it, palms flat, eyes tracing the pattern of the tiled backsplash like it might offer some kind of answer.

Naomi's words linger, curling around me in the quiet. *You deserve someone who reaches back.* It's such a simple sentence. Obvious, even. But it lands somewhere deep. Somewhere I've been avoiding.

Because when *was* the last time David reached for me? Without a motive. Without whiskey in his veins. Without it being about smoothing things over or saving face.

I've been carrying so much. This relationship, this house, Mia's entire world, my future. Juggling it all like a one-woman balancing act. And somehow, I've kept convincing myself that if I just try a little harder, bend a little further, it'll all fall into place. That if I keep folding myself into the shape he wants, he'll look at me the way he used to. Like he actually sees me.

But what if he's not looking? What if he stopped looking a long time ago?

I rub my hands over my face, chasing away the sting building behind my eyes.

Eventually, I straighten, switch off the kitchen light, and move toward the stairs. My body feels slower. My breath a little tighter. But I climb anyway.

The house gives out as I move through it. Floorboards shift beneath my steps. The hallway clock ticks. Outside, the faint rustle of tree branches scrape against the window at the top of the stairs.

Darkness cloaks the hallway upstairs. I don't want to disturb the stillness, so I leave the light switched off, and I don't want to name whatever this feeling is building in my chest.

The bedroom door is ajar, and I ease it open, half-expecting to find the bed empty, the glow of David's office still visible under the door down the hall.

But he's here. Already asleep. Curled onto his side, arm tucked under the pillow, the duvet pulled halfway up his chest. His face is turned toward the door, the sharp lines of his jaw softened in the dark. He looks peaceful. Almost boyish in sleep. Beautiful even.

I stand in the doorway for a few moments longer than I need to. Just... watching. Letting the doubt settle into something duller. Something I can hold.

Then I tiptoe through the room, changing into one of my oversized sleep shirts. Soft cotton. Faded edges. Comfort in the familiar.

I slip beneath the covers, careful not to jostle the mattress. The crisp cotton sheets are smooth against my skin and the space beside me holds the warmth of his body. I roll onto my side, facing away, the scent of his skin faint but familiar, and close my eyes.

Then, the weight of his arm, a comforting pressure, settles around my waist.

The contact startles me for a second. His palm, warm as summer stone, rests steady against my stomach, guiding me back into his embrace.

I let him hold me.

His breath is steady at my neck. The weight of his presence is grounding in a way that almost tricks me into believing everything is okay.

A stray tear glides down my cheek, falling onto my pillow. Then I close my eyes, allowing myself to lean into the moment.

His hand moves without hesitation, slipping beneath my shirt like it's done it a hundred times before. Fingers skim the curve of my hip, trail along the edge of a rib, climb higher in slow, deliberate strokes.

"I'm sorry, Ellie." He murmurs, voice barely above a whisper.

I don't answer. Because I don't know if it's an apology for snapping at me, or for something bigger.

But when his lips press against my neck, lingering there, trailing lower, heat blooms inside me.

He slides his hand up my stomach until his fingers find the curve of my breast. His touch, feather-light.

I turn toward him and our mouths meet halfway. Slow at first, exploratory, then deeper. Hungrier. He kisses like he's trying to reclaim something, and I let him. I don't overthink it.

Because part of me wants this too. Or needs it, maybe.

Needs the closeness. The confirmation.

Maybe if I give enough, he'll stay.

Maybe if I stay close, he won't pull away again.

My fingers curl into his hair as his hand finds my thigh, gripping, grounding. He palms my ass and tugs me closer, our bodies aligning in slow, measured waves. The heat builds between us—familiar, muscle-deep, but still just out of reach.

He pushes the fabric of my sleep shirt higher, hands roaming like they used to. Like he already knows the map of me. I let my eyes fall closed. Let the sound of his breath in my ear drown out the quiet doubts still whispering at the edges of my mind.

Because in the dark, it's easier to forget.

There was a time this felt like love.

When closeness meant connection.

When the weight of his desire made me feel seen. Wanted. Chosen.

But now? Now there's distance even in the heat. A hollowness behind the pull.

Like we're reaching for each other through fog.

I close my eyes. My breath stutters. And I wait for it to feel like something more. To feel like it used to. To feel real.

Even though somewhere deep down, I already know how this ends.

With me lying awake after.

Staring at the ceiling.

Wondering how something can feel so familiar... and still leave me feeling so far away.

CHAPTER 12

when the music stops

KIERAN

THE TOUR'S FINALLY OVER—SIX long months—and the moment my boots meet solid ground, the weight of it hits me. No more swaying floors beneath my feet, just unmoving pavement pressing up through worn soles. My body registers the stillness before my mind can even catch up. My shoulders scream, my legs throb, and sweat clings to my skin in a sticky film. It all lands at once.

And with it, the exhaustion.

Not the kind that makes you want to crawl into bed and disappear. No, this is different. It's bone-deep, sure, but it's earned. Worn like a medal. The tiredness that follows a high you never want to come down from.

Last night's show? *Wild.*

Another sold-out venue. Our third this week.

What used to be rooms crammed with a hundred—maybe two hundred—faces pressed against the stage has turned into something else entirely.

Last night, it was over fifteen hundred. A packed-out hall, the kind that echoes even before the music starts. Balcony seats. Security barriers. A lighting rig that looked like something from a bloody awards show.

And they came for *us*.

A crowd so loud we could barely hear ourselves on stage. People screaming lyrics back like they'd been waiting their whole lives to let them out. Like our songs weren't just ours anymore — but theirs too.

The lights, the heat, the pulse of it all still buzzes at the back of my skull.

I can still feel the bass vibrating through the soles of my feet, even now.

Like my body hasn't quite accepted that it's over.

That the stage is behind us and not beneath me.

But for now, the adrenaline's gone, and we're standing in a hotel corridor, waiting to meet with Nick, when all I want is a hot shower and a bed that doesn't sway with motion. The door swings open, and we shuffle into the conference room like a pack of sleep-deprived zombies. The energy is all muted groans and slumped shoulders, a collective exhaustion that needs no explanation.

We look like hell.

Nick's already standing at the head of the room, bright-eyed and bushy-tailed. Grinning like a man who's definitely not been surviving on 3am petrol station snacks and thirty-minute naps. His blazer is crisp, his shoes are polished, and his optimism is borderline offensive this early in the day.

"Fellas," he says, clapping his hands together like he's about to deliver a wedding toast nobody asked for. "I just want to say. I'm beyond proud of what you've done over the last few months."

We mutter a few tired thank-yous under our breaths.

"The entire country knows your names now. Hell, you've made a mark bigger than any of us could've imagined this last six months. And I'm thrilled to tell you..." He lets the moment hang, milking it. "The label officially wants to sign you for an album."

A beat of stunned silence. Then… *"LET'S GOOOOO!"* Ryder launches out of his chair like he's been tasered, fists in the air, grabbing Luca's shoulders and shaking him like he's trying to resuscitate him.

Luca just smirks, shrugging him off. "An entire album?" he says, looking at Nick. "Guess we're stuck together a little longer, mate."

Theo leans back in his chair, arms folded, smug as ever. "He'd be lost without us."

Ryder's still vibrating. "We have to celebrate. Big night. Champagne. Fireworks. A private island…"

"Let's scale it down, Bezos," I cut in, but I'm grinning too.

Nick holds up a hand, still smiling. "Before you start designing your own yacht, let me add one more thing."

We all quiet down.

"You've earned this. Every single one of you. The shows, the interviews, the photoshoots. You've killed it. And now?" He spreads his arms wide. "You get the rest of the year off."

The room falls still.

"A break?" Luca echoes, like the words are in a foreign language.

Nick nods. "Yeah. Go. Rest. Be with your people. Live a little. You'll hit the studio fresh in the new year."

And just like that, relief crashes over me like a wave. I hadn't realised how tight my chest had been. How much I've been holding in. The deadlines, the pressure, the endless movement… all of it loosens.

A break. Three months. Time to be Kieran. Not just Kieran from the band. It's exactly what I didn't know I needed.

I pull out my phone and fire off a quick text to Dad.

> Tour's done. Break till January. Labels signing us.

DAD [08:37]

> Brilliant news, Kieran. Well done, son! Never been more proud of you.

I stare at that for a moment. Let it sink in. Let it matter.

"*HELL YEAH!*" Luca crows, tossing his phone onto the table like he's just won the lottery. "I'm already booking a flight to Italy, baby."

"Make that two! I'm coming with you," Theo says, dead serious. "Your nonna loves me."

"She's *my* nonna," Luca says, shaking his head.

"She said I have nice hair," Theo grins.

"She also said you eat like a stray dog," Luca fires back.

"I took that as affection." Theo shrugs. "I swear to God, I'm going to hibernate for the next three months. Wake me up when it's January."

"Can't wait to see the feral little swamp creature you emerge as," Luca says, kicking the leg of his chair.

Theo flips him off without moving. "Joke's on you. I'll be well rested and hotter."

The laughter that erupts around the table is the good kind. The kind that scrapes the stress out of your lungs, the kind that makes you feel like yourself again. It's messy and stupid, and honest.

For the first time in months, it feels like we're not bracing for impact. Like we're just... us. Four idiots who somehow turned noise into something people care about.

This moment?

Yeah.

This one's ours.

The sun's already dipping by the time we stumble out of the hotel. After the meeting, we all just... collapsed. There was no champagne toast, no rooftop party, no ridiculous backstage blowout like we used to dream about. Just this strange, heavy quiet that none of us quite knew what to do with.

We sprawled out on the beds, or any spare bit of floor not covered in bags, eating greasy takeaway and scrolling mindlessly on our phones, while the silence stretched between us like an old jumper. Worn out, but weirdly comforting.

We're not used to stopping. We're used to chaos, to noise, to motion. Standing still feels a little too much like free-fall.

Theo's the one who cracks through the moment, flopping onto the floor with a dramatic groan and waving his phone in the air like a flag.

"*Boys*," he announces, eyes gleaming, "there's an end-of-summer bonfire happening down at Coral Point tonight. Locals, music, drinks. Real low-key. Last blowout before everything shuts down for winter."

I raise an eyebrow. "Coral Point?" The name doesn't ring any immediate bells.

Theo tosses his phone at me, and I catch it. A quick search later, I piece it together. It's a small village close to where we are. Tucked near the edge of the Lakes, all private beaches and craggy little coves.

The photos are all misty coastlines and low, rolling hills. It looks... peaceful. Hidden.

The kind of place you could disappear into for a night.

We look at each other. Don't even need to vote.

"YESSS BOYSSSS!" Ryder yells, knocking over his takeaway as he jumps up, already halfway to the door.

Because, of course, we're not starting our first night of freedom by being responsible.

Not yet.

The drive to Coral Point doesn't take long.

The hotel receptionist sorted us a minibus after Theo sweet-talked her with that grin he saves for getting what he wants. It's nothing fancy. One of those beat-up local shuttles with peeling upholstery and a rattle in the dashboard that comes and goes like it's got a mind of its own. But it gets us from A to B.

Theo claimed the front seat, naturally. He's half-turned around, knee on the seat, chanting directions to the driver like we're in some kind of low-budget road rally. "Left! No—the next left! Straight! Well... straight-ish! Right!"

The driver, a wiry guy with grey hair and patience worn thin, just grunts now and then, steering us through the winding roads like it's all part of the deal.

In the back, chaos brews. Ryder's trying to hijack the speaker with a playlist that sounds like a bad school disco circa 2003, cueing tracks with deadly seriousness. Luca keeps wrestling the phone back, switching songs with a sigh that says he's questioning every life choice that led him here.

I stretch out as far as the seat will let me, head tilted against the window. The cool glass vibrates faintly, a low hum against the jarring bumps of the uneven road. A chill clings to its surface. Outside, the hills blur past. Soft slopes, dry-stone walls, and flashes of the lake catching the last of the evening sun.

The driver pulls up near a faded wooden sign that reads *Coral Point Cove*. We pile out of the minibus—the door clanging shut behind us. My boots sink into the sand as soon as I step onto the beach, the warmth from the day still lingering in the air.

It isn't a big tourist spot. Not the flashy kind, anyway. It's tucked along the west coast, a hidden strip of sand with a handful of flashy cabins dotting the shoreline, a few weathered shops still open with hand-painted signs and twinkling fairy lights. A scattering of locals and tourists roam the beach, trailing footprints through the cooling sand.

The heat clings, heavy and damp, but the breeze off the water cools the sweat at the back of my neck. I roll my shoulders, shaking off the leftover tension from the tour, letting the ground steady me.

The guys scatter almost immediately. Theo's already deep in conversation with someone near a taco truck, Luca flips his sunglasses down like he's going incognito (he's not), and Ryder is already halfway through charming a group of sun-kissed girls by the cooler.

But I hang back for a second and breathe it in.

The night carries that unmistakable mix of salt on the breeze, wood smoke curling through the air, and the faint, sun-warmed scent of skin after a long day. The fire crackles up ahead, casting flickering shadows across the crowd as the day turns to dusk. Laughter rises and falls in easy waves, people dancing barefoot, drinks in hand, glowing under the sway of the beach lanterns strung overhead.

I don't need to be surrounded by people tonight. But there's something about the vibe here that feels right.

It's easy. It's real.

We start getting recognised. Just a few fans at first. Hesitant smiles, shy glances, the occasional *"are you...?"* followed by a squealed *"I knew it!"* It's not overwhelming. Just ripples of attention. Some selfies. Some thank-yous.

I nod toward the fire, where a few acoustic guitars are already being passed around by a group of uni-aged kids huddled on the sand. One's strumming something out of tune, the others are laughing too hard to care.

"C'mon," I say, smirking. "Let's give 'em a show."

Luca raises an eyebrow. "You serious?"

Theo's already peeling off toward the group. "We're borrowing these," he calls over his shoulder, not even pretending to ask.

By the time I catch up, Theo's got a beat going on an upside-down bucket, and someone's shoved a half-decent guitar into my hands. Ryder's crouched beside an abandoned, battery-powered keyboard, brushing off a light dusting of sand, fiddling with the keys like it's some ancient artefact.

Luca accepts a guitar from a guy in a bucket hat, who just grins and says, "Please make it sound better than I did."

"No promises," Luca deadpans, but he's already tuning it by instinct.

"This was supposed to be chill, Kieran," he mutters, shooting me a look. "We were supposed to be chill."

Ryder's grinning like a devil. "And yet, here we are. Making chaos out of a drum bucket and a student keyboard."

Theo's tapping spoons on the rim of his new *'drum,'* head bobbing like he's at Glastonbury. "Face it, we don't know how to not play."

I strum a few chords, the strings rough and familiar beneath my fingers. "It's not a gig. No lights. No label. No pressure. Just music."

And that's all it takes.

We crash our way through a rough, sprawling take on *Sweet Disposition*. Someone yells *Hands Down*, and Luca's already in before the rest of us catch up, the whole circle belting the chorus like a drunk, overenthusiastic choir.

Yellow turns into a raw, half-broken cover of crooked harmonies, breathless laughter, no one quite in key. And when someone shouts

Mr. Brightside, we ruin it in the best possible way, howling the lyrics into the dark like it might save us.

We slip a few of ours into the mix, just the ones that matter. The ones that hit differently when you strip them back and play them without the noise. No stage, no lights, no crowd roaring the chorus. Just chords in the dark, voices low, and something honest sitting in the space between.

And now we're just sitting in the afterglow. Sweaty, smiling, and pleasantly wrecked. People scatter around the fire in loose rings, swaying, chatting, sipping whatever drinks they've dragged down from the cabins and shops lining the dunes. The flames crackle in bursts, casting gold across the dunes.

I sink into the sand, legs stretched out, hands braced behind me. The warmth clings to my palms, the last of the day's heat tucked into the grains. Overhead, the stars are showing, faint freckles scattered across a sky slipping from blue to black.

To my left, Luca's still noodling on the borrowed guitar, fingers wandering without purpose. Ryder's locked into a game of tonsil tennis with some blonde like it's an Olympic sport. And Theo, God help us all, is hammering out a full rhythm on a cooler lid with two mismatched spoons in his own world.

"Percussion gremlin with zero shame," I mutter, grinning.

Theo doesn't even flinch, just smacks the spoon against the crate again and points at me like he's issuing a challenge. "You wish you were this cool."

Honestly? I do.

I lean back again, letting the hum of the night blur at the edges until…

"Excuse me?"

I blink, looking up.

She's maybe early twenties, blonde hair tucked under the hood of her sweatshirt, trainers half-buried in the sand. She clutches her phone, fingers fidgeting with the hem of her sleeve, her face a mix of awe and total panic.

"Hey," I say. "What's up?"

She steps forward hesitantly. "I—I don't want to interrupt. I just. I wanted to say thank you."

I sit up straighter. "For?"

She exhales like she's been holding her breath for hours. "*Lightyears*. That song got me through a bad time. I don't think I'd be here if I hadn't heard it when I did."

Everything inside me stills.

It's always like this—raw, disarming, impossibly humbling. No matter how many times it happens, it never stops flooring me. Not because of ego or pride, but because it's *real*. Because someone, somewhere, was holding on by a thread... and our music was there when they needed something to hold on to.

I lean forward slowly, elbows resting on my knees, trying to meet her where she is. "Hey," I say, soft but steady. "I'm really glad you're here."

She nods once, a quick jerk of the chin like she doesn't trust herself to speak.

"But what you just said?" I add gently. "That was *you*. Not us. The song might've been there in the background, might've helped you breathe for a bit, but you're the one who made it through. Don't ever give that away. *You* did that."

She blinks fast, swiping the sleeve of her hoodie under her eyes. "Yeah?"

"Yeah," I nod. "We wrote that song when everything felt like it was falling apart. Luca got the riff down in one take, but the lyrics... those were all the shit we didn't know how to say out loud. So we put it in the music. I think we just hoped someone out there would hear it and feel a little less alone."

She lets out a sound—part laugh, part breath, part something fragile breaking loose—and hugs her arms around herself like she's trying to stay anchored.

"I don't mean to get all emotional..."

"Don't apologise," I say, shaking my head. "Seriously. This? This is the best part of what we do. Not the shows. Not the charts. *This*. Getting to meet someone who connected with the music."

She hesitates, voice small. "Can I... get a picture?"

"Course you can," I say, already moving. "Come on."

She crouches beside me in the sand, and I slip my arm gently around her shoulders—nothing overdone, just a real, solid moment. We both smile for the photo, and when she steps back, she lingers.

"Thanks," she murmurs. "For not brushing it off. For saying that."

I look her in the eye. "Never would. You're still here. That means everything."

And I mean it.

Because beneath the noise and chaos, that's the heartbeat of all of it. Not just survival—but *connection*. Strangers meeting in the ruins, saying: *I made it through, and so did you.*

She melts back into the crowd, and I sit there for a moment longer, the quiet settling around me like a second skin. Gratitude pooling low in my chest.

I tip my head back and let the stars blur above me, the night sinking in slowly. It's the kind of night that clings to your skin, humming somewhere in your bones.

And then, movement. Just at the edge of my vision.

Naomi?

A flash of firelight catches her stride. Sharp. Certain. She's weaving through the crowd like she's on a mission, drink in one hand, the other mid-gesture as she talks to someone I can't see. All focus. All fire.

I blink, almost disbelieving.

She's lit by the beach lanterns, their sway casting golden edges along her hair and cheekbones. Hoodie half-zipped, sleeves shoved up, chin tilted like she's ready to throw down if someone so much as breathes wrong. Classic Naomi.

My heart kicks up, urgent and clumsy.

I sit up straighter, eyes sweeping the crowd. Past the fire, past the guys, past the silhouettes dancing near the shoreline with shoes dangling from their fingers.

I'm searching for her.

Because if Naomi's here tonight…

She might be, too.

CHAPTER 13

when worlds collide

ELLIE

I DID IT! FIRST-CLASS honours degree.

The words don't feel real. Not yet. Like I've wandered into someone else's story, and they forgot to kick me out of the spotlight.

I'm not used to this part. The win. The finish line. But this time... I made it.

The weight I've dragged for years. Hospital shifts, coursework I barely understood, microwave dinners that passed for meals, endless nights studying after Mia went to sleep, and the quiet fear that I was always one step from failing has lifted.

But, still. *Staff Nurse Carter.* I bite back a grin. It still doesn't feel real.

No more unpaid shifts. No more 4 a.m. breakdowns over essays or care plans. No more praying I'd make it through another thirteen-hour shift without crying in the loo or half-falling asleep on the drive home.

No longer the student. No longer the girl tiptoeing through imposter syndrome with a clipboard and borrowed confidence. I earned this. Every bleary-eyed lecture. Every missed moment with Mia. Every second-guess and every shift where I questioned if I was cut out for this.

It's terrifying. And freeing. And something close to pride hums low in my chest, steady and sure.

My phone buzzes nonstop in my bag, stuffed with messages from classmates, tutors, and family. Mum even cried when I shared the news, her voice cracking in a way it rarely does. Mia practically tackled me the second I walked through the door, squealing and clinging like I'd come home with a puppy and a tray of cupcakes.

And now here I am, sitting across from David, watching a candle flicker between us. The golden glow dances in his eyes as he lifts his glass.

The restaurant is intimate. Dim lighting, crystal glasses, linen napkins you feel guilty using. A string quartet plays somewhere in the corner, soft and unobtrusive. Couples murmur over tasting menus, and a waiter glides past carrying a bottle of wine I can't pronounce.

It's beautiful. Sophisticated. Carefully curated. And just a little… too much.

These places have never been my scene. It's like I'm one wrong fork away from a *Pretty Woman* moment. But David fits here. Slides into it like a tailored suit. So I sit a little straighter. Smile politely. Try not to let it show.

"I'm so proud of you," David says, voice steady, eyes clear. He lifts his glass, then takes a sip. "You've worked so damn hard for this, Ellie. You deserve it."

My throat tightens. For a second, I can't even speak.

I remember this version of him, the one who knew how to show up. The one who'd buy my favourite chocolate without asking. Who'd book places like this *just because*. The man who made me feel like the centre of his world.

It's disorienting, remembering how easy it was to fall in love with him.

"Thank you," I murmur, tucking a strand of hair behind my ear. "It still doesn't feel real."

His gaze lingers like it used to. Like he's proud. Like he means it. And then, without warning, he stands, smoothing down his shirt, and extends a hand toward me. "Dance with me."

I blink. "What?"

A small smile tugs at his lips. "Dance with me," he repeats, glancing toward the open space by the quartet. A few couples sway in a slow, effortless rhythm, like they were born knowing how.

"David," I say, "you hate dancing."

"I hate *bad* dancing," he says, eyes glinting. "But if you recall, I happen to be pretty good at it."

And just like that, I let him lead me from the table. His hand settles at the small of my back. Warm and certain. His other finds mine, our fingers lacing effortlessly.

The music is soft. Some classical arrangement I don't recognise, all gentle tides and rising swells. I let myself melt into it. Into him. Into the moment. His body is familiar. The cadence of our steps easy.

It's been so long since we've done anything like this. Since we've felt like this. And part of me aches at how natural it still is, how quickly the weight disappears when his arms are around me and we're swaying beneath the glow of chandeliers.

"You're really doing it," he murmurs, voice low against my ear. "Your dream. You should be proud of yourself."

I close my eyes. Breathe him in. Try to hold on to the parts of us that still work, even if they feel fewer and farther between.

Then, somehow, I find my voice. "Actually, I planned something," I say, pulling back just enough to meet his eyes. "A bit of a double celebration. To mark this moment. And your birthday coming up."

His brows lift. "Oh?"

"I booked us a cabin," I say, the words small but steady. A nervous smile tugs at my mouth. "Next weekend. Mum and Dad said they'd have Mia. No work, no distractions. Just us."

He doesn't respond straight away, and the pause stretches long enough that his silence says everything. Until he sighs, dragging a hand down his jaw.

"Ellie..." And there it is. Not a no. Not yet. But I can already feel the shift in the air.

He doesn't respond right away. Just rubs the back of his neck, jaw tensing, enough to make my stomach clench.

"Can we even afford that right now?" he says, eventually. "Things are really tight."

The words hang heavy in the air.

My fingers tighten around the edge of the counter. "I've been saving," I say, quietly but firmly. "For months."

He raises an eyebrow, sceptical. "From where?"

I draw in a slow breath. "The café. My weekend shifts. Tips. And a bits from student loan payments—I didn't spend all of it. Just scraped what I could, here and there."

A beat passes.

David exhales through his nose, the way he does when he doesn't want to say something out loud. Like that makes it less real. His silence is louder than any argument.

"I appreciate it," he says, each word chosen like it might go off in his hand. "Really. It's thoughtful. But it's just... bad timing. Work's insane right now. I've got a massive deal closing. I can't step away. Not even for a weekend."

The disappointment hits low, solid. Like a rock dropped into my stomach. I try to keep my face neutral. Try not to let the sting show. "You're always working," I mumble, trying not to sound like I'm accusing him, even if part of me is. "I just thought maybe we could use some time. It's been so long since we did anything like this."

He doesn't answer straight away, just lets the moment stretch, eyes fixed somewhere just past my shoulder.

"I know," he says. "I know it's been hectic. I just don't have the bandwidth for anything else right now."

"*Bandwidth?* Even for me? You don't think we *need* this, David?" I ask, quieter this time. "Even a little?"

His mouth presses into a tight line. "It's not about need, Ellie. It's about priorities. And right now, I can't afford to lose focus."

I look at him for a long moment, studying the man across from me. The clean lines, the calm surface, the way he's already pulling back. I could keep pushing. Could ask him to try. To meet me halfway. But what's the point?

So, I pull the edges of myself back in.

I nod, swallowing around the tightness creeping into my throat.

"Of course," I say, pulling my voice into something polite. Manageable. "I should've just asked before I booked it."

He squeezes my hand gently. "You should still go, though. It's paid for now." He says, voice easy, like he's solving a simple problem. "Take Naomi. Or Mia. Make it a girls' weekend. Go celebrate."

It's a nice suggestion. But it's not the point.
I wanted time with him.
But I don't say that. I just do what I always do.
I shrink. I smile.
"Yeah."
He kisses my forehead.
But the moment is gone.
Again.

The following weekend, the car is packed, the snacks loaded, and Naomi's Ultimate Girls Trip Playlist is already blasting at a volume that could be classified as a public disturbance.

We haven't even hit the motorway, and she's already declared it a no skips masterpiece. An unapologetic mess of early 2000s pop, questionable power ballads, and one dubstep remix I'm refusing to acknowledge until it's too late.

The first chorus of *Wannabe* hits before we're out of the car park, and Naomi's already scream-singing with the windows down. By the time *All by Myself* comes on, she's clutching her chest like she's in the final round of *Britain's Got Talent*.

Mia and Claire are in the back seat, tangled in friendship bracelets, crisp packets, and some heated teenage debate about whether bucket hats are iconic or criminal. Naomi's in the passenger seat, sunglasses the size of dinner plates perched on her nose, hair tied up in a scarf that's one hundred per cent more aesthetic than functional.

And me? I'm behind the wheel, windows down, sea air sneaking in more with every mile.

There's something about driving away from everything that's been weighing me down. From the silence with David. From the hollow ache of polite disappointment, I can't bring myself to voice. From the cabin I booked for two, that's now a girls' trip.

It's not what I pictured. But maybe it's what I need.

Naomi turns the music down just long enough to announce, "This trip is for chaos, and I will be accepting no further input on the matter."

"Mate," I say, laughing, "you're literally the only one who's said anything."

"Exactly." She flashes me a wink. "Visionary leadership."

Claire leans forward from the back, twirling a strand of her braid around her finger. "Do we have a mood board?"

Mia, without missing a beat, holds up her phone. "I made a Pinterest folder. There's glitter. And sunsets. And lifeguards."

Naomi nearly chokes on her smoothie. "That's my girl."

We're not even halfway to Coral Point before the car is echoing with off-key harmonies, demands for second breakfast, and a full-blown, courtroom-level debate about whether Avril Lavigne counts as punk or pop.

Naomi threatens to yeet herself out the window when Mia calls her *vintage*.

It's loud and chaotic, and it's perfect. And for the first time in what feels like forever, I feel... lighter.

The closer we get to the coast, the more everything seems to open up, like the world's loosening its grip.

The road winds through the hills in lazy curves, stitching the land together with tarmac and blind corners. Every bend reveals something new—lakes flat as poured glass, trees pressed close to the banks, ancient and thick, their branches dripping in late-summer green. Sunlight flickers through the canopy above, catching the dashboard in bursts of gold before vanishing behind leaves like it changed its mind.

Naomi's got half her body out the window, hair everywhere,

yelling that she's *absolutely one with nature now*, while Mia and Claire take turns arguing over who's spotted more sheep and trying to outdo each other's photo angles.

And then the hills fall away.

Coral Point rolls into view like it's been waiting for us. This absurd little postcard of a place. The road spills us out into narrow, cobbled streets, cottages stacked like they've been there forever, painted in soft, impossible colours. Turquoise. Lemon yellow. Coral, obviously. Every windowsill bursts with flowers, like the buildings are trying to out-bloom each other.

The air changes, too. Thicker, saltier, threaded with seaweed, warm stone, and something sweet I can't place. Maybe fudge. Or fresh bread. Or just the kind of sugar that clings to the air in places like this.

Beyond the rooftops, the ocean stretches wide and dark, the horizon smudged with distant hills. The waves chase each other in a rhythm I feel somewhere low in my ribs.

It's messy. Weathered. Rough in all the ways that feel honest. And God, it's beautiful.

As we roll into town, Naomi leans dramatically out of the window and yells, "WE HAVE ARRIVED!" like we're about to liberate a small nation on horseback.

No one pays her the slightest bit of attention, which somehow only makes her more pleased with herself.

Mia and Claire cheer from the back seat, craning to spot a gelato shop or a beach hut with decent Wi-Fi as we roll past a weathered wooden sign that reads *Coral Point Cove*, the paint chipped, the letters faded by sun and salt.

Just beyond it, we pass a battered old minibus parked half on the verge, the kind that's survived one too many chaotic journeys. The side panel's dented, one hubcap's missing, and someone's scratched '*MV was 'ere'* on the back door.

I blink, a half-smile tugging at my mouth. It feels like a place time has forgotten. And maybe that's the point.

The road narrows even more, threading between knotted old

trees and scrubby wildflowers before tipping us out by a quiet corner of the shoreline.

I ease the car onto the gravel drive, the tyres crunching as I pull up outside our cabin, just a few steps from where the beach gives way to tufts of grass and pale, weather-beaten sand.

The cabin itself is small, tucked between two crooked pines. It rises with a peaked roof and wears its soft, silvery-grey wood like a weathered coat, its sun-bleached shutters framing wide glass windows that catch the light. The salt-kissed air softened and shaped it into something both rustic and effortlessly elegant.

And then, silence. Not heavy. Not awkward. Just peaceful. The kind of silence that doesn't ask anything from you. It just lets you be.

Naomi throws her door open like she's arriving on the set of her own beach-themed soap opera, arms stretched wide. "Okay, ladies. Let's unpack and do something that costs too much and contributes nothing to our personal growth."

"Shopping?" Claire suggests.

"Shopping!" Naomi confirms.

We spend the rest of the late afternoon doing the most cliché tourist things imaginable, and I love every second of it.

We drift through a string of tiny shops that all smell of sandalwood and pot-pourri, where every shelf is overflowing with hand-poured candles that cost more than my phone bill. Shell necklaces hang from driftwood displays, T-shirts scream terrible puns like '*Seas the Day*', and somewhere in the corner, there's a display of wind chimes clanging in the breeze.

Naomi tries on at least six pairs of novelty sunglasses, including a pineapple-shaped pair she insists are *weirdly flattering*, before abandoning them all with a sigh.

Meanwhile, Mia and Claire find matching shark tooth bracelets and behave like they've discovered ancient treasure. They're already planning to wear them *forever*, which, in teenage time, means until Tuesday.

I let Naomi talk me into a hoodie that says 'I Heart Coral Point' in glittery letters.

"I *cannot* wear this," I say, studying it as I hold it up.

"You absolutely can," she fires back. "And you will. It's giving unhinged coastal mum and aunt. I'm obsessed!"

God, give me strength.

We wander along the seafront, ice creams in hand, and find a spot to perch on the boardwalk. The afternoon sun bounces off the water, turning the fishing boats into lazy silhouettes bobbing in the glittering blue.

By the end of the afternoon, I'm sun-drunk and smiling so hard my cheeks hurt. It's like today exists in a world of its own.

Then, as we're strolling past a fish and chip shop, something flaps against the window, catching the corner of my eye. A poster taped to the glass. Sun-bleached around the edges, corners curling in the breeze.

End of Summer Beach Party!
Music · Food · Bonfire
"One Last Night of Summer Magic"

My feet drag to a halt.

There's something about the messy lettering and the promise of music and fire under the stars that tugs at something low in my chest.

Naomi, ever the bloodhound for a vibe shift, doubles back. She follows my gaze, reads the poster once, and whips her head toward me with a look of sheer triumph.

Her grin is criminal. "Say. Fucking. Less."

"Mia..." I protest, half-laughing, half-hoping for a miracle.

But before I can even finish the sentence, Mia waves me off as though she's the adult and I'm the one who needs supervision. "We want a night in, Mum," she declares from behind a fistful of shopping bags. "Movie marathon. Popcorn. Zero adult supervision."

I raise an eyebrow. "You're thirteen, not seventeen."

Mia just grins, unbothered. "Semantics."

I blink, trying to process the role reversal of my thirteen-year-old daughter inadvertently telling me to go out and have fun. "I don't know..."

Naomi is already sliding her sunglasses off dramatically. "Ellie," she says, placing both hands on my shoulders. "I love you. But I am officially staging an intervention."

"Oh no."

"Oh yes." She gestures to the girls. "They will be fine. We'll make a stop at the rental place for snacks and DVDs like it's 2006."

Mia raises an eyebrow from the back seat. "We have Netflix, you know."

"Please. You haven't lived until you've experienced a local DVD rental shelf organised entirely by vibes and guesswork." Naomi turns her attention back to me then. "Plus, they both have phones. The cabin is, what, a spit's throw from the beach?"

"Stone's throw," I correct.

Claire nods. "Spit's probably more accurate."

Naomi ignores her. "Come on. When was the last time we went to a beach party together?"

I open my mouth.

"Exactly!" she cuts me off before I can even say anything. "It's been years. And we have just accomplished major life goals. We qualified. I…" she pauses. "Successfully flirted with two hot paramedics this week. We deserve some fun."

"What happened to the junior doctor?"

She brushed me off. "Old news!"

I'm already smiling, even as I shake my head. "You're relentless."

There's a stubborn part of me that wants to resist. To stay safe. Predictable. But another part says maybe it's time to step off the track I've been running on for years. Let go. Just for one night.

"Fine," I say, laughing despite myself.

"YES!" Naomi fist-pumps the air.

"MOVIE NIGHT!" Mia yells, throwing both her arms in the air like she's casting a spell.

Claire claps, and I sigh in defeat. But I'm still smiling.

Before Naomi and I abandon the next generation to their fortress of sweets and spreadsheets, we make one crucial stop: the local rental shop.

It's like stepping into a time capsule. The place smells of dust and vanilla air freshener, the kind that's meant to smell inviting but mostly smells like regret. Battered DVD cases, hand-scrawled staff picks, and faded movie posters cram the narrow aisles. There's a flickering neon sign above the counter that reads *Be Kind, Rewind*. Fighting a losing battle against the twenty-first century.

The man behind the till looks like he's been here since the dawn of cinema and might be the last line of defence in the battle against streaming.

Mia and Claire dive into the snack aisle like gremlins released into the wild.

"We need a classic," Claire announces, clutching a jumbo bag of popcorn.

Mia holds up *The Parent Trap* triumphantly, her eyes shining. "Sold!"

I press a hand to my chest, mock-sniffling. "Proud parenting moment."

At the till, we dump a frankly alarming pile of snacks: sour worms, chocolate buttons, three different types of crisps, and something labelled "cola-flavoured drink."

The man doesn't even flinch. Just raises a slow eyebrow. "You havin' a party?" he asks in a gravelly drawl.

"Movie night," I say. "Two teenagers."

He gives a slow, solemn nod. "Godspeed, love."

We drop the girls back at the cabin, their arms already overloaded with snacks and DVDs like they're prepping for a three-day siege.

Mia and Claire set to work, burrowing into the sofa with blankets and building a snack fort so structurally sound it could survive a coastal storm. *The Parent Trap* menu is already looping on the TV, and the smell of buttered popcorn fills the small living room.

I linger in the doorway, arms crossed, trying—and failing—not to fuss.

"Phones on," I say, giving them both a look. "Not on silent. If anything feels off, or if you need anything, even if you just hear a weird noise... you call me. Got it?"

Mia rolls her eyes with the practiced patience of a teenager. "Yes, Mum," she says, in perfect deadpan harmony with Claire.

I narrow my eyes. "I mean it."

Mia tosses a piece of popcorn at Claire, who catches it in her mouth like a trained seal. "We'll be fine. We've got food, movies, and zero desire to interact with actual humans tonight."

Claire nods. "We have a schedule."

Naomi peeks her head around the door, grinning. "They're more organised than we ever were."

"No offence," Mia pipes up, grinning at me, "but you're the ones we should be worried about. Don't do anything too cringe."

I clutch my chest. "I'll have you know, I am the height of sophistication."

"Yeah, in like... 2007," Mia teases, laughing.

I throw a cushion at her, and she ducks, still grinning.

Satisfied—sort of—I step back and pull the door closed behind us, the warm glow from the windows spilling onto the porch.

Naomi slings an arm around my shoulders as we head toward the path leading down to the beach. "Ready to party like we're twenty-one again?" she asks.

I laugh, shaking my head. "We were barely functional then."

She shrugs. "Still iconic though."

And just like that, we walk into the night, the sound of the ocean pulling us closer.

The beach is alive by the time we wander down toward the sand.

It's only a five-minute walk from the cabin, but something about the quiet trek through the trees makes it feel like stepping out of one world and into another. I carry my flip-flops in one hand, the soles knocking together as I pad barefoot down the weathered path.

Music thrums low in the air, carried on the sea breeze. A lazy, acoustic vibe that seeps into your bones without asking permission. As the sun sets, the sky slips toward navy, with streaks of orange fading at the horizon, revealing the stars that blink into view.

The bonfire is the heart of it all, flames licking toward the sky, casting everyone in soft golds and deep shadows. Around it, the crowd moves in loose circles. Couples swaying to the music, groups huddled around coolers, and battered beach chairs. String lights zigzag between weather-worn poles, their glow warm and inviting, like someone bottled up the last gasp of summer and strung it across the night.

The air smells like salt and smoke, and frying dough. Someone's juggling marshmallows near the fire, and someone else is attempting to start a beach-wide game of rounders with a small bat.

Naomi bumps her shoulder into mine, grinning like she's a teenager again. "This is a vibe." And I have to agree. It's messy and loud and imperfect, and somehow exactly what I didn't know I needed.

I curl my toes into the cool, soft sand, its fine grains a soothing caress against my skin. Somewhere, a wireless speaker coughs to life, and the music shifts into a song I half-recognise, something raw and summery.

I glance around, half-expecting to feel out of place. Too old, too stiff, too something. But the energy here demands nothing from you. It just welcomes you in, barefoot and messy and exactly as you are.

Naturally, Naomi fit right in. She's already clocked the churro stand, a man in a linen shirt handing out drinks in plastic cups, and a knot of girls who are laughing so hard they're crying.

She throws a look over her shoulder at me. "You coming, or are you just gonna stand there looking pretty?"

I laugh, flipping her off, and follow her into the crowd.

The night feels stretched out ahead of us. Loose, wild, and full of possibility.

Naomi disappears toward the toilets, passing me her drink and promising to be exactly *'two Beyoncé songs'* worth of time. I linger where the firelight softens the edges of the crowd, holding both cups, unsure where to stand.

I take a slow sip of the drink she handed me. Something cold, sweet, and a little fizzy. I let it settle on my tongue as the air wraps around me. The music shifts to something softer, a lazy acoustic riff that tugs at the edges of my thoughts.

I'm threading my way toward the firelight, drinks balanced precariously in my hands.

I turn. Step forward. And crash straight into someone's chest.

Solid. Warm. Immediate.

The impact jolts the cups, sloshing cold liquid over my hands. I stumble back, muttering an apology, but firm hands catch my elbows before I lose my footing.

"Shit, I'm so sorry…" I start, my voice already flustered, ready to disappear into the sand out of sheer embarrassment.

But then I look up, and in that instant, the music, the firelight, everything just fades. It's as though something mutes the world, leaving only this moment.

Ice-grey eyes. Messy dark hair.

For a moment, we just stare at each other, caught in a moment that felt timeless.

His fingers coil around my arms, and it hits me somewhere low and stupid in my stomach, just like it always does.

He blinks once, as if he's trying to convince himself I'm actually here. "Ellie?" His voice is a little hoarse, a little stunned, like he hasn't said my name in a long time and doesn't trust how it feels.

I swallow down the chaos rising in my chest and find my voice. "We really have to stop meeting like this," I laugh.

Something shifts in his expression. A flicker of surprise. And then, unmistakably… a grin that wrecks me a little more than I care to admit.

Kieran Hayes, smiling at me like the whole bloody beach just disappeared around us.

CHAPTER 14

tides of tension

KIERAN

Ellie's here. Hoodie, jean shorts, sea salt clinging to her hair, moonlight brushing her skin. And those legs. Long, sun-kissed, and ridiculous. Somehow, even better than I remembered.

"What are you doing here?" She asks, her voice lighter, touched with surprise and something warmer underneath.

I laugh, still half-stunned. "Could ask you the same thing."

She shrugs, tucking her hands into the front of her hoodie. "Supposed to be a girls' trip," she says, smiling. "Naomi, Mia, one of Mia's friends. But then we saw the poster for the party and, well. Here we are."

That soft sparkle in her eyes floors me, and I can't help the grin that pulls across my face. "Fate's got a hell of a sense of humour."

She huffs a laugh, shaking her head. And then, like a damn hurricane, Naomi whirls in. "What in the *flying* shit-balls?!"

I turn just in time to see her charging toward us, expression a full tragedy of disbelief. Ellie groans beside me, pinching the bridge of her nose and laughing under her breath. She slips just out of arm's reach. I already miss her without meaning to.

Naomi stops dead a few feet away, throwing her hands up dramatically. "*Seriously*?! You? Here? Of *all* places?!"

I flash her a crooked grin. "Hey, Naomi."

She points between Ellie and me like she's solving a murder case. "Of course it's you. *Of course.*"

Ellie's still laughing, covering her face like she can't believe it either.

Naomi flicks her gaze between us one more time, then folds her arms with a smug, shit-eating grin. "You two are *actual* magnets. It's disturbing."

I chuckle low in my throat, rubbing the back of my neck, because... she's not wrong.

Naomi hooks her arm through Ellie's and tugs her forward. "Alright. Come on. Music, drinks, this vibe? It's criminal not to lean in."

I catch Ellie's eye as she lets Naomi lead her a step ahead. She throws me a small smile, one that lands dead-centre in my chest.

I fall into step beside them without thinking.

The party surges louder ahead of us, and the bonfire throws gold sparks into the night. Theo is laughing so hard he nearly spills whatever horror is in his cup. The guys are wild, loose, and electric.

I call out over the music, "Look who I found."

Luca's head snaps around, and the grin that explodes across his face is nothing short of chaotic joy. "Ellie Carter! As I live and fucking breathe."

Before she can even respond, Theo hurtles toward her like a human golden retriever, lifting her clean off the ground in a bear hug.

"FUCK YES!" he howls. "This night just got better!" He spins her once before setting her down, then turns and slaps a double high-five into Naomi's palms. "You both look dangerously hot. I'm intimidated."

Naomi flicks her hair like royalty. "You should be."

Ryder's sprawled in the sand, the same blonde from earlier now firmly settled on his lap, her laugh high and breathy against his neck. He lifts his drink with a lazy grin, eyes catching the firelight. "Ladies," he drawls. "Welcome to the chaos."

Luca slings his arm around my shoulders and leans in close

enough I can smell the rum and bonfire smoke on his skin. "It's like gravity, man," he mutters, smirking. "You and her."

I roll my eyes. "Don't start."

He just grins wider. "Too late."

And for the first time in too damn long, it feels like we're all exactly where we're supposed to be.

The next hour is a blur in the best possible way. Laughter spills across the sand, blending into the crackle of the fire and the soft crash of the tide.

Theo invents a game called *Fireball Volleyball* that involves nothing more than someone hitting a half-deflated beach ball into the flames and then screaming when it catches fire.

Ryder starts an impromptu dance-off near the wireless speaker. Luca somehow gets roped into judging it, completely deadpan, holding up makeshift scores made from discarded napkins.

Someone passes around glow sticks. Naomi wears hers like a crown. Theo strings two together like nun-chucks and nearly takes someone's head off.

And Ellie? She is *glowing*. The firelight dances across her skin, catching in her hair, turning her into something almost unreal. She moves through the crowd with that soft smile, always quick to laugh, always half-glancing toward me when she thinks I won't notice.

I notice. Of course I do.

We're barefoot, half-drunk on cheap tequila and sea air. Theo tries to climb onto someone's shoulders and immediately topples them both into the sand. While Naomi leads an aggressively chaotic conga line around the fire-pit.

I watch Ellie twirl under the fairy lights with Luca, arms thrown up, her laugh spilling freely into the night. She's so close now. Close enough to touch. Close enough to break me clean open.

One of the guys from earlier passes the guitar around again, and I find myself reaching for it without thinking. And, like muscle memory, my hands find the strings.

The chords fall easily under my fingers, the notes carrying into the firelight. People sway without thinking. Conversations dip, the energy pulling tighter, sweeter.

I see Ellie out of the corner of my eye, settling cross-legged a few feet away, her chin resting in her hand, watching me. And God help me.

I strum through a few chords. Something familiar, something I know will draw her closer without even trying. And sure enough, she shifts toward me, slow and curious. I move the guitar out of the way and pat the sand between my legs, giving her a look that says, *come on then*.

She smirks, then closes the short distance between us, dropping down so close that the slightest brush of her knee against mine sends a jolt straight through me.

I tilt the guitar toward her and place it in her lap. "You ever played before?"

She shakes her head, tucking a strand of hair behind her ear. "Always wanted to," she admits. "Never had the time."

I shift slightly as she settles in front of me, warm and close and entirely too much, all at once. "Time's overrated." I adjust the guitar in her lap, move close enough that my chest brushes her back, and reach around her, guiding her hands into place.

My touch is light, but it's enough to make her still. "Here," I murmur.

She lets out a laugh. "I'm probably going to be awful at this."

I lean in, breathing in the perfume that clings to her skin. Her hair shifts in the breeze, brushing my cheek, and beneath it lingers a trace of lavender, clean and subtle, like she's just stepped out of the shower hours ago and it never quite left her.

"You'll do just fine. Trust me." I guide her fingers gently, the tips of mine brushing over hers. Her hands are soft and warm, tentative but willing. My pulse trips, a thrum behind my ribs I can't seem to ignore. "Look," I murmur, curling her fingers just slightly. "You want enough pressure to press the string, but not so much that you crush it."

"You make it sound easy."

"It is," I say. "Especially when you've got a good teacher."

She glances over her shoulder at me, a half-smile playing on her lips. "Cocky."

I smirk. "Confident."

She plays another soft note, and I hum in approval. "You're a natural," I say, and the word lands softer than I meant it to. Then she turns her head just enough to look up at me from under her lashes. Her hair brushes my cheek. Soft, wild, and dizzying in a way that completely wrecks my ability to think straight.

My throat tightens as her smile curves slow and dangerous. Her body leans into mine like we've always fit this way, like the years in between never happened.

This is it. This is the line. And I'm dancing right on the edge of it.

One breath closer, and I could taste her skin. If I tilt my head just slightly, my mouth would be on the curve of her jaw, the hollow of her throat. I could fall into her without looking back.

But then she shifts—not closer. Away. Subtle, deliberate. Like she feels the charge in the air and needs to cut it dead before it sparks.

She doesn't meet my eyes, doesn't need to. That quiet retreat says enough.

A reminder. A boundary. One I've got no business flirting with.

Because she's not mine.

Not anymore. Not ever, maybe.

She's engaged. Living a life that doesn't include me. And I'm sitting here like some lovesick idiot who forgot the way she smiled at me in another lifetime doesn't mean a damn thing now.

God, I feel like such a dick.

So caught up in the ghost of what we were, in my own want, I didn't stop to consider what it might look like.

What it might *mean*.

This isn't a movie. There's no swelling music or grand kiss. There's just me—reaching for something that isn't mine—and her, stepping away with the kind of grace I should've shown first.

I run a hand down my face. The air feels colder now. Heavy with everything I didn't say.

And maybe that's for the best.

So I pull the moment back into my chest and let it burn there, silent and unspoken.

"ELLIE CARTER. DRINKS. NOW!" Theo, with his impeccable timing, yells from across the fire.

Ellie laughs, then untangles herself from the guitar. From me. I let her go, even though my heart stays caught in the space she leaves behind. And then she's gone, swept away by Theo and Ryder.

I sit there, hands ghosting over the strings where hers had been, every nerve in my body lit up and aching. And as I glance up at the sky, at the stars scattered recklessly and bright over the water, I exhale slowly.

Fuck. I'm so far gone.

A few minutes later, Naomi drops into the sand beside. She folds her legs neatly, stealing the last of my drink without even asking.

I don't even bother fighting it. I'm too busy trying to get my heart to settle back into something resembling a normal rhythm.

Naomi says nothing at first. Just sits there, letting the music and laughter wrap around us like static. Then, softly… "So…"

It's not a question. It's a door she's holding open. I rake a hand through my hair and let out a rough breath. "So," I repeat.

"You okay?" she asks, turning to look at me properly. Her voice isn't teasing now. It's real. Steady.

I don't answer right away. Because yeah—I'm surrounded by friends, the fire's warm, my body's still humming from playing music. But no, I'm not okay, not even a little. "Fine." I shrug, trying to play it off. "Just tired."

Naomi snorts. "That's cute. Lie to someone else, Hayes."

I exhale hard through my nose. "Nothing's going on."

"Nothing?" she repeats, cocking her head, voice dry as sand. "Because it looked like something from where I was standing. And my vision's elite."

I look at her then, and she's already got that look on her face. The one that says *don't even try it. I'm ten steps ahead of you.* So, I drop the act.

"I'm falling for her," I admit, voice cracking a little. "Again. Still. Whatever the fuck this is."

I scrub a hand over my jaw, trying to find the words that fit the size of it all. "But she's with him," I say. "She's tied to him. And I hate it because..." I break off, shaking my head. Naomi waits. "I don't think she even knows how unhappy she is."

She's quiet for a while. Then she says, gently: "She knows."

My gaze snaps up.

"She knows," she repeats, slower this time. A hint of meaning behind the words. "She's scared," Naomi says eventually, her voice low. "And she's tired. And she's been surviving for so long she doesn't remember what it feels like to just... be happy."

I glance at her, throat tight.

"You see her laugh," Naomi continues. "You see those moments when she's free. But you don't see the hours she spends holding everything else up. Mia. Uni. Her parents. Keeping the peace with David. Pretending she's not drowning half the time."

I close my eyes, the ache blooming deep in my chest.

"She doesn't let people see it," Naomi says. "Doesn't know how. She'll get there, but she's not ready yet. Just... be patient with her," she says. "She trusts you. More than you realise. Just give her space to come to you. And she *will* come to you, Kieran."

I nod, staring at the fire like it might have answers tucked between the flames. "I'll be waiting."

"Good." Naomi bumps her shoulder against mine, soft but solid. "She needs someone that will be."

A gust of wind kicks up from the water, carrying the smell of smoke. I watch the fire crackle, feel the empty space Ellie left behind like a ghost against my skin.

I'll wait for her. For as long as it takes.

The first thing I notice is the god-awful pounding in my skull. The second is the unmistakable taste of tequila and regret coating my tongue.

I groan, one arm flung over my face as I shift against the hotel mattress. My eyes stay screwed shut, like that might somehow hold back the nausea lapping at the edges of my stomach.

How the hell did I get back here?

Bits and pieces shuffle through my memory like a broken slideshow. The beach. Ryder shoving another beer into my hand. Theo daring Luca into a shot competition neither of them should've accepted.

Ellie, sitting between my legs like it was the most natural thing in the world. Her hands curled around the guitar I'd dropped in her lap. That laugh. Ringing through the air as she fumbled her way through the chords.

The way the rest of the world faded into the background until it was just us, tangled in the easy gravity of something too big to name.

The way she pulled away when I was dangerously close to crossing a line.

I force my eyes open, instantly regretting it as the ceiling glares back like a personal attack. My hands drag down my face in protest.

Across the room, an obnoxious snore cuts through the silence like a chainsaw. I tilt my head and spot Ryder sprawled across the sofa, one leg hanging off the side, arms akimbo, still fully dressed. Dead to the world.

Christ.

What time is it?

I reach instinctively for my phone on the nightstand, squinting against the blast of light from the screen. 11:47 a.m. Not ideal. But not tragic.

Just as I'm about to drop the phone back onto the bed, a notification flashes across the screen.

> ELLS [11:49]
> Hope your head isn't suffering too much today 😂

Another follows before I can even blink.

> ELLS [11:50]
> Also! Naomi says she hates you for getting her involved in that last round of shots.

A breath of laughter escapes me. If Naomi looks anything like I feel, I understand her outrage.

> Tell Naomi I regret nothing. She made her choices. Hope you get home safe.

I hover for a second, thumb tapping the edge of the phone. Only a few seconds pass before her reply lands.

ELLS [11:53]

Setting off later. Naomi is no longer living, laughing or thriving. That's for sure! And I've felt better lol.

I chuckle again, sitting up now, back protesting. My head's still a war zone, but this stupid little conversation, bright and easy, helps.

> So what you're saying is you're both unfit for human interaction today?

ELLS: [11:56]

Already accepted my fate. Bed and hydration are severely calling my name.

> True survival mode then?

ELLS [11:56]

😂😂 yeah

What about you?

I glance across the room. Ryder hasn't moved, except to dramatically flop one arm over his face, like he's shielding himself from the memory of his own choices.

> Currently watching Ryder battle for his life in his sleep. It's touch and go but I think he'll make it.

ELLS [11:57]

I'm rooting for him.

Warmth blooms low in my chest, and I slip the phone into my pocket. Ryder's death rattle of a snore fills the room, and then he shifts, eyes squinting like he's just regained consciousness in a post-apocalyptic wasteland.

"Water," he croaks, like it's his dying wish.

I raise an eyebrow. "Use your legs, dickhead."

"Dying," he rasps.

"Good."

He flips me off blindly, doesn't even lift his head. I shake mine, dragging myself upright and padding barefoot over to the mini fridge. I grab a bottle, toss it across the room, and it lands with a satisfying thud on his stomach.

He grunts but barely reacts, cracking it open with a groan and taking the tiniest sip known to man.

I lean against the dresser, rubbing a hand over the back of my neck. "Where the hell did you disappear to last night?"

"Bro," he mutters, voice as rough as gravel. "Do not ask me questions until I can feel my face again."

I huff out a laugh, taking a long pull from my own water.

That's when my phone rings. I take it out of my pocket and frown down at the screen, expecting Luca's or Theo's name to pop up. But it's not them.

It's Mrs. Patel.

I sit down, my stomach dipping like the floor just tilted under me. She has lived across the road from my dad for as long as I can remember. She's basically family, always checking in on him when I'm gone. But she never calls me.

On the second ring, I swipe to answer. "Mrs. Patel?"

"Kieran." Her voice is tight. Breathless. But it sounds urgent. "It's your father."

The air leaves my lungs. "What happened?" My voice comes out sharper than I mean it to.

"He's been taken to hospital."

Blood rushes in my ears, roaring like a wave crashing over me. "What... what's wrong?"

"It's his appendix," she says, her voice shaking. "It burst this morning. I called the ambulance, they got to him in time, but he's in surgery now."

Surgery. Jesus Christ. My mind blanks, then spins. Thoughts scatter, useless.

I'm moving before I even register it. Grabbing at my jeans with shaking hands, hoodie caught inside-out, yanked over my head in a rush. My bag's barely zipped. I don't check what's inside. I don't care.

Shoes. Where are my shoes?

There, half under the bed. I shove my feet in without socks, without thought, heart pounding like it's trying to punch its way out of my chest.

The room tilts. My hands are clammy. My lungs can't seem to fill. I just need to get home. I just need to go.

"Bro?" Ryder's voice is suddenly clear. Hangover forgotten.

I glance at him. My grip tightens around the phone. "It's my dad."

His face drops. He's upright now, alert, like someone flipped a switch. "Shit. What's going on?"

I tell him everything. Mrs. Patel. The emergency. The surgery. It spills out fast, too fast. My voice is tight, breath clipped at the edges, like I'm trying to outrun the panic clawing up my throat.

In my mind, I can already see it. Dad lying there alone, hospital sheets too white, machines blinking at his side.

And I wasn't there.

It's been months. Hell, well over a year if I stop lying to myself. I've been on the road, buried in shows and noise and deadlines, telling myself I'd call later. Visit next month.

Now he's in the hospital, and I'm not there. The guilt hits, burrowing into my chest like a fist made of iron.

He's on his own. And he shouldn't be.

"I need to get home," I say, the words tumbling out as I swing my bag over my shoulder.

But before I can move, Ryder is on his feet. "Let's go," he says, already shoving his wallet and phone into his pocket.

I stare at him, caught in a blur of panic. "What?"

"You think I'm letting you do this alone?" He shoots me a look. "No chance, mate."

"Ry, you don't have to—"

"Shut up."

I blink. The sharpness in his voice cuts through the fog in my head.

He steps in front of me, arms crossed, face serious in a way that silences everything. "Kieran, I've seen you break bones, fight off food poisoning, and play through the worst flu I've ever witnessed. But you suck at handling shit when it comes to your dad." His tone softens, but he doesn't budge. "So yeah, I'm coming. I'll call Nick, see if he can sort us a car."

I let out a shaky breath. My chest is still tight, but I don't argue. Because he's right. And I need him.

I nod. Quiet, but grateful as hell.

He claps a hand to my shoulder and squeezes. "Good. Now let's go."

CHAPTER 15

where it ends

ELLIE

THE LATE MORNING AIR CARRIES that soft saltiness that clings to your skin and doesn't quite let go. From the porch, I can just make out the girls down on the beach—two silhouettes flitting back and forth along the shoreline, bare feet kicking up sand, their laughter carried faintly on the breeze.

Mia's in my *"I Heart Coral Point"* hoodie that Naomi demanded I buy yesterday, hair a mess, dragging some poor excuse for a kite along behind her. Claire's got the bucket and spade, like they've reverted to being six again instead of thirteen. They're sun-drenched and free and utterly oblivious to the weight pressing behind my ribs.

Naomi hands me a mug of tea and collapses onto the seat beside me with a dramatic groan. She's in her sunglasses, even though the sun's barely peeking over the horizon.

"Remind me again," she mutters, "that we are *far* too old to drink like that."

I smirk, wrapping my fingers around the mug. "We are definitely too old to drink like that."

"My liver knows. My dignity knows. But my brain?" She shakes her head. "That bitch still thinks we're twenty-one and bulletproof."

I huff out a soft laugh, the warmth from the tea slowly thawing the cold inside my chest. "You were a machine last night. Until you fell off that log dancing to ABBA."

Naomi groans into her sleeve. "Ellie. *Please*. That wasn't me. That was Patricia."

I glance sideways at her, the laugh escaping before I can hold it in. "Patricia? Is she the one who—"

"I swear to God, Eleanor, if you don't stop talking…"

I can't help it. I burst out laughing, the sound cracking through the quiet like sunlight between clouds. Naomi groans again, but she's grinning now too, her cheeks flushed with the start of a hangover or maybe just the memory.

For a while, it's easy. Just us, sitting barefoot on old porch chairs, the ocean glittering at the edge of the world. The aftermath of the bonfire still clings to my skin—smoke and salt and the sweetness of toasted marshmallows. And there's a kind of clarity in the air, like the night burned something out of me.

Not joy, exactly. But something close.

Naomi lifts her sunglasses and rests them on her head. Her tone shifts—quieter now. "So."

I don't look at her. "So?"

She nudges my leg with hers. "Are we going to talk about why this turned into a girls' trip instead of the weekend you planned with David?"

My stomach knots and I hesitate. "He cancelled last minute. Something urgent came up with work."

She stares at me for a moment. "And the truth?"

I roll my eyes. "Naomi…"

"Come on, Ellie. I know when you're spinning it pretty."

I let out a hollow breath, because there's no point trying to defend him to her. "He talked his way out of it."

Her silence says everything.

"He said he wanted me to go, to enjoy it anyway. Said I deserved a break. But really?" I shake my head. "He couldn't pull himself away from work for one night. One bloody night."

Naomi exhales, slow. "Ellie…" Her voice is quieter now, but there's an edge to it. "When are you going to wake up?"

I blink. "To what?"

"You planned a weekend away, and he couldn't even be arsed to show up. And you're still making *excuses* for him. Still carrying the weight of this relationship like it's all on you."

I press my fingers to my temples. "I'm not—"

"You are," she says, cutting in. "And I get it. I do. You've built a life together. There's history, a million reasons to stay. But Ellie… you're not *happy*. And I'm tired of watching you disappear inside yourself just to keep the peace."

Her words land sharp. Too close to the truth.

I stare out at the horizon, where the sea swells gently beneath a hazy blue sky, and say nothing at all.

Finally, I mutter, "It's not that simple, Nay."

Naomi lets out a soft, incredulous laugh. "God, Ellie. You're like a record on repeat."

I bristle, but she doesn't stop.

"It's *never* that simple. That's always the excuse. You keep talking about Kieran like he's this safe place—like he's *air* and you've been underwater for years. And still, you keep going home to the man who's *drowning* you."

I blink hard, throat tight. "That's not fair. And you know it."

Her expression softens, but only slightly. "Isn't it?"

"We're just friends," I say, and even I hear how hollow it sounds.

"Do you really believe that?"

I open my mouth, but nothing comes out.

She watches me carefully. "Because I don't think you do. Not really. And I don't think he does either."

I look away.

She doesn't push. Just keeps her voice low. "You planned this weekend away to try and salvage something that's already breaking apart. And when he bailed, you acted like it was fine. Like a girls' trip was the plan all along."

My voice is thin. "Because I didn't want to waste it."

Naomi shakes her head. "You're not wasting *the trip*, Ellie. You're wasting *yourself*."

That lands deeper than I want it to. I stare down at the mug in my hands, the rim smudged with gloss, and suddenly I feel hollow. Like all the scaffolding I've built around myself is shaking loose.

"I know, Naomi. I *know*, okay!"

The words burst out of me, raw and sharp, louder than I mean them to. My chest heaves with the weight of them, my eyes burning. "You think I don't see it? That I haven't been swallowing it down every fucking day? I feel like I'm cracking open, Nay. Like if I stop moving, stop pretending for even one second, everything will fall apart."

Naomi doesn't flinch. She just reaches over, her hand settling over mine with a quiet steadiness that makes my throat ache even more.

"I'm scared," I whisper, voice barely there now. "I don't know who I am without all of this. Without holding it together."

"I know," she murmurs. "God, Ellie. I know."

I shake my head, hot tears spilling over. "I just want to feel like myself again. Like I did last night. Like I matter."

Naomi's voice is soft, but certain. "You *do* matter."

I let out a shaky breath, pressing the heel of my hand to my eyes.

"I hate seeing you dim yourself like this," Naomi adds gently. "Especially when I've seen you *lit up*. I love you, even when you're a pain in the arse. And I'll keep loving you, even when you don't know how to love yourself."

Before I can say anything, she's on her feet and pulling me into a hug—tight and warm and unrelenting. Her arms wrap around me like armour, and something in me caves. I sink into it, burying my face into her shoulder, breathing in her familiar scent of jasmine and sugar.

"I'm serious, Ellie," she murmurs into my hair. "You've got to promise me something."

I nod, unable to speak past the lump in my throat.

"Promise me you'll start listening to your heart," she says, voice fierce now, the kind of fierce that comes from love. "Not the guilt. Not what's familiar or easy or looks good from the outside. Just… what you *want*. What you *deserve*."

I nod again, tighter this time, the promise pressing hard against my ribs.

"And stop *lying* to yourself," she adds, pulling back just enough to look me in the eyes. "You're allowed to choose more. You're allowed to *want* more."

The silence that follows isn't heavy anymore.

It's honest.

Held between us like something sacred.

It's been hours of winding roads and motorway hum, but I finally turn onto the drive—headlights painting lazy arcs across the porch before blinking out. The engine ticks and cools beneath the bonnet, and for a moment I just sit there, hands loose on the steering wheel, breathing in the hush.

Then I see David's car. Parked up like it never left.

Weird. He wasn't supposed to be home until tomorrow.

I glance into the rearview mirror. Mia's still curled up, hoodie drawn tight around her like a cocoon, hair wrap slightly askew, bracelet-laden wrists resting against her tote bag.

The ache that builds in my chest is slow and deep. This weekend gave her something bright to hold on to. And maybe it gave me something too. A reminder that lightness is still possible, even after everything.

I reach back and brush my fingers lightly over her shoulder. "Come on, bug," I whisper. "We're home."

Mia stirs, scrunching her face into a yawn, blinking blearily at the window.

"Straight to bed, yeah? And be quiet, David might be in bed." I say.

"Okay." She says through a yawn, grabbing her tote and hoodie in a tangle of limbs as she gets out of the car. She pauses halfway up the path, then rushes back, wrapping her arms around me before I've even opened mine. "Thanks for the best weekend ever, Mum," she murmurs, her voice soft with sincerity.

My throat tightens immediately, tears stinging unexpectedly at the corners of my eyes. I squeeze her back, pressing a kiss to her temple. "Anytime, sweetheart."

She trails up the path, dragging her overnight bag behind her, and I follow at a slower pace, my hand reaching for the keys in my jacket pocket.

I unlock the door and it swings open on familiar hinges, the hush of home wrapping around me. It's dark inside. Quiet. The kind that makes you think maybe this weekend brought us something. A bit of space. A reset, even.

But then I hear it.

Low, steady, unmistakable—David's playlist drifting down the stairs.

That curated mix of acoustic covers and polished indie beats he plays when he's trying to unwind. Or distract. Or disappear.

I flick off my flip-flops in the hallway, shrugging out of my jacket. My arms are sore from the drive. My body is heavy in that good, slow way. I can still feel the warmth of the beach, the music in my bones, the buzz of laughter from a circle of people who made me forget that the rest of my life was still waiting for me.

By the time I lock up and reach the upstairs landing, Mia has already cracked open her bedroom door, spilling a warm sliver of lamplight into the hallway. I pause there, leaning against the frame, watching her for a second.

She's already curled beneath the duvet, face half-buried in her pillow, hoodie still on, the covers pulled up to her chin. I study her for a moment, and my heart aches with a love so fierce it almost hurts.

I back out, pulling the door closed behind me gently, and turn toward my bedroom at the far end of the hall, the promise of sleep tugging at me with every heavy step.

I open the door quietly, without thinking. No reason to hesitate. No reason to brace. But the second the door swings open, the air shifts.

My brain doesn't register it right away. The room smells... unfamiliar. Like perfume that doesn't belong to me. Like sweat and skin, and something lived-in, recent. The bedside lamp is on, but it's dim. Turned low, like a secret.

And then I hear it.

A low, rhythmic creak of the mattress.

I freeze on the spot.

The noise stops me in my tracks before my eyes even find the source. But when they do. My world cracks wide open. There's a *woman* in my bed.

Suddenly, I'm nowhere and everywhere all at once, and the realisation hits like a blow, knocking the air clean out of my lungs.

His body moves slowly and almost deliberately, his hands braced against the mattress as hers skim over his back. His mouth is at her shoulder, his breath ghosting over her skin. Their bodies lay tangled in the sheets, as if they had been there for a while.

I watch it happen. As though it's not happening to me. Like I'm floating above it, separate, watching someone else's life implode in slow motion.

David moves again. His hand slides up her side, her back arches, and she lets out a soft, pleased sigh. And that sound? It *shatters* me.

Something cold and sharp lodges itself between my ribs. My breath stops. My stomach churns. And all I can do is stand there while everything inside me detonates.

The sheets shift again, and then David turns his head. His eyes meet mine. And it hits him. The recognition. The horror.

He jerks back like he's been electrocuted, stumbling off her like he's only just remembered who he is. The woman gasps, startled, scrambling to cover herself with the twisted sheets.

I look at her.

Straight into her eyes.

She's blonde. Long hair, tanned limbs, red lipstick smudged across a mouth that still looks swollen from kissing. Her cheeks are flushed, skin golden and glowing in the low light.

She stares back at me, wide-eyed and frozen, clutching the sheets to her chest like that'll make a difference now.

But it doesn't matter what she looks like.

Because *he* is the one who promised me forever.

David stares at me like he's still trying to make sense of what he's seeing, like he's searching for the version of me that isn't shattered on the inside.

"Ellie..." he breathes, his voice raw, wrecked. "Shit—"

But it's too late. Too fucking late. My body floods with something wild, primal, and suffocating. My chest tightens so violently that I can't breathe. I don't even remember backing away. All I know is that I'm moving.

His voice follows me, panicked. "Ellie—fuck. Just wait..."

The door shuts behind me, and I'm already moving—down the stairs, through the hallway, past the kitchen, fingers fumbling with the lock on the back door.

I don't stop. Don't breathe.

I just need out.

The door creaks open and I storm onto the patio, the night air slamming into my chest like a wake-up call. Cold. Real. Sharp around the edges.

I brace my hands on the garden table, knuckles white against the wood, trying to pull myself back into my body. Trying not to scream.

Then I hear it. The back door creaks open behind me.

"Ellie," David calls, voice low but sharp at the edges—like he's trying to keep the neighbours from hearing.

I don't turn. Not yet. The gravel crunches under his bare feet as he steps onto the patio, sweatpants dragged on, chest bare, hair wild and damp with sweat. His mouth opens around words he hasn't formed yet, hands lifted like I'm some skittish thing he might spook.

"Ellie," he says again, closer now. "Just listen—"

That does it. I spin around, heat rising fast up my throat, rage surging to the surface like a bruise pressed too hard.

"*Listen?*" My voice cracks on the word. "To what, David? More lies? More carefully rehearsed excuses?"

He flinches. Just barely. But I see it.

"I wasn't thinking," he says, hands still raised in some weak, helpless gesture.

"Oh, that much is fucking clear," I snap. My whole body is shaking. My heart is crashing against my ribs like it wants to break free.

"I made a mistake. I didn't mean for this to happen—we were working, I had too much to drink." he breathes, wrecked. "I love you so much, Ellie. I'm so sorry baby."

"No! You don't get to say that." My voice breaks on the last word, barely a whisper now. "Not anymore. You fucked someone in my bed, David. *Our* bed. *For fuck sake!*" My voice is loud now, sharp.

"I swear to you, I'll do anything to fix this," he says, desperation clawing at every word. "We can get through this, Ellie. I know we can. Just stay. *Please.* Don't walk out on what we have. Not like this."

And then he says it. The words that change everything.

"You have nowhere else to go."

I blink, and my chest goes still. David's face pales. He knows the second the words leave his mouth that he's crossed a line.

I look at him. *Really* look at him. And I see the fear of losing control in his eyes. The way he tries to turn my lack of options into his leverage.

I shake my head slowly, something dark and hollow curling in my stomach. "Wow," I whisper. "You really think that, don't you?"

He stammers. "Ellie, that's not, I didn't mean..." But he did. And we both know it.

David's still reaching for me. His voice softens, taking on that tone again. The one he always uses when he's trying to reel me back in. The one he knows works.

Used to work.

"Ellie, come on," he says, his voice barely above a whisper now. "Don't do this. You're upset. You're hurt. I get it, I do. But we can fix this. We can come back from this. You just, you need to stay. Just for tonight."

He steps closer, his hands held out like something fragile. "Please," he murmurs, "if not for me. Then for Mia."

My breath catches. And that's it. That's the card he's played. Mia.

He says her name like it's a lifeline. Like she's his golden ticket. Like I wouldn't burn down the world for that girl.

I close my eyes, just for a second. Long enough for the grief to rise in my throat, thick and hot and impossible to swallow.

My jaw tightens. I look up at him again. "Fuck you, David. You don't get to use her against me."

David flinches, guilt washing over his face. "I'm not," he says, but it's a lie. A weak one.

"Yes," I whisper, "you are."

The silence between us is loud now. So loud, it rings in my ears.

I should leave. I should walk out that door tonight and never look back. But I can't. Not yet. Not like this.

Because it's not just about me.

Mia is upstairs, asleep in the world I've tried so hard to make feel safe. A life I've built brick by careful brick—packed lunches, clean uniforms, goodnight kisses—even when everything inside me was falling apart. I've fought to give her stability, to shield her from the mess, from doubt, from the kind of heartbreak that lingers.

And I won't be the reason it all crumbles in the middle of the night.

I won't let him be the one to explain what she wakes up to.

So, I do the only thing I can. I turn. I don't wait for him to follow. Just shove the back door open, and step into the kitchen. My footsteps echo in the hush. Everything feels still. Like the house is holding its breath.

I move through the kitchen, past the counter where I used to leave notes, where dinner used to wait under foil. Through the hall where his shoes are still kicked to the side, like nothing's changed. My hand trails the bannister as I climb the stairs, each step heavier than the last.

I pass our bedroom without pausing. His bedroom now.

The guest room is at the far end. Dark. Still. Untouched. And I'm suddenly thankful for the extra space.

I slip inside and shut the door behind me. No photos on the walls. No echoes of laughter or arguments or love gone stale. Just a bed, a dresser, and a quiet that expects nothing from me.

The door clicks shut as my back hits it, and I slide down, legs folding in until I'm curled on the carpet. I fist my hands into the fibres like they might hold me together. Then my breath comes in short, shallow bursts. Sharp at first, then unraveling into full-body sobs that tear their way out of me like they've been waiting too long.

I cry until my throat burns. Until my hands go numb. Until I can't tell where the grief ends and the rage begins.

Because it's not just about what he did. It's every lie I told myself just to stay. Every time I swallowed doubt. Every time I smiled through the ache, or convinced myself that love was supposed to hurt a little if it was real.

I bury my face in my hands and sob harder, the sound muffled but relentless. Because I wanted so badly to be loved without conditions. And now I'm not sure I even know what that looks like.

My mind spirals, spinning through memories so fast it feels like whiplash.

Late nights in the kitchen, David pressing kisses to the back of my neck while I cooked. Sunday mornings tangled in sheets, the smell of coffee between us, him whispering stupid jokes that made me snort into the pillow. The nights he'd pull me into his lap when he thought I was worrying too much, his arms a protective cage around me.

I think of every moment we laughed, every look he gave me that felt so real. Every time I defended him and convinced myself the distance between us was temporary. That the loneliness in my own bed was normal. That loving someone meant enduring the bad seasons.

I press my palms against my eyelids until the worst of the shaking passes.

Until the room steadies around me.

CHAPTER 16

home again

KIERAN

Hospitals always smell the same. Too clean. Like someone tried to scrub trauma and grief out of the air and failed miserably.

We move down the endless corridors, our footsteps dull on the tile floors. I hate it here. Always have.

It reminds me of being eleven years old, sitting on cracked vinyl chairs while adults whispered around me, pretending I couldn't hear the word cancer being traded like an unavoidable truth.

But this time, it's different. This time, when I push open the door to Dad's room, he's awake. And he's *smirking*, right at me, like he's won something.

"Jesus, boy," he rasps, voice rough but amused. "If I'd known all it took to get you home was a blown appendix, I'd have booked it in months ago."

The tension snaps out of my chest so fast it leaves me dizzy. I let out half a laugh and cross the room in a few fast strides. "Don't think it works like that, old man. Maybe just send a text next time, yeah? Less dramatic."

Dad shifts against the pillows, wincing but grinning. "Wouldn't have had the same effect though, would it?"

Behind me, Ryder ambles in, doing his best impression of

someone who isn't still hungover. "Dunno, Bri," he says, hands shoved in his pockets. "A promise of free beer might've got him home quicker."

Dad chuckles, the sound low and warm. "Good to see you both. Even if you do look like you lost a fight with a tequila truck."

Ryder drops into the chair with a groan. "Never drinking again, just to be clear."

I shake my head and drag a chair closer to the bed. Dad's paler than usual. His hair's sticking up in tufts, like he's been battling with the hospital sheets. But he's still here. That's all I care about right now. "You scared the shit out of me," I admit, voice low.

Dad's eyes soften a little. He reaches out, squeezing my forearm with a strength that doesn't quite match his battered frame. "Takes more than a dodgy organ to get rid of me, son." he says, voice rough and reassuring.

Ryder kicks his boots up onto the foot of the bed like he owns the place. "So what's the verdict, Bri? They reckon you'll survive?"

Dad groans, scratching absent-mindedly at the dressing taped to his side. "Apparently so. I'm stitched up like a damn teddy bear. The real tragedy is the food though. If they try to feed me one more bowl of that flavourless soup, I swear I'll walk out dragging the IV stand with me."

Ryder snickers. "Bet Kieran could smuggle you in a burger or something. Man's sneaky when he wants to be."

Dad raises an eyebrow. "Yeah? And here I thought all he was good at was looking moody and breaking guitar strings."

I feign offence. "Wow. I drive halfway across the country, drop everything to be here, and this is the welcome I get?"

Dad chuckles, then sighs as he rubs at his temples. "Still can't believe you came straight here. Must be the first time in history you've not been late for something."

"Can't be late when you don't have a choice, old man."

He gives me a long look at that. One of those dad looks. His eyes are softer now, a little glassy.

"Still," he says. "It's good to see you, sprout."

That ache hits me again. Low and deep. Because it has been too long. And now, here we are. Hospital beds, IV drips, and things I should've seen coming.

I shift in my chair, not sure what to do with my hands. "Yeah," I say, voice low. "It's good to be home. Despite the circumstances."

He nods, the silence settling between us, like he understands more than I'm saying.

She's got a trolley with her—clipboard, blood pressure cuff, the works—and she gives us a look that says visiting hours don't mean move-in.

She wraps the cuff around Dad's arm, inflates it with a few quick pumps, then presses a thermometer in his ear like she's done it a hundred times already today. He doesn't protest, just rolls his eyes at me over her shoulder.

We get the hint. Time to go.

I clap Dad on the shoulder. "I'll be back tomorrow."

"Bring edible food," he calls after me. "Or don't bother!"

Outside, the air smells like wet tarmac and cheap coffee from the vending machines. Ryder falls into step beside me, hands in his jacket pockets.

We say nothing for a long moment. And then he bumps his shoulder into mine. "You good, bro?"

I let out the breath I didn't realise I'd been holding, and my shoulders drop, tension bleeding out inch by inch. "Yeah." I pause. Swallow. "Better now."

He nods once. Simple. No fuss. No digging.

"Hey," I say, quieter this time. He looks over. "Thanks. For coming with me Ry. For just being here."

Ryder shrugs, but it's softer than usual. "Where else would I be?"

I nod, throat tight.

Sometimes it's not the big gestures. It's the quiet loyalty. The showing up without needing to be asked. The kind of friend who sits with you in silence when the words are too heavy.

The rental bumps along the narrow country roads, headlights cutting sharp lines through the dark. Ryder's in the passenger seat, fiddling with the heat, and I keep one hand on the wheel, the other flexing in my lap.

He'd called Nick the second I got the news, sorted us out a car in ten minutes flat, no questions asked. I didn't even have to ask. Just one look, and Ryder was already moving.

Outside, the world blurs—crumbling stone walls and fields shrouded in a heavy, starless night sky. A chilling wind whispers through the tall grass, carrying the scent of damp earth through the open window.

This is Rosemere. Where I learned to ride a bike, kissed a girl behind a shed, and wrote my first half-decent song in the back of a textbook.

It's tucked into the crook of the east coast, and the village feels like it's been here forever. Half farmland, half fog, closer to sheep than anything resembling a skyline. The type of place where time stretches out. Where life moves slower, like it's got nowhere urgent to be.

And right now, I need that.

I ease back in my seat, sinking into the headrest, and let my eyes flick to the window as the village pulls nearer in soft, familiar fragments.

And just ahead. That same battered sign, swallowed by ivy, still clinging to its chipped welcome like it's been waiting.

Welcome to Rosemere.
Population: Small.
Spirit: Stubborn.

It's like time folded in on itself. Like I never left.

Ryder's slumped beside me, head tipped back against the window, headphones hanging loose around his neck. He's awake but still giving me space without making a thing of it.

I'm grateful for that. Because my chest is a mess of things I can't untangle right now. Relief, guilt, nostalgia so sharp it cuts.

The closer we get, the tighter everything pulls.

The road dips into a hill, hedgerows closing in on either side like the dark's folding in. Moonlight glints off the branches, silvering the leaves, turning everything soft and ghostlike.

I remember this stretch. The way I used to bike it with the lads, legs burning, heart hammering, wind slicing through us like we were invincible. Always chasing something. Always running from something else.

Then the road curves, pulling us into the arms of the village. The crooked post office, with its roof still slouching to one side. The green where we used to boot a football around until the light gave out and someone took a ball to the face. The weathered stone cottages, the old stone pub, and a single flickering streetlamp clinging to life.

I don't realise I'm white-knuckling the gear stick until Ryder nudges my arm.

"You alright, mate?"

I nod, forcing my fingers to loosen. "Yeah. Just feels weird. Coming home like this."

He hums under his breath. Not quite agreement. Not quite disagreement, either. Just understanding.

By the time I pull up outside Dad's farmhouse, the sky's already gone black—thick with low clouds that block out the stars, pressing down like they've got weight. The fields are cloaked in shadow, the only light coming from the porch lamp casting a soft, amber glow across the gravel.

The white stone walls are half-lost under a tangle of ivy, and the garden gate is still hanging on by one rusted hinge. There's a welcome mat that hasn't looked new in over a decade, and a pair of muddy boots left neatly to one side. The kind of details that shouldn't hit this hard, but do anyway.

It used to be a working farm before dad retired. Now it's more bones than business. Just a few old stables at the side, mostly empty except for a couple of rescued horses. The barn's still standing, though God knows how.

But the allotment out back? That's where he spends most of his time these days. Rows of veg and stubborn weeds, radio on full blast, soil up to his elbows. He says it keeps him moving. Gives him something to grow that doesn't talk back.

I sit there for a moment longer, engine ticking cool beneath the bonnet, the porch light flickering faintly in the mirror.

Home. In all its quiet, scruffy glory.

And God, I've missed it.

But Dad's not here. And it's the first time I've ever come back to this house without him waiting.

Ryder exhales behind me. "This place hasn't changed a bit." His voice is soft.

I nod, fingers tightening around the strap of my bag. "Yeah."

Ryder's already out of the car by the time I even get the key out of the ignition, hauling our bags onto the front step like he's done it a hundred times before.

Because he has.

Every summer when we were younger, every long weekend, every breath between gigs or chaos—we ended up here. No matter where the road took us, it always circled back to this front door.

It meant something to both of us. Still does. Especially to Ryder. He didn't grow up with stability, not really. But he crashed here like it was his, like the house knew his name and never asked questions.

The visits got fewer once the band took off, once the road started demanding more than it gave back. But the feeling doesn't fade. The pull's still there, baked into the bricks and beams.

If there's anywhere Ryder knows better than a stage, it's this place.

"I swear, every time we come back, I consider just moving in," he says, slinging his bag over his shoulder and eyeing the front door like it might open itself.

I snort, shifting my guitar case in my grip. "Yeah? Gonna trade the tour bus for early mornings, horse feeding, and fence repairs?"

Ryder shudders. "Absolutely not. I'll supervise, though. I look good in flannel."

"You're insufferable."

"And yet, I'm your favourite."

I roll my eyes, but let the smallest grin slip. Then I push the front door open and step inside. The familiar creak of the floorboards beneath my boots is like a welcome home on its own.

The air smells like it always has. Old wood, laundry powder, and the faintest whiff of smoke from the fireplace that never quite stops clinging to the walls. It hits before I've even taken my shoes off. Like a memory. Like a hug. Like a punch to the ribs.

I drop my bag by the stairs. It lands with a dull thud that echoes louder than it should in the quiet. I stand there for a second, just breathing. Trying to steady the rush in my chest.

The coat hooks by the door are still crooked. One hanging a little lower, bent just enough to remind me of the day I came home from school in a mood and yanked my bag off so hard the whole rail came down. Dad never properly fixed it. Said it gave the place character.

The rug's more worn than I remember. Faded in the middle, threads curling at the edges where Buddy had decided the entire house was his personal scratching mat as a kitten. Chaos in a fur coat. I side-eye the kitchen, and sure enough, there he is. Sprawled across the worktop like he pays rent, tail flicking with all the smug satisfaction of a creature who knows he owns the place.

Mum's photo on the hallway table, same frame, same spot. Her smile frozen in that moment before everything shifted. Bright. Steady. Like she knew how to keep us all upright. I reach out, thumb brushing her face.

Everything's still here. Exactly where it should be.

Ryder kicks off his shoes and beelines for the kitchen. "Alright, I'm raiding the fridge. Don't even try and stop me, Hayes."

I wave a hand over my shoulder. "If you find anything edible in there, I'll be impressed."

His voice calls from the other room, "I once ate a week-old petrol station sandwich. I fear nothing, my friend."

I chuckle under my breath and turn toward the stairs. My legs know the way before my brain does. Two steps at a time, left at the landing, third door on the right. My fingers wrap around the doorknob and twist. And just like that, nostalgia hits me square in the chest.

The room is a time capsule. Posters still cover every inch of the wall. Classic rock legends layered over one another like a shrine to chaos. A few corners are peeling. Some have a mix of blu-tac and Sellotape holding them up.

But it's all still here. Untouched.

Old notebooks and a few dusty guitar picks clutter the desk. There's a cracked mug holding a handful of pens that haven't worked since 2015.

In the corner, propped against the wall, is my first guitar. Cherry red, a little scuffed around the edges, but still intact. Still mine.

I step over to it, run my fingers along the fretboard. Dust clings to my fingertips like time itself doesn't want to let go.

Old trophies from school music competitions line the shelves, their plastic gold figures still frozen mid-guitar solo. I remember every single one. Every late-night practice. Every show Dad sat in the front row for, pretending not to tear up when I played.

And the photos. *God*, the photos.

I reach for one frame on the dresser. An old band shot, from when we were just four idiots with bad haircuts and a dream. None of us knew what the hell we were doing, but we believed in it. In us. We played in pubs, backyards, and shitty festival slots. But we were together. That counted for something. Still does.

The bed creaks as I drop onto the mattress, the springs familiar and forgiving. It's lumpy in the same places it always was, and somehow, it still fits me like it remembers every song I ever wrote in it.

I grab the remote and flick on the TV without bothering to check the channel. A cooking show blinks to life. Close-up shots of glossy berries tumbling into glass bowls, steam curling off saucepans like something seductive.

The narrator purrs through the speakers, her voice low and syrupy. "The strawberries should be ripe and bursting, their juices yielding at the slightest pressure…"

I blink. *Okay*.

She continues, unbothered, as a spoon sinks into whipped cream with the reverence of a love scene. "And now, we gently coax it into the martini glass… just to the point of collapse."

I glance toward the window like it might offer a buffer from whatever soft-core fruit content I've tuned into.

"You want it bulging at the rim, trembling, but still holding shape."

Jesus Christ. I lunge for the remote and mute it, cheeks burning despite the fact that I'm the only one in the room. The screen flickers in silence, a single strawberry rolling dramatically across a porcelain plate.

But it fills the silence just enough to let me be.

I lean back and close my eyes. And then, soft padding and a gentle thud steals my attention.

I open one eye. "Hey, Buddy."

The old tabby strolls into the room like he owns the place, tail flicking, eyes half-lidded with that signature feline smugness. He hops onto the bed with zero hesitation, stretches out beside me, and starts kneading the blanket like it personally wronged him.

His purring starts almost instantly. I run a hand over his fur, slow and rhythmic, and my chest finally unclenches.

For the first time in what feels like months, my body stops. Stops bracing. Stops rushing. Stops pretending I'm not completely and utterly exhausted.

And as Buddy curls into my side and the TV murmurs in the background, I let the weight of the day melt into the mattress.

Let myself breathe.

Let sleep take me under.

CHAPTER 17
it isn't black and white

ELLIE

THE CAFÉ WASN'T PART OF the plan this week. But the thought of staying home—of pacing the same rooms, hearing the same silence—made my skin itch. So I called Brenda, asked if she needed a hand, and she didn't hesitate. Just told me to come in.

A few months ago, I thought I'd have my first nursing position lined up by now. I worked my arse off for that degree. Sacrificed sleep, sanity, and so much more.

But reality had other ideas.

Despite every headline screaming about nurse shortages, there are barely any openings. And the ones that do exist? They're hours away, rotational positions I don't want, or in specialties I don't want to settle for.

So, I wait. Float. Exist. A severely overqualified barista.

The sound of the coffee machine hisses through the air, steady beneath the low hum of conversation and the occasional clatter of plates. The scent of fresh pastries, warm bread, and ground coffee beans wrap around me like a blanket I can't quite feel. Comforting in theory, not in practice.

I keep myself busy. Wiping down counters, restocking sugar dispensers, counting out the till like I might find a version of myself buried under the coins. Anything to keep my mind from spiralling. Because if I stop, even for a second, it all comes rushing back.

The bed. The sheets. David's body moving against hers like it was second nature.

My jaw clenches and I scrub at an invisible stain on the counter —harder than necessary.

I pour another cup of coffee and listen to the scrape of cutlery, the world continuing like it hasn't even noticed mine's unravelling.

At least here, everything is simple. Predictable and calm.

"Ellie, love, come sit for a minute."

I glance up to see Brenda watching me from behind the pastry counter, concern etched into the fine lines of her face. Her silver-blonde hair is tucked into a neat, low bun, stylish but effortless, like everything about her. Crisp white shirt, soft grey cardigan, sleeves pushed up like she's ready to tackle the mess she sees in front of her.

I force a smile, too tight to be convincing. "I'm fine, Bren. Keeping busy, that's all."

She doesn't move. Simply crosses her arms and raises one brow. It's one of those looks that strips away your bullshit before you've even finished speaking. "You've been keeping too busy," she says plainly. "You're barely stopping long enough to breathe, let alone eat. And I haven't seen you look this tired in a long time."

I swallow, the dishcloth twisting in my hands like it's absorbing the guilt. "I just... I don't know. I don't know what I'm doing anymore."

Before I can say anything else, she tugs me into one of the corner booths and places a steaming cup of tea in front of me. The same way she always did when the world felt too loud.

My fingers wrap around the mug, clinging to the heat.

Back then, the first sip always brought comfort. Now it just burns. Too hot, too sharp, and too real.

"Alright," Brenda says, sliding into the seat across from me. "Out with it."

I blink. "What?"

She lifts a brow, her voice even. "Darling girl, I've known you since you were a teenager. You think I don't notice when something's not right?"

She nods toward the mug, still untouched in my hands. "You've been floating around this place like a ghost all week, and I'd bet my almond croissant recipe it has something to do with that man of yours."

The breath leaves my lungs like someone's punched it out of me. My grip tightens on the mug. I should tell her. I want to tell her. To tell someone. But the words sit heavy in my chest, unmoving. "Things... aren't great," is all I manage, voice flat.

Brenda doesn't look convinced. "How not great?"

I shake my head, eyes falling to the surface of the tea as the steam curls into the air like a question I can't answer. "I don't really want to get into it right now."

Her brows draw together, clearly weighing her next move. But then she exhales, reaches across the table, and gives my hand a gentle squeeze. "Okay," she says softly.

No pressure. No judgement. Just Brenda, steady as ever. "What about your parents?"

A bitter laugh escapes before I can stop it. "Are you kidding? I don't need reminding how much of a disappointment I am right now. It won't be a conversation, Brenda. It'll be a performance review. A tally of every mistake I've made, like they've kept all the receipts."

Brenda's lips press into a thin line. She doesn't need to say anything. That look is enough. "Ellie, that's not true."

I shrug, staring down at my hands, picking at the skin around my thumb. "Isn't it?"

She sighs and leans forward, taking both my hands in hers. Her grip is warm. Steady. The way it always is when I feel like I'm falling apart. "Ellie, love, when will you stop punishing yourself for your past? Every choice you've made led you here. Look at you! You have Mia—a remarkable girl who *adores* you. You have a degree. Made it through when most people would've given up. You're exactly where you're meant to be, even if it doesn't feel like it yet."

Her words sit heavy on my chest, too full of truth for me to brush away.

"I wish I knew what came next," I whisper. "Because right now? I've got no idea." I break off, swallowing hard. "I'm tired, Bren. So fucking tired."

Brenda gives me a small, reassuring smile. Her eyes, kind but unwavering. "Oh sweetheart. Sometimes not knowing is the first step to figuring it out. Life doesn't follow a straight line. You're still moving forward, even if the road's a little bumpy."

The knot in my chest pulls tighter. I nod slowly, the heat of the tea finally seeping into my skin.

Brenda runs a hand over her forehead, sighing through her nose before fixing me with a look that's far too knowing. "Whatever this is... it breaks my heart to see you going through it alone."

I don't answer. But her words stay with me, lingering long after she gets up to tend the counter.

I know I'm not alone, and I know I have people who care—Brenda, Naomi, even Mia, in her own way, always watching with those wide, too-knowing eyes.

But there's something about saying it out loud. About admitting that my life feels like it's collapsing in on itself. It would make it too real. Too permanent. And worse. It would make me look like I haven't learned a damn thing.

I press my fingertips to the side of the mug, grounding myself in the fading heat. My eyes drift to the door. Part of me wants to bolt. The other part wants to crawl into Brenda's kitchen and hide.

And then, stitched into the fabric of my thoughts, I think of Kieran. We haven't spoken since the morning after the bonfire. I've seen his name flash across my screen a few times, but I haven't replied. Not because I don't want to—because I don't know how.

The lines feel blurry now—smudged by everything that's happened since. I told myself it was better this way. Easier.

But I can't help this quiet pull in my chest. An ache for the person who sees me. Who doesn't ask for more than I can give.

I want to talk to him. But what would I even say?

Hey, sorry I disappeared. Life's falling apart. Wanna unpack my emotional trauma over coffee?

Not exactly light conversation.

So, I stay silent. Let the thoughts pass like clouds.

And stare down into my tea like it might show me a version of myself that still knows what the fuck she's doing.

By the time we pull into the driveway, the sky is turning gold. Long shadows stretch across the pavement, cast by the low-hanging sun. The air has that unmistakable edge—a quiet crispness that says summer's finally giving way to autumn.

Mia hums along to the song still playing on her phone. Her school blazer crumpled in the back seat and her fingers toying absently with the friendship bracelet Claire made her last weekend.

She'd burst out of the school gates full of chatter about art class and the kid who had a biro explode in his mouth. I'd done my best to keep up, to nod in the right places, to laugh where I was supposed to. But now, as I kill the engine and the quiet settles in around us, the weight returns. Heavy. Inevitable.

David's car is already in the drive and my stomach sinks—he's home early.

All week, I've managed to avoid him. Slipping through the cracks of our shared routine like smoke. He doesn't usually get back from the office until seven, and I've made sure I'm tucked away in the guest room long before then.

I pick up my phone from the passenger seat and stare at the message on the screen.

> DAVID [14:45]
> Babe, can we talk this out? Barely seen you all week. I miss you.

I'd assumed he meant later. Tonight. When Mia was in bed and I had time to steel myself.

But no. He came home early.

Mia taps my arm, breaking my spiral. "Mum?"

I blink, dragging my gaze back to her face.

"Can I go to Claire's?"

I nod, my voice catching in my throat. "Yeah, love. Course you can. But drop your bags in first."

She smiles and climbs out, already humming again.

When we step inside, I notice it immediately. The house smells different. Not the usual faint trace of coffee, laundry detergent, and whatever remnants of lunch Mia's left in her school bag.

No. This is sharp. Deliberate. Vanilla and fresh flowers. Manufactured comfort.

Mia kicks off her shoes, already halfway through another sentence. "I told Claire I'd bring my science project round. We're finishing it for next Monday."

Before I can even respond, she bolts up the stairs, her rucksack bouncing behind her. A second later, I hear her door thud open, then the creak of her wardrobe. Business as usual.

I stay in the hallway for a breath longer than necessary, keys still in my hand, coat still on.

The living room door is ajar.

He's in there. I know it without looking.

And still — I look.

Candles. Jesus Christ. He's lit bloody candles. There's one flickering on the coffee table and another on the windowsill, next to the plant I keep forgetting to water. A wine glass sits untouched by the arm of the sofa. He's cleaned, or at least tidied. Throw blankets folded. Cushions plumped. It's like walking into a stage set.

Mia barrels down the stairs like gravity's only a suggestion. "Got it!" she shouts, almost losing her footing halfway down. "Claire's gonna freak out when she sees it, it actually exploded earlier but I fixed it — look!"

She skids to a halt in the hallway, cradling the monstrosity like it's a newborn. It's a papier-mâché volcano, lopsided and streaked with orange food colouring. Bits of foil cling to the base, and there's glitter stuck to her forehead.

"Jesus," I murmur. "It's enormous."

"I know! We're gonna add dry ice if her mum lets us. Smoke

effects and everything." She's buzzing, cheeks flushed, full of that giddy energy that only thirteen-year-olds and caffeine addicts possess.

I nod, trying to match her brightness. "Be careful walking with it, yeah?"

She leans over awkwardly to kiss my cheek without letting go of the volcano. "Love you!"

"Have fun, bug."

And then she's gone—shoulder first through the door, practically hopping down the front steps, project wobbling like it might go off again.

The silence that follows is thick.

I turn back toward the living room.

The candles flicker.

And I step inside.

He's there. Sat on the edge of the sofa, elbows resting on his knees, fingers laced like he's trying to hold himself together with them.

David Sinclair, poster boy for control. Always pressed. Always polished. Tailored trousers and just the right aftershave.

But not tonight.

Tonight he's in grey sweatpants and a fitted crew neck tee, the kind that clings to every line of his too-perfect body. Barefoot. A rare five o'clock shadow softens his jaw, like he forgot to care—or wanted me to see that he didn't.

He doesn't look up right away. Just stares at the floor like it might hand him a script. Like he's searching for the version of this where I don't walk out.

I say nothing.

I hang my coat on the back of the chair even though I want to keep it on. Keep my keys in my hand. Keep one foot out the door.

He finally speaks, voice low, throat-wrecked. "Thanks for coming in."

It's so absurd I almost laugh. Like this is a bloody dinner reservation I'm late for.

I stay standing, arms crossed tight over my chest. "I live here."

His eyes flick up at that—briefly. Bloodshot. There's something desperate in them, but it's buried deep. Like he's still managing the optics, even now.

"Will you sit?" he asks, voice barely above a whisper.

"No."

It comes out flat. Not cruel, not emotional. Just... final.

I stay rooted to the spot, arms folded. The only sound is the quiet tick of the clock and the soft flicker of a candle behind him.

"I—I don't even know where to start," he says, scrubbing a hand over his face. "It didn't mean anything, Ellie."

I don't move. Don't even blink.

He nods like he expected that. Like he knows the line won't cut it, but he's got to say it anyway. "I was drunk. It was stupid. One mistake. One night. I swear, it's never happened before, and it will never happen again."

Still nothing from me.

He shifts, palms dragging down his thighs. "I know that doesn't help. I know it's not enough. But I need you to understand—it wasn't about you. It never was."

I watch him.

The slump in his shoulders. The mess of his hair. The regret drawn tight in the lines around his eyes. He looks ruined. Not performative. Not theatrical. Just... wrecked.

And the worst part?

Some small, pathetic part of me aches for him.

The man I built a home with. The one I shared my body, my child, my whole life with. I know every inch of him—how he takes his coffee, the sound of his laugh when he's half-asleep, the way he over-waters the basil and swears it's thriving.

Now he's sitting there, broken and sorry and soft in places he never used to be.

That old, ugly instinct in me wants to reach out. To *fix*. To forgive.

But I don't.

I look at him. Really look at him.

And I say the truth, as quiet and honest as I've ever said anything.

"You *broke* me, David." My voice is low. Honest.

His eyes squeeze shut. And then he's moving—up off the sofa, crossing the space between us in two quick steps.

His hands cup my face—gentle, but firm. Like he's trying to hold me close. Keep me here. Keep me his.

His eyes search mine, wild and glassy. Our foreheads almost touch.

"I know, Ellie. I know." His voice cracks. "But don't give up on us. We can fix this. I'll do anything. Tell me what you need."

His thumbs tremble against my cheekbones.

I don't move. My hands hang limp at my sides while he clings to me like I'm the only thing keeping him upright. His breath is warm against my skin. His aftershave clings to the air between us—familiar, expensive. The bottle I wrapped in tissue paper for his birthday last year.

"I'm sorry," he breathes. "I'll never stop being sorry. You have every right to hate me. To leave. But I love you. I love you so much it hurts, and I don't know who I am without you."

And just like that, I feel it.

The slow, traitorous give of my walls softening under the weight of his voice. The way his words curl their way into the rawest parts of me—gentle, poisonous, effective.

I know what this is.

I know how it works—how someone can dismantle you kindly. With love in their eyes. With trembling hands on your skin. With words that sound like repentance but taste like rewrites.

And still, I can't stop it.

The doubt creeps in, slow and careful.

Maybe it wasn't that simple. Maybe he didn't mean to. Maybe I should've done more. Been more. Maybe this doesn't have to be the end.

He's in my head.

Twisting the truth with tears and tenderness. Making me feel guilty for being hurt.

And the worst part?

Some dark, exhausted part of me wants to let him.

Because if he's sorry—*truly* sorry—then maybe we don't have to burn it all down. Because what he's saying... it sounds like love. Like accountability. Like the man I fell for before the distance. Before the silence. Before the betrayal.

I want to scream at myself to wake up.

But I just stand there, drowning in the softness of a man who knows exactly how to play me.

And I hate myself for it. Because this isn't black and white. It's grey and raw and murky as hell.

"Ellie," he whispers.

But the way he says my name—like it's the last thread holding him together—undoes something in me. Something small and stupid and tired.

His hands stay on my face, brushing over skin gone cold. His eyes are glassy, searching mine—begging for a version of this where I choose him.

Tears spill down his cheeks.

Then I feel it—

That first betrayal of my composure, sliding hot and slow down my face.

Because seeing him like this—this broken, this bare—*breaks* something in me.

Not out of love. Not out of forgiveness.

Just the sheer weight of it. The history. The grief of watching something I once believed in fall apart right in front of me.

His hands don't grip anymore. They hold. Like he already knows I'm halfway gone.

"I just—I don't know, David. Honestly." The words fall from my mouth like ash. "I don't know how to move past it."

He shakes his head, almost frantic. "You don't have to know. We'll work it out. I'll prove it to you—every day, Ellie. I'll earn you back."

And for a second, I almost nod.

Almost let the warmth of his promise pull me back into the illusion.

But something shifts.

Something old and fierce and buried deep suddenly claws its way to the surface.

And I hear a voice—*my* voice—cutting through the noise.

"I don't I trust you," I say, quiet but clear. "Not anymore."

He flinches. Barely. But I feel it.

"I want to. God, I *want* to," I admit, voice cracking. "But I can't pretend this didn't change something. That it didn't *break* something."

He opens his mouth, but I shake my head before he can speak.

"You want me to say it'll be okay," I murmur. "But I don't know that it will. I don't know *how* to make it okay."

For a moment, he looks at me. Like he doesn't recognise the version of me that won't bend.

Then something changes.

It's subtle. A flicker in his expression. A breath that comes too sharp. His hands fall away from my face.

"You don't *know*," he repeats, voice flatter now. Like the emotion's been ironed out of it. "Ellie, I've been standing here owning up to everything. I'm trying to fix this. But you—you're not even trying to meet me halfway."

I blink. "David—"

"You've already decided. You're standing there, looking at me like I'm a stranger. Like everything we've been through means nothing."

"You *cheated* on me, David." I snap.

"I *know*! And I've said I'm sorry. I've told you I'll do whatever it takes. But you're punishing me for being human. For slipping, once, after *everything* I've done for this family."

I flinch.

He sees it—and softens his tone. "I didn't mean it like that. I just—Ellie, I've carried a lot. The hours. The pressure. Supporting you through uni, making sure Mia has everything, keeping this house running—"

"I never asked you to—"

"You didn't *have* to," he snaps, then reins it in. "You didn't have to ask. I *wanted* to. Because I love you. Because I wanted this life with you. But now you're ready to throw it all away?"

I stare at him. But my silence only invites more.

"I even helped you patch things up with your parents! Do you think they'd be playing happy families now if it wasn't for me holding the middle?"

I feel my jaw clench, but I can't speak.

"I've loved Mia like she's mine, made sure she's safe, supported, *happy*—and now you're ready to walk out on all of it?"

"I'm not walking out on Mia."

"No," he says tightly. "But you're still blowing her life apart. Her home. The version of family she knows."

I stare at him, throat tight, pulse thudding.

He steps in again, hands brushing mine, tone softer now. Persuasive. "I'm not trying to hurt you, Ellie. I'm trying to show you what we have. What you'll lose if you go."

His eyes flicker over mine. "You think starting over's going to be easier? You think someone else is going to come in and love her like I do? Or love *you* the way I have? What you're doing is walking away from something *good*, just because it got hard."

And there it is.

The twist.

The part where my pain becomes the problem. Where his betrayal becomes my blame to carry.

Where *I* become the one who's breaking us—all because I won't pretend it never happened.

And finally, I see it.

He's not fighting for me. He's fighting to stay in control of the story.

I wrap my arms around myself, the silence between us stretching thin and brittle.

"I don't even know who you are anymore," I say quietly. "I can's see past what you did. I've tried. I've really tried. But I don't think there's a version of this we can come back from."

I turn before he can answer, before he can rearrange his face into something that might undo me.

I walk away.

And just as I reach the hallway, I hear it.

The sharp smash of glass.

Then the dull, violent thud of something hitting the wall—or the door.

I don't stop to look.

I keep walking.

One step. Then another.

And somewhere deep in my chest, beneath the fear and the ache and the guilt that still clings like smoke, a flicker of something steadier burns.

Resolve.

A quiet, trembling truth I haven't had the courage to name until now.

I don't want to be someone who stays because it's easier.

I don't want to keep choosing someone who didn't choose me.

Not anymore.

CHAPTER 18

between beams and silence

KIERAN

"Why do you pack like you're emigrating, Bri?" Ryder huffs, wrenching open the boot of Dad's taxi, hauling out bags like he's moving a five-person family into a luxury resort. "You were in hospital for three fucking days, not off filming *Survivor*."

Dad scoffs from inside the car, already unbuckling himself with a groan. "It's the hospital, not a bloody spa retreat. And that bag's got my good slippers in it. Don't bend them."

I stifle a laugh and move to the passenger side. The gravel crunches under my boots, the house casting a familiar silhouette in the late afternoon light.

My shoulders ease without me even noticing. "Alright, come on, old man," I say, offering a hand. "Let's get you inside."

"I can walk just fine, thank you very much." He waves me off. "Lost an appendix, not a leg."

"Could've fooled us with the way you've been milking it," Ryder shouts from the porch.

Dad glares at him, but there's a smirk pulling at the corner of his mouth. "Keep mouthing off and I'll have you mucking out the stables first thing tomorrow."

"Is that a dare?" Ryder mutters, dragging the last bag through the front door with a dramatic thump.

I shake my head, laughing as I help Dad out of the car and up the steps, even though he's pretending he doesn't need the help.

He's moving slowly, but he's up, and he's home.

Inside, Dad exhales as he sinks into his favourite armchair like it's a throne. Well-earned and missed. His eyes flutter shut for a second, like being home is enough to ground him. "Ahh," he mutters, voice gravelly. "That's more like it."

Ryder appears in the doorway, wiping invisible sweat from his brow. "Right. That's my second good deed of the month. I expect food, appreciation, and at least one framed photo of me on the mantel."

Dad peeks one eye open. "You'll get a sandwich and a clip on the ear if you're lucky."

"Can't wait."

I roll my eyes and head into the kitchen. The air smells faintly of lemon cleaning spray and something warm. I flick the kettle on, muscle memory kicking in, grabbing three mugs and lining up the tea bags. Just the right splash of milk in Dad's—the way he likes it.

Halfway through making the tea, I glance out the window. Ryder's in the garden, tossing a stick for Buddy like he thinks the bloody cat might chase it.

Spoiler: he won't.

Buddy sits a few feet away, perched like the king he is judging a court jester, eyes half-lidded and unimpressed. I can practically hear his thoughts from here: *You absolute clown.*

I grin to myself, shaking my head as I bring the mugs into the living room. "Here you go," I say, handing Dad his. "The sacred blend."

He takes a sip and sighs, sinking deeper into his chair. "Mmm. Tastes like actual tea. That crap in the hospital tasted like it could've been brewed in a boot."

"Probably was," I smirk, collapsing onto the sofa opposite him.

Ryder saunters back inside, brushing stray bits of grass off his jeans. "Alright, I've got questions," he announces, pointing toward the backyard. "What's with all the tools and that pile of wood near the fence? I nearly tripped over a rogue hammer. Are you secretly building a trebuchet, Bri?"

"Right... I'm not just gonna pretend I know what a trebuchet is. That a real thing or did you make it up?"

Ryder snorts. "Big arse catapult. Chucks boulders."

"Ah." I nod, slow. "So like... medieval Angry Birds?"

"You are *painful*, mate." Ryder groans from across the room.

Dad chuckles, setting his mug down with a soft clink. "I've been working on the old barn. She's seen better days. Thought I'd finally get round to fixing her up. Turn it back into proper storage space again."

He shifts in his chair, a little sheepish. "Progress has been... slow."

"Slow?" I echo, raising an eyebrow. "Dad, it's been falling down since I was fifteen."

"And it's still standing, isn't it?" he shoots back, eyes twinkling.

Ryder flops into the armchair beside me with a theatrical groan. "That thing's one gust of wind away from collapsing. What are you even planning to do with it?"

"Reinforce the structure, replace a few beams, lick of paint. Nothing fancy," he says, waving a hand. "I've got a plan."

I glance between him and Ryder and something sparks in my chest. "Well, lucky for you," I say, "you've just had two very capable, albeit questionably skilled, labourers delivered to your doorstep."

"I don't like where this is going," Ryder mutters under his breath.

"Oh, come on," I nudge his leg with my foot. "We're here, aren't we? May as well make ourselves useful. We'll get it sorted in no time."

"I didn't sign up for a barn renovation, mate," he says flatly.

"Stop your whining. It'll be fun."

"Unbelievable," he groans. "This is manual labour disguised as wholesome bonding."

I laugh, letting my head tip back against the sofa, taking in the scene. Dad smirking into his tea. Ryder scowling half-heartedly. The house creaking in the background like it's breathing again. I've got my dad. I've got Ryder. And we've got a crumbling barn that might just be a project worth throwing ourselves into.

The sun had long since set by the time I excused myself for the night, leaving Ryder and Dad still hunched over some makeshift blueprint for our impending barn renovations. Complete with Dad's questionable sketches and Ryder's expert-level sarcasm.

Their laughter follows me up the stairs, a low hum of something steady and good.

I push the door to my bedroom open, the hinges creaking like they always do, and step inside. It's quiet in here. Peaceful.

I move to where my guitar rests against the wall. Lift it, and run my fingers over the strings once, then twice, feeling the vibrations settle into my chest.

I sit on the edge of the bed and start strumming. Nothing planned, just letting my hands move, following the sound wherever it wants to go. The chords are soft. Melancholic. Something between a memory and a question.

My mind drifts, and before I know it, Ellie's face is there, hovering behind the notes. The image of her under the lights at the beach. Her laugh echoing over the music. The way she looked at me like I still mattered.

It's been a little while since we talked. The last proper message was before everything with Dad went sideways. I meant to follow up. Meant to check in. But the timing was off, and then the days just kept folding into each other.

I set the guitar beside me and reach for my phone, thumb hovering over her name in my messages.

I hesitate, not because I don't want to talk to her, but because I do. And I miss her. Not afraid to admit it.

Hey you. Miss catching up. How you doing?

I stare at the message for a second before hitting send, set the phone down on the nightstand, and pick up the guitar again—letting my fingers drift back over the strings.

The room fills with sound, the melody weaving itself around the quiet. I follow it wherever it wants to go. Notes turning sadder, a little more searching. A tune that says more than I know how to put into words.

I should be tired. I *am* tired. But the music keeps me anchored. Keeps the noise in my head from swallowing me whole.

Eventually, the sound blurs. My fingers slow. My eyelids droop, heavy with the kind of tiredness that isn't just physical. It's emotional. A weight I've been carrying for weeks now, long before Dad ended up in the hospital.

I lay the guitar on its stand and reach for the lamp when a knock sounds at the door. It creaks open, and Dad appears, silhouetted against the soft glow of the hallway light. "I've missed hearing that at all hours," he says, voice low and warm. "Whatever you're playing. It's good, son."

"Thanks, Dad." I smile, surprised by the flicker of emotion that rises in my chest. "Just noodling around."

He leans casually against the doorframe, arms crossed. "You always did have a way of making even noodling sound like something more."

I shrug, trying to play it off. "Comes with the territory, I guess."

He watches me for a beat longer, then pushes off the frame. "Don't stay up too late. We've got a barn to tackle in the morning, and I'm not carrying you and Ryder through the whole thing."

"Wouldn't dream of it."

"Goodnight, son."

"Night, Dad."

He closes the door behind him, and the room settles back into quiet.

I flick off the lamp and the glow vanishes, replaced by the soft blue stretch of moonlight across the floorboards.

I slide beneath the covers and stare up at the ceiling.

Then, because I'm weak, I reach for my phone one more time.

Her name's still there. The message marked as read.

Still nothing back.

I tell myself it's nothing. She's probably busy. Tired. Distracted. But something twists in my chest, anyway.

I close my eyes. And sleep, relentless and heavy, finally pulls me under. Ellie's name still echoing somewhere between the last note and the first dream.

The next afternoon, Ryder and I are elbows-deep in the barn renovation project, which is looking less like a forgotten health hazard and more like something a person might choose to walk into.

It's early October, and though the trees are turning, the sun's pushing through the clouds like it's still clinging to summer. The air's warm, humid even, and the heavy lifting has both of us sweating. The scent of sawdust and cut pine fills the space, sunlight slanting in through the open barn doors in wide, golden streaks.

My shirt's plastered to my back. Ryder's hair looks like it lost a fight with gravity somewhere around hour two. Still, we're making progress. And for the first time in a while, my head feels quiet.

It's good being out here. Doing something with my hands. No pressure, no noise, no headlines. Just the ache of muscles, the scrape of timber, and Ryder's endless complaints filling the air.

Dad is embracing his self-appointed role as supervisor, parked on the back porch in his favourite chair with an iced tea in hand, offering direction like he's hosting *Grand Designs: Rural Chaos Edition*. "Left a bit, Ryder! You're as crooked as a politician!" he yells, cupping his hands around his mouth like a football coach.

Balanced precariously on a ladder, Ryder lets out a long, theatrical sigh. "You trying to get me killed out here?" He shifts, the ladder creaking. "I will haunt you, Brian Hayes. I swear to God."

I can't help the grin stretching across my face. "You heard the man," I call up, handing him another plank. "Try not to bring down the entire government while you're at it."

Ryder grabs the wood with exaggerated force. "Ha-ha. Hilarious," he mutters, squinting against the sunlight. "Why don't you climb up here and risk *your* life, pretty boy?"

"And miss the show down here?" I shake my head. "Not a chance."

The barn's bones are old, weathered beams, flaking paint, memories wedged into every creaky board. But it's solid underneath. It just needs time. Patience. A bit of care.

On the makeshift workbench, an iPad propped against a paint can buzzes to life—I answer the call. Theo's face fills the screen, sunglasses on, sprawled in a lounge chair under the last of a bright Italian sun. "Oh look," Ryder mutters. "The idle rich."

Theo lifts a lazy hand in greeting, smirking. "You two look like you're dying."

"Feels like it," I say, wiping my forehead with the hem of my shirt.

"We've upgraded from 'barn disaster' to 'mild structural hazard,' though, so that's something."

The screen shifts and Luca appears, holding up an obnoxiously large cone of gelato like he's cradling a newborn. "Tell me you're jealous," he says, lowering his sunglasses.

Ryder groans. "Mate, I would sell Kieran's soul for one of those right now."

"Rude," I mutter.

"You'd get over it."

Theo leans closer to the camera, grinning. "You're rolling around in dirt and calling it productivity."

"It's called craftsmanship," I deadpan. "Very rustic. Very authentic. Extremely sweaty."

Dad chuckles from the porch, raising his glass in salute. "Don't let them get to you, boys. They're just jealous they're missing out on all this fresh air."

"Careful, Ryder," Theo adds. "That hammer's not a toy."

Luca nods solemnly. "You're about as stable as a one-legged stool up there."

Ryder flips them off, hammer still in hand. "You're lucky there's an ocean between us."

The laughter that follows is effortless. Easy in the way that only comes with time and love. It settles into my chest, warm and grounding.

I pull out my phone, half to escape the heat, half out of habit. The lightness of the moment dims. Still no reply.

I stare at the screen for a second longer than I mean to.

Come on, Ellie...

I tap out another message.

> Just wanna make sure everything's ok?

I stare at it like it might slap me for being soft. Then hit send anyway and shove the phone back in my pocket like it's suddenly radioactive.

No big deal. Totally casual. Not like I've checked the thread... what, five times today? Six, max.

"*She'll reply,*" I tell myself. "*She always does.*"

Then I grab a hammer and try to look like a man who absolutely did not just whisper at his phone like a moron.

"Oi!" Ryder shouts, waving a tape measure like he's conducting an orchestra.

"Kieran, stop daydreaming, we've got a barn to save!"

"Yeah, yeah," I mutter, catching the tape mid-air as he tosses it down. "Calm down before you fall and break something."

We work until the light fades, the air cools, and shadows stretch across the overgrown grass.

Hammers thud. Laughter bubbles. Every so often, Dad calls out a suggestion like he's building the next Taj Mahal.

Eventually, he hauls himself up from his throne with a stretch. "Alright, lads. I think you've done enough damage for one day."

"I second that," Ryder says, descending the ladder like a very tired koala. "I need food. And a nap. In that order."

Together, the three of us head toward the house, the scent of Dad's beef stew curling through the air—rich and savoury, all red wine and rosemary. It drifts out the kitchen window like a homing beacon, tugging us in by the stomach.

I feel the day in my bones. In the dirt under my nails, the bruises on my hands. But I also feel something else. Peace.

Still, as we reach the back steps, I check my phone one last time. Nothing.

I swallow the disappointment. Tell myself I don't have the right to feel it.

Not when she's with someone else. Not when I'm the one standing on the outside, waiting for a door she's under no obligation to open.

I shake off the thought, but it clings, sticky and stubborn.

I follow the smell of stew inside, the ache of missing her settling into a place I don't know how to reach.

The kitchen smells like home. Rich and hearty, like every stew Dad's ever made. The windows are fogged from the heat and the radio hums some low country tune in the background.

Ryder beelines for the fridge like he owns it, grabbing two beers and tossing one my way. "Cheers to surviving manual labour," he says, cracking his open.

I raise mine, clinking the glass necks together before taking a sip. "To functional barns and dysfunctional friendships."

"Oi," he says, but he's grinning.

Dad ladles stew into mismatched bowls like a man who believes in hearty portions and second helpings before you've even finished the first.

We eat around the kitchen table, swapping stories, complaining about sore muscles, tossing out the occasional jab about each other's so-called 'construction skills.'

Ryder insists he was the backbone of the operation. Dad says the barn survived in spite of him. I choke on my beer laughing.

But underneath it all, a tiny ache thrums in my chest. Because even in this comfort, even in the quiet, she's still there.

CHAPTER 19

the dam breaks

ELLIE

MY PARENTS' HOUSE LOOKS THE same as it always has. Clean to the point of sterile. Cold. Perfection that doesn't breathe.

The pristine living room with its immaculate white sofa no one ever sits on. Symmetrical lamps. Art on the walls that's tasteful, but hollow. A sharp, artificial citrus scent fills the air—as though masking something rotting underneath.

Everything is curated. Controlled. Designed to be looked at, not lived in.

I don't even know why I came. If Naomi wasn't visiting her own parents, I'd be pouring my soul out to her instead. Wrapped in a blanket, wine in hand, crying over pasta covered in a devastating amount of cheese.

But she's gone. And I'm here. Sitting at the kitchen table like I'm seventeen again, stomach tight, waiting for reassurance that never comes.

Desperate. *Pathetic.*

Mum perches on the chair opposite like she's conducting an interview, not having a conversation with her daughter. Legs crossed precisely at the ankle. Manicured hands resting on the table, one thumb brushing idly over her wedding band.

She doesn't look at me at first. Just scans the room, eyes flickering over surfaces, searching for something out of place.

"You know, Eleanor," she says finally, voice clipped and cool, "it feels as though we're having this same conversation every few years."

I flinch at the formality in her tone. *Eleanor.* Always Eleanor when she disapproves.

"What do you mean?" I ask, pulling my cardigan tighter around myself like I can shield against the words I know are coming.

"I mean," she says eventually, "there's always… something. Some drama. Some emotional decision. You say David cheated on you. That things haven't been right for a while. But are you *sure* it's what you think it is? That it's really as bad as you're making it out to be?"

I blink, stunned. "Am I *sure*?"

She lifts a brow—measured and unbothered. Like I'm the one creating chaos where there is none.

Dad clears his throat from across the room. He's been standing by the window this whole time, hands buried in his pockets like he doesn't know what to do with them.

He moves toward me slowly, face softer than mums, but still cautious. That same tired worry I've seen my whole life—like loving me is a balancing act.

"Ellie, sweetheart," he says gently, leaning against the other end of the table. "Of course we'd never turn you away. But we're… concerned. You've always been reactive. You make decisions quickly. We just want you to take a breath before you do anything drastic. Think about Mia. About everything you've built."

My heart clenches, a tight, mean fist inside my chest. "I *am* thinking about Mia," I breathe. "I think about her every minute of every day."

"We're not saying you're wrong," Mum cuts in, adjusting the hem of her blouse even though it's already perfectly pressed. "But David's always been there. He's given you a good life. Are you really prepared to throw that away over a mistake?"

I stare at her. "A *mistake*?"

"Relationships aren't perfect, Eleanor," she says quietly. "You don't just walk away when they get difficult. You work at them. You compromise."

I laugh—sharp, bitter. "You think I haven't compromised? I have *sacrificed*. I've twisted myself into shapes you'll never understand. And he took all of it. Every last bit."

Dad shifts uncomfortably, but says nothing.

"You live in a fantasy," she replies, her voice thinning. "You expect some perfect version of love that's not real. Real love requires patience."

My hands tremble, fists curled in my lap. "So what? I should stay with someone who lies, manipulates, and cheats—because that's what commitment looks like to *you*?"

Dad exhales, shifting again like the conversation is too heavy to stand beneath.

"No one's saying you have to stay," he says, low. "We're just saying—be sure. Mia needs stability. And you've struggled before, Ellie. We don't want to see you go through all of that again."

"I'm not struggling," I snap. "I'm *fighting*. For her. For me. And I thought, just once, you'd see that."

Mum clasps her hands together tighter, her wedding band flashing like a warning. "We don't want you to throw away something that could still be repaired."

"He's not a broken *chair*, Mum. He's a man who made a thousand choices that hurt me." My breath catches. "And Mia deserves better than that. *I* deserve better than that."

She doesn't answer. But her composure shifts—just slightly.

She can feel it slipping. The neat version of my life she's clung to, unravelling at the seams.

She reaches out, voice low. "Ellie, please. We're trying to protect you."

I meet her eyes—steady, unflinching.

"You're not protecting *me*," I whisper. "You're protecting the idea of me. The version of me that finally looked acceptable once David entered the picture. The version you could brag about."

Her hand drops.

"I spent years trying to be that version," I say, voice shaking. "But she's not real. And I don't think she ever was."

The silence that follows is sharp. Cold and final.

Things are good between us when my life is good. When I make sense. When I make them proud. But the second I unravel—even a little—they turn sour.

I stand abruptly, my chest tight, throat aching with frustration.

Mum pales, her composure slipping just enough to show the cracks.

Dad shifts beside her, caught between discomfort and guilt.

"Ellie, we just don't want to see you hurt again," he says softly.

"I *am* hurting, Dad." My voice rises, splintering. "David is hurting me. *You* are hurting me."

It cracks out of me before I can stop it. Raw. Loud. Final.

Tears prick at the corners of my eyes, but I don't look away. I *make* them see it.

"Everything I do is for Mia. Every decision. Every fight. Do you honestly think I'd risk all this if I wasn't absolutely sure I couldn't keep living the way I was?"

They don't answer.

And their silence—the same one that's lived between us for years—says everything.

I walk toward the door, every step heavy with disappointment. But under the ache, something harder sets. Like steel cooling in my bones.

As I open the door, I speak without turning back.

"I'm not staying with someone who breaks me just to keep *your* illusion intact."

Then I step out into the fading light, pulling the door shut behind me with a soft but final click.

The ache doesn't leave with me. It clings to my skin, sinks into my bones, and follows me all the way to the car. Just another weight I've learned to carry.

The streetlamps blur past in streaks of orange and white. My hands tighten around the wheel—knuckles pale under the dashboard glow.

I don't even know why I bothered going.

I didn't want a dramatic reckoning or some grand intervention — I just needed somewhere to land. A place to breathe. Somewhere quiet to figure out what I wanted. How I wanted to move forward.

But the second I walked through that front door, I saw it — the shift. The caution in their eyes. Like they'd already decided who they were going to be in this story, and it wasn't the people standing beside me.

They could see I was hurting. Could hear it in my voice. But none of that mattered as much as preserving the image. The illusion they've spent years carefully stitching together — the almost-son-in-law with the pressed shirts and effortless charm. The fixed-up version of their messy daughter.

I should've known better.

I *did* know better.

Deep down, I knew before I even knocked.

I exhale through my nose, changing lanes as the petrol light flickers to life.

Of course. One more *fucking* thing.

I pull into the nearest station and slot the car into a bay. The air outside is sharp, biting at my cheeks as I lift the pump.

I fill the tank on autopilot, my head buzzing with everything and nothing at once. Inside the shop I grab a bag of Mia's favourite sweets, those ridiculous fizzy rainbow strips she pretends to hate but eats by the handful.

The thought of her rolling her eyes and trying not to smile softens something in my chest.

At the till, the man scans everything, and I reach for the joint account card.

Tap.

Declined.

I frown. Try again.

Declined.

"Weird," I mutter, switching to my personal debit card instead. That one goes through instantly.

"Bloody contactless," I add under my breath, forcing a tight smile at the cashier as I scoop the sweets into my coat pocket.

But I'm not laughing it off this time.

Same card, same flash of awkwardness. David's voice rings in my head. *Technical glitch, bank error, nothing to worry about.*

Then a cold, quiet question lodges in the back of my throat.

I tuck the sweets into my coat pocket and head back to the car, trying to convince myself it's nothing. That it's just another thing to deal with later.

But unease crawls under my skin all the same. A tiny, sharp stone caught in the seam of my certainty.

The house feels different when I get home. Like someone has vacuumed all the air out and left the shell behind.

Mia's staying at Claire's tonight, and without her here, the place feels… wrong. The lights are dim. The air is heavy. No music. No laughter. No warmth.

Just silence.

David's car isn't in the drive. Working late again. A phrase so overused it's lost all meaning.

I step inside, letting the door click shut behind me with a soft thud.

My footsteps creak on the floorboards as I head for the stairs, each one slower than the last. I drag my hand along the banister, fingertips trailing the smooth grain like it might anchor me. Like if I let go, I might just float off into the silence.

My pulse stutters as I reach the landing and stop.

David's office door is slightly ajar. A faint blue glow spills through the crack, pooling onto the carpet. The computer hums quietly.

He never leaves it on.

He never leaves it unlocked.

A chill skates down my spine and I hover in the doorway, uncertainty prickling at the back of my neck.

A warning.

A dare.

Still, my feet move of their own accord.

The door creaks as I ease it open, the sound soft but stretching in the stillness.

Inside, everything is painfully precise. Papers stacked with military neatness. Pens lined up like they're reporting for duty. Even the phone charger's coiled tight, snake-like and watching.

I hesitate. This feels like a violation. An intrusion. But something deeper pushes past the guilt.

My fingers hover over the mouse, breath tight in my throat.

What am I even doing?

At first, I see nothing unusual. Work emails. Appointment reminders. Subscriptions he never reads.

I almost laugh. Maybe I *am* paranoid. Maybe my parents' judgment rattled me more than I thought. But then an untitled folder catches my eye.

It's full. Overflowing.

Something cold trickles down my spine.

I click.

And the floor drops out from under me.

It starts with a single email — one I almost don't open. A line of unread notifications buried beneath appointment reminders and online shopping promos. But something about the subject line hooks my gut.

Payment overdue: Immediate action required.

I click it. Then another. And another.

Debt collectors.

Past-due notices.

Overdraft warnings stacked like kindling.

Statements from credit cards I've never used.

Loans I never even knew we had — some dated back months. One over a year ago.

All in David's name.

Some in both of ours.

A quiet roar builds behind my ribs.

There's a second loan. Then a third. Then a fourth.

One tied to the car. One attached to a personal line of credit.

And then —

I freeze.

One flagged in bold red type. Secured against property.

I click into it.

And there it is. Cold and clinical.

Money borrowed against the house.

Our house.

The one I bought on my own. The one I fought for—brick by bloody brick—after Mia was born. The one place that was mine, until he convinced me to put his name on the mortgage. Said it was safer that way. Said we were building a future together.

And now—

Now it's collateral.

I blink once, twice, trying to force the blur away, but it clings.

Everything on the screen swims, numbers warping like they're underwater. Except they're not soft and blurred. They're sharp. Precise. Cruel.

The declined card at the Foundry. The petrol station.

That wasn't a glitch.

Wasn't contactless being temperamental.

Wasn't an issue with the bank.

It was the first crack.

The first clue I refused to see—because believing him was easier than looking for the truth.

My hands move before my thoughts can catch up. Scrabbling, frantic, fingers slipping on my phone screen as I fumble to find the banking app.

It's not there. *Of course it's not.*

David said I didn't need it. Said it only stressed me out. That I deserved a break. That peace of mind was worth more than watching every penny. He said he'd keep an eye on things—handle it from his end.

And I let him.

"For fuck sake, Ellie!" I whisper-shout to myself.

I re-download it, fingers trembling so badly I miss the App Store search twice.

My thumb hovers over the login screen, coiled so tightly it's like my lungs have forgotten how to work.

Error.

Incorrect username or password.

"Shit!" I hiss.

My hands move before my thoughts can catch up. Scrabbling, frantic, as I type *bank* into the search bar of David's emails and there they are. Dozens of them.

Thank Christ for paperless banking.

I click the most recent one — October.

And there it is. In black and white.

£3.84.

The figure stares back at me like a slap.

That's it. That's all that's left. The account we've used for groceries. For bills. For Mia.

I scroll through the transactions, heart hammering so loud I can barely hear. Payday loans. Withdrawals I don't recognise. Casino charges. Betting sites. Direct debits I never authorised.

Each new entry slams into me like a blow.

How long has this been going on?

How many lies has he told?

How could I have been so fucking stupid?

I look back to the untitled folder, scroll some more, hands trembling. And then I see it. Tucked innocently between the mess:

Your Hotel Booking Confirmation.

I click. And it feels like the bottom falls out of the world.

David's name. Two guests. A reservation at a boutique hotel hours away.

Booked just days ago. And beneath it:

Alicia Bennett.

The breath leaves my lungs. The screen swims.

I click further. Email chains. Flirtatious messages. Inside jokes I don't understand. Weekend plans. Explicit content.

His name. Her hearts and winks.

It wasn't one mistake or some drunken lapse—it was deliberate. Planned. Nurtured.

He *chose* her. Over and over and over again.

I stumble forward, catching my hip hard on the sharp corner of the desk. Pain jolts up through the bone—hot and sudden—but it barely registers. Everything else is louder.

Irrelevant.

My stomach heaves, like something inside me is turning to acid.

I slap a hand over my mouth, breath hitching fast and shallow. Like it's not meant to be in me anymore.

I lurch into the hallway, crashing against the wall like I'm drunk. The paint's cool under my palm, but nothing feels real. The floor bucks beneath me. The walls bend and blur.

He took everything.

Everything.

I barely make it to the guest room. Legs giving out halfway to the bed, and I crash down onto the edge with all the grace of a marionette whose strings have been cut.

My hands won't stop. They shake like they're searching for something to hold on to, but there's nothing. Not anymore.

And my chest. *God*.

It won't open wide enough. The air comes in broken pieces. Like my ribs forgot how to be a cage, and now they're just knives.

I grab my phone, but it takes three tries to unlock it, my vision too blurry.

Naomi's name glows at the top of my contacts. She'd come. She'd drop everything. But she's with her family. With people who love her.

I scroll again. Past my parents. Past the people who'll tell me to be practical. Who'll tell me to compromise. Who'll pick his side without even meaning to.

There's no comfort there. No softness. Not for me.

Not anymore.

My thumb keeps scrolling, aimless. Until it lands…

Kieran.

Not at the top. Not the easiest. But the only name my heart clings to like instinct.

I don't think. I don't breathe. I just press the call button.

The phone rings once. Twice. Three times. Each ring a heartbeat. Each one a razor slicing across my nerves.

Just as I'm about to hang up, too raw, too scared. He answers.

"Ells?" His voice is low. Rough with sleep. But it's him.

And that's all it takes. The sound of my name on his lips is like a dam breaking open.

CHAPTER 20

Somewhere Safe

KIERAN

THE PHONE RINGS, SHATTERING THE silence of my room. I jolt upright, heart already pounding before I even see the screen. It's late, too late for anything good. I blink the sleep from my eyes, throat dry, nerves prickling.

The minute I see her name, everything else vanishes.

I swipe to answer with trembling fingers, pressing the phone to my ear, already braced for the worst. But nothing could have prepared me for what I hear next.

"Ells?"

My voice is barely a whisper, thick with sleep and fear. I sit up straighter, already bracing for something I can't name.

Then I hear it.

A sob—violent and broken, ripped straight from her chest. It knocks the air right out of me.

"Ellie—" I choke on her name. My heart lurches like it's trying to reach her through the phone.

She gasps again, breath jagged and frantic. "Kieran—I don't know—" The words collapse in her throat.

Fuck.

I'm on my feet without thinking, pacing like movement might somehow close the distance between us.

"Ellie, sweetheart—breathe," I say, forcing calm into my voice when all I want to do is scream. "You're okay. I'm right here, alright? I've got you."

But she can't. I can hear it—she's not just upset, she's *drowning*. Gasping like she's trying to claw her way out of her own body. And it kills me.

It fucking kills me.

My chest is caving in. A useless ribcage, doing nothing to contain the ache ripping through me.

"I can't…" she sobs. "I can't—I don't know what to do. Everything's—everything's falling apart…"

"Shh." I soothe, voice lowering, trying to steady her. "You're okay. Just breathe with me, yeah? You can do that. In… and out. I'm right here with you, Ellie. Just breathe."

I pace another length of my bedroom, fingers tightening around my phone.

Every stuttered breath on the other end feels like it's cracking me open. I'd give anything—*anything*—to be there right now. To ground her. To take even an inch of this pain from her.

But I can't do any of that.

All I can do is keep my voice steady. Something solid for her to hold on to. I don't even know what I'm saying. I'm not sure the words even matter. I just keep speaking, soft and low. I count her breaths. Whisper her name like a prayer. Give her everything I can give, even with the miles between us.

Because right now, she doesn't need solutions. She just needs to feel *held*.

I'd give anything to hold her.

"In… and out," I murmur. "That's it. Just keep breathing. I've got you."

I press my palm to my own heart, trying to match her rhythm. "That's it, baby. You're doing so good. You're not alone. I'm right here."

And I mean it. God, I *mean* it.

A minute passes. Maybe two. Her crying softens just enough that I can hear the quiet hitch in her breath.

"Kieran…"

My name, from her lips, undoes me. I want to reach through the speaker and wrap her up. Carry her home. Keep her safe from every last thing.

"I'm here," I whisper. "Right here."

"I don't know what to do," she says, voice small and ruined. "I can't stay here. Everything's ruined. Mia—I can't do this to her."

I swallow hard, throat burning.

She's not just breaking. She's splintering. And I can't catch the pieces fast enough.

"You don't have to explain anything, Ellie," I say, trying not to let my voice crack. "Not right now. Just tell me what you need. Tell me where you are."

"I'm at home. David's not here. Mia's at Claire's." Her voice shivers. "I just… I needed to hear your voice."

Christ.

My lungs seize again.

A fresh sob breaks free on her end, and I let her have it. Let her fall apart without trying to glue it back together too soon.

"I'm so tired, Kieran. So fucking tired. Of pretending. Of being strong."

Tears burn behind my eyes. I close them tight, fist curling at my side.

"You don't have to fix anything tonight," I tell her. "You don't have to carry it all. Just let me help."

Silence settles again, heavier now. I wait, heart hammering like it's counting seconds wrong.

"I don't have anywhere to go," she breathes. "Naomi's away. My parents—I can't go to them."

Something inside me snaps clean in half.

And suddenly, I know.

This is it. The thing I've been waiting for without realising it. Every late-night text. Every half-finished song. Every restless ache I couldn't name.

It was always leading here.

To her.

Her voice, broken and brave, reaching for me in the dark.

And I'll be damned if I let her fall now. She called me. She *chose* me. And I will never not choose her.

I press the phone tighter to my ear, my chest burning with the weight of it all, and say the only thing that matters.

The only thing she needs to hear.

"Come to me."

And fuck, I've never meant anything more in my life.

Not just for tonight. Not just for this breakdown. For every night she ever cried alone. For every time she was told to settle for less. For every time she carried the weight of the world and smiled through it.

I don't tell her any of that yet. I don't need to.

The promise is already there, in the silence between us, in the steadiness of my voice, in the way I will tear the world apart before I let it hurt her again. For her, I'd move mountains, rearrange the stars, do whatever it takes to make her happy.

"What? Kieran, I…" She says, like she misheard.

"Just… come to me, Ellie." I repeat.

"Right now. Or in the morning. Whenever. I'll come get you. I just… I want you here. I *need* you here."

The line is silent again. My heart beats against my ribs like a warning.

Then I hear her breath. A quiet, trembling breath.

"Okay."

The world outside is still wrapped in darkness, and I haven't slept since she hung up the phone. Not even close.

The lamp hums low beside me, casting long shadows across the floorboards, and every minute that passes feels like it stretches a little tighter over my chest.

She was coming. Said she needed to grab Mia, and then she'd be on the road. Windrush Hollow to Rosemere. Four hours, even less with the roads being empty at this hour.

If I had to guess, she'll get here around three. It's 2:45 now.

The front porch light is the only glow in the dark, casting a soft pool across the drive. I've been sitting here in the living room, half pacing, half staring out the window, heart lodged somewhere in my throat.

I keep telling myself she's coming. That she's safe. That she's just taking her time.

But when you've heard someone break like that, when you've felt it through the phone line. Patience feels like trying to hold your breath underwater.

Every second stretches thin, taut, unbearable.

Her voice plays on a loop in my head. The way it splintered, the way it broke. And every time it echoes, it makes it harder to breathe.

I'll never forget the sound of it. I don't *want* to forget the sound of it.

Because if she trusted me enough to fall apart like that, to reach for me when she had nothing left, then I'll spend the rest of my life proving she was right to.

I move to the window again, heart hammering. My palms ache from clenching and unclenching them at my sides. Every time a set of headlights flickers down the empty lane, my breath catches, and every time it's not her, it guts me a little more.

What if she changed her mind?

What if she's stuck somewhere?

What if something happened?

The worry coils tighter with every second. And then the crunch of tyres on gravel cracks through the silence.

I'm on my feet before I even think about moving. Barefoot, ignoring the cold bite of the tiles against my skin, I yank the front door open.

Headlights sweep over the driveway, cutting through the cold, misty air. The entire night holds its breath with me as the car rolls to a stop. Relief crashes over me so hard my knees buckle.

I step out onto the porch, the night air sharp against my skin, but

I barely feel it. My whole body locks on to the car door. The moment it creaks open. The second she steps out into the muted glow of the porch light.

Ellie moves like the world's been weighing her down for too long. Like it's still clinging to her—even now.

Her hair's pulled back in a messy knot, her hoodie hangs loose around her small frame, and her face. *Jesus Christ.*

She looks wrecked. And still. She's the most beautiful thing I've ever seen.

Then Mia tumbles out of the passenger side behind her, bright-eyed and clutching a stuffed unicorn, practically vibrating with excitement even in the middle of the night.

That contrast, it breaks me. The innocence and the devastation standing side by side.

Mia unburdened.

Ellie carrying it all.

They're here. They're safe. They're mine to protect now.

Somewhere beside me, Ryder appears, barefoot and bleary-eyed, rubbing the back of his head. "Care to explain?" he mutters under his breath, still rough from sleep.

I exhale, the tightness in my chest easing the smallest fraction. "Honestly?" I say, voice rough. "I don't even know what's happening."

Ryder follows my gaze, clocking Ellie, clocking Mia. And all the sleepiness falls right off him. His face softens. "Well," he mutters. "Whatever it is... looks like you did something right, mate."

Ellie catches my eye. For one endless heartbeat, the whole world quiets, just the two of us standing there with years of words lodged between us.

Then, carefully, she nudges Mia forward.

Ryder glances at me, then at Ellie, reading the room in about two seconds flat. He turns to Mia with a crooked, easy smile. "Hey, you must be Mia. I'm Ryder."

Mia gives a quick nod, the edges of her mouth lifting, still a little wary but curious.

"You probably don't want to stand out here all night," Ryder says, backing toward the door. "Come on. Kieran's dad has the biggest biscuit barrel I've ever seen, and I make a cracking hot chocolate."

Mia hesitates for half a second, glancing at Ellie for permission. Ellie gives a faint nod, her smile tight but grateful. "Go on, bug. I'll be right behind you. Kieran and Ryder are very dear friends of mine."

Ryder raises an eyebrow, his expression suspicious as he leans towards me. "*Dear friends*, huh? Did you hear that, Kieran? We've been upgraded."

I shoot him a pointed look, my tone mockingly stern. "Ryder, behave yourself, please."

He smirks, unfazed, turning his attention back to Mia as they head inside.

And then it's just us. Ellie standing on the gravel drive, clutching her bag, her shoulders drawn up like she's still carrying every heavy thing she couldn't leave behind.

"Hey, you," I say softly, my voice rough with the effort of not saying more.

"Hey," Ellie breathes, forcing a fragile smile that barely masks the turmoil she's fighting to contain. Her gaze flickers between the ground and my face, as though she's afraid her composure might shatter if she looks too long.

The second Mia's out of sight, the mask she's been holding cracks wide open.

I step down off the porch, moving slowly, not wanting to startle her. "Ellie," I whisper, unsure whether to close the gap.

Her hands tremble where they grip the strap of her bag. She tries to speak, but it's like the words won't come. And then she lets the bag fall from her shoulder, and a broken sound rips out of her chest.

Her throat works. Once. Twice. And in a voice so small it almost gets lost in the wind.

"I don't know if I can do this, Kieran."

And fuck...

That's it.

That's the sound of someone who's spent every drop of strength holding themselves together for the sake of everyone else. Someone who's reached the edge and is terrified of what's on the other side.

I close the distance without even hesitating.

She crumples into my arms, her forehead pressing against my chest, her whole body trembling so hard I can feel it through my ribs.

I wrap her tight in my arms, but I say nothing.

Her hands fist into the fabric of my hoodie, desperate, clinging. She's not crying, not exactly, but there's a rawness to the way she's breathing that guts me.

Her legs give way beneath her. I sink to the steps, bringing her with me, settling her between my knees, tucking her against me like I could somehow shield her from the whole damn world.

"I've got you, Ellie," I whisper into her hair.

She nods. Her hands twisted in my hoodie.

I press my forehead against hers and close my eyes, letting the moment settle, feeling the full weight of her in my arms. Cradled into me. This is more than a hug. It's surrender. It's trust. It's her finally letting go and choosing me to fall into.

I swear I've never been surer of anything in my life. Because this —her body in my arms, trembling but here, breathing but breaking —is the moment everything makes sense. All of it.

I say nothing else. I don't rush her. I just hold her. One hand tracing slow circles over her back, the other wrapped around her shoulders like I can keep the world at bay just by staying close.

Like maybe, I can be the quiet that everything else wasn't.

Ellie sits perched on one of the stools at the kitchen island, her fingers tracing slow, aimless circles into the worn wood surface.

Her eyes drift across the room, taking in the chipped cupboards, the faded cream walls, the ivy creeping across the windows. But nothing seems to land. She looks pale. Hollowed out. Like someone who's been holding their breath for so long, they don't trust the air anymore.

Behind me, the kettle hums, steam curling into the soft hush of the early morning.

I move around the kitchen on autopilot—mugs, coffee, milk. But my attention never leaves her. There's still tension in the curve of her shoulders, a tightness that even the warmth of the room can't loosen.

"This place is beautiful," she says after a while, her voice low, almost shy. Her eyes sweep the kitchen again, softer this time. "It feels... peaceful."

I smile as I pour the water, the scent of tea filling the air. "Yeah," I say. "Growing up here was..." I glance out the window, letting the memories settle. "It was simple. A good place to be a kid."

She turns back toward me, something flickering in her gaze. Curiosity. Longing. Maybe both.

"I can picture it," she murmurs. "I bet you had all the freedom in the world."

Leaning back against the counter, I fold my arms across my chest. "I did," I say, grinning a little. "Dad let me run wild most of the time. Riding horses, climbing trees—*falling* out of trees. Pretty sure I gave him a few extra grey hairs."

The softest laugh slips out of her, a small precious thing, and my chest tightens. Even tired. Even broken open like this. She's still Ellie.

"You make it sound like a dream," she says, a wistfulness threaded through her voice.

I cross to her, setting the mugs down on the worktop and sliding one toward her.

She eyes it like I've handed her poison. "Black?" she says, raising an eyebrow.

"You said you needed caffeine." I grin.

She takes a sip anyway, then pulls a face like it personally offended her.

I chuckle. "Was that a wince or a spiritual crisis?"

"A little of both," she mutters, pushing the mug away. "Got any milk?"

I find a half-full bottle of milk and splash a bit into her mug. "Better?" I ask, sliding it back to her.

She looks at it, eyeing me over the rim, then looks back at the mug like it's still suffering. "That's adorable," she says dryly. "You think that counts as milk."

I raise a brow. "That was milk."

She sets the mug down and levels me with a look. "You gave it a suggestion of milk. A whisper. Like it's in witness protection."

I laugh, already reaching for the bottle again. "Alright, alright. How much milk does it take to stop you judging me?"

"Enough to make it look less like tar," she says, smirking.

I add enough to make her happy and she wraps her hands around the mug, satisfied with herself.

Adorable.

"You're lucky, you know," she says then. "This is a special place."

I take the stool across from her, our knees almost brushing under the counter.

"Yeah," I say. "I know. Didn't always see it when I was younger, though. Back then, all I wanted was to get away."

She smiles, small but knowing. "Funny how that works."

"Yeah." I tilt my head, watching her.

"The older I get, the more I realise how much this place shaped me."

She nods, thumb brushing the side of her mug. And something in her posture shifts. A little less braced. A little more here. "Well," she says, voice steadier now, "I can see why. It's beautiful, Kieran. Really."

"You and Mia are welcome here as long as you need," I say softly. "I mean that, Ellie. No rush. No rules."

She blinks fast, looking down at her hands. I catch the smallest tremor in her chin before she presses her mouth into a tight line, holding it back.

Then, she reaches across the island. Her fingers brush against mine. Light and uncertain. Testing. I turn my hand over, let her find her own grip. The warmth of her touch anchors something deep in me.

"Thank you," she whispers.

It's just two words. But it sounds like surrender. Like relief. Like trust cracking through the fear.

We sit there in the stillness. Not awkward. Not heavy. Just quiet.

Footsteps shuffle down the hallway, slow and deliberate. The familiar creak of the floorboards tells me who it is before he even appears. Ellie notices too.

I feel the way her body tenses, her hand slipping away from mine, like a reflex she hasn't learned how to undo yet. She reaches for her mug, fingers wrapping around it.

Dad appears in the doorway, blinking against the soft morning light spilling through the kitchen windows. His hair's sticking up in soft grey tufts, his dressing gown thrown half-on like he gave up halfway through getting dressed.

There's a moment where his gaze falls on Ellie and he hesitates. "Oh," he says, voice still rough with sleep but warm underneath, "didn't realise we had company."

He smiles the way only my dad can. No suspicion. No judgement. Just that quiet, steady welcome that's built into the bones of this house.

I step around the island, rubbing a hand over the back of my neck. "Dad, this is Ellie. Ellie, this is my dad, Brian."

Ellie rises to her feet, polite but uncertain. She smooths her sweatpants with one hand and offers the other out, her smile small but genuine. "It's lovely to meet you, Brian," she says, her voice soft. "Kieran's told me a lot about you."

Dad's face softens. He crosses the kitchen in a few strides, taking her hand in both of his like he's greeting an old friend, not a stranger standing in his kitchen at the crack of dawn. "Well," he chuckles, "any friend of my boy's is more than welcome here. Especially if you're putting this smile on his face before sunrise."

Ellie lets out a small laugh, and the tightness in her shoulders loosens just a fraction. "Thank you," she says, meaning it. "I appreciate it. I... kind of showed up without warning."

Dad waves that off with a grunt, like it's the most ridiculous thing he's ever heard. "Don't be daft. This house is built for people who need it."

And something shifts in Ellie's face. Something fragile and aching. It's there for just a second before she blinks it away. But I see it. That flicker of longing. That tiny part of her that's starved for this kind of unconditional welcome.

"Thank you, Brian," she says again, quieter this time.

Dad squeezes her shoulder. "No thanks needed. You're family now."

He claps me on the back as he passes, shooting me a look that says, *"We'll talk later"* without a hint of menace. Just understanding.

"I'll be out back if you need me," he calls over his shoulder. "Don't let him burn anything important."

"I'll do my best," Ellie replies, a smile tugging at the corner of her mouth.

We listen to the creak of the floorboards as he disappears down the hall.

The house settles again and Ellie exhales, setting her mug down with a soft clink. Her gaze lingers on the doorway like she's trying to memorise the moment, store it somewhere safe.

"He's lovely," she says eventually.

I smile, nudging her foot under the counter. "Yeah. I got lucky."

She looks at me then, really looks. And I know she sees it. The home. The safety. The love that built this place.

And maybe she's starting to believe there's space for her here too.

There's still so much unsaid between us. So many questions I want to ask, stories I want to hear, pain I want to carry for her. But I don't press. I just stay here, in this moment, holding the quiet with her.

Whatever she needs, however long it takes. I'll be here.

CHAPTER 21

a place to land

ELLIE

MY EYES FLUTTER OPEN, AND for a moment, I don't know where I am.

Then it hits me—all of it. The heaviness in my chest, the unfamiliar weight of the duvet, the smell of pine and something citrus clinging to the air. Not home. Not David's. Kieran's.

The last twenty-four hours spill in like floodwater—my parents' cold disbelief, the sick thud of truth when I opened David's computer, the way my hands shook as I called Kieran. And the way he caught me.

No questions. No judgement. Just that one quiet command—

"Come to me."

Like there was no version of this where he wouldn't want me.

And *God*, the way he said it—low and certain, no hesitation—like I was his to protect.

It lodged somewhere deep inside me, quiet and warm. A lighthouse in the wreckage.

I close my eyes again, just for a second. Just long enough to pretend I'm still floating in that quiet space between knowing and breaking.

The room is awash with soft morning light, spilling through the half-open blinds in long stripes of gold that stretch across the bed like fingers. There's a stillness here, one that's gentle and unfamiliar. A silence that doesn't make me brace for impact.

I breathe in. Bergamot, soap, and something else. Something warm and worn in—so undeniably *him*. The scent wraps around me like a memory, and I pull the duvet tighter, burying my face into the pillow, letting it hold me just a little longer.

It's been so long since I slept like this. Deep and dreamless. Without the jittery dread of what tomorrow might bring or the relentless loop of thoughts I can't silence. I'd forgotten what it feels like to wake up not already exhausted.

My gaze drifts around the room. Every inch breathes Kieran—the battered guitar leaning against the wall, shelves crammed with old records, faded books, crooked frames of frozen moments.

My phone buzzes against the nightstand. I reach for it reluctantly, the vibration slicing through the quiet.

> DAVID [07:23]
> Babe where are you? We need to talk.
> Call me.

Twelve missed calls sit beneath it.

The cold creeps back, chasing out the warmth like smoke through a cracked window. The illusion of peace slips. I lock the screen and set the phone face-down, pushing it aside.

Not now.

Not here.

The door creaks open. I shift, propping myself up as Mia peeks inside, curls a tangled halo around her sleepy face. She rubs at her eye, an oversized t-shirt swallowing her frame.

"Hey, bug," I whisper, lifting the duvet.

She doesn't hesitate. Padding across the room in socked feet, she climbs into bed beside me, curling into my side like she used to when she was little and scared of storms. I wrap my arm around her, anchoring myself in her familiar weight.

"Morning, Mum," she mumbles, voice thick with sleep. She rests there for a moment, fingers toying with the duvet, before she lifts her head, eyes searching mine.

"Mum... what are we *really* doing here?" Her question slices clean through the quiet.

I brush a strand of hair from her forehead, my hand trembling slightly. "We're just taking some space, sweetheart. Just until I figure things out."

She nods, but the crease between her brows deepens. "How long are we staying?"

I swallow the lump rising in my throat. "I don't know yet, sweetheart."

There's a pause. Heavy and quiet. "Is it... because of David?"

The air leaves my lungs in one harsh exhale. I blink, throat thick, heart cracking a little under the weight of her words. I forget sometimes how much she sees. How much she understands without me ever having to say a thing.

"Partly," I admit. I tilt her chin until our eyes meet. "But mostly, it's about finding what's best for us. For you and me."

She watches me for a long moment. Then simply says, "Okay." And burrows back into my side. "I love you, Mum."

Tears sting behind my eyes. I press a kiss to her curls, holding her tighter. "I love you too, bug. More than anything."

We stay there for a little longer, letting the peace of the house wrap around us. Then my stomach betrays me, rumbling loudly enough to make Mia giggle. "Hungry?" she teases, nudging my side.

I roll my eyes, laughing as I sit up, stretching the last traces of sleep from my body. "Starving. How about you? Want to see what we can find in Kieran's kitchen?"

Mia nods, slipping from beneath the sheets. She smooths her tangled curls back with both hands, flashing me a playful grin. "Definitely. Think they'll have pancakes? Or waffles?"

"I don't know," I say, smiling as I pull myself out of bed. "But we can have a look."

She springs out of bed, tugging her hair into a messy bun as she leads the way downstairs, her footsteps whispering against the worn wooden steps. The house holds that soft, lived-in smell of wood, earth, and something yeasty, like fresh bread.

In the kitchen, light spills across the scarred counters. Mia beelines for the fridge, throwing it open with a delighted squeak. "Mum! They've got everything! Eggs, bacon, milk, even strawberries!"

"Looks like we're making breakfast for everyone," I say, grabbing eggs and flour.

It's strange how natural this feels. My hands work automatically, pulling bowls, whisking batter, moving through the steps with an ease I forgot I had. Mia shifts onto a stool and starts slicing the strawberries with the careful focus only a thirteen-year-old can muster. Her tongue peeks out at the corner of her mouth, the way it always does when she concentrates.

"You know," I say, cracking another egg into the bowl, "I don't remember the last time we cooked together without rushing."

Mia glances up, smiling. "That's because you're always working or at uni. But we can do it more now, right?"

That small, hopeful look on her face undoes me.

"Absolutely," I promise. "We can." And we will.

The first pancake sizzles in the pan, the smell rising like something holy. Mia slides her strawberries across the counter and sneaks one into her mouth.

"These smell awesome," she says between bites. "Even better than Brenda's."

"Don't let her hear you say that." I grin, flipping the pancake. "But, I did learn from the best."

The moment breaks as a sleepy voice calls from the hallway. "Oi, Kieran!" Ryder's voice carries, loud and theatrical. "Ellie's making pancakes. *Actual* pancakes. She's a keeper, mate!"

I roll my eyes, stifling laughter, as he appears in the doorway, all bed hair and smug expression. "Good morning to you too, Ryder."

He snags a strawberry from Mia's bowl and she swats at him. "Those are for the pancakes!"

"Apologies," Ryder says, holding his hands up. "I didn't realise I was stealing precious cargo."

"Hands off Mia's strawberries," I warn, playful.

He gives her a wink.

A moment later, Kieran—who insisted on sleeping on the sofa—walks in, and all coherent thoughts vacate my brain.

He's rumpled and golden in the morning light, wearing only low-slung pyjama bottoms, sleep-mussed hair sticking up in every direction. Strong arms. Broad shoulders. Defined chest. A trail of dark hair disappearing beneath the waistband…

And on his side, just to the left of his ribs, a small tattoo catches my eye. It catches my breath mid-thought.

I can't quite make out what it is from here. Just the curve of something intricate, delicate. A tangle of lines and soft edges that weave together like they mean something. Like they matter.

A fresh, traitorous flutter sparks low in my stomach, the same stray butterfly that keeps surfacing whenever he's near.

I snap my gaze upward, cheeks flaming, and his eyes meet mine. Dark and amused. And of course he's smiling. Like he's caught the exact direction of my gaze and isn't the least bit sorry for it.

Bastard.

"Pancakes, huh?" he says, moving toward the coffee machine and preparing mugs for everyone. "You're spoiling us."

Ryder leans against the counter, grinning. "Look at this. Mum and Dad making breakfast together."

"Ryder." I groan.

"What? It's domestic bliss."

Brian appears then, smiling as he surveys the bustling kitchen. "Is that pancakes I smell, or are you lot just teasing an old man?"

"Morning, Brian," I say, stacking pancakes. "Hope you don't mind us invading your kitchen. I'll make sure we replace everything we've used. I just wanted to do something nice, to thank you for letting us stay."

Brian waves a hand, his eyes crinkling at the corners as he offers me a reassuring smile. "Nonsense, Ellie. While you two are here, this place is your home too. Use whatever you need. And besides," he says, glancing around the bustling kitchen with genuine fondness, "you have no idea how much I've missed this. Having the house full of noise again is better than any thank you."

Something cracks open in my chest at the ease of his acceptance. "Thank you," I say, my voice small but sincere. "Really."

And I mean it. I don't remember the last time someone said I was welcome without conditions.

"Careful, Bri," Ryder pipes up, stacking another pancake onto his plate and flashing a mischievous grin Brian's way. "Keep up that sentimental talk and we'll have to find you a job writing greeting cards."

Brian shoots Ryder a mock glare, shaking his head in amused exasperation. "Watch it, son. I'm not above grounding grown men."

"You wouldn't dare." Ryder gasps, clutching a hand to his chest in mock horror. "Who else would you rope into your DIY projects?"

Brian raises a brow, fighting off a smile. "I'm sure I could find some other unfortunate soul."

Kieran clears his throat, breaking through the playful banter with a warm smile. "Alright, enough emotional chats before breakfast. Pancakes are getting cold, and I don't know about you lot, but I take breakfast pretty seriously."

Ryder nods, already drowning his pancakes in syrup. "Seconded."

Brian chuckles, glancing at Mia with amusement. "Better get used to these two, Mia. They don't leave room for hesitation at breakfast. It's a survival-of-the-fastest type situation around here."

Mia giggles, grinning as she looks around the table. "I think I can keep up."

Kieran catches my eye then, a gentle reassurance in his gaze as he passes me a plate. "You alright?" he asks, leaning closer for a moment.

"I think so," I whisper, letting out a slow breath as I meet his eyes, feeling steadier with each passing moment.

We all settle at the table, plates piled high, coffee cups steaming. And for the first time in longer than I can remember, it feels like home. Not just because of the house—but because of *them*. The warmth, the laughter, the peaceful rhythm of being wanted without having to earn it. Not the sort of home you perform for. The kind built by the people who see you, and let you stay anyway.

Much later in the afternoon, Kieran and I sit outside on the porch swing, wrapped in a blanket he draped over my shoulders without a word. Mia's laughter drifts through the open window, Brian's voice weaving between it as they battle over chess.

Kieran passes me a glass of wine and keeps a beer for himself, fingers brushing mine as he leans back. That easy silence falls between us again. The kind that isn't awkward, just... patient.

"She seems happy," Kieran says, voice quiet beside me. "Dad's in his element. He used to do the same thing with me—but I was a sore loser."

"It's sweet," I whisper, wrapping my fingers around the stem of my wineglass.

Kieran turns toward me. "So, how are you holding up?"

I inhale, letting the air settle in my lungs before I exhale. "I don't even know," I admit, staring down at my wine. "Part of me feels like I *should* be falling apart. But out here... I feel like I can breathe. Which just makes me feel guilty."

Kieran says nothing at first, but his hand edges closer on the blanket between us—close, but not touching. "You don't have to carry it all, Ellie," he says. "Not here. Not with me."

The words hit harder than I expect. I blink against the sting at the corners of my eyes. He says it like it's obvious. Like I'm not a burden. Like it's allowed—to lean on someone and not apologise for the weight.

"I didn't think I'd find this much peace here," I murmur, my fingers tightening around the glass. "Not after everything. But I do. And that scares me."

Kieran nods like he understands, his gaze fixed on something far off. "Being scared doesn't mean you're doing the wrong thing."

Through the window, Mia beams as she shouts, "checkmate!" and Brian groans, throwing his hands in the air. I laugh before I can help it, and Kieran turns to glance at me, a small flicker of something warm in his eyes.

"She's going to destroy him."

"She already has," he murmurs. "And he's loving every second."

I glance at him. For a long moment, we just sit there, breathing the same air, wrapped in the same silence.

"I'm not expecting you to lay it all out," he says. "You don't owe me anything. But when you called me the other night…" He pauses, jaw tightening. "I've never felt so *useless* in my life. Hearing you like that, knowing I couldn't just… hold you—it killed me."

I look away, throat tightening.

"I want to be here for you, Ellie," he continues, quiet and steady. "Whatever that looks like. I'm not going anywhere. I need you to know that."

I close my eyes for a second, the weight of his words landing square in my chest. His certainty. His care. And me, not knowing how to hold either without flinching.

"I've spent so long convincing myself I didn't have a choice," I whisper. "That I just had to endure it. For Mia. For the version of life that looked right from the outside." My voice trembles. "But being here… seeing her laugh, seeing me laugh—it's like I'm remembering parts of myself I thought were gone."

Kieran doesn't flinch. Doesn't look away. Just listens.

"But this isn't forever," I pause. "We're guests. I can't just—stay here like it doesn't cost anyone anything."

I pause, swallowing hard. "Because it *does* cost something. Space. Time. You. And I'm already… too much."

The words scrape raw on their way out, but I can't stop them.

"I hate feeling like a problem people have to solve. Like someone you make room for out of obligation," I whisper. "And I *knew* you'd answer—I knew you'd show up. That's why I called you. Because in that moment… I needed you."

My voice trembles. "But even *needing* you feels selfish. Like I've dragged you into something heavy and broken when you didn't ask for any of it."

Kieran's grip doesn't loosen. If anything, it steadies me.

"You didn't drag me into anything," he says, low and sure. "I *want* to be the person you call. I want to be here—exactly where I am. With you."

He reaches out then, covering my hand with his. His thumb strokes across my knuckles in slow, grounding circles.

"You're not a guest in my life, Ellie," he says. "You never were."

The words undo something in me. They pull loose the threads I've worked so hard to keep knotted. I don't know how to respond. I don't even know how to believe him. So, I just let the moment stretch out.

Then my phone buzzes in my pocket, sharp and jarring.

I don't need to look to know who it is.

But I do anyway.

And the pit opens in my stomach all over again.

> DAVID [19:03]
>
> Ellie enough of this. Stop acting childish and come home. We need to talk. Now.

It's all there. The tone. The control. The veiled threat hidden beneath the illusion of reason.

I lock the screen, slipping the phone back into my pocket like it burns. The quiet between us thickens again. But this time it feels different. Heavier.

"I'm sorry," I murmur.

Kieran just shakes his head. "Don't be."

When I look at him again, his eyes haven't changed. No judgement. No pity. Just quiet understanding.

He sees me.

All of me.

And somehow, he's still here. Still choosing to be here.

And God, I don't know what I've done to deserve it.

CHAPTER 22

string lights and sunsets

KIERAN

Dusky evening light spills through the high garage windows, soft and amber, casting long shadows across the floor. The chill is damp and bone-deep, and the stubborn scent of engine oil clings to the walls like something half-remembered.

Not much has changed.

The old posters still curl at the edges, faded and peeling from paint-cracked corners. The same threadbare rugs lie scattered across the concrete—just enough to muffle footsteps and soften the echo. Cables snake between amps and speakers like ivy, some so frayed they violate at least three safety codes.

Ryder's already in his spot by the old garage door, his keyboard set up on the same battered folding table we've used since we were just starting out. A half-empty mug of coffee perches on a cracked speaker beside him. He looks right at home. Like this space, this chaos is woven into his DNA. And—it is. For both of us.

I grab my guitar from its wall hook, fingers brushing over the wood out of habit, before I strum a few quiet notes. I sink onto the sagging bench across from him, the one with our initials carved into the edge from a night we barely remember.

It's not glamorous. But it's ours. Always has been. We've written more proper music here than anywhere else.

"Alright," I say, running a few more chords. "Let's go again. But come in earlier this time, let it build slower. I want it to feel like it's sneaking in."

Ryder gives a salute, fingers already finding the keys. "Roger that."

We settle into it. Him catching the rhythm—me shifting the melody, letting it move and breathe however it wants. It's fluid. Unspoken. The kind of ease you only get when someone knows how you play before you do. Years of gigs, late-night rewrites, and midnight panic have shaped this.

We stumble a few times. Try a new fill. Mess up a transition. Laugh. Swear. Start over.

It's perfect.

Ryder leans back, scrunching up his face. "Okay, that was rough. Not *entirely* my fault, but still."

I snort, muting the strings. "We'll tighten it up. That verse doesn't sit right anyway."

He stretches, spine cracking as he lifts both arms overhead. "So," he says, casual as hell, eyes sliding to me, "you and Ellie."

I blink. "What about us?"

He shrugs, but there's a look on his face. Mildly amused, mostly nosy. "She's here. You've been smiling like you're in a bloody toothpaste ad. Seems like something worth poking at."

I rest the guitar across my lap and exhale. "It's not like that."

"Mhm." He sips his coffee. Waits.

I rake a hand through my hair. "She's been through hell, Ryder. I don't even know how deep it goes yet."

"And yet, here she is. With you."

"She's not here *with* me," I say, quieter this time. "She didn't come to pick up where we left off or fall into anything new. She's here because she had nowhere else."

Ryder sits forward, losing the teasing edge. "You think that makes it mean less?"

I glance up.

"She chose this place, Kieran. She chose you when she broke. Not her parents. Not her best mate. *You*. That means something."

My throat tightens. "It just... it kills me. Seeing her like that. Pretending she's fine when she's clearly not."

He's quiet for a beat, then nods. "So be the person who makes her feel like she doesn't have to pretend."

I let the words settle, finding their own place in my chest.

"You care about her," Ryder says, but it's not a question.

"More than I should," I admit. "But I'm not gonna be another thing that complicates her life. She needs space. And someone who's just... there."

Ryder taps the rim of his mug and nods once, solemn. "Well, lucky for her, she picked the right place to crash."

He lets the last few notes of his melody hang in the air, his fingers hovering over the keys. I lean back, stretching out my legs, the guitar resting across my chest.

"Barn's starting to look bloody decent now," he says, glancing out the cracked garage window at my dad, who's brushing a final coat of paint across the old doors. "Feels wrong not celebrating it somehow."

I smirk. "What, like a ribbon-cutting ceremony?"

Ryder rolls his eyes. "Nah, idiot. I'm talking old-school. Food. Fire pit. Some tunes. Like we used to before we got fancy and half-famous."

I raise an eyebrow at him, glancing at the grey-streaked sky. "It's barely ten degrees out and you want a *barbeque*?"

"If it's not raining sideways, it's grilling weather," Ryder says. "Adds flavour. Builds character. Gives the sausages a real sense of hardship."

"You're an idiot."

"An idiot with a plan."

I let the idea settle. And then I think of Ellie. Of how she looked today. Soft and quiet, but lighter. Mia giggling with dad. That rare peace you don't realise you're craving until you find it.

"Alright," I say. "Something small. Simple. A bit of light."

Ryder raises an eyebrow. "You mean fairy lights and heartfelt speeches?"

"Fuck off."

He leans back, laughing. "What if we got the boys back? One flight from Italy, they'll be here in no time."

"You reckon they'd come?" I ask, surprised by how much I want that. Want them all here, in one place.

"They'd be on the next flight if you asked," Ryder says, dead certain. "Tell 'em it's a reunion. Band bonding. Emotional wellbeing. Whatever makes it sound important."

"We should call Naomi too," I say after a moment. "I think Ellie needs her."

Ryder nods, all teasing gone now. "Do it. She'll want to be here."

He's already pulling out his phone before I've decided. "I'll take the clowns," he mutters. "You get the responsible adult."

I smirk, lifting my phone and stepping out into the sun-soaked yard while he dials Theo and Luca. I can already hear his opening line. "Alright, you international men of mystery, pack your bags. We're resurrecting the yonder years."

I shake my head, then focus on the screen. Thumb hovering over Naomi's name. Ellie didn't want to disturb her. But this isn't about interrupting a trip. It's about giving Ellie something she might not ask for, but needs.

I press call.

"Naomi speaking. If you're calling to tell me Mia's gotten into street fighting, I swear to God..."

"It's Kieran."

There's a pause. A shift in the air, like she's stopped mid-step. "Oh." Her voice softens, the snark peeling away. "Kieran. What's going on?"

"She's here," I say, my voice low. "Ellie. With Mia."

Another pause. Then a gust of breath, like she's stepped outside or stopped pacing. "Fuck sake, Ellie," Naomi mutters. "I knew something was off. Hasn't replied to any of my messages all week."

"She's coping," I say. "But only just. She's putting on a brave face I think."

The silence stretches across the line, weighted now, heavier than before. "I bet she is." Naomi huffs, sounding frustrated.

"She got here two days ago."

"She left him," Naomi says eventually. It isn't a question.

"Yeah," I say. "Well... I think. Not for me. Not for anyone else. She just... I don't think she could take it anymore. I don't know the full story."

Naomi exhales again, like she's fighting off every instinct to storm over. "It's about bloody time. That man's like mould, always creeping in no matter how much you scrub."

I almost laugh, but it dies quick. "It wasn't easy for her," I say. "Still isn't."

"Of course not," she snaps, but there's steel under the heat. "And I bet she's blaming herself, isn't she? Acting like this is her mess to fix. Like she's inconvenient."

I press a hand to the back of my neck. "Pretty much."

There's a soft sound, like she's dragging a hand over her face. "Where are you?" Naomi asks.

"Rosemere. My dad's place. We're doing something tomorrow night, something small. Thought she could use something easy."

"I'm coming. Text me the address," Naomi says, no hesitation. "But don't tell her. She's probably convinced she doesn't deserve anyone showing up for her right now."

I smile despite the ache behind it. "She'll be glad."

"And Kieran?" Her voice dips quieter. More real.

"Yeah?"

"Thank you. For being there for her."

I swallow around the lump in my throat. "Said I would be."

I hang up just as Ryder bursts out into the yard, phone in hand, grin smug as hell. "They're coming!" he declares. "Flights booked. Theo's already making a playlist. Luca asked if there'll be garlic bread."

"Fucking idiot," I mutter, shaking my head, a laugh bubbling out of me.

And just like that, something settles deep in my chest. A sense of things falling into place. Not everything. Not all at once.

But enough.

The next day, the barn is a full-blown construction zone.

Luca and Theo arrived about an hour ago. They wasted no time declaring the barn *a vibe waiting to happen*. Now they're elbows-deep in boxes of cables and battered decorations, operating with the kind of confidence only people with no plan whatsoever can manage.

The evening sun slants through the open double doors, catching on the rafters where fairy lights are half-strung, tangled, and stubborn. An old speaker system wheezes out a playlist Theo swears is *curated to evoke nostalgic serenity*. Luca's already questioned what the hell that's supposed to mean, *twice*, and been ignored both times.

Ryder's perched on a ladder, muttering under his breath as he struggles to hook fairy lights onto one of the ceiling beams.

"Tell me again why I'm the one dangling from death's doorstep?" he grunts.

"Because you're the youngest," Luca calls from the floor, half-buried in a pile of tangled extension cords.

I'm crouched by the firepit just outside the barn, coaxing kindling into something that might catch. Smoke curls into the air, the scent already clinging to my clothes.

It's been too long since we did something like this. Before the touring, before everything got big and serious. Back when music and late nights with dad were enough.

Just as I lean back on my heels, the front door bangs open, and a blur of pink and denim barrels down the porch steps.

Mia stomps across the grass, eyes wide and sparkling with excitement. She halts to a stop in front of me, nearly toppling into the crate of firewood. "Can I help?" she asks, vibrating with the need to be useful.

I glance at her, this force of nature wrapped in stubbornness and heart. "Absolutely—Ryder!" I shout toward the barn. "New recruit reporting for duty!"

He leans over the beam to squint down at us. "Can she untangle forty metres of fairy lights and not complain?"

"I'm very patient," Mia says, folding her arms like she's just been handed the keys to the company.

Ryder sighs, dragging a hand down his face. "Alright, come on then. But if you mess up my system."

"You don't have a system," Mia interrupts, skipping past me toward the barn. "You've got a mess. And no symmetry."

Ryder glares after her. "I'm being bullied."

"By a thirteen-year-old," I call, tossing another log onto the fire. "Tough break, mate."

Mia disappears into the barn, her voice already floating back, giving Ryder what sounds like an unsolicited lecture on light distribution and spatial balance. He tries to argue, but she steamrolls him with a confidence that would put an architect to shame.

I grin, sipping from my beer bottle as the fire catches. Warmth seeps into my bones, but not just from the flames. From the sound of them. The life. The messy, noisy, heart-full kind of life that only happens when you stop worrying about the rules.

Then I feel it. That shift. A ripple in the air, like the whole world holds its breath for a second.

I glance up and everything else fades. Ellie's just stepped out of the house.

The sunset catches her first, throwing gold across her hair where it falls loose around her shoulders. She's wearing a soft peach dress, the hem fluttering just above her knees, paired with an oversized cardigan that looks like it was made for comfort, not show. It hangs off her frame in that perfect, careless way. Like she doesn't even know she's the most beautiful thing I've ever seen.

She moves across the grass, her bare toes curling in the cool dirt, her hands tucked into the sleeves of her cardigan. The breeze lifts the fabric of her dress, just enough to tease, just enough to undo me.

It's not just the way she looks though, Christ, that alone would be enough to bring a man to his knees.

It's the way she carries herself. Soft. Tentative. Like she's not sure she's allowed to take up space here, in this moment, in this skin. Like she's been surviving so long she forgot how to just *be*.

And all I want is to pull her in, wrap her up, and tell her she's allowed to take up every inch of it. Every breath. Every heartbeat. Every piece of my stupid, wrecked heart if she wants it.

"Hey," she says, her voice carrying over the wind.

I rise to my feet, heart pounding like I've just been knocked sideways. "Hey," I manage. Every word I know has abandoned me. She's short-circuited my whole system.

"You look... nice."

Theo coughs behind me and it sounds suspiciously like *"understatement."*

Ellie raises an eyebrow, smirking like she knows what I'm struggling to say. "Just nice?" she teases, her voice lilting in that way that used to wreck me years ago and still does.

I step closer without thinking, voice dropping low enough that it's just for her. "You're beautiful, Ellie. You look like something people write songs about."

She freezes, the words catching her off guard and then her cheeks flush this soft, breathtaking pink. She ducks her head, shy but smiling, like she doesn't quite know what to do with the compliment.

That shy smile? It wrecks me. It finishes what the dress started and carves out the last bit of self-control I had left.

Behind us, Luca whistles low under his breath, and Ryder, who's been watching despite pretending to argue with Mia, mutters, "Oof. Smooth, mate."

I barely hear them. Because right now, it's just her.

Ellie Carter, standing in the last light of the day, looking unsure and gorgeous, real and happy.

And fuck, if I wasn't already completely gone for her...

I am now.

Every part of me knows it.

There's no pulling back. No cooling off. No pretending anymore.

I'm hers.

Even if she doesn't know it yet.

CHAPTER 23

barefoot on the grass

ELLIE

"There," I say, securing Mia's braid with a hair tie and brushing a few stray strands behind her ear. "All done."

She beams at me in the mirror, tilting her head side to side to inspect the result, then hops down from the bed, smoothing her dungarees like she's stepping onto a stage.

No hesitation. No second-guessing. Just pure, unfiltered joy as she bolts down the stairs with a shout of, "Theo! Don't start the marshmallows without me!"

I shake my head, smiling despite myself. Still amazed at how easily she's settled here. How quickly she's folded herself into this space like she's always belonged.

Like we both have.

My smile lingers as I stand, smoothing down the front of my outfit. A simple tea dress I haven't worn in years, rediscovered while rooting through my wardrobe and thrown into my bag on a reckless whim. It skims on my thighs, dips just enough at the neckline, hugs curves I'd almost forgotten I had. For a moment, standing there with nothing to cover me, I feel exposed. Before I can think too hard about it, I reach for the battered cardigan Brenda knitted for me years ago and pull it on, grounding myself in the familiar weight of it.

The buzz of my phone yanks me out of the moment.

I freeze, my stomach knotting instinctively before I even look at the screen.

> DAVID [17:06]
>
> Where the hell are you Ellie? I'm done being patient. You owe me a conversation. You're blowing this way out of proportion.

I sit back on the edge of the bed—phone heavy in my hand, thumbs hovering over the keyboard as that familiar war rages inside my chest.

But then something sharper cuts through the noise.

Not rage. Something steadier. *Clarity.*

I breathe out, fingers trembling as I type.

> I found the emails, David. You don't get to tell me what I've seen or how I feel anymore. I need space. Please don't contact me again.

I stare at the message for a long time. Pulse thrumming in my ears. Every muscle braced for impact.

And then hit send.

It lands like a match on dry earth. Immediate. Irrevocable.

His response comes fast. Too fast.

> DAVID [17:08]
>
> Ellie please. It's not what you think. You don't know the full story. I can explain.

Of course he can. There's always an explanation, a loophole, a reason it's not as bad as it seems—as long as I'm willing to twist myself small enough to believe it.

My jaw tightens. I type again without letting myself second-guess.

> No. You don't get to twist this. You lied. Over and over. I'm done being the one who has to bend to your will and fix the mess.

Send.

Without hesitation, I power the phone off. The screen goes black in my hand. I drop it onto the nightstand like it weighs a thousand pounds.

There's silence. Not the buzzing, anxious kind that fills a room when something's about to break.

This silence is freeing. Like opening a window after a storm.

I stay seated for a moment longer, letting the quiet settle into my skin. Letting it stitch me back together, thread by thread.

Then, slowly, I push myself up from the bed and cross to the window.

Outside, the world glows gold and alive. The sun spills over rooftops and tangled gardens, catching on dewy leaves and clotheslines and the tops of cars down the street.

And for the first time in a long time, I want to be in it. I want something real. Something that's mine.

Right now, I don't have all the answers. But I know this much — I'm choosing me. Not out of defiance. Not out of fear. But because I finally believe I deserve more than existing.

And maybe something in me has started to trust that I'll find it.

The barn behind me glows with soft amber light, Theo's playlist trickling through the open doors in soft, lazy waves. There's laughter somewhere behind the trees, the kind that spills out without restraint, the kind you want to bottle for later.

I pull my cardigan tighter around myself, stepping across the yard into the open arms of evening. The sky above is a slow-blooming canvas of colour. Molten gold bleeding into fiery pink, the edges bruising into deep violet where the first stars are just beginning to blink awake.

Kieran is crouched beside the drinks table, arranging a row of mismatched bottles with Theo, who's more interested in cracking open another beer than maintaining any sort of system.

Luca is locked in a fierce, silent war with a stubborn folding table, dragging it across the grass with all the patience of a man defusing a bomb.

Behind them, the barbecue hisses to life. I turn to find Brian manning the grill, tea towel thrown over one shoulder, flipping sausages with care.

He hums under his breath. A low, tuneless melody that somehow stitches itself into the evening air. And when he glances over at the noise unfolding around him, his whole face softens.

"Smells amazing," I call out, brushing my hands down the front of my dress as I wander closer. "Need a hand?"

Brian glances over, a twinkle in his eye. "Nah, love. I've got it. You just enjoy yourself." He pauses, taking in the scene. The chaos, the clatter, the fairy lights sagging in uneven sways overhead. His smile grows softer now. "It's been a long time since this place felt full like this."

There's something about the way he says it. Something that tugs at a part of me, still bruised and unsure.

I step in closer, noting the tightness in his shoulders, the way his weight's favouring one leg.

"You're not overdoing it, are you?" I question, not wanting to overstep but unable to quiet the concern. "You're not that long post-op, and I know standing for too long can knock you sideways."

Brian chuckles, but there's no offence in it. "Just an appendix, Ellie. They whipped it out, stitched me up, and sent me on my way. I'm good."

I narrow my eyes. "You say that like it was a tooth. You had major abdominal surgery, Brian. Your body's still catching up."

He chuckles. "Kieran said you'd be keeping an eye on me."

"And he wasn't wrong," I say, only half teasing.

His smile holds, a little glassy around the edges. "You really are a nurse through and through, eh?"

"Occupational hazard," I shrug.

Brian's eyes crease with something fond. "I promise, I'm fine. If I feel like I need to rest, I'll sit down. Scout's honour."

Before I can respond, Kieran materialises at my side, his arm brushing against mine as he sets a bottle down on the table.

The contact is brief, but it grounds me. Roots me to the earth.

"You alright?" he asks, voice pitched low just for me.

I nod, blinking against the sudden tightness in my throat. "Yeah," I murmur.

He studies me for a beat longer than necessary and then nods, a small, private smile pulling at the corner of his mouth. "Good," he says, voice warm. "Because this? This is the kind of night you don't forget."

The words settle in my chest, sinking deep. And for the first time in what feels like forever, I let them.

The soundscape shifts... the crackle of embers from the barbecue, the low hum of a speaker drifting through the barn doors, the clink of glasses and the occasional peal of laughter rising into the dusk.

I glance toward the drinks table where Kieran is now laughing at something Theo's said, head tipped back, eyes crinkling at the corners. There's a looseness to him tonight. An ease I don't think I've ever seen in the crowded snapshots of his life I used to catch from a distance.

Kieran glances up then, catches my eye across the lawn, and holds it. There's no smile this time. Just something quieter. And that stubborn butterfly in my chest—the one that's been fluttering uncertainly for days—gives a small, certain kick against my ribs.

A sharp blast of a car horn slices through the moment, jolting the low buzz of the garden into sudden motion. Everyone's heads snap toward the drive just as a taxi rattles to a stop, kicking up a swirl of dust that glows gold in the last slanting rays of sunlight.

For a moment, we all just stand there, caught between confusion and curiosity. Then the back door of the taxi flies open with a dramatic flair, and out tumbles Naomi in all her chaotic, glorious, unapologetic energy.

Signature sunglasses, red lipstick, leopard-print scarf whipping behind her like she's just stepped off a film set, and a duffel bag slung over one shoulder like she's about to start a revolution.

She plants herself on the gravel, throws her arms wide, and bellows, "Right! Which way's the barn raising, and do I get a hat, or do I just light something on fire?!"

For half a second, there's stunned silence. And then the whole yard erupts into laughter. The kind that bubbles up too fast to hold back, scattering into the cooling air like sparks from the fire pit.

I'm already moving across the grass toward her before I even think about it. "Naomi?" I gasp, grinning so hard it hurts.

"Surprise!" she crows, slamming the taxi door shut and strutting toward me with all the reckless confidence of someone who has never once questioned if she belongs.

Theo meets her halfway, arms open wide like he's greeting a long-lost sibling. "You're a menace," he declares as she launches herself into his arms.

"You're just jealous I arrived with style," she retorts, planting a smacking kiss on his cheek before releasing him and turning toward Luca with a pointed finger.

"And you. I expect at least three cocktails by sundown. I didn't suffer a bumpy countryside Uber ride for warm lager."

Luca gives a mock bow, the corner of his mouth tugging into a grin. "Your wish is my command."

Kieran lifts her duffel bag with one hand, smiling like she's just slotted a missing piece back into the day and she grins through all of it, sharp and sunlit. Completely at home.

Ryder's leaning against the barn, one leg hooked behind him, beer in hand. His eyes flick to Naomi as she walks across the yard. "Nay," he says, winking.

Naomi doesn't miss a beat. "Ry."

Then, her eyes find mine and the theatrics drop. She strides the last few steps and pulls me into a hug that's all arms, warmth and fierce, steady grounding.

Not gentle. Not hesitant. The sort of hug that says: *You're not alone.*

"You're here," I murmur, the emotion catching hard in my throat.

"Where else would I be?" she says, squeezing tighter. "You think I'm letting you go through this on your own?"

Before I can answer, there's a blur of motion to my right. Mia barrels across the lawn, braids bouncing, a blur of pink and freckles, all limbs and energy. "Naomi!" she cries, her voice cutting across the twilight like a spark.

Naomi spins, arms already open. Mia launches into her without hesitation, and Naomi catches her, laughing as she stumbles back a step under the force. "You didn't tell me you were coming!" Mia beams.

Naomi turns, arms already open. "Figured I'd better show up before you replaced me with one of Kieran's rockstar mates."

"Too late," Ryder declares, suddenly beside them with an arm slung around Mia's shoulders. "She's already chosen me. Bonded over fairy lights."

Mia snorts, pleased with herself. "He says I've got 'superior coordination skills'."

"She does," Ryder confirms. "Outshone me in every department. It's a bit humbling."

The laughter swells again, and it wraps around the entire group like another layer of the gathering night.

Through it all, Kieran lingers by the drinks table, watching with a quiet, steady smile that lands somewhere deep in my chest.

And somehow, in all this chaos, all this light. I feel something settle inside me. I'm not just existing anymore. I'm living again.

And it's because of *him*.

I drift toward Kieran before I can think about it, drawn like a thread pulling taut between us.

He doesn't look at me right away. His attention lingers on Mia and Ryder, who are now trying to convince Naomi to help hang a paper lantern from a wobbly ladder.

But I can feel the shift in him as I step closer.

"You had something to do with her being here, didn't you?" I say, keeping my voice low so it doesn't carry over the noise behind us.

He shifts his weight, mouth pulling into a sheepish half-smile. "Maybe."

I raise an eyebrow. "Maybe?"

He drags a hand through his hair, messing it up even further, and lets out a breath. "She needed to be here," he says. "You needed her. I didn't think you'd ask... so I asked for you. I figured... if it were me, and I was going through something, I'd want my person close. And Naomi's yours."

A beat passes between us. The noise around us dips just enough for the moment to feel private. Like the night has made space for it.

"I didn't want to make it harder," I say quietly. "Didn't want to burden anyone."

He steps closer, close enough that the heat of him cuts through the chill between us. "You're not a burden, Ellie," he says, and there's something fierce in his voice now. "You never were."

I look away, blinking fast, swallowing against the lump rising hard in my throat. "Thank you," I manage, the words soft but steady. "I don't think I realised how much I needed her until she got out of that taxi."

His eyes soften too, and he gives a small, almost bashful shrug, like it's no big thing, like showing up for me isn't extraordinary.

But it is. It's everything.

"I just wanted you to have something good," he says. "Even if it's just one night."

Somehow, I believe him. In this strange, beautiful, unsteady new beginning that doesn't feel so impossible anymore. And for a moment, I just stand there, taking it in, letting it land.

I sink into one of the old deck chairs pulled up around the fire-pit, tugging a faded plaid blanket over my knees. The fire's burning low now, its glow flickering gold across the garden like the night itself is breathing out, finally exhaling after a long, full day.

Everything has softened. Bellies are full. Hearts feel lighter. The buzz of laughter hums through the air, wrapped in the scent of wood smoke and scorched marshmallows.

From where I sit, I can see the whole evening unfolding like a snapshot I'll want to tuck away forever.

Mia is curled up on a hay bale nearby, her legs tucked beneath her, Buddy snoozing at her side like a fluffy little guardian. Ryder has just finished tucking a blanket around her, gentle for someone who was halfway to doing an aggressive worm across the garden two hours ago.

His usual chaos has quieted into something softer, something almost protective.

Near the drinks table, Naomi is holding court, animated and wild as she waves her hands in grand gestures, arguing about something I can't quite make out. Either way, she has the guys in the palm of her hands.

Theo's hiccupping with laughter between sips of beer, Luca's pretending to be scandalised, and Naomi's cheeks are flushed pink from wine and glee.

And Brian, bless him, is still pottering around like the quiet heartbeat of it all, gathering empty glasses with one hand, humming something soulful under his breath.

Every so often, he stops to adjust a lantern or poke at the fire — the flames dancing up to meet him like old friends. There's peace in him tonight. A kind of calm that feels stitched into the stars overhead.

It's perfect. Not in the curated, posed way David always insisted things should be. It's the perfect you don't plan for — it just happens. The kind you fall into, without even realising how much you needed it.

Then... I feel him before I see him. The soft crunch of boots against grass. The shift of the air around me. Kieran moves into my periphery like he belongs there, hands tucked into the pockets of his hoodie, firelight highlighting the stubble along his jaw in molten gold.

He doesn't speak right away. Just stands there, close enough that the edges of our spaces blur, and it's all I can do not to stare. Because he's devastating like this: backlit by firelight, hair a little messy, his soft hoodie clinging to the breadth of his shoulders, faded denim slung low on his hips. He's all easy warmth and quiet strength, and the sight of him winds something tight and aching low in my stomach.

It's stupid how just the simple way he's standing there can make me feel like the ground might shift right out from under me if I'm not careful.

His gaze sweeps across the lawn, taking it all in, and then lands on me. "Looks like they're holding up alright," he says, nodding toward the chaos near the drinks table.

"For now," I reply, tucking the blanket tighter around me. "Give it twenty minutes and someone's going to start a very bad rendition of '*Wonderwall.*'"

He chuckles low in his throat, the sound curling around the edges of my heart. "My money's on Naomi. She's had her eye on that speaker all night.

I laugh, soft and genuine.

For a moment, we just sit there in the firelight's warmth, the evening settling deeper around us.

And then he shifts, only slightly, but enough that it feels deliberate. An invitation. A spark. "Come dance with me," he says, voice low.

I blink up at him. "What?"

He holds out a hand toward me, palm open, patient. "Just one," he says, that familiar, boyish smile tugging at the corner of his mouth.

The breeze lifts the edges of my cardigan. Somewhere nearby, a slow song winds through the night air, wrapped in the glow of fairy lights and firelight.

I should say no. I should retreat into the safety of stillness.

But looking at him with his hand outstretched and his eyes steady. It's impossible to lean away from it.

So I slip my hand into his, and he pulls me to my feet, like we've done this before in another life.

Kieran's fingers close around mine, warm and sure. The heat of him sinks straight through my skin. The callused press of his palm, the rough brush of his fingertips, the quiet steadiness in the way he holds me.

He leads me toward the patch of grass strung with fairy lights, the music from the barn spilling out in soft waves. His hand moves to my waist with the same careful reverence, the other still cradling mine like it's something precious.

We sway together, barely moving, just enough to call it dancing. His thumb brushes over my knuckles, tracing invisible circles that feel more intimate than any kiss. I rest my free hand on his chest, feeling the slow rise and fall of his breathing beneath my fingers, the steady heartbeat of him.

He smells like smoke, bergamot, and clean cotton, and it wraps around me, blurring the rest of the world. I tilt my head against him and let someone else hold the weight with me. Just for a moment. Just until it feels a little less heavy.

"You having a good night?"

I nod against his chest, my throat too tight for anything else.

When I glance up, he's already looking at me. Like whatever I'm carrying, he's already decided he's strong enough to help shoulder it.

I feel his hand shift ever so slightly at my waist, fingers slipping beneath the open edge of my cardigan. His thumb finds the thin fabric of my dress—barely a touch, barely a breath—and still, my whole body stills. My breath catches like it's snagged on a wire. His hand is warm and steady, the kind that undoes you. And I feel it. Not just on my skin, but somewhere deeper. Like a spark catching a thread. Like the beginning of something that could burn.

I close my eyes for a second, trying to hold on to this moment. Because it's... different. Not flashy or overdone. This? This is barefoot on the grass, stars overhead, laughter that's real and easy. It's comfort. Peace. This is *him*.

There's a pull in my chest, low and insistent. Not fear. Not guilt. Something rawer. The need to tell him. To say it all out loud. Because he deserves to know. Because maybe saying it will make it real. And maybe once it's real, I can let it go.

My voice catches in my throat for a second. But he waits, patient as ever, like he already knows I'm searching for the words.

"Hey," I whisper, tightening my fingers where they're curled in his hoodie.

He leans down a little, his forehead brushing mine, his voice low and careful. "Yeah?"

I swallow, the fire crackling somewhere behind us, the rest of the world slipping further away. "Is there somewhere we can go?" I ask. "Somewhere quiet?"

For a heartbeat, he doesn't move. Just looks at me like he's reading every thought tangled behind my eyes. And then he nods, the smallest, softest movement. No questions. No pressure. Just the same open hand he's been holding out to me since the moment I called him.

"I know a spot," he says gently, his thumb brushing once more over the back of my hand. "Come on."

And without letting go, he leads me away from the firelight out toward the darkened fields where the stars gather like witnesses.

CHAPTER 24

almost

KIERAN

I DON'T SAY MUCH AS I lead her away from the garden. I don't have to. Her hand in mine is enough. The shape of it, and the way she lets me hold it, lets me guide her even now, says more than any words ever could.

I give her fingers a gentle squeeze. Not rushed. Not coaxing. Just steady. Just here.

We cross the lawn in silence, the night folding in around us. It's cooler now, the warmth of the fire giving way to the crisp edge of autumn air. The ground crunches softly beneath our steps, damp grass and gravel mixing underfoot as we reach the back gate.

The moon hangs low above the trees, swollen and golden, casting everything in a silver haze. It spills across the field like light poured from a cracked bowl, glinting in the dew, catching in the folds of her cardigan, turning her hair to spun glass in the dark.

She still doesn't speak. Just walks beside me, our hands linked, her skin cool from the breeze. But I keep my grip steady.

The house disappears behind us as we cross into the open field. The grass gets longer out here, swaying in soft waves beneath the breeze, and up ahead, the tree comes into view.

My tree.

The one I've known since I was a kid. The one I used to run to when the world got too loud. Gnarled roots breaking the earth like old bones, branches stretched wide like it's holding the sky open.

"This was always my spot."

She doesn't answer right away. Just turns her head, taking in the view. The lake shimmers below us, glassy and still. Fireflies blink along the edge of the reeds. Somewhere far off, a frog croaks once and falls silent.

When she speaks, her voice is small, but not weak. "It's beautiful."

"Yeah," I say, still watching her. "It is."

We sit down together beneath the old oak. Our shoulders brush as we lean back against the bark. I shift, tucking one leg underneath me and hooking my other arm over a bent knee, steadying myself without thinking. She wraps her cardigan tighter around herself, pulling both knees toward her like she's trying to disappear into the fabric. Her fingers toy absently with the hem of her dress, tracing invisible patterns into the soft cotton.

She's so quiet that if I were anyone else, I might fill the silence. But I don't. I wait. I let her be.

And then, when she's ready, she says it.

"David cheated on me."

The words land like a punch to the ribs.

She exhales slowly, and I watch her fold in on herself just slightly. The way her shoulders dip, the tight edge in her voice. It's like saying it costs her something physical. Her next breath comes thinner, more brittle.

"It was the night we got back from Coral Point," she whispers. "I came home, walked into our bedroom, and he was in bed with someone else. He thought I was coming back the next day."

My spine goes rigid against the bark. My jaw locks. Fury rises, hot and fast, blurring the edges of my vision.

She doesn't cry. Doesn't flinch. She just stares out at the lake, unmoving. But the way she holds herself, like she's balancing on the last fraying thread of something she hasn't dared to let unravel, *guts* me.

I shift closer, not touching her yet. Just near enough that if she needed someone to lean into, I'd already be there. "Have you told anyone else?"

She hesitates, then shakes her head. "Only my parents," she says, voice tight. "But it fell on flat ears. Like they heard me, but didn't *hear* me."

Her throat works around the silence.

"I haven't even told Naomi," she admits. "I couldn't. I felt — ashamed. Like if I said it out loud again, it would make it more real. Like maybe it was my fault for letting it get this far."

She goes even quieter. "But it wasn't just the cheating, Kieran."

She pauses... and then it begins.

Not all at once. In slow, jagged pieces. Like ice cracking underfoot — sharp, sudden, impossible to stop once it starts.

She tells me about the lies. The gambling. The manipulation. The slow erosion of trust. The emails. The debt collectors. The loans against the house. The bank account he drained down to nothing while she kept putting dinner on the table and sweets in Mia's coat pocket.

She talks about the way he wore her down. The slow, grinding collapse of her confidence. The manipulation that made her doubt her own instincts until silence felt safer than speaking.

Her voice stays quiet, almost clinical, like she's reciting someone else's story. But every word feels like a shard of glass driving deeper into my chest.

And I just sit there, letting it wash over me. Every broken piece. Every unspoken hurt she's stitched in to herself for years.

Because the worst part isn't the cheating. It isn't even the lies. It's that he made her believe she had to endure it. That she wasn't allowed to want more.

When she finally runs out of words, she just sits there. Small and still, like the weight of it has hollowed her out.

My hands are fists against my knees, every instinct in me screaming to fix this, to go back in time and rip her out of that house the first moment he made her feel less than whole. But I can't.

All I can do is be here.

Now.

I shift closer, careful not to startle her, and speak low, rough. "Ellie... none of that is your fault."

She pauses, and when she speaks again, her voice is brittle. "I saw the signs. Not that he was cheating—not that. But that it wasn't healthy. And I stayed anyway. I kept pretending. Kept defending him. And the second I stopped, it all crumbled." She swallows hard. "And when it did, I felt like the weakest version of myself. Like breaking under it meant I'd failed."

I don't rush to fill the silence. I just watch her. And my heart cracks open for her all over again.

"You didn't fail," I reassure her. "You stayed because you loved him. Because you thought you were doing the right thing—for Mia, for yourself. That doesn't make you weak. That makes you human."

She blinks rapidly, like she's trying to stop the tears before they fall. I shift a little closer, my voice low, steady.

"And now you're here. Picking up the pieces. You're not broken, Ellie. You're *brave*."

She says nothing. Just sits there, rigid and aching in the half-light, like the weight of it all might cave her in.

So I reach for her hand. Slow. Careful. I don't thread my fingers through hers—just rest my palm against the back of her hand, warm and steady. My thumb brushes once across her knuckles.

Her breath stutters, and for a second, I think she might pull away.

But then—her fingers turn, curling up into mine with a grip that's not strong, but *certain*.

She leans in, forehead pressing lightly to my shoulder, and I feel her exhale—slow and shaky—like it's the first breath she's taken in hours.

"I don't know why I said it now," she murmurs, a voice so small it nearly disappears. "I wasn't even planning to."

"I'm glad you did."

"I feel like if I say it, it'll become real," she whispers. "And I'll have to face what it means. What I let happen."

"No." My voice is firm, low. I shift fully toward her now. "Don't do that. Don't carry it like it's yours to own. This is his mess, Ellie. Not yours. Never yours."

She drops her gaze to our hands, fingers twisting with mine. "I spent so long convincing myself it was just stress. That the distance was normal. That if I worked harder, he'd come back to me." Her voice breaks again, lower now, almost a breath. "I made excuses until there were none left."

Gently, I reach out and cup her face, the familiar shape of her drawing me in like a tide I can't fight. My thumb finds the tiny heart-shaped mole just below her left cheekbone, so familiar it hurts, and I brush over it without thinking, like my hand remembers even after all this time.

"Listen to me." I murmur, softer now. "That man broke every promise he made to you and still found a way to blame you for it. That's not love, Ellie. That's cowardice. That's cruelty."

For a second, her chin wobbles. A sharp flash of grief in her eyes. But she swallows it down like she's done a thousand times before.

I lower my voice even more. Barely above a whisper. "I hate that you carried all of this on your own."

The breeze catches the edge of her cardigan, carrying the scent of her skin. Sun-warmed petals, a hint of musk, and the slow, golden sweetness of vanilla. I breathe it in like it's the only thing anchoring me.

And then, so soft I almost miss it…

"Kieran?"

I look up instantly. "Yeah?"

Her voice shakes, but the words come clear. "Will you just… hold me?"

There's no hesitation. No thought. I open my arms, and she moves in to me without a second's pause.

But she doesn't just lean.

She climbs into me. Straddles my lap, curling in to my chest like she's trying to disappear there. Her cardigan pools between us, her knees bracketing my hips, and her arms hook tight around my shoulders like she's scared she'll float away if she doesn't anchor herself.

And I hold her. I hold her like it's the only thing I was ever made for.

Her breath stutters against my throat, sharp and shallow. She clutches the back of my hoodie like it's a lifeline, her whole body trembling with the silent force of what she's finally letting herself feel.

And then, the first tear. Hot against my skin. Heavy with everything she's never said.

And it wrecks me.

I tighten my arms around her, cradling the back of her head, whispering nothing but steady breaths into her hair. No rushing. No fixing. Just holding.

Her breathing slows eventually, but she doesn't let go. Neither do I.

I keep my arms locked tight around her, feeling every shudder, every broken tremor of breath against my chest. I press my mouth into her hair, letting her know without words I'm here.

After a while, she shifts, her fingers loosening from my hoodie and moving higher until both hands cup my jaw. It's so gentle it almost undoes me. Her thumbs brush over the stubble along my cheeks, tentative and trembling, tracing the corner of my mouth like she's not sure if I'm real. Her touch is heartbreakingly soft, so careful, it feels like worship and devastation all at once.

I stop breathing when the pad of her thumb grazes my bottom lip. Slowly, so fucking slowly, she leans back enough to look at me. Her eyes are glassy, rimmed with red, but they don't hide. They burn. Fierce and raw and alive.

"I don't know what this is," she whispers, her voice cracking right down the middle. "I don't know what I'm feeling, Kieran. It's too much… I don't understand any of it."

I cover her hands with mine, steadying them against my jaw. My fingers curl gently over hers, holding her in place. Holding us in place.

"I do," I say, rough and certain. And fuck, I mean it. I let my forehead fall to hers, closing my eyes against the flood of feeling rising too fast to name.

I feel her breath catch against my mouth, but I keep going, every word carved from the centre of me. "I want you, Ellie. Every part of you. Not the perfect pieces. Not the polished ones. You. As you are. Right now."

My hands slide up the curve of her back, slow and reverent, until my palms cradle the nape of her neck, feeling the wild thrum of her pulse under my fingertips.

"I've wanted you since the moment I saw you four years ago," I say, my voice roughening. "And not just the version I knew then. Every version of you. The woman you've become. The mother. The fighter. The one who still shows up with kindness even when the world's tried to rip it out of her."

I pull in a slow breath, feeling her trembling in my hands, and the truth falls from me, raw and easy. "I tried to move on. Tried to forget. But the truth is... I never stopped thinking about you. Not really. It's always been you."

Her breath hitches against mine, and I feel the shift. The way something inside her bends toward me, fragile and fierce all at once.

I move just slightly, angling her closer.

"And right now?" I breathe, my voice gravelled with everything I'm holding back, "all I want is to kiss you until you forget every time he made you feel like you weren't enough. To touch you like you deserve. To show you. With my hands, my mouth, every part of me, that you're not too much. That you're everything."

For a second, she just looks up at me under the silvered glow of the moon, her eyes wide and uncertain as her hands tighten against my jaw.

And I swear, if I wasn't already hers, completely and hopelessly. This would've been the moment that finished me.

"I want to hear the way you sound when it's me making you come undone, Ellie." I breathe, my forehead pressing closer to hers now. "I want to rewrite every lie he ever burned into you and make you remember what it feels like to be wanted for exactly who you are."

Her lips part in a shaky breath and for a heartbeat she leans in.

It would be so easy. So God damn easy to close the gap, to give in to the wildfire roaring between us.

And *fuck*, I want to.

But I don't. I won't. Not like this. Not when she's still bleeding.

Instead, I press the faintest kiss to her forehead. "But not tonight, baby."

Her body trembles in my lap, and I gather her closer, wrapping my arms around her.

"You've been through hell. And you're allowed to heal. You're allowed to take your time. You don't owe anyone a thing."

She shudders out a breath, the fight bleeding out of her bones as she melts into me again. I don't rush it. I don't ask for more. I just hold her until I feel her breathing even out against my chest.

"When you're ready—truly ready. I'll be right here. And I promise, I'll show you how to feel *everything* again."

I kiss the crown of her head and tighten my arms around her once more, swearing to myself, as long as she needs me, I'll never let her fall again.

CHAPTER 25

catching me softly

ELLIE

We walk back toward the barn slowly. Everything's quieter now. The fire has burned down to embers, the lights dimmed, and the music faded into low static, barely a whisper in the air. Only Brian and Luca are moving about the garden, gathering empty glasses and folding up chairs, their voices murmuring in the dark.

Kieran keeps my hand in his the whole way. Neither of us is speaking. Neither of us needing to.

The house glows faintly in the distance, porch light buzzing against the cold. Inside, the warmth wraps around us like a second skin. The old wood creaks under our steps as he leads me up the stairs, his thumb brushing the back of my hand every few seconds, like he's making sure I'm still here.

When we reach his bedroom door, he hesitates, then looks at me.

I meet his gaze, heart thudding quietly against my ribs. "Stay with me?" I ask.

The words are soft, almost swallowed by the house settling around us. But he hears them.

He lifts an eyebrow, tilting his head slightly. Not smug, just surprised. Like he's making sure I mean it. And that look alone makes something in my chest ache in that too-full, too-fragile way.

"I mean," I start, stumbling over my own words as heat creeps up my neck, "just… you've been on the sofa and… you don't have to. If you don't want—"

"Ellie…" he interrupts, mouth curving into that knowing smirk that makes me weak at the knees, "if you want to get me in your bed, you only need to ask, baby."

I roll my eyes, but the blush betrays me. That strange mix of affection and vulnerability cracking me wide open. "It's not about that. I didn't mean—"

"Hey," he whispers, reaching for my waist and pulling me in slightly. "I'm just playing with you."

Then, he reaches past me, nudging the door open with his shoulder and glances back at me, voice a gentle hush now. "C'mon."

The room is dark when we enter, the only light spilling in from the wide windows facing the fields. The moon is full and low, casting everything in a silver-blue wash. It catches the angles of Kieran's face. The firm line of his jaw, the curve of his mouth, and it turns him almost unearthly. Like something pulled straight out of a dream.

I stand there quietly, drinking him in.

He doesn't speak, just lifts his hand and curls a finger, beckoning me to him.

I go.

He watches me the whole time, eyes steady and soft around the edges, as the space between us shrinks. When I stop in front of him, he lifts his hands slowly and finds the edge of my cardigan. He doesn't tug, just waits. An unspoken question lingering in the space between breath and heartbeat.

When he finds no hesitation, he slides the cardigan down my shoulders with a quiet patience that makes my chest ache, and the fabric whispers down my arms before pooling at my feet.

He circles around me slowly, hands trailing along my waist until they pause at the small of my back. He doesn't rush or assume, he just waits for any sign I've changed my mind.

When he finds none, he leans in, brushing a feather-light kiss to my bare shoulder.

It's not a tease or a question, just a promise.

His lips linger for half a second longer than necessary, and I feel it like a pulse humming just beneath my skin. My breath catches, but I don't pull away. If anything, I lean into him ever so slightly.

Kieran exhales as though he's been holding that breath all night. Then he finds the zipper, and the sound of it sliding down echoes in the stillness between us.

As the fabric loosens, it slips down my spine, then falls away completely. Gathering at my feet in a soft, quivering heap, like the moment is exhaling with us.

I turn to face him, now in nothing but the sheer lace slip I wore underneath, bare feet on the wooden floorboards, heart hammering against my ribs.

He steps back a fraction, drinking me in, not with hunger, but with something almost appreciative.

Then, without breaking eye contact, he reaches for the hem of the hoodie he's wearing and tugs it over his head in one clean movement.

And, *oh God*.

Hello abs.

I try not to stare, but it should absolutely be illegal for someone this emotionally available to possess such a thing.

His mouth twitches like he knows exactly what he's doing. "Arms up," he says quietly, voice low, and I almost keel over on the spot.

I obey, and he eases the hoodie over my head, pulling it gently down my body and smoothing it over my shoulders like he's wrapping me in himself. The fabric is warm and smells faintly of him.

He tugs the sleeves down past my hands, adjusting the hem where it pools mid-thigh. Then, before I can even breathe properly, he leans in and presses a kiss to the tip of my nose.

I close my eyes at the feel of it. Something so small. So devastatingly tender, I almost come undone.

Kieran takes my hand and leads me to bed without a word. We climb under the covers like it's the most natural thing in the world, and he pulls me into him with a careful strength that makes every broken part of me settle.

I curl into his chest, tucking my body against his warmth. I can feel his heartbeat beneath my cheek, steady and sure. "Thank you," I whisper against his skin, the words catching at the edges of my breath.

His arms tighten around me, a fierce gentleness.

"I'm yours, Ellie," he breathes, voice breaking slightly as he kisses my forehead. "Always have been."

And just like that, wrapped in him in the dark, with the whole broken, beautiful world outside the walls. I let myself fall. Deeper than I ever have. Into the safest, calmest sleep I've ever known.

The porch swing creaks as I ease onto it, pulling the faded blanket over my knees with a soft sigh. Naomi's already there, sunglasses pushed up into her hair, one hand wrapped around a mug of coffee like it's the only thing keeping her upright.

She barely glances at me at first. Just hands me a second mug, steam curling into the cool morning air between us.

But then her gaze drifts lower. To the baggy hoodie swallowing me whole. To the hem of what is unmistakably a lace silk slip peeking out beneath it.

Her brows shoot up above the rims of her sunglasses. "Well, well, well," she drawls, a slow grin spreading across her face. "Looks like someone had an eventful night."

I choke on my first sip of coffee, heat rushing up my neck. "It's not what you think."

Naomi tips her head, mock-serious. "Really? Because you're sitting here looking like a rom-com heroine after a night of sin. Hoodie three sizes too big, suspiciously mussed hair, bare legs in October…" She gestures lazily at me with her coffee. "And I'm supposed to believe you spent the night playing Monopoly?"

I groan, dragging the blanket higher over my lap. "Naomi."

"What?" She bumps her knee against mine under the blanket, smirking. "I'm just saying. If the hoodie fits…"

I can't help it. I laugh. A genuine laugh, rolling up from somewhere low in my chest.

"Seriously though," Naomi says, her voice softening, "you look… lighter."

I glance down at the sleeves bunched over my hands, the faint, familiar scent of Kieran clinging to the fabric.

"Yeah," I whisper. "I feel it."

Naomi leans back, pulling her sunglasses down over her eyes, and the porch swings gently beneath us. The morning hums, low and easy around the house. And I let myself lean into the safety, the lightness, the tiny but certain beginning of something new.

Something for *me*.

"I swear, I had like… three drinks. Why is my head beating out of my skull?" Naomi shifts the conversation in that chaotic way she does, sunglasses now crooked on her nose as she clutches her coffee like it's the last holy relic on Earth.

I snort. "That's a blatant lie."

"Don't start with the I told you so. I'm fragile." She groans, dragging the blanket over her head.

"You never learn."

She peeks out just enough to glare at me. "I learn selectively."

I laugh, but the sound fades into something softer. My head falls back against the swing, and I let the quiet stretch between us, loose and easy.

"I told Kieran everything last night," I mumble.

Naomi shifts, lifting her sunglasses just enough for our eyes to meet. "Everything?"

I nod.

She sits up a little straighter, her hangover clearly forgotten. "How do you feel?"

"Exhausted," I say honestly. "But lighter. Like… something's finally shifting."

She watches me, patient and steady.

"There's more, though. Stuff I haven't even told you yet." I hesitate, shame curling hot in my chest. "I wanted to. I nearly called you a dozen times, but I just…"

"Hey." Naomi reaches for my hand, curling her fingers around mine. Her thumb brushes my knuckles, grounding. "I'm here now."

I swallow hard. "I found him in bed with someone else."

The words land like stones in the space between us.

"But that's not all." I chime in before I let her speak. "I found emails, Nay. It wasn't just once. It was never just once. He tried to tell me it was a mistake and I *believed* him. And the gambling? It's so much worse than I thought. There's nothing left, Nay. Nothing."

Naomi's hand tightens around mine. She takes a long sip of her coffee, jaw locked, eyes burning. "That rat bastard."

A laugh escapes me, but somehow, it's exactly what I needed.

"I've been so *stupid*," I whisper.

"Stop that," Naomi says immediately, firm. "You're not stupid, Ellie. You trusted him. You stayed loyal. That's not stupidity, that's love. He's the one who wrecked it."

I blink hard, staring down at our hands. "But I stayed. I kept making excuses even when it felt wrong."

Naomi opens her mouth, but I press on, the words scraping raw on the way out.

"And part of me…" I hesitate, hating how it twists in my gut. "Part of me feels like being here makes me a hypocrite. Like I'm no better than he is. Like somewhere along the line, I broke something too and just kept pretending it wasn't there."

Naomi doesn't rush in. Doesn't plaster it over. She just watches me, steadily.

"Even though we haven't… even though nothing's happened that shouldn't have." I glance down at the hem of the blanket, tugging it between my fingers. "I can't pretend I haven't felt it. Felt something. For months now. Creeping in when I wasn't looking."

The words hang between us, heavy and sharp.

"You're not him, Ellie," she says finally, voice low and fierce.

I shake my head, throat burning. "Aren't I, though?"

She squeezes my hand hard enough that it grounds me, brings me back to the moment. "You didn't wake up one morning and decide to hurt him. You woke up every morning trying to save something he was already setting on fire behind your back. There's a huge difference."

The tears burn again, but they feel different now. Less shame. More release.

"You're allowed to grieve what you hoped it would be. And you're allowed to move toward something better. You don't owe him your loneliness, just because he made you feel small."

I nod slowly, breathing through the weight in my chest. "I'm sorry I didn't tell you first."

Naomi squeezes my hand tighter. "You don't need to be sorry. You've been carrying all this for so long, trying to stay strong for Mia. And then someone finally saw you. Really saw you. Of course it all came out."

She smiles, small but sure. "I'm glad it was him."

My voice breaks into a whisper. "Who'd have thought after all these years. He'd be the one to catch me when I fell apart."

Naomi leans back, the ghost of a grin playing on her lips. "Honestly? I'm not that surprised."

I blink. "You're not?"

She shrugs, like it's obvious. "Ellie, you two were always magnetic. Even back then. I watched you orbit each other that entire week, like you didn't even realise you were doing it. Like you were pulled together by something bigger than you."

A breath escapes me. Soft and trembling at the edges.

Naomi's smile tilts wistfully. "You think I didn't notice how different you were that week? How different you are now? You glow when you're around him."

I look away, blinking the sting from my eyes.

"So yeah," she says softly. "It makes sense that it's him. That after all the bullshit… the person who sees you. Really sees you. It's Kieran."

The truth of it settles deep, somewhere under my ribs.

"Of course," Naomi adds, a smirk tugging at her mouth, "I was expecting tattoos and a tragic man bun. But this version's alright, I guess."

A laugh bursts from me. Half-snort, half-sob. "You're such a dick."

"Yeah, yeah." She bumps her shoulder into mine.

For a long moment, we just sit. The swing creaks. The breeze tugs the blankets tighter around us. The weight between us, heavy but shared now, finally feels a little lighter.

"I don't know where I go from here," I say at last. "It's been good to get away, but I can't hide out here forever."

Naomi stays quiet, just listening.

"I already pulled Mia out of school for the week. I have to go back… but I can't go back there. Not to that house. Not to him." I pause, forcing the words out. "Nay… could we stay at yours? Just for a bit? Until I figure shit out?"

She doesn't even blink. "Ellie. Of course. Jesus."

Relief swells so fast, it nearly knocks the breath from my chest.

"Take the spare room," Naomi says, squeezing my hand. "Hell, take my bed. I'll sofa-surf if I have to."

The tears prick again, but this time they taste like gratitude. "Thank you," I whisper, the words thick and raw.

"You don't have to thank me," she says gently, tucking a piece of hair behind my ear the way she used to when we were sixteen and heartbroken. "You just have to keep going. One step at a time."

I nod, a breath shuddering out of me. Then I lean into her shoulder and close my eyes. Just for a moment. Just long enough to borrow some of her steadiness.

"Now," she announces, clearing her throat dramatically. "Let's go pack before I get all misty-eyed and start quoting Adele or some shit."

When we make it down the porch steps, the driveway is alive with motion. Bags being shuffled, car doors flung open, Buddy staging a protest by refusing to leave the front seat.

Ryder slams the boot shut. "Alright, that's everything packed. I deserve a pint and a back massage."

"That could be arranged," Naomi winks, perching on the edge of the passenger seat. One leg crossed over the other, sunglasses in place, chin tilted like a queen surveying her domain. "If you're nice."

Ryder pauses mid-stretch, clearly surprised by her tone. I catch the flicker of a grin he tries — and fails — to hide.

"I can't wait to see Claire again!" Mia's voice rings out as she circles the car like she's got rockets strapped to her feet, her tote bag bouncing off her hip. "Mum, can I stay up late tonight?"

I cross my arms and raise an eyebrow. "That depends. Are you going to eat all your veggies for the rest of the week and stop leaving wet towels on the bathroom floor?"

She groans, already climbing into the car. "Emotional blackmail! Naomi — help!"

"Sorry, kid. Team mum all the way." Naomi grins over the roof of the car.

"Betrayed," Mia sighs, slumping dramatically into her seat. "In broad daylight."

I laugh, closing the door gently behind her. Just as I turn, the front door creaks open again.

Brian steps out, drying his hands on a faded tea towel, his usual flannel shirt half-tucked into jeans, glasses perched haphazardly on top of his head like he forgot they were there.

He takes in the scene. The buzzing energy, the loaded car, Naomi and Ryder still flirting at full volume, and then his eyes land on me. "Well, now," he says warmly, something tugging at my chest. "Didn't think I'd be sad to see my house get quieter, but here we are."

I meet him halfway across the gravel, and when he opens his arms, I don't hesitate. I step into them, letting his steady presence anchor me for just a second longer than I meant to. "Thank you," I murmur, voice thick again. "For everything. For letting us stay, and not asking questions."

He pulls back slightly, his gaze gentler now. "I don't know what you're going through," he says, voice low and certain, "and I'm not gonna pretend to understand the weight of it all… but I've been watching that boy of mine all week." A knowing smile tugs at the corners of his mouth. "It's clear as day how much he cares about you. The way he looks at you. Like he's already made up his mind."

My throat tightens, but I say, quietly, "I don't know what I did to deserve him."

Brian huffs a soft laugh. "Ellie, sometimes people just see each other. No games. No performance. Just truth."

He glances toward the car, then back at me. "Girlfriends have come and gone over the years. A few I liked. Most I didn't. But this? Whatever this is?" He shakes his head, his smile softening. "This is different. I've never seen him like this."

I swallow, blinking hard. "I don't even know what this is, Brian," I admit, barely above a whisper. "My life, the mess I'm in… I just don't want to mess everything up."

Brian nods, like he's not surprised. "Then take your time. But, Ellie, don't push it away just because you're scared. Just let it be real." He rests a hand gently on my shoulder. "You've got a good one there. And from where I'm standing, it looks like he's ready to wait as long as you need."

My breath shudders out of me, and I manage a small, watery smile. "Yeah."

"You're both welcome back anytime," Brian adds, voice a little rougher now. "Door's always open. But look after yourself and that girl of yours, yeah?"

I nod, but before I can say anything else, the front door swings open again.

Kieran steps out, carrying the last of the bags. His hair is a mess. Soft and tousled, like he's run his hands through it all morning. There's a quiet stillness in him that hasn't faded since last night, like he's walking around with part of my story now. Holding it carefully.

He crosses the driveway in a few long strides and drops the bags at Ryder's feet. Ryder doesn't miss a beat, hoisting them into the car with a grunt.

Kieran turns to me then, eyes locking with mine. He says nothing at first. Just closes the distance and pulls me into a hug, one hand curling protectively around the back of my neck.

I let myself lean into him. Just for a moment. Just long enough to memorise this.

"Thank you," I whisper into his shirt, knowing he hears it.

He pulls back slightly, hands settling at my waist. His eyes are so soft, it almost undoes me. "You're gonna make me all emotional," he murmurs, trying for a smirk. "Not a good look."

I laugh under my breath. My heart still feels full and fragile all at once.

Then he reaches up, tucks a piece of hair behind my ear, and says, "Everything I said under that tree... I meant it. Every word. And you can hold me to that promise."

I frown a little. "What promise?"

His grin curves slowly. "The one where I said I'd make you feel everything."

A rogue butterfly kicks inside me, and I open my mouth to respond, but before I can, he cups my face, gentle and certain, and leans in.

His palms are warm against my cheeks, thumbs brushing lightly beneath my eyes, like I might shatter if he's not careful.

And then he kisses me. Not rushed. Not hungry. Just a kiss. Closed lips, soft and certain.

But it unravels something inside me all the same.

My breath catches. My fingers curl instinctively into the front of his shirt, gripping him like my body's afraid to let go.

It's not about heat, not yet. It's something steadier. Truer. Like he's placing a piece of himself in my hands and trusting me not to break it.

When he finally pulls back, his forehead lingers against mine. His breath mixes with mine, warm and steady.

He's smiling. Soft and unguarded. "When the time's right... you're *mine*, Carter."

And the way he says it—it's not a question. It's another promise.

Behind us, Naomi beeps the car horn. "All aboard the heartbreak express!"

I laugh, shaking my head and pulling away as Kieran lets me go.

Gravel crunches beneath my boots as I walk to the car, heart still thudding against my ribs. Already strapped in, Mia dramatically waves to Buddy, as if the cat might follow us home.

I slide into the driver's seat and barely get the door shut before Naomi grins at me like she's about to combust.

"Okay," she says, shifting in her seat, "what the *fuck* was that?"

I just shrug. And sigh. Dreamily. "It was... something."

Naomi lets out a squeal. "Alright, we'll debrief on the road. But first..." she plants her feet on the dash with a flourish, "we need snacks."

As we pull away, I glance out the window. Kieran's still standing by the front steps, one hand lifted in a lazy wave, that soft smile still lingering on his face. In the rearview mirror, the farmhouse gets smaller and smaller until it's hidden by a curve in the road.

As the music starts, something upbeat and nostalgic, the countryside rolls past us in a blur of gold and rust, the colours of early October bleeding into each other. The hedgerows whip by like brushstrokes, and overhead, a pale, cloudless sky stretches in front of us.

For a moment, I let myself feel it.

The quiet.

The warmth still blooming low in my chest.

I can still feel the ghost of Kieran's kiss on my lips. The steady pressure of his hands, the way I held onto his shirt like I didn't want to let go. Like some part of me already knew what he was offering.

My fingers tighten slightly on the steering wheel. Because it's not just about the kiss.

It's about being seen. Chosen. Without conditions. Without having to earn it by shrinking myself.

I lean back into the headrest, watching the world blur past. And slowly, inevitably, the weight of what's waiting creeps in.

The house I left. The wreckage David made of our lives. The mess I still have to walk back into.

I have no actual plan. No job. No fixed place to stay beyond Naomi's generous offer.

But I'm not going back to pretending.

Not to silence.

The knot in my stomach tightens with every mile. A quiet dread, humming like background noise, louder the closer we get to the life I left behind.

You've got a good one there. He's ready to wait.

Maybe that's enough for now. And maybe I don't have to know how this ends.

Maybe — I just have to keep moving forward.

CHAPTER 26

four rooms and a bean bag

KIERAN

I SIT AT THE KITCHEN island, hunched over a lukewarm cup of coffee I've already reheated once but haven't drunk. The silence presses in from all sides. No laughter spilling in from the barn, no thud of Mia's boots stomping across the floor, no clatter of mismatched mugs or late-night toast runs. Just the soft ticking of the kitchen clock and the distant hum of the wind brushing through the trees outside.

The seat across from me is empty. The one Ellie claimed every morning this week, hair still damp from the shower, curled into a hoodie she borrowed and never gave back.

It's stupid, but I keep glancing toward the hallway. Like she'll come padding in barefoot, stealing toast off my plate.

She's gone.

I don't even notice Dad enter the room until he slides a fresh mug across the counter toward me. The scent of proper coffee cutting through the fog in my brain.

"You look like a man whose soul just left in a hatchback," he says, settling onto the stool opposite mine with a grunt.

A quiet laugh escapes me. "Something like that."

He doesn't push. Just takes a slow sip of his coffee and leans back, like he's got all the time in the world.

"She's going through a lot, Dad," I murmur, running my thumb along the rim of my mug. "But I just, I don't know, I want to be there. Not from a distance. Not as some guy she used to know."

Dad nods, eyes steady on mine. "You always were rubbish at watching from the sidelines."

That earns a ghost of a smile. "Did I ever tell you how we met?"

"At the hospital, wasn't it?"

I shake my head. "That was the second time. First was Sound Busters. Four years ago. Remember when we played that small set? I saw her. Sounds insane, but I felt it. Like I already knew her. And then..." I trail off. "She was gone."

Dad lets out a long breath. "So that's what had you moping around like a sodden puppy for months."

I blink. "You noticed that?"

"Son, you walked around like someone had unplugged your soul. Ryder thought you were dying. I figured it was girl trouble. Didn't think it was that deep."

I grip the mug tighter. "I didn't even get her last name. No number. Nothing. It was like she never existed. Until I saw her again."

He studies me, then leans forward, forearms braced on the counter. "Fate's a stubborn bastard, Kieran. Doesn't care about timing or clean breaks. When something's meant to come back around, it does. Might take four years and a hurricane of drama, but it always finds its way."

The words land heavy in my chest. "You believe that?" I ask.

He doesn't hesitate. "I believe in you. And I believe that if someone keeps showing up in your life, after all this time and through all this chaos, you don't wait for the stars to line up. You make your own damn constellation."

It hits deeper than I expect. I crack a small grin. "That's poetic."

"Write it into a song and make me rich."

"Deal." I pause. "So what now?"

"That's your call, son. But I'll say this. Don't sit still. You've done the waiting. If she needs space, give her that. But if this is something real? Be where she is. Show up."

I rake a hand through my hair, exhaling slowly. "I've been thinking about getting a place in South Havens. The boys are up for it too. Change of scenery might do us all good. Somewhere to settle when we're not on the road."

Pride flickers behind Dad's smile. "You've been chasing something for years, son. Maybe now's the time to start building something instead."

His words stay with me long after the coffee's gone cold.

After he heads out to feed the horses, I stay sat here, nursing the silence.

Then I pull out my phone, thumb hovering, before tapping the rental app I've been stalking — South Havens already in the search bar.

I scroll until something catches my eye. Clean lines, tall windows, modern. Big enough for the boys. Space to breathe.

I don't overthink it. I just hit *schedule viewing* and text Luca.

> Found a place in South Havens. Viewing this afternoon. If we leave now we can make it.

LUCA [10:17]

> You serious?

> Deadly. Don't make me go alone or I'll accidentally rent a shoebox with bad lighting.

LUCA [10:18]

> FFS 😳 Give me twenty and a bacon roll.

I smile. He's been staying at the inn in town since the barbecue, but he's the best option for this. Luca's got an annoyingly sharp eye for detail, and I trust his judgement. Even if he pretends not to care.

I'm already moving, something in my chest loosening, like momentum clicking into place.

South Havens is as beautiful as I remember.

The sun hangs low in the sky, casting long shadows over the pavements, turning shop windows into gold-tinted mirrors. There's a cool bite in the air. The kind that sneaks in under your collar, not sharp enough to sting yet, just enough to make you wish you'd grabbed an extra layer.

The streets are busy. School kids, couples wrapped up in coats with takeaway cups steaming between their hands, everyone going about their day. Life here thrums low and steady, a different rhythm to the one I'm used to.

Luca and I round the corner toward the apartment, both of us stretched thin from the drive. Traffic hit just as we rolled into the city. One wrong turn and a shouting match with the sat-nav later, and we barely made it on time.

"Next time, I drive," Luca mutters, finishing the last of his lukewarm petrol station coffee.

"Next time, just let me handle the roundabouts without screaming," I shoot back, shouldering open the gate to the building.

"I shouted once."

"It echoed, Luca. Birds scattered."

He glares at me, but there's a smirk tugging at his mouth as we approach the building. Clean brick, curved glass balconies, tasteful black awnings. "Alright," he says, adjusting his jacket. "Let's see if this overpriced hole is as tolerable as it looked online."

"Optimism," I deadpan. "So rare. So fragile."

I press the buzzer and step back, hands jammed in my jacket pockets. A second later, a voice crackles through the intercom — female, upbeat, estate agent-y. "Come on up, I'll buzz you in."

The door unlocks with a clunk, and Luca pushes it open, raising an eyebrow at me.

The lobby's sleek and sterile, all pale wood and polished tiles, smells like eucalyptus and fresh paint.

We take the lift to the top floor, and when the doors slide open, the estate agent's already waiting — clipboard in hand, blazer sharp.

"Kieran, Luca? I'm Beth. Feel free to have a proper look around — I'll hang back out here, give you space to take it all in."

Luca flashes her a grin. "Cheers, Beth."

She nods, stepping aside as the apartment door clicks open.

We both pause.

"Shit," Luca breathes, stepping inside.

It's massive. Two floors. Floor-to-ceiling windows. Cool-toned woods and matte black accents. A floating glass staircase cuts a clean line up one wall. Polished concrete floors softened by oversized rugs.

The kitchen is sleek and minimal. Built-in espresso machine, double oven, a wide island lined with bar stools.

"It's like a bloody Airbnb for grown-ups," Luca says, wandering deeper in.

I trail after him, moving toward the living room.

The light here hits differently. Soft and golden as it filters across the L-shaped sofa and low coffee table. There's a wall-mounted speaker system, plenty of space to host a writing session, and tucked somewhere just beyond the buildings—the ocean.

I could see us here. All of us.

Theo sprawled across the sofa in the sun. Ryder turning the balcony into a jungle of questionable plants. Luca setting up a vinyl station and threatening anyone who touched it with greasy fingers.

And me.

Writing songs. Brewing a decent cup of coffee. Waiting for something that doesn't feel impossible anymore.

"You're actually serious about this." Luca says, stepping out onto the balcony. But it's more of a statement than anything else.

I follow him, leaning my shoulder against the doorframe, letting the cool air graze my skin. The street below buzzes with late afternoon life. Kids weaving between parked cars, someone dragging a stubborn spaniel on a lead, the salty tang of the ocean curling up over the rooftops.

"Yeah. It's big enough for all of us," I say, shrugging. "And it's quiet."

Luca gives me a look that's part amusement, part something sharper. Like he's seeing more than I'm saying. "This wouldn't have anything to do with a certain nurse and her kid, would it?"

I roll my eyes, but there's no heat behind it. Just honesty. "I want to be closer, yeah," I admit. "Not to crowd her. Not to... force anything. I just…" I break off, dragging a hand through my hair. "I don't know. After everything she's been through…" I exhale, the weight of it curling tight in my chest. "I don't want to be four hours away if she needs me."

Luca sips his coffee, his gaze steady on the horizon. He doesn't rush me. Just waits, patient like he always is when it matters.

"I'm not expecting anything," I add quietly. "Not some fairytale ending. Not for her to magically be ready. Christ, I don't even know if she'll want me around once she really starts putting her life back together." I let out a humourless laugh. "But I'd rather be here, close enough to show up, than sit on my arse at home wondering if she's alright. Even if all I ever get to be is a friend standing in her corner."

Luca snorts into his coffee. "Yeah, alright. And I'm the King of bloody England."

I shoot him a look. "I'm serious."

"So am I," he says, raising an eyebrow. "Mate, you're about as subtle as a freight train. Friends don't look at each other the way you two do. Not unless they're very confused or very in denial."

I groan, tipping my head back against the doorframe. "It's not like that."

"It's exactly like that." Luca grins. "I mean, fuck, you practically imprint on her like a baby duck every time she walks into a room."

I shake my head, but I'm smiling now, the tension bleeding out of me under the weight of his teasing.

"It's not about labels," I say after a minute. "It's about being where I'm supposed to be. She might never pick me. I get that. But it won't change the fact that I... I choose her. Even if all I ever get to do is stand by and hope she finds her way back to herself."

Luca watches me for a beat longer, something softer flickering behind his grin. Then he claps a hand on my shoulder, solid and grounding. "Alright, mate. Sounds like you've thought it through."

"I have."

He squeezes once before letting go. "Still think you're a lovesick idiot. But you're our lovesick idiot."

I bark out a laugh, the knot in my chest loosening a fraction.

The breeze tugs at the edge of Luca's jacket. For a long moment, he just watches the street, the way the last light catches on the windows and the sea beyond.

"Also, for the record," he says, a smirk tugging at his mouth, "if you get us kicked out of this place for a romantic rooftop serenade, I'm absolutely telling the landlord I warned you."

I grin, bumping his shoulder with mine. "Deal."

We step back inside and Luca's already poking around the kitchen drawers, pretending not to care while quietly inspecting the hinges.

I linger for a second longer in the living room, letting the weight of the place settle into my bones.

This isn't just somewhere to crash between gigs. It's a choice. A reset.

I pull out my phone.

> Found a place in South Havens.

ELLS [15:37]
Wait... WHAT?? You're actually here?

> Will be when it's all sorted. Big place. Even got my own balcony.

ELLS [15:39]
I can't believe you're moving to the city. What happened to life on the road?

> Apparently all I needed was sea air, decent coffee, and one good reason to stay.

ELLS [15:40]
Well. Welcome to South Havens, rockstar. Can't wait to see how long you last without setting off the fire alarm 😂

> Challenge accepted.

I pocket my phone, a grin still tugging at my mouth.

The momentum doesn't just feel good.

It feels right.

The apartment came together faster than I expected.

The moment we left the viewing and spoke to the boys—we called the agent. There was already a queue of interest. Young professionals, a newlywed couple, some influencer who just wanted the balcony for content.

But Luca worked his magic, all charm and compliments. And within forty-eight hours, the place was ours.

From that point on, it's been non-stop. Total chaos. But somehow —it's the good kind.

And now? I'm standing in the middle of our new living room, coffee in hand, watching Ryder crash through the door with his suitcase and Theo puffing behind him, hauling a bean bag he apparently refused to part with.

"Whose idea was it to fetch a bloody bean bag the size of a Mini Cooper?" Ryder huffs, helping Theo wrestle it through the door in a true *Pivot* moment.

"It has sentimental value," Theo calls back, now dragging a laundry basket filled entirely with snacks, a lava lamp, and three tangled phone chargers. "Also, it moulds to my stress."

"What moulds to my stress," Luca mutters from the kitchen, "is the idea of moving into an apartment with three grown-ass men and watching it turn into a teenage boy's fever dream in under forty minutes."

I lean against the island, coffee still in hand, grinning as the chaos explodes around me.

The place is already losing its minimalist edge. Bags kicked halfway into rooms, empty takeaway boxes stacking by the sink, someone testing the Bluetooth speaker with an aggressively bad playlist.

"I swear I labelled everything," Ryder groans. "Why do I have three blenders?!"

"A man can never have too many blenders," Theo says, dropping the bean bag in the middle of the living room like he's placing a crown jewel. "This spot gets the most sun. It's mine now."

"It's a bean bag, not a sun lounger."

"You can pry it from my cold, Wotsit stained hands."

Ryder opens another box, pausing before holding up a blackened chunk of something vaguely metallic. "What the hell is this?"

Theo squints. "Oh. That's my toaster."

Ryder looks horrified. "Why does it look like it survived a war?"

Theo shrugs, completely unbothered. "I'm not saying I meant to light it on fire. But here we are."

I lean against the counter, grinning as Ryder mutters something about insurance premiums and spontaneous combustion.

Luca finally gives up trying to maintain any order and slouches onto the sofa with a resigned sigh. "Just don't spill anything on the rugs. Or the fridge. Or literally anything I might have to clean."

Ryder flicks on the espresso machine with a triumphant flourish. "See, this is why we moved in together. Domestic bliss."

"And," Theo adds, pointing a solemn finger at me, "a lovesick frontman who may or may not have orchestrated this entire relocation as part of an emotionally charged long game."

I raise a brow, deadpan. "That's slander."

"It's correct," Luca says without even opening his eyes.

I shake my head, a smile tugging at my mouth. "You're lucky I like you lot."

"We know," Ryder grins, already unpacking a keyboard with the delicacy of a brain surgeon.

The banter continues, filling the space like music.

Eventually, I slip away from the noise, heading down the hall to the room I quietly claimed after the viewing.

It's not the biggest, but it's bright, angled ceilings and a wide skylight that throws sunlight in soft streaks across the floorboards.

My guitar case leans in the corner. A stack of lyric notebooks sits beside the bed.

I drop onto the edge of the mattress and exhale, letting the hum of laughter and low music drift through the cracked door. I lie back on the bed, arms folded behind my head, staring up through the skylight.

The light's fading fast, dipping toward dusk, and the glass curves the sky into a soft blue frame overhead.

For years, life's been loud. Gigs, flights, hotel check-ins at 3 a.m. The constant churn of motion. Barely a breath between soundcheck and the next city.

And I loved it. Still do.

But somewhere along the line, I started craving something else. Not to leave the road behind. But to have somewhere to come back to.

I sit up and drift back into the living room.

Luca's sprawled on the sofa with a book balanced across his chest, eyes closed, but definitely still listening. Ryder's curled into the corner chair like a human marshmallow. Theo's fully nested in the bean bag, head tipped back, half-snoring already.

It's not clean. It's not quiet. But it's ours.

A place to crash. To write. To breathe. To escape to when the road gets too loud.

I take a slow sip of my coffee and look around at the boxes and bags, the half-hung coat hooks, the IKEA tools Theo's definitely been using wrong.

No screaming fans. No deadlines. No tour bus humming through the night.

I don't feel like I'm chasing something anymore.

I feel like I've landed.

CHAPTER 27

when the mask slipped

ELLIE

It's only been a week since we left Rosemere, but it already feels like a lifetime ago. I should feel grateful. Safe. Like I'm home.

But sometimes I still catch myself standing in the hallway of Naomi's flat, waiting for the sound of a car pulling into the drive, or for the weight of something I can't quite name to press in around my chest.

If this is home, it's not the kind I recognise yet.

A few days ago, I went back to the house. Just long enough to grab some clothes for Mia, her schoolbooks, the soft blanket she refuses to sleep without.

And thankfully, David wasn't there. Because I'm not ready for that conversation. Not yet.

I haven't even found the courage to text my parents. I know I should at least let them know where we are. But every time I try, the words catch. I can already hear their voices in my head. Heavy with disappointment masked as concern.

I don't have the strength for that. Not now.

And... I miss Kieran. His presence anyway.

The quiet way he listened. The way he made space for me, demanding nothing in return.

I still can't believe he's here. In South Havens. Just a short drive away. Part of me wants to see him. More than I want to admit. But I also don't want to be the girl who runs from one mess straight into someone else's arms.

He deserves more than that. I deserve more than that.

I'm happy for him. And the band. Really, I am. They've got this new place, new momentum, new beginnings.

But I'm still here. Trying to remember how to start over.

Somehow, Naomi's flat already smells like home. If I let myself believe it. Vanilla candles. Leftover takeaway. Her signature expensive shampoo that makes the whole bathroom smell like an overpriced spa.

Mia's treating it like an extended sleepover. Her stuff is scattered between the spare room and the living room floor. Her school blazer is draped over the back of Naomi's armchair like she owns the place.

She doesn't ask too many questions anymore. I think she knows I don't really have the answers yet.

As for me. I'm still adjusting.

The days are falling into rhythm. Sort of. I make breakfast. Pack Mia's lunch. Drive her to school. Come back and open my laptop like I'm about to find a new life tucked inside my inbox.

But there's nothing.

I stare at job listings and half-formed applications. Rewrite my CV. Save files I never submit.

All the while, the clock keeps ticking. I'm getting by for now. Scraping through with the café shifts and the savings I kept tucked away in a separate account David never had access to—*thank God*. It's not much, but it's enough to buy me a few weeks. Maybe a month, if I'm careful.

If nothing comes through before then, I'll have to suck it up and take a rotational at the hospital with Naomi. Hospital wards aren't for me. I know where I want to be, where I belong, but I might not get the luxury of being able to make that decision.

Naomi's been incredible, though. She just hands me a glass of wine at the end of the day and lets me talk when I need to and stay silent when I don't.

She's always been like that. Loud and chaotic on the surface. Soft and steady underneath. I don't know what I'd do without her.

I wish I could say things have been quiet. That I've had the space to breathe. To think. But my phone tells a different story. David's messages are still coming. Shorter now. Sharper. No more apologies. Just demands.

You can't ignore me forever.

We need to talk.

You're being dramatic.

Each one twists deeper under my skin, and I haven't responded to any of them. But my fingers hover over the screen every time. Like some part of me still expects him to change.

He won't. I know that.

But it doesn't feel over.

Not yet.

It's late by the time the flat finally settles into quiet. Naomi's at work and Mia is down the corridor, humming under her breath, half-ignoring her homework.

I'd offered to help. She'd rolled her eyes and told me I'd ruin her flow. Which, to be fair, might not be entirely wrong. The last time I tried to help with Year 9 maths, we both nearly cried and one of us swore at a fraction.

(It was me. I swore at a fraction.)

So now I leave her to it and pretend I'm not mildly traumatised by simultaneous equations.

I'm curled up on Naomi's saggy old sofa, blanket over my knees, *Titanic* playing in the background even though I've seen it a thousand times. And yes, I'm still furious they let Leo freeze when there was plenty of room on that fucking door.

It's one of those rare moments where everything feels... still. Almost normal.

There's a soft knock at the door. I pause the movie and sit up straighter, glancing toward the hallway.

Maybe it's Mrs. Norris looking for her cat again. Poor thing had a habit of hiding behind the plant pot by the old lift. I'd helped her find him twice this week already.

I smile faintly, shove the blanket off my legs, and pad across the living room barefoot.

I don't even look through the peephole. Just unhook the latch and pull the door open.

And there he is.

Standing in the hallway like he owns it.

Tailored coat. Polished arrogance. The weight of old habits settling into the air between us.

My body reacts before my mind can catch up. Cold in my stomach. A spike of nausea behind my ribs.

I move to shut the door immediately. I don't even want to talk to him right now. He stops it with his foot. "Ellie," he says smoothly.

And before I can think, before I can even breathe, he pushes it open and steps inside. "Don't you think it's about time you came home, sweetheart?"

His voice is calm. Measured. That careful tone he always uses when he wants to sound rational. Reasonable. The tone designed to make me question myself.

I step back automatically, instinct tightening every muscle in my body. "I'm not coming back, David. It's over."

He smiles. But it doesn't reach his eyes. "Come on, Ellie. Let's not make this harder than it needs to be."

My hand curls into the hem of my jumper. I take a breath, sharp and steady. "How did you even know I was here?"

He laughs. "It wasn't hard. I don't know why I didn't check here sooner. Naomi's place was the obvious choice, wasn't it? You two are stupidly inseparable. Didn't you think I'd figure it out eventually?"

That chill slips lower down my spine.

I glance past him. To the door, the window, the phone, scanning without even meaning to. Calculating.

"You've made your point," he says, stepping further into the flat like he owns it. "I gave you space. But dragging this out. It's childish, Ellie."

"I'm not dragging anything out," I say. My voice is tight. But steady. "I'm protecting myself. And Mia."

"She doesn't need protecting from me!" he snaps.

And that's when I smell it. Whiskey. Thin and sour, clinging to the edges of his breath.

My pulse kicks up hard. The wall behind me kisses my shoulder without me even realising I've moved.

His smile stays fixed. But it's different now. Sharp around the edges.

"You don't get to play the victim here," he says, his voice lowering. "I made mistakes. I admitted that. But this?" He gestures to the room, to the space between us. "Running away. Hiding in someone else's flat like some martyr. It's not noble, Ellie. It's *pathetic*."

My throat tightens. But I stand my ground. "I left because you lied. You cheated, David. You gambled away everything we built. What else was I supposed to do? Stay and keep pretending it was fine?"

His jaw ticks. "I said I was going to fix it... I told you I'd sort everything out. But no, you couldn't even give me that chance, could you?"

He steps closer. I don't flinch. But inside, my whole body is vibrating.

High alert. Every instinct screaming.

"You had to go crying to your friends and drag Mia into it," he says through gritted teeth. "You don't get to paint me as the villain just because you got scared."

"I didn't get scared," I force the words out. "I got tired, David. Tired of being lied to. Tired of being managed. Tired of being made to feel like it was my fault every time I asked you to be honest."

"You're twisting this," he snarls.

"No." I lift my chin. "I'm finally seeing it."

And then the mask slips. For a breath, a heartbeat, he looks almost startled.

And then...

The rage floods in. It happens fast.
Too fast.
Before I can even react, he lunges. Fingers clamping around my wrist, yanking me off balance, and slamming me back into the wall. The impact rattles up my spine, knocking the breath from my lungs.

I gasp, sharp and instinctive, my heart spiking into my throat.

My free hand flies up, shoving hard against his chest, but it's like trying to move a brick wall. His body cages mine against the plaster, the heat of his anger pressing down on me.

He looms over me, wild and furious, his eyes blown wide, pupils swallowing the colour.

"You *do* this," he spits, voice low and vicious, "you push and push until everything breaks."

"David," I rasp, struggling against his iron grip, panic clawing up my throat. "Stop."

But he doesn't stop. He leans in closer, a mockery of intimacy, squeezing harder just to show he can. Just to show I can't stop him.

"You always make things harder than they need to be," he growls, his fingers grinding into bone.

As he speaks, he shoves in closer, chest crushing against mine, forcing me back harder against the wall until it feels like the air is being squeezed from my lungs.

"You think you can do this without me?" he spits, his breath hot against my cheek. "You'd be nothing if I hadn't stepped in. Nothing without me dragging you through."

His words hit harder than his grip. Each one sharp. Precise. Designed to wound.

"I gave you everything," he sneers. "And this is how you repay me? Playing the victim? Pretending you don't need me when you never made it through a single day on your own."

My heart slams against my ribs, but I keep my mouth shut.

Because I know how this game works. He talks, he digs, he twists.

There's no space left between us. No room to move, no room to breathe.

Inside, something cracks. Not fear. Not submission. Something colder. Clearer. A knowing. Because he's wrong. I'm still standing. And I won't let him tear me down just to feel taller.

"David." My voice breaks, shatters, but somehow it doesn't waver. I meet his eyes, even as tears blur mine. "Let. Go."

A long, brutal beat. His grip holds steady, digging in, the threat unspoken but heavy in the air between us.

"Let. Go." I say again. Firmer this time.

And then finally.

He lets go.

Not gently. Not apologetically. He throws my wrist aside like something dirty, something used up.

I stumble back, clutching the aching joint to my chest, fighting to stay upright as the wall lurches sideways around me.

David just stands there, chest heaving, jaw set, like he's the one who's been wronged.

And in that breathless, broken space between his fingers falling away and the ache blooming in my wrist. I know.

This is the line. The one I can't uncross. All the lies. The gaslighting. The apologies soaked in guilt.

I spent years trying to hold it together. Trying to understand him. But this? There's no fixing this. Whatever thread was left between us —it snaps clean and final. And just like that, I was done listening.

He stares at me, hands trembling, chest rising and falling in short, sharp breaths. "I didn't mean…"

"Get out," I say. Stronger this time.

His mouth opens again, but I don't care. I turn, yank the door wide with shaking fingers, and stare him down with everything I have left.

"*Now!*"

For a second, he doesn't move.

Then he storms past me without another word, the scent of whiskey trailing behind like a warning.

The door slams shut behind him.

And just like that. He's gone.

I stand frozen, back against the cold plaster, legs folding beneath me like they don't know how to hold me anymore. My wrist throbs in time with my heartbeat, sharp and rhythmic, and my shoulder screams where it had hit the wall.

All those years, he never laid a hand on me. Not like that. It was always words. Calculated silences. Manipulation. Guilt wrapped in apology. Gaslight laced with charm.

But this? This was something else.

And now I'm sitting on the floor in my best friend's flat, heart still racing, with the evidence of him etched into my skin.

The soft scuff of bare feet breaks the quiet.

My head snaps up.

Mia stands at the edge of the hallway, framed by the glow from the bedroom light. She's clutching the edge of the kitchen counter, her sleeve slipping down her arm, curls a wild, messy halo around her face. Her eyes are wide. Too wide.

"Mum?" she says, small and unsure.

Oh God.

I scrub at my face with the sleeve of my jumper, realising too late that my cheeks are wet. I don't even remember crying.

"Bug..." My voice breaks. I clear my throat and try again, gentler. "It's okay, sweetheart. I'm okay."

She inches forward, glancing at the door, then back to me. "Was someone here?"

I nod once. "Just a visitor," I say. "It's alright now."

She doesn't look convinced. But she comes to me anyway. Slow, cautious steps. Like she's approaching something fragile.

When she reaches me, she sinks down beside me without a word. Her body presses into my side, small, warm and trembling just a little.

I wrap my good arm around her, pull her in, and kiss the crown of her head. She burrows in closer.

For a long moment, we just sit there. Then, her voice, barely above a whisper. "Did he hurt you?"

If I wasn't already broken, that one sentence would have shattered me.

I squeeze my eyes shut. Press another kiss to her hair. "I'm okay, baby. It was just... an argument."

A lie wrapped in a softer truth.

She nods against me. Still too young to know when not to believe me.

She asks no more questions. Just stays curled into my side, as if her body knows better than her mind how much I need this.

Eventually, Mia's breathing slows, heavy and even against my side.

I untangle myself carefully, easing her upright. "Come on," I whisper, brushing the hair from her face. "Let's get you to bed."

She nods sleepily, letting me guide her down the hall, her fingers clutching the hem of my jumper like she's afraid I might disappear if she lets go. In her room, she climbs into bed without protest. No complaints, no stubborn bargaining, just a quiet compliance that squeezes something deep and aching in my chest.

I tuck the blanket up around her shoulders, smoothing her curls back from her forehead. She blinks up at me, half-lidded, something raw flickering in her eyes. Something far too old for her years.

"I love you, Mum," she murmurs.

My throat tightens painfully. "I love you too," I whisper back, kissing the soft skin of her forehead. "Always."

I sit beside her until her breathing evens out completely, until the furrow in her brow finally smooths, until she drifts away to somewhere softer than this night deserves. When I finally leave her room, I close the door with a soft click and lean against it for a moment, trying to catch my breath.

The flat feels colder now. Empty and full all at once.

I drift back into the kitchen on autopilot, filling a glass of water from the tap. I stand there a while, staring out the window at the darkness pressing against the glass. My reflection stares back, hollow-eyed, tension in every line of her body. A ghost of a girl trying to remember how to be solid again.

I take a slow sip, one hand braced against the counter like it might hold me upright.

I don't know how long I stand there. Long enough that the rest of the world seems to fade, swallowed by the quiet hum of the fridge, the soft creak of the pipes.

I walk back into the living room and the TV's given up entirely, frozen on Netflix's passive-aggressive little box of judgement.

Are you still watching?

A stupid question. Because if I was, I'd be watching. Not standing here, questioning my life choices while a faceless algorithm throws shade.

Even streaming services know I'm spiralling.

My wrist throbs—a dull, pulsing ache beneath the surface. I cradle it in my lap, pulling the sleeve of my jumper back to take a proper look. Skin flushed, slightly swollen. No obvious deformity, range of movement intact. Likely a mild sprain. Ice, elevation, pain relief, rest. I catalogue it like a checklist, the nurse in me kicking in even as everything else unravels.

I sink into the sofa, wrap the blanket back around my shoulders, and let myself go quiet.

The silence isn't peaceful this time. It's waiting. And when the lock clicks open, I don't startle. I just breathe. The familiar shuffle of boots. The clatter of keys dropped into the bowl. Naomi's voice, tired and dramatic, cutting across the quiet.

"If one more grown man tells me he's scared of needles while bleeding on my crocs," she calls from the hallway, "I swear to fucking God, I'm transferring to a desk job and taking up bird-watching…"

She stops mid-sentence. I don't turn around. I can feel her noticing the sharp shift in the air, the wrongness of the silence.

"Ellie?" Her voice is softer now, threaded with something sharper than exhaustion.

I turn slowly. She's already moving. Crossing the living room in three strides, crouching in front of me, scanning my face like she's cataloguing every crack and fracture.

I open my mouth, but nothing comes out.

Her gaze drops to my wrist, the bruise already starting to darken, and she swears under her breath, low and furious.

"Was he here?" she asks. Her voice is low, steady. Lethal.

I nod. Just once.

Naomi's jaw tightens so hard I can see the muscle jump. She

presses a hand to her mouth, like she's physically restraining herself. "That piece of..." She cuts herself off. Breathes.

Her hands find mine, gentle but unyielding, grounding me. "What did he do?"

I hesitate. Her hands tighten around mine. "Ellie. *Tell* me."

I swallow, voice catching. "He grabbed my wrist." The words feel small, like if I make them tiny enough, they'll hurt less. "It wasn't — he didn't hit me. It was just..."

"Ellie," she says again, fiercer now. "Don't you *dare* try to shrink it."

The tears come again, sudden and hot. I wipe at them uselessly. "I didn't want to scare Mia," I whisper.

Naomi's face softens, her whole body breaking and rebuilding in a heartbeat. "She saw?"

"After," I murmur. "I told her it was an argument."

Naomi doesn't speak right away. She just looks at me and I hate how well she sees through me. Then, softly, "Ellie... has he ever done anything like this before?"

I shake my head without thinking. "No. Never."

She doesn't blink. "Ellie."

I meet her eyes, throat tight. "I promise you, he's never touched me before. He's lashed out before, but he's never hurt me."

There's a pause. Just a beat. But it stretches, heavy and quiet, filled with everything I'm not saying.

Naomi exhales, low and shaky. A sound tangled with too many things to name. Relief. Rage. Heartbreak.

Then she pulls me in without another word. Arms tight, fierce, like she can hold me together by force if she has to. She wraps me up so tight I can feel the hammering of her heart against mine. She holds me like she's trying to stitch me back together by sheer force of will.

"You're safe now," she murmurs fiercely against my hair. "I've got you."

Eventually, Naomi pulls back, just enough to look me in the eye. Her hands stay on my arms, grounding me, like she's afraid I'll float away if she lets go.

"You have to do something about this, Ellie." She says quietly. No drama now. Just certainty. A steady, immovable wall of it.

I lower my gaze, staring at where our hands are still linked, her thumb brushing over my knuckles in a slow, steady rhythm. I can't find my voice. Can't make myself say the words aloud.

I don't even know what I'd say, or who I'd even tell. He grabbed my wrist. He shoved me into a wall. He said it wasn't his fault. Would they even listen? Would they think I was overreacting?

The thoughts spiral fast, a knot of shame and fear tightening in my chest until I can barely breathe.

Naomi's grip tightens. "This is the part," she says softly, "where you stop handling everything on your own."

I nod. Just once. Small and shaky.

Her shoulders loosen a fraction, some of the tension bleeding out of her. She lets go of my hands, rising to her feet, dusting invisible crumbs from her jeans like she's gearing up for battle.

"Right. First things first. Tea, chocolate, and then we make a plan in the morning."

A stunned laugh rattles out of me, half-sob, half-relief. "You're so dramatic."

Naomi grins, already heading for the kitchen. "Damn right. I've been waiting years for my moment to stage a full emotional intervention. Let me have this."

She disappears into the kitchen, clattering around like she's physically beating back the silence.

I stay curled up on the sofa, blanket pulled tight around my shoulders, the weight of the last hour pressing heavy into every bone.

I can hear her muttering to herself as she moves. Something about needing the good tea, not the dust in the box by the microwave, and where the hell did she put the chocolate biscuits.

It's so normal, *so Naomi*, that it anchors me more effectively than any pep talk could have.

When she returns, she's carrying two steaming mugs and a packet of chocolate digestives tucked under one arm like contraband.

She flops down onto the other end of the sofa, shoving a mug toward me with all the gentleness of a bulldozer. "Drink. Sugar is basically medicinal at this point."

I take the mug with both hands, fingers wrapping around the warmth, and sink deeper into the cushions.

Naomi doesn't push. She just sips her own tea, legs tucked under her, hair falling loose over her face. She turns on the TV and watches it idly, some rerun flickering across the screen, acting like this is any other late night.

And somehow—*impossibly*—it helps.

I don't drink the tea right away. Just sit there, breathing it in, letting the normalcy of the moment wrap itself around me.

And for the first time all night, the silence doesn't feel suffocating.

CHAPTER 28

now that i found her

KIERAN

"And that's when Theo tried to bribe a customs officer with a signed drumstick and a bag of Haribo."

Laughter explodes across the room. Ryder nearly chokes on his coffee. Theo raises his hands like he's accepting an award, and Luca just shakes his head like he's aged ten years in that single memory.

"I maintain that he appreciated the gesture," Theo says. "He just didn't understand my vision."

"You tried to pay off a border agent," Luca says flatly, "with *sweets*, Theo."

"It was Haribo Tangfastics, mate. I was offering him the good stuff."

We're midway through recording an episode of Off the Record with Max and Jules, a behind-the-scenes music industry podcast we somehow agreed to appear on. Their living room's resembling a makeshift studio. Mics, wires, pop shields, and those oversized noise-cancelling headphones that make you feel like you're hearing your own thoughts in surround sound.

Max grins behind his mic. "Honestly, this is already my favourite episode. You guys are chaos."

"Controlled chaos," Ryder says proudly, adjusting his mic like he actually knows what he's doing. "We're very professional now. We even have matching mugs."

"Only because I stole them from the last green room," Theo adds with a shrug.

Jules leans forward with a smirk. "Serious question. You've just wrapped your first successful UK tour and taken a step back from the madness. What made you settle in South Havens?"

Luca jumps in first, like he always does. "We needed a break. A proper one. Not three days off where we're still answering emails from a ferry."

"Also," Ryder says, "I was one parking ticket away from snapping and throwing myself into the sea."

I chuckle, but my fingers tap lightly on the arm of my chair. "We just wanted something that felt real again. Less noise. More space to think. Write. Live."

"New music coming?" Jules asks, her notebook half-forgotten in her lap.

"We're not putting pressure on it," Luca says. "Back in the studio in the new year. We'll see where the vibe takes us."

"And until then?" Max raises a brow.

"We breathe," Theo says, for once not joking. "Get our heads straight. Spend time where it matters."

There's a pause, a beat of quiet as the room settles around that sentiment. I feel all three of them glance my way, not overt, but unmistakable. I give the smallest shrug, a smile tugging at the edge of my mouth.

"Alright," Max says, clapping his hands together. "Last question. The big one. We ask every guest."

Jules leans in dramatically. "What's your current personal soundtrack? The song that sums up where you are right now."

Theo groans. "Every bloody time."

"Come on, Kieran," Luca says, sly smile firmly in place. "You go first."

I pause, thinking about lying. About saying something upbeat or cryptic or clever. But the truth catches in my throat, too big to swallow. "*Now That I Found Her*," I say quietly.

Max hums in approval. "Oof. That's deep."

"Yeah," I murmur.

The room falls silent for a moment. Not awkward, just full. Heavy with things that don't need to be said aloud.

And then Ryder, blessedly, dives in with something ridiculous about his current obsession with vintage disco ballads, and the moment passes, laughter filling the air again like we hadn't all just felt the shift.

After we wrap up, pose for the obligatory group photo, and sign the wall in the hallway like some rite of passage, we spill out into the crisp evening air. The city buzzes around us. Horns, voices, the faint thump of a baseline leaking from an open window somewhere up the street.

For a second, I just stand there. Let it sink in. The tour. The move. The plans we'd casually talked about in that living room like they weren't a dream anymore. It feels good. Real. Like something solid underfoot.

Then my phone buzzes. I tug it from my pocket, thumb already halfway to unlock it.

> ELLS [16:44]
> ~~Hey. Something happened.~~

Three words.

But they hit like a sucker punch. My stomach drops. My chest goes tight. The street noise fades under the thrum of blood in my ears.

I stop walking.

"Kieran?" Luca calls from a few steps ahead. I don't answer. Just stare at the screen.

"Everything alright?" Ryder asks, doubling back when he catches the look on my face. I nod slowly, even though nothing about me feels steady. "I don't know yet."

I'm already dialling. The phone rings once. Twice.

"Hey," Ellie answers, her voice soft. Rough around the edges, like she hasn't slept. Like she's holding something in with both hands and it's still threatening to spill.

"What happened?" I ask, sharper than I mean to. "Ellie, are you okay?"

A pause. A breath. I can hear something in the background, Mia's voice maybe, or the clink of a glass? But mostly it's the silence between her words.

"It's nothing, really," she says too quickly. "Just… a terrible night."

My jaw tenses. "Ellie."

"I promise, I'm fine," she says again, gentler this time. "But… would it be okay if I came to see you?"

I don't hesitate. "Yeah. Of course. You want me to come get you?"

"No, it's okay. I'll come to you."

Another beat. A crackle of unspoken things. "Okay," I say, lowering my voice. "I'll be here."

The line goes quiet a moment later, but the weight of her voice stays with me. Heavy. Fragile. Like she's finally run out of ways to pretend.

I look up at the sky—the buildings, the unfamiliar streets I've only just started calling home—then I turn toward the apartment, already moving.

Whatever this is, it isn't nothing. And I'll be damned if I let her convince herself it is.

When I get back, I can't rest.

The apartment is too quiet. Too still. Which is saying something, considering Ryder's installed a blinking neon sign over the coffee machine that reads *CAFFEINATE OR DIE*, and Theo's beanbag still occupies a corner of the living room like some sort of lounge gremlin shrine.

I texted Luca five minutes after Ellie had hung up.

> Need the place to myself for a bit.

LUCA [17:04]
Say no more.

He always knows when not to ask questions.

Now, I'm pacing. Back and forth across the living room, my boots dragging just slightly over the rug, carving an invisible path like I can somehow walk the anxiety out of my chest. I keep glancing at the clock, even though barely five minutes have passed.

The late evening light spills through the windows, turning everything a little washed-out, a little faded. Dust floats in the beams of sunset. The corners of the apartment feel stretched, like the space itself is holding its breath.

I've tidied without thinking. Folded the blanket on the sofa. Moved Theo's shoes out of the hallway. Lit the vanilla candle on the coffee table.

I don't know what she'll need tonight.

But I want her to feel safe. I want her to walk in and feel like she can breathe.

I drag a hand through my hair for what feels like the hundredth time and cross to the window again, checking the street even though I know she'll be buzzing from downstairs, not strolling up like a scene from some old movie.

My hands are clammy. My heart hammers against my ribs, each beat sharp and restless. I don't know exactly what I expected from the phone call. Maybe for her to tell me it was work. A flat tire. A bad day at school pickup. Something manageable. Something small.

But it wasn't the words she said. It was how she said them. Low. Measured. Like someone trying not to set off an alarm inside their own chest.

You don't send a message like *Hey. Something happened* and then brush it off unless you're carrying something too big to name.

And the fact that she wants to come here, to me, tells me everything I need to know.

Whatever it is... she doesn't want to be alone with it.

The buzzer rings. It cuts through the apartment like a blade, slicing straight through the fog in my head.

I freeze for half a second. My hand half-raised. My breath locked somewhere between my lungs and my throat. Then I move. Cross the room in four long strides and press the intercom.

"Ellie?" I say, trying to keep my voice even.

A pause. Then: "Yeah."

I hit the door release, the buzz filling the stillness, and step back. I leave the front door open just enough to lean there and wait.

The hallway is quiet. The hum of the lift climbing floor by floor buzzes in the distance. A soft mechanical sigh as it slows.

Then the doors open. And there she is.

She steps out like she's not entirely sure she belongs in her own body. That damn cardigan wrapped around her like a blanket, sleeves pulled over her hands, head bowed like she's bracing against a wind that hasn't quite arrived yet.

Her eyes shift, and something catches in them, like a thread pulled loose. The tight line of her shoulders falters. A breath leaves her, soft and unguarded, and in that moment, I see it. The weight she's been carrying. The way she sags with the quiet recognition of me.

"Hey, you." I say softly.

"Hey," she echoes, barely more than a breath.

She exhales slowly, like she's been holding her breath the whole way over. I step back and open the door wider without a word. She brushes past me, close enough that her sleeve catches my arm. Just the smallest touch, and yet I feel it everywhere.

She pauses just inside the hallway. Like she isn't sure if the walls will welcome her or trap her.

Her shoulders dip slightly. A breath, not a release.

"You want a drink?" I ask, already halfway toward the kitchen because standing still feels unbearable.

She shakes her head. "No. I just… I just want to sit, if that's okay?"

"Of course," I say, motioning toward the sofa.

She crosses the room slowly, every movement cautious, and curls into the cushions like she's trying to make herself small. Cardigan sleeves pulled farther over her hands. Knees tucked up. Her gaze fixed somewhere I can't follow.

I sit beside her. Not too close. Close enough.

I don't touch her. I don't fill the silence with words. I just stay steady, an anchor if she needs one.

And then, after a long moment where the only sound is the soft hum of the city beyond the windows, she speaks.

Her voice is so quiet, I almost miss it.

"He came to Naomi's flat."

The words slice through the stillness like a blade. My whole body goes taut. But I don't move. Don't speak. I force myself to stay still, to stay soft, even as every instinct inside me sharpens to a knife's edge.

She doesn't look at me. Just keeps staring straight ahead, her voice small and clinical, like she's reading a weather report instead of recounting something that split her wide open.

"He just... walked in. Like nothing had changed. Like he still had the right to."

I clench my hands into fists against my knees, trying to bleed the fury out through my knuckles without making a sound.

She speaks in fragments after that. Hesitant. Halting. Telling me about the way he acted, like she owed him a conversation. How he forced his way inside. The twisting guilt he tried to wrap around her like a net. And then...

"He grabbed me."

The words wreck me.

She says it like it doesn't matter. Like she needs to flatten it down before it flattens her. But her fingers curl tighter into the sleeves of her cardigan, pulling them up to her knuckles.

"Pushed me," she says again, softer this time, like saying it smaller will make it hurt less.

I stay exactly where I am. Still. Anchored. Because if I move, I'm not sure I'll be able to hold the anger back.

She tells me Mia came out afterward. That she saw enough to ask if he hurt her.

And Ellie. *God, Ellie.* She lied. Told her no. Because that's who she is. The one who protects everyone else, even if it leaves her bleeding.

When she finishes, the silence between us is so heavy it feels like another person in the room.

I let it stretch. Let her have it. Let her feel whatever she needs to without pushing her.

Then, voice low and careful, I say, "Can I see?"

She hesitates, and for a second, I think she might pull back. Retreat. Fold herself smaller. But then she extends her arm toward me.

I reach out, just as slowly. Take the edge of her sleeve between my fingers and ease it back.

The bruise blooms across her wrist, dark and swollen, the skin mottled with purples and sickly yellow. It clings to her like something branded, fingers etched in flesh, a mark he left behind without asking. A signature she never gave permission for.

It stops me cold.

A flush of heat surges through me, sharp and instant, like a match to dry leaves. My chest locks tight, breath snagging behind my ribs, and for a second, I swear they might crack from the strain.

I lower the sleeve gently, like the bruise might shatter under my touch. My hands retreat to my lap, useless, trembling with something that wants to be violence. I flex my fingers to keep from clenching them into fists. But I can't give in to that. Not here. Not now. Not when she's beside me, too quiet, too still.. What she needs isn't rage. It's safety. And right now, that means staying still, even when everything in me wants to burn.

"I don't…" I try again, my voice rougher now, ragged with helplessness. "I don't know what I'm supposed to say right now, baby."

She doesn't respond. Just watches me like she's waiting for something to crack.

And God, I want to fix it. I want to take the pain out of her hands and carry it myself. But I can't, not unless she lets me.

"But this isn't okay," I say, more firmly now. "What he did, what he's still doing, it's not okay, Ellie. You know that right? And you don't need to minimise it. Not to me. Not to yourself. This isn't just some heated argument. It's not normal. It's not something you deserved."

She looks away, her lips pressed into a tight line, her fingers curling inwards like she's trying to disappear.

So, I shift closer. I cup her face gently, guiding her to look at me. Her eyes are glassy, brimming with tears that haven't yet fallen.

"You don't have to carry this alone," I tell her. "You didn't do anything wrong. You don't have to keep making excuses for his choices. You don't have to keep hiding."

She swallows hard. Her voice trembles. "I just... I needed to be near you. You make it stop. You make it quiet, Kieran. You make all the bad stuff just... go away."

My breath catches. Because I get it. I've felt it too. That pull toward someone who makes the noise die down. And hearing it from her, it unravels me.

I press my forehead to hers, gently, and stay there. Not kissing her. Not touching beyond the anchor of her face in my hands. Just being here.

"I hope you know how proud I am of you," I whisper.

She draws back slightly, like she didn't expect that. Like those words land heavier than anything else I've said.

"I mean it," I add, voice thick. "You could've buried this. You could've smiled through it and let it eat you alive. But you didn't. You came here. You let me in. You let someone see it."

Her eyes shimmer. Her lips part like she might speak, but the words don't come.

"You're the strongest person I know," I say. "And I hate that you had to be."

She exhales shakily. One tear slides down her cheek, and I catch it with my thumb, brushing it gently away.

"I know you're scared," I murmur. "I know this feels broken. But you're not doing this alone. You haven't been for a long time. I hope you see that."

She doesn't respond. Doesn't need to. Because she leans into me. Just enough. And I hold her there for as long as she needs.

She stays curled into me long after the words have dried up, tucked beneath my arm, her fingers lightly curled in the fabric of my hoodie. The way someone holds on when they're not ready to let go entirely, but they're trying to believe they can.

My thumb brushes over her shoulder in slow, steady strokes,

anchoring her to the here and now. Every few seconds, she exhales like she's releasing something she's been holding for far too long. Her whole body feels different now. Less rigid. Less guarded. Not unbroken, but beginning to settle.

The bruise is still there, hidden just beneath the fabric, but it doesn't own this moment. Not now. Not with her head on my shoulder and the quiet steadiness of her breathing against my side. What matters is that she came. That she told me. That she let herself rest.

I tilt my head and let my chin settle into her hair, the soft scent of lavender wrapping around me, anchoring me like a lifeline I didn't know I needed. It's not the easy kind of closeness we've shared before. There's no teasing, no warmth laced with laughter. This is quieter. Heavier. Real in a way that leaves no room for anything but truth.

This is what it means to be someone's safe place. And maybe that's all I need to be for her right now. Not the one who fights. Not the one who fixes.

Just the one who stays. And for as long as she needs somewhere to land, I'll be right here. And I'm not going anywhere.

CHAPTER 29

a line in the sand

ELLIE

Rain taps a slow rhythm against the kitchen window, soft and steady like a warning. The sky's that dull grey that settles low and heavy, pressing against the rooftops. Inside, the toaster clicks, the kettle hums, and Mia's voice cuts through the quiet like it always does. Sharp, dramatic, and too awake for a Monday morning.

"I swear my maths teacher has it out for me. Three pop quizzes in one week? That's not education, that's psychological warfare."

I slide a breakfast bar into her rucksack, zip it shut, and hand her a waterproof jacket. "Please wear it, they serve a purpose, Mia."

"I make no promises."

A car horn bleats outside. I cross to the window and nudge the curtain aside with the back of my hand. Callum's car idles at the curb, wipers sweeping in lazy arcs.

He came.

I'd called him over the weekend, just to ask if he could help now and then, maybe take Mia to school once or twice. I wasn't expecting much. A vague excuse, maybe. But he hadn't hesitated. No drama, no edge. Just *"Yeah, of course."*

And now here he is. On time, no less. There's a first for everything.

We've come a long way since we were teenagers, mostly in separate directions. Even so, it's something.

"You sure you've got everything?"

"Lunch, P.E kit, looming sense of academic doom. Yep."

I open the door, and the chill hits. Cold, damp, and tinged with the smell of wet tarmac and leaf mulch. I press a kiss to her cheek, pulling her close for just a moment. "Be good."

She rolls her eyes but gives me a quick squeeze. "You too, weirdo."

I watch her jog down the path and climb into the car without looking back. One last wave, and then they're gone, swallowed by mist and rain.

The door clicks shut behind me, and then silence settles around the flat.

I drift through the kitchen, mug in hand. I keep finding myself in mindless motion, like if I keep walking between the sofa, the sink and the hallway mirror, I won't have to face the truth sitting at the bottom of my gut.

My wrist still aches beneath the sleeve of my jumper. The bruise has bloomed into something dark and sickening. I took a photo of it that night. Two, actually.

I don't know why I did it. But in some ways, I do. Because somewhere deep down—beneath the doubts—something is shifting. And I'm tired of waiting for him to twist things until they sound like my fault.

I turn away from the window, my mind already made up. I'm not going to file a complaint or press charges. Not yet. But I want to know where I stand.

I grab my car keys from the bowl by the door, shrug on my jacket, and move before I can change my mind. The flat feels too small, like the walls are pressing in, urging me out. I lock the door behind me with shaking hands, the cold metal biting into my palm, and make my way to the car.

The station sits at the end of a long, narrow stretch near the town centre, hunched between a solicitor's office and a row of council buildings. Rain comes down in thick sheets, blurring the world outside into smudges of grey and shadow.

I sit in the car longer than I mean to. Engine off. Doors locked. The heater hums against the cold, but it doesn't take the edge off. Rain drums hard against the windscreen, loud and relentless, distorting the building ahead until it looks like it's sinking underwater.

I've made it this far. Dressed. Parked. Present. But still, my hands won't let go of the steering wheel. Fingers clenched, knuckles white, like letting go might unravel everything I've held together.

What if I'm making this bigger than it was?

What if they think I'm wasting their time?

I swallow hard, shake my head, and force myself to move. One hand unclenches. Then the other. I gather my bag, phone already tucked into the outer pocket, with the photos queued and ready.

Inside, the waiting area is harsh and sterile. The receptionist doesn't glance up as I approach, her eyes fixed on the glowing screen in front of her. Her fingers tap the keyboard in a slow, mechanical rhythm, like she's been doing it for hours. Across the room, someone flips through a battered magazine, pages turning with a sound too loud for the quiet. But all I can hear is the steady tick, tick, tick of the wall-mounted clock behind the desk, and beneath it, my heart pounding in my ears.

The receptionist is polite. She doesn't ask questions. Just takes my name and tells me to wait.

So, I do.

Until a uniformed officer appears from the hallway and calls my name.

I stand and follow her down a narrow corridor that smells faintly of disinfectant. The carpet is thin and worn, the lights above flickering just enough to make my eyes ache. She leads me into a small interview room. Beige walls, no windows, and a table that looks like it was dragged in from a storage closet. In the centre sits a lone box of tissues, perfectly placed, like an afterthought dressed up as comfort.

The officer closes the door behind me with a soft click and

gestures to a chair. She looks as though she's in her late thirties, her blonde hair pulled back into a clean, no-nonsense ponytail, uniform pressed. There's something composed about her. Practiced, but not cold.

"Thanks for coming in," she says, sliding into the seat opposite me. Her tone is clipped, but not unfriendly. She pulls a notepad from a leather folder and clicks a pen into readiness. "My name's Officer Palmer. I understand you'd like to speak to someone about an incident?"

"Yes." My voice comes out smaller than I want it to.

She nods, not impatiently, just waiting. I fumble with the strap of my bag, then dig out my phone and set it on the table.

"I'm not here to file a complaint," I blurt. "Not… formally. I don't want to press charges. I just…" I glance down at my hands, then force myself to meet her gaze. "I need to know what my options are. What I'm allowed to do."

Palmer watches me for a moment, then gives a slow nod. "Alright. Why don't you tell me what happened?"

So, I do.

Quietly. Carefully. Every detail I can manage.

I tell her about the messages. About him showing up uninvited. The way he pushed into the flat. How he grabbed me. I tell her Mia was there. That she saw the aftermath. That I told her it was nothing because I didn't know what else to say.

But once the words start, they don't stop.

I tell her about the other things. The parts that don't leave bruises. How he used to gaslight me so I'd end up apologising for things I hadn't done. How he'd disappear for nights on end, only to come back with excuses that didn't quite add up. But if I questioned them, I was the paranoid one. How he'd build me up in front of others, only to tear me down behind closed doors.

"It's always been words. Quiet manipulation I thought I was imagining. He made me believe I was imagining it, anyway. That I was paranoid. But… he's never…" I add. "It's the first time he's ever put his hands on me."

Palmer doesn't interrupt. She just listens. Occasionally writes something down. But mostly, she just holds the space.

When I'm done, there's a long silence.

She leans back, fingers still curled around her pen. "I'm really sorry you went through that."

I blink, throat tight. I wasn't expecting kindness. Not like that.

"But just so you're aware." Her tone shifts, softer, but laced with the weight of policy. "Under current legislation, harassment is only a criminal offence if it's repeated behaviour. Two or more incidents. And unless a formal threat was made, or there's ongoing contact."

My chest tightens. "So, because this was the first time he—"

"I'm not saying it doesn't matter," she cuts in, lifting a hand. "It does. But in the eyes of the law, we're limited in how we define certain types of abuse. Especially when it's emotional or psychological."

She taps her pen against her notepad. "Even with the bruising… it's not that we don't take it seriously. It's that one incident doesn't meet the threshold for criminal harassment."

My pulse spikes. "You're telling me nothing can be done unless he comes back and does it again?"

Palmer's expression tightens, just slightly. The professional mask flickers. "I understand how frustrating that sounds."

"No," I say, sharper than I mean to. "You don't. I came here because I was scared. Because I thought speaking out was the right thing to do. I shouldn't have to bleed for it to count."

A silence stretches between us.

I drop my eyes, staring at the edge of Palmer's notepad. There's a smudge of blue ink near the corner where her thumb must've rubbed against the paper. It's small. Unremarkable. But I can't stop looking at it. Something about the messiness of it grounds me.

Palmer exhales. Then, she puts the pen down beside the smudge.

"You're right," she says, quieter now. "The system isn't always good at recognising control. Or fear. Not until it escalates. We should be better. But we work within the definitions we've been given."

Something inside me sinks.

Palmer leans forward, elbows resting on the table. "But you are not powerless, Ellie. There are things we can do. Things that build a record. That give you something to stand on if it ever happens again."

I meet her eyes. There's something different there now. Not pity. Not distance.

Just honesty.

"What can I do?" I ask, my voice tight but steady.

"You can file a report," she says. "It won't launch an investigation, and he won't be notified at this stage. But it creates a paper trail. If he contacts you again, or if he turns up, we'll already have context. You won't be starting from zero."

She picks up her pen again, but her voice stays gentle. "It's not always about what we can do today. Sometimes, it's about what we'll have in place tomorrow."

The words land hard in my chest. Real. Solid. Like a rope I didn't know I needed to hold on to.

I nod. "Okay," I say. "Let's do that."

Palmer finishes logging the last note from my report, her fingers tapping on the keyboard as the low hum of the station fills the space between us.

I could leave now. I've done what I came to do. But still, I sit there, my hands curled tight in my lap, the words pressing against the back of my teeth.

I shift in my seat. "There's something else."

Palmer looks up, her gaze steady. "Of course."

I wet my lips, nerves buzzing just beneath my skin. "We own the house together. David and I. We're not married, but both our names are on the mortgage." My voice tightens around the words. "When I left, I took Mia. We've been staying with my friend. But we can't stay there forever. I want to go home. But I don't know if I can."

Palmer sets down her pen, giving me her full attention. "You have every right to return," she says. "If your name is on the mortgage, he can't prevent you. And unless there's a court order barring access, which there isn't, you're entitled to be there."

I nod slowly, but it doesn't loosen the knot twisting tighter in my chest.

"But he has the same rights," I murmur. "Doesn't he?"

Her pause is small but telling. "Yes," she says. "He does. You're both co-owners."

I press my hands harder into my thighs to keep them from shaking. "So if I move back in... and he shows up?"

"You can ask him not to," she says. "And if he refuses, or if he causes any kind of disturbance, you document everything. If you feel unsafe, you call us. That would constitute a breach of the peace."

"But that's only if it gets worse," I whisper. "Only after he's already there."

Palmer's mouth presses into a thin line. "I know it's not enough. I know it feels like you're being asked to carry all the risk. But you're not powerless, Ellie."

I lift my head, and she leans forward, her voice low but steady. "What I suggest is this. You get a message to him in writing. Calm, clear, and factual. Tell him you intend to return to the house. That you've spoken to the police. That you do not want him to return, given the circumstances. Make it official."

I hesitate, the thought of reaching out to him turning my stomach. "And if he ignores it?"

"Then you've built your foundation," she says. "Every message. Every ignored boundary. Every incident. You're creating a record. You're making it harder for him to pretend this is something it's not."

I sit there a moment longer, absorbing her words. The heaviness in my chest hasn't gone. But beneath it, there's a flicker of something else. Resolve.

I nod. "Okay," I say quietly.

Palmer offers a small, tired smile. "One step at a time."

The station doors hiss shut behind me, and I step out into the grey afternoon. The air is sharp and damp. It's stopped raining now, but the air still carries that metallic bite. I pull my jacket around myself and pause for a second at the top of the steps, my breath misting in front of me.

For a moment, I just stand there. Letting the sounds of the town wrap around me. Car tyres hissing on wet tarmac, the distant rumble of a bus, a child's laugh from somewhere unseen. The world feels both too big and too small all at once. Like I could disappear into it if I'm not careful.

I reach into my bag, my fingers brushing the folded leaflet Palmer gave me. The resources, the numbers, the small practicalities of safety printed in neat bullet points. The paperwork tucked beneath it. Proof that today wasn't all in my head. Proof that I was seen.

It doesn't fix everything. But it's something. It's a beginning.

I square my shoulders against the chill and head toward the car, my boots splashing through shallow puddles along the kerb. The key fob is cold in my hand as I unlock the door and slide into the driver's seat—the familiar smell of the heater kicking in as I turn the engine on.

I sit for a minute, my hands resting on the steering wheel, the silence pressing in close. My heart's still thudding, but it's not panic anymore. It's the leftover adrenaline of having stood my ground.

I went. I spoke. I didn't let myself back down.

The clouds above are still thick when I pull away from the kerb, but the sun is trying to break through. Soft light nudging through in pale streaks, turning puddles into scattered reflections of gold and grey. I drive through town with the radio low, more static than song, a quiet hum beneath the gentle swish of tyres on wet roads. The streets blur past, familiar, but off-kilter. Like I'm seeing them through someone else's memory.

By the time I reach Naomi's flat, my body feels like it's been hollowed out and refilled with something sharp and unfamiliar. Not fear. Not even anger. Just certainty.

I park outside, kill the engine, and gather my things. My bag, the paperwork tucked inside, my keys clutched tight in my palm. Each small movement feels deliberate. Like laying down stepping stones across a river.

I climb the stairs, one hand trailing the worn railing, the other still gripping my keys like a tether. When I reach the landing, I pause for a moment outside the door to the flat. The lights inside glow through the frosted glass. Home. At least for now.

I take a breath, unlocking the door and pushing it open with my shoulder.

Naomi doesn't even blink when I walk in. She's curled on the sofa, wrapped in a blanket, a half-finished glass of wine perched on the armrest beside her. She lifts an eyebrow in greeting, then holds up the bottle with a silent offer.

I nod. A small, tired smile tugging at the corners of my mouth.

Without a word, I shrug off my jacket, kick off my boots, and cross the room to sink into the sofa beside her. She pours without asking, passing me the glass with a nudge to my arm.

I take it, the first sip warming a place in me I hadn't realised had gone cold.

We sit there for a minute, the TV buzzing in the background, the rain tapping against the windows.

"You went?" Naomi says, her voice low.

I nod again, feeling the truth of it settle heavier in my bones now that I'm back here. "Yeah."

She doesn't push. Just waits.

So, I tell her. About Palmer. About the report. About the plan. About how the law feels like it's balanced on a knife's edge, but at least now there's something written with my name on it. Some small protection carved out of the noise.

When I finish, Naomi sets her glass down with a soft clink. "You did good, Carter," she says, squeezing my knee.

And even though it shouldn't make me cry, even though it's just one simple thing. Somehow, it does.

Because I did. I did something good today. I did something for myself.

We stay like that for a while. No rush. No pressure. Just two glasses of wine, the buzz of the TV, and the quiet hum of the rain thickening outside.

Naomi shifts, stretching her legs out and nudging me with her foot. "You know what you have to do next, right?"

I already know. I've known since I left the station. But the thought of it makes my stomach knot. "Yeah," I murmur. "I have to tell him."

Naomi sits up a little straighter, pulling a battered notebook from under the coffee table. "Right. We're doing this. No emotional essays. No loopholes. Just facts."

I laugh under my breath—more of a huff—but it still cracks something lighter into the room. I tug the blanket tighter around my shoulders, balancing the glass on my knee.

Naomi flips open the notebook to a clean page, pen poised like she's about to cross-examine me. "Alright. Start with the basics. What do you want him to know? Without giving him any room to twist it?"

I think for a second, then say, "That I'm going back to the house. That I want him gone. That I've spoken to the police."

Naomi scribbles, muttering under her breath. "Good. Firm. Now add a timeline. Otherwise he'll drag it out forever."

"Seven days?" I offer.

"Perfect." She underlines it twice. "Anything else?"

I hesitate. Then shake my head. "No threats. No emotional bait."

"Exactly." She jots a few more words, then hands the notebook over to me. "Here. Read it."

I tuck my glass aside and take the notebook, my fingers brushing the rough edge of the paper. Naomi's handwriting is strong. Certain. Like she wrote it knowing I could stand behind it.

The message is brief. Direct. No room for misunderstanding.

David,

Following recent events, I've sought legal advice and spoken to the police. I will be returning to the house with Mia. I am asking that you do not return.

Please collect your belongings within the next seven days.

For clarity: this is not a pause or a break. I am ending our relationship.

I do not want further contact unless it relates to the house. If you come to the property uninvited, I will report it.

Ellie.

I read it twice. Then a third time.

It's not cruel. It's not cruel because it's true. And that's something I'm ready to stand behind.

I reach for my phone, copying it word for word into a message. My thumbs hesitate over the keyboard for a beat, one last flicker of old habit. The urge to soften it. To make it easier for him. To leave a door cracked open.

But no.

I'm done leaving doors open for someone who never once thought about what it cost me to hold them.

I press send.

The message blinks out of existence, absorbed into the ether between us.

Done.

Naomi watches me for a long moment, her face softer now. "How do you feel?"

I breathe out, slow and shaky.

"Terrified," I admit. "And... lighter."

"Good," she says, reaching over to top up my glass like we're celebrating. "You deserve to feel lighter."

I take the wine, but I don't drink it yet. I just sit back on the sofa, feeling the exhaustion slip into my bones now that the adrenaline has nowhere left to go.

Out there, somewhere, David will read that message. Maybe he'll ignore it. Maybe he'll rage. Maybe he'll do nothing at all.

But here, in this moment, I'm safe. I'm heard. I'm not alone.

I tuck the blanket higher, let my head tip sideways until it rests against Naomi's shoulder. She doesn't flinch or shift away. She just leans into me too, warm, solid and steady, as the storm outside thickens into proper rain.

I exhale, letting it all settle. Then I close my eyes, just for a moment, and let myself rest.

I don't have to carry it all tonight.

Tomorrow will come.

And I'll be ready.

CHAPTER 30
frostbite and freedom

KIERAN

I shoot off a text while I stand barefoot in the kitchen, phone in one hand, coffee mug in the other.

> You've got half an hour. I'm picking you up. Dress warm.

The reply comes quicker than I expect.

ELLS [10:01]
Half an hour?? You can't just give a woman 30 minutes if she doesn't know where she's going.

I smirk into my mug, thumbs already flying across the screen.

> Think scarves. Maybe boots. Definitely not heels.

ELLS [10:02]
Is this a kidnapping?

> Technically yes. The good kind. No ransom required.

ELLS [10:03]

Do I at least get snacks?

> Chips. Guaranteed. Possibly vinegar. Maybe even a battered sausage if you behave.

ELLS [10:05]

Sausage? 😇

I stare at the message, grinning like an idiot.

> Jesus, Ellie. It's 10am and your mind's already in the gutter?

ELLS [10:06]

You put it there 😇

> I mean that wasn't my plan. But if that's what you want I can make arrangements.

ELLS [10:07]

KIERAN 😳

> Just being supportive.

ELLS [10:09]

You're filth. And if there's no tea involved, I'm filing a formal complaint.

> Your complaint has been noted. Still picking you up in 30.

She doesn't reply after that, but the read receipt gives her away.

I grin to myself, draining the last of my coffee before tugging on a jacket and grabbing the keys off the hook. I don't even have a destination in mind. Just… open air. Space. A breath away from everything that's happened.

Exactly thirty minutes later, I roll to a stop outside Naomi's building, engine idling beneath my palm as I drum light fingers on the steering wheel.

The front door swings open before I even reach for my phone. She's right on time.

Ellie steps out into the crisp air, her coat cinched tight at the waist and a scarf looped hastily around her neck, one end still dangling as she wrestles it into place. Her cheeks are already pink from the cold, her hair half-windswept, and the second I see the faint tug of a smile at her lips, something in my chest unclenches.

She spots me, eyes narrowing like she's half-suspicious and half-amused, and crosses the pavement with that same no-nonsense stride I remember from four years ago. Back when she thought I was trouble and let me flirt with her anyway.

She climbs into the passenger seat, pulls the door shut, and fastens her seatbelt with a flick of her wrist.

"Well," she says, arching an eyebrow as she tugs her scarf higher. "I'll give you this. You're irritatingly punctual."

I smirk, glancing sideways as I pull away from the curb. "Some of us like to be on time when we're kidnapping people."

She huffs out a laugh and settles into her seat, head tilting back as the city blurs past the window. "You realise that's not the reassuring statement you think it is, right?"

"Too late," I say. "You're in now. No refunds."

For a few minutes, we drive in comfortable silence. The town slowly thins around us. Coffee shops giving way to parks, parks giving way to wide skies and long strips of coastline road. There's something grounding about the way she sits beside me, legs crossed at the ankle, fingertips brushing the hem of her coat like she's still fidgeting the weight of the week out of her bones.

She glances over at me. "Alright. But seriously... what is this? Where are we going?"

I glance at her, then back at the road, a small smile tugging at the corner of my mouth. "It's not about the where."

She shoots me that look. The one that says *if you get all poetic-songwriter on me right now, I swear to God*. But she doesn't press. She just watches me.

"This is just—something," I say after a beat. "A moment. For you. Because you've been through hell. And you're still standing.

Still showing up. You've handled more than most people could even imagine, and I don't think you realise how amazed I am by you."

Her breath hitches a little, but I don't let it linger. I don't want this to become another heavy moment for her to carry.

"But today's not about that," I say quickly. "It's not about him, or the system, or the next steps, or the weight of it all. Today's just a breath. Just a stupid little drive to somewhere that you get to be Ellie again. Not the strong one. Not the mother. Not the nurse struggling to find a job."

I glance over at her, meeting her eyes. "Just... you."

She says nothing at first, just stares at me with something soft and stunned flickering behind her eyes. Like she doesn't know what to do with that kind of space. Then she lets out a slow breath and leans her head against the window. "I don't remember the last time I got to be just me," she murmurs.

I nod, keeping my hands steady on the wheel. "I remember you, Ellie. Before everything. The you that laughed so loud it turned heads. The you who made everything around her brighter without even trying."

Her breath catches, just a little, but she doesn't look away.

"I remember that girl," I say. "And I figured... maybe she could use a morning that wasn't about holding everything together."

There's a beat of silence between us. Not heavy. Just full.

And then she shifts in her seat, eyes glinting with something familiar.

"Kieran..."

I shoot her a quick look and cut in before she can get any further. "Alright, alright, that's enough of the heavy stuff."

She blinks, startled into a small laugh.

"First stop Brenda's," I say, flicking the indicator on. "I'm starving and craving a croissant."

The café is quieter than usual for a Saturday. Just the inaudible murmur of conversation, the occasional hiss of the coffee machine, and the gentle clatter of crockery. The air is thick with the scent of warm pastries, mingling into something that wraps around us like a blanket.

I'm halfway through an almond croissant, flakes everywhere, when I glance up and catch Ellie smiling.

Not at me.

At Brenda, who's perched on the chair opposite her like a proud aunt who's been waiting all month to fuss. There's something easy between them. Familiar. Like Ellie never left, like this place just folded around her the second she stepped through the door.

"You look tired, love," Brenda says, not unkindly. "But there's something else in your eyes that's different."

Ellie ducks her head, fingers curled around her mug of tea. "It's been a long week."

Brenda reaches across the table and gives Ellie's hand a gentle squeeze before leaning back again, as if that alone might be enough to anchor her. "Well, I'm glad you're here. This place isn't the same without you."

They fall into conversation like nothing's changed. Mia, Naomi, some risotto disaster that ended in *"emergency noodles."* Ellie's laugh bubbles out, soft and warm, and something in my chest eases.

I don't say much. Don't need to. Watching her like this with her shoulders lower, her eyes clearer, I just sit in it. Let myself witness it. Her voice has that lighter edge again, the one I've missed. Not performative. Not weighed down. Just hers.

She doesn't tell Brenda everything. Not the hard stuff. But she doesn't need to. There's a rhythm in the way she holds her tea now, like it's comforting. And her smile, God, it's quieter than usual, but it's real. A softness threaded with exhaustion, sure, but there's peace there too. Flickering in the quiet.

She doesn't even realise how strong she looks. But I do. I see every inch of it.

I stand, brushing flakes off my hoodie and draining the last of my coffee in one go. "Drink up, buttercup," I say, nudging the base of Ellie's mug with a grin. "We're not done yet."

She arches an eyebrow, suspicious. "Oh no. What now?"

I smirk. "You'll see. Come on."

She groans but gets to her feet, offering Brenda a quick hug and a promise to stop by again soon. Brenda watches her go with that same fond smile, already back behind the counter, hands moving with muscle memory through a tray of croissants.

Ellie pushes through the door, the little bell jangling overhead. Cold air rushes in, tugging the warmth away with her.

I move to follow, already half-turned when I hear her voice.

"Kieran…"

I stop. I glance back toward the counter. Brenda's already moving, folding paper bags with precise ease, but she looks up just long enough to catch my eye.

"Thank you."

Two words. Quiet. Honest. But there's a knowing expression on her face.

I nod once, then turn and step out after Ellie.

Outside, the cold air hits hard. The wind coming off the water stings our cheeks, but the sky is a wide, washed-out blue, and the sun glares off the sea like a spotlight.

Ellie tugs her coat tighter around her and burrows down into her scarf. "You know," she mutters, glancing sideways at me, "next time you decide to play tour guide, a weather warning wouldn't kill you."

I huff a laugh and bump her shoulder with mine as we walk. "Where's your sense of adventure?"

She groans dramatically. "Frozen. Somewhere between the café door and my rapidly numbing toes."

I laugh. "It's a beach. In England. In October. What exactly were you expecting? Sun loungers and mojitos?"

Ellie shoots me a look like I've offended her. "Preferably, yes."

But the edge of her mouth twitches. And I catch it, the tiniest smile curling at the corners. The way she exhales a little easier. The way her step falls into rhythm with mine.

We walk for a while, the crunch of pebbles beneath our boots the only sound between us. The sea rolls in gently, lazy and rhythmic, the tide pushing and pulling in a constant hush. The cold air wraps around us in bursts, sharp against our cheeks, and I swear my ears are going numb—but I don't care. Not when she's beside me like this. Close enough for our shoulders to brush every few steps.

We settle on a low stone wall just above the dunes—the ocean stretching wide in front of us, steel-grey and endless. The horizon blurs into the sky, the whole world softened by salt air and that strange hush that only happens at the coast.

She draws her knees up, chin tucked into her coat, scarf pulled comically high around her jaw, but I say nothing. She looks peaceful. Windswept and flushed and so heartbreakingly real.

The wind whips across the shore, catching her hair and tossing it across her face in loose strands. She closes her eyes and leans into it, like the sting of the cold is some kind of relief. Like she's letting it scrub something clean inside her.

Then, she looks down toward the shore, at a small group of people in wetsuits. "No sane person is voluntarily getting in that sea in this weather. I don't care how spiritual it's supposed to be. Cold water therapy is a scam."

I glance over at her, grinning. "I'm starting to think your sense of fun's a summer-only subscription."

She snorts, eyes still closed. "My sense of fun doesn't involve frostbite, thank you very much."

The breeze picks up, sending a fine spray of sea mist into the air. I don't even flinch. The quiet between us is soft now, not heavy. Like we're both settling into it. Letting it hold us.

Her phone buzzes.

Ellie jumps slightly, fumbling it out of her coat pocket, brows furrowing as she unlocks it. The wind drags across her face, but she doesn't seem to notice. She just stares at the screen. Frozen.

I sit up straighter, pulse spiking before my brain catches up. "Ellie?" Her name tumbles out of my mouth instinctively, pushed by the sudden shift in her posture, the way she goes still, phone clutched tight, breath held like she's waiting for the world to tilt.

She blinks. Slowly. Like she's not sure if what she's seeing is real.

Then her eyes flick up to mine, wide and stunned, her mouth parting around a single word. "Kieran."

Her voice is soft, breathless, like saying my name makes it more real.

She looks down at the phone again, holding it like it might vanish if she blinks too long. "He's gone. David. He's gone. I just got a message from him."

For a second, everything stills. My heart stutters, caught somewhere between hope and caution, like it doesn't know which way to fall. I search her face, and that's when I see it, really see it.

Relief breaks across her features in slow, unsteady waves, like she doesn't quite trust it yet. Her shoulders drop, her mouth trembles. Not with fear this time, but something closer to joy. Like air filling lungs that haven't known peace in too long. There's colour in her cheeks, a spark in her eyes that hasn't been there in weeks. She exhales, shaky and overwhelmed, but smiling.

"What kind of message?" I ask.

She doesn't speak at first. Just hands me the phone.

> DAVID [13:24]
>
> I've made arrangements to vacate the property. I'll be staying elsewhere for the foreseeable future. I trust this will give you and Mia the space you need. Please keep me informed regarding any formal steps moving forward. I'd appreciate it if we could keep this civil and contained. David.

It's polite. Calculated. Every word carefully chosen to sound reasonable. Safe. But I see it for what it is, he's covering his arse. Playing nice now because he knows there's a record. A paper trail. Because Ellie finally took back the narrative.

Still. He's gone.

I look up just in time to catch it, that moment the news fully hits her. Her lips part, her breath catching like she can't quite take it in.

Then she laughs. This sharp, half-disbelieving sound that turns into something bright. She squeals, high-pitched and completely unguarded, and before I can process it, she launches herself at me.

I barely stay upright as she crashes into my chest, arms flinging around my neck, her whole body shaking with something fierce and wild. Relief. Joy. Everything she's been holding back, spilling out in this one ridiculous, beautiful hug.

I wrap my arms around her tight, grounding her as she laughs into my shoulder, and I press a kiss to her temple without even thinking. "I'm so happy for you, Ellie."

She pulls back just enough to look at me, eyes wide and shiny, disbelief still written across her face like she doesn't trust it's real.

Then.

Plip.

A raindrop lands on her cheek.

She blinks and we look up. Another hits the bridge of my nose. Then three more follow, fat and sudden.

"Oh, for fuck's sake," I mutter, glancing up at the sky as it darkens.

Ellie grins, sudden and bright, and before I can react, she whips off her jacket and bolts, letting her scarf fall to the sand behind her. She's running across the damp sand like some kind of coastal maniac.

"Ellie!" I call after her, laughing even as rain starts properly falling. "You're going to freeze!"

"Worth it!" she yells back, curls sticking to her cheeks, arms flung out like wings.

I chase her, and rain soaks through my jacket in seconds, cold and insistent. She's spinning like a storm, and I run straight into it.

I catch her from behind, arms sliding around her waist as I lift her off the ground. She screams and laughs, thrashing lightly as I spin her in a wild circle.

"Put me down!"

"No chance," I grin, holding tight.

We stop, breathless, the rain falling in steady curtains now. Her hands flatten against my chest as she turns in my arms, face upturned, eyes locked on mine.

She's soaked. Smiling. Rain dripping from her lashes. And I've never seen her look more alive.

She's so gorgeous it hurts.

Her hands curl into my jacket. Her lips part, just slightly.

I reach up, fingers brushing the wet strands of hair from her cheek, tucking them gently behind her ear. Her eyes flutter, her breath stutters, and my heart is thudding so hard I can barely hear the sea anymore.

But then she shifts. Her expression breaks into a grin, wide and wild. "This calls for chips," she says.

I blink. "*Seriously?*"

She nods, water running down her face. "Extra salt and vinegar!"

"You're soaked."

"So are you."

And despite the storm, despite the ache building somewhere in my chest that doesn't quite know what to do with all this, I laugh.

"Alright," I say, letting my forehead rest against hers for the briefest second. "Chips it is."

CHAPTER 31

the family i chose

ELLIE

I DIDN'T EXPECT DAVID'S MESSAGE to come without arguments. No passive-aggressive jabs. No guilt-tripping follow-up texts disguised as concern. Just a neatly written message, as if this was always going to be simple.

And it should feel like relief, the ending I've been aching for. But it leaves a strange taste in my mouth. Like I've waited so long for the next fight that its absence makes me feel off balance.

Still, I won't lie to myself. Not now. The ease of it makes my stomach twist. The way he backed away, suddenly respectful and polite. I see straight through it. The fear, now that he knows I've started putting things in writing. That I've stopped apologising for seeing him clearly.

But I'm not dwelling on it. Not anymore. There's no point in trying to find meaning in his silences, or morality in his retreats. He's gone. That's all I need to know.

And this? This is the start of something. Of moving forward. Of choosing my own version of stability—not just for Mia's sake, but for mine.

Because I've spent years putting everyone else first. Holding myself together in the background of someone else's chaos.

Not anymore.

Not this time.

Today, I'm walking back into that house for myself.

I pull into the driveway—the tyres crunching over the familiar patch of gravel I once resented for always needing weeding. The house rises in front of me like a memory I haven't decided what to do with yet. The curtains are drawn. The porch light is off. From the outside, it looks untouched, like it's been holding its breath.

Mia's not with us. Brenda offered to take her for a few hours, claiming she'd teach her how to make her famous scones, which probably means they're already covered in flour and eating dough straight from the bowl. I'm grateful. For the distraction. For Brenda. For all of it.

Naomi's in the passenger seat beside me, her fingers drumming against her thigh like she's trying to keep herself from reaching over and squeezing mine. Kieran's in the back seat, his presence steady and solid like it always is.

My people.

I kill the engine and rest my hands on the steering wheel for a second longer than necessary. Naomi says nothing. Neither does Kieran. They just wait. No pressure. No theatrics. Just there.

I glance at Naomi, and she gives me a small nod. A *you've got this* without making a big deal of it.

Before I can move, Kieran's already out of the back seat, circling around the car. He opens my door without a word, offering me a hand. Not because I need it to stand, but because it's a ritual now. A silent promise: *I'm here.*

The cold air bites first, threaded with the damp, heavy scent of fallen leaves. I tug my coat tighter around me and step onto the path, the key heavy and unfamiliar in my coat pocket. We walk the rest of the way in silence, and when we reach the door—I pause. The keys bite into my palm where I've been gripping them.

Kieran's voice is low beside me. "You alright?"

I nod, but my voice comes out smaller than I mean it to. "Yeah. Just… weird, I guess."

I take a breath, square my shoulders, and step up to the door.

The lock sticks, like it always bloody does, but after a little wiggle and a muttered curse under my breath, it clicks. My fingers tighten around the handle.

And then I push the door open. It creaks with a low groan, and the house exhales around us like it's been holding its breath, too.

The smell hits first. Faint dust, a hint of stale polish, something floral still clinging to the air from the diffuser I left on the hall table. It's familiar, but distant. Like it belonged to another version of me.

The hallway stretches ahead, unchanged. Same photo frames on the wall. Same stack of post on the sideboard. One of Mia's shoes still wedged under the radiator, where she kicked it off in a rush and we never moved it.

But there's something off, too. Like the house knows it's been in limbo. Like it's waiting for someone to decide what it becomes now.

I step forward, then another, each footfall louder than it should be. Naomi and Kieran follow, letting me lead.

I check the front room first.

The curtains are still drawn, but enough light seeps through to cast thin slats of grey across the floor. It's colder in here. Emptier.

He's gone.

The jacket that always hung from the banister? Gone. The decanter on the shelf that I hated but never moved? Gone. His laptop bag?

All of it. Gone.

I let out a breath, the kind you don't even realise you're holding until it spills out of you. "He's actually gone," I say, half to myself.

I look around. Letting my gaze move around the room. The space looks wrong without his things, but not in a way that makes me want them back. Just in a way that makes the air feel different. Lighter. Like even the walls are trying to figure out what comes next.

I walk through the rest of the house with a steadier step. The hallway. Upstairs.

No trace of him.

The wardrobe has gaps now, his side emptied. The bedside drawer on the left is open and bare. The bathroom's missing his razor, the aftershave I used to love on him before everything soured.

But still. No notes. No mess. No confrontation. Just… gone.

When I make my way back downstairs, Naomi's in the kitchen, surveying the space with her arms folded.

"We've got some serious work to do," she says, wrinkling her nose at the stack of dirty dishes in the sink and the smell of something long-expired creeping out of the fridge.

"I'll put the kettle on," Kieran says, already moving toward it.

I step further into the kitchen and stop cold. It's not a bomb site. But it's not clean either.

The sink is full. Plates crusted over, mugs stained with tea. Bottles of whiskey lined up like trophies on the worktop, two of them empty and tipped over like no one could be bothered to right them.

I move toward the kitchen table. The placemats are askew, shoved aside in a hurry. There's a faint ring of coffee staining the wood.

The laptop's gone, but its presence still lingers. A rectangle of cleaner wood, a faint border of dust. A small groove where the charger always dragged against the edge.

The ghost of his habits.

I tug one chair back—the legs scraping against the tiles and something slips out from underneath.

I crouch, steady fingers reaching for it.

A betting slip. A few odds scrawled in the margins in handwriting I know better than my own.

I close my fingers around it. The paper crinkles, sharp and dry, in my palm.

Naomi's sorting through the fridge. Kieran's stacking plates by the sink. Moving through this space like it already belongs to me again.

I walk to the bin, flip the lid, and drop the slip inside.

Just like that.

He didn't leave it out on purpose. He missed it. Dropped it. A final oversight in a life built on secrets so tightly packed they crumbled under their own weight.

But I saw it. And that's enough.

I turn back to the table, taking it all in one more time. The empty spot where his laptop lived. The coffee stain. The faint scuff on the chair where he used to hook his ankle.

Proof of presence. Proof of absence.

And I feel it, that shift again. It's subtle. But solid.

I don't feel sad. Or rageful. Or nostalgic. I feel done. Done pretending. Done excusing. Done waiting for something to change.

And somewhere inside that quiet knowing, I find the smallest ember of peace.

Naomi and Kieran stayed for most of the afternoon. We blitzed through the rooms like a well-oiled machine. Bin bags, surface spray, an unspoken agreement to throw out anything that didn't spark joy or belonged to a version of life that no longer fit.

Naomi swore at the dodgy hoover. Kieran fixed the hinge on the back door like it was no big deal. They kept the mood light. Like they knew I needed progress without pressure, momentum without weight.

And when they left, it wasn't a goodbye. It was a *"see you later,"* a bottle of wine tucked into the fridge, a door left open for whenever I needed to step through it again.

Now, it's just me and Mia.

We're curled on the sofa, wrapped in a throw blanket that still smells faintly of Naomi's washing powder. She's still in her school uniform, knees drawn up beneath her, hot chocolate cradled in both hands. Her hair's a little wild from where she yanked it free of her ponytail, and she's staring at the TV with that glazed-over expression that says she's not really watching it at all.

I shift closer, tucking a stray curl behind her ear. "Hey, bug?"

She glances up at me, alert. Waiting. Like she already knows something important is coming. I clear my throat, grounding myself. "So, I wanted to talk to you about something."

She nods, quiet and steady. "Is this about David?"

"Yeah," I say gently. "It is."

Her fingers tighten around the mug.

"You know how we've been at Naomi's for a while? And before that, with Kieran?"

Another nod. Slower this time.

"Well... the reason we left is because some some things David was doing—how he was treating me—they weren't okay. I didn't see it at first. Or maybe I didn't want to. But I should've left sooner. I know that now."

She looks down at her drink, stirring the marshmallows until they dissolve into froth. "Did you fight?"

I pause, choosing my words carefully. "It's complicated. There were a lot of things I didn't realise weren't normal. And I need you to know, it's not your job to worry about it. What matters is that we're here. And we're safe."

She nods again, but her brow furrows. "So... you broke up?"

"Yeah," I whisper. "We did."

Silence stretches between us for a moment, taut but not heavy. "Is he coming back?" she asks, her voice small.

I shake my head. "No. I made that clear. And if he does show up or tries to contact us, I'll handle it. It's just us now. Like it was before."

Mia leans her head against my shoulder, the top of her head warm against my neck. She says nothing at first, just lets out a soft breath that settles against my skin like a sigh she's been holding in for days.

I rest my cheek on her hair. "I'm sorry, Mia. I know things have been... a bit rough."

"A bit?" she says, pulling back just enough to look up at me, her brows drawn. "You've been crying in the kitchen when you think I'm asleep. You forget stuff. You never sing in the car anymore."

I let out a shaky breath, half a laugh and half a sob. "You noticed all that?"

"I'm not a baby, Mum." She shrugs, like she's been holding this in for a while. "I know something's been wrong. I didn't know what to do... so I just tried to be extra good."

"Oh, sweetheart." My heart cracks wide open. I cup her face, brushing her hair behind her ear. "You're perfect, just the way you are."

"You're different lately," she says. "Better. Not all better, just… not as sad. I like it."

I nod, pressing a kiss into her hair, holding her a little tighter. "I feel it. Like I can breathe again."

She snuggles in again, arms wrapping around my middle. "I'm glad you're okay, Mum."

The words land like a stone in my chest. Gentle but heavy, full of all the things she's too young to carry but somehow has, anyway. I blink hard, swallowing around the lump that rises in my throat.

Outside, the rain starts again, soft and rhythmic against the windows. Inside, we stay wrapped in the blanket's warmth, the quiet hum of the TV flickering in front of us.

It's not perfect. It's not over.

But it's ours.

The knock comes just as I'm reaching for the remote, Mia still tucked in against me, her head resting on my shoulder. We're halfway through some baking show neither of us is really watching, mugs of half-drunk hot chocolate cooling on the coffee table.

Mia sits up straighter, her eyes flicking toward the door. "Was that…?"

"I've got it," I say, dropping the remote onto the arm of the chair as I pad barefoot down the hallway.

My heart ticks a little faster. Not with fear. With something like anticipation. Like a string already pulled tight, waiting to be tugged.

I reach for the door handle on instinct, muscle memory taking over before my brain catches up. But then I freeze, hand hovering just above the metal as a flicker of unease twists in my stomach. I draw my hand back and take a step closer to the door instead, pressing my eye to the peephole.

Theo's grinning face is pressed comically close to the glass, a pizza box balanced in one hand, a six-pack of beers dangling from the other.

"You gonna let us in or what, Ellie-Bellie?" he calls through the door. "It's pissing it down and my hair's doing unholy things."

I laugh, a full-on belly laugh, and unlock the door, pulling it open.

Theo barrels in first like a golden retriever in skinny jeans, rain dripping off the hem of his jacket. "She's alive!" he declares, heading straight for the kitchen like he's been here before.

Naomi's right behind him, shaking out her umbrella and grinning. "You didn't think we'd let you spend your first night back on your own, did you?" she says, tugging off her coat and kicking her boots onto the mat.

Kieran's next. He steps inside slower, steadier, his eyes locking on mine for a beat longer than the others. He leans in and presses a kiss to my cheek. Soft and fleeting, but enough to make my stomach do a ridiculous little flip.

"Hey, you," he murmurs.

"Hi," I say, unable to keep the smile from tugging at my lips.

Luca and Ryder follow, arms full of snacks and board games and a suspicious-looking bottle of something that looks like tequila.

Lord. Pray for my carpets.

"Hope you like chaos," Ryder grins, holding up a half-squashed bag of popcorn.

"Because we brought a lot of it," Luca adds, already unloading everything onto the kitchen counter like a man on a mission.

I blink at the lot of them, dripping water onto my freshly cleaned floor, filling the house with noise, warmth, and the scent of melted cheese.

"You're all insane," I say, but the smile won't leave my face.

Naomi plops onto the sofa beside Mia, tugging her into a quick side-hug and asking about school. Theo hijacks the TV, pairing it to his phone, and moments later, his Spotify playlist hums through the speakers. Meanwhile, Ryder is crouched in the corner, trying to get the fireplace going, although I know it's mostly decorative. Luca takes over in the kitchen like he's been appointed logistics officer, opening cupboards, claiming the best serving plates, arguing with Kieran over which drink belongs to whom.

And me?

I just stand in the middle of it all for a moment. And breathe.

This house used to feel like a pressure cooker. A place where I had to shrink myself to survive. Now… it feels wide open. Full of mismatched voices, obscene jokes, and the people who stitched me back together when I couldn't see the cracks forming.

I don't need to do anything tonight. I don't need to explain. Or justify. Or carry the weight of everything that's happened.

I just get to be here. With them. The people who show up, stay late, and make everything feel better.

CHAPTER 32

fuck it

KIERAN

THE LIVING ROOM LOOKS LIKE a bomb's gone off in a craft store and a takeaway.

Pizza boxes are stacked like a leaning tower of regret on the coffee table, crusts abandoned like forgotten promises. Someone —definitely Theo—has left a bag of popcorn in the corner, half-spilled and ignored. Blankets drape over every surface like they've given up trying to be folded.

In the middle of it all—a bead explosion.

Ellie's curled up in the armchair, cardigan cocooned around her like a second skin, talking with Luca and Theo. Her face is relaxed, her laugh easy, and I can't stop looking at her.

But I'm not sitting beside her. I'm cross-legged on the floor with Mia, who's threading tiny plastic beads onto a string with the precision of a brain surgeon.

"No. Stop, stop!" she slaps my hand away like I've just committed bead-based treason. "You're doing it backwards."

"That's possible?" I look at my jumble of string and colour. "You said blue, then yellow."

"Yes, but look!" she says, nudging it toward me. "If you do yellow now, it throws off the whole pattern. You skipped one. Look."

She gestures at my mess of mismatched colours like it's offended her.

I just shrug and let her fix it.

There's something calming about the way she moves through the task. Quiet and focused, completely absorbed.

A crash echoes across the room.

"*OW*. Bloody hell, Naomi! Was that necessary?"

"If you'd moved your foot like I told you, I wouldn't have had to elbow you in the spleen!"

I look over just in time to see Ryder sprawled across the rug, coiled beneath Naomi, who's still clinging to the Twister mat like a warrior in battle.

"I think I pulled something," Ryder groans.

Naomi grins, flushed and victorious. "My sympathy has left the fucking building."

Luca sips his beer like he's above it all. "You two realise you're one round of Jenga away from foreplay, right?"

Naomi throws a cushion at his head. "Jealousy's a disease, Luca. Get well soon."

Laughter erupts, filling the room like it belongs here.

"Okay," Mia says, focused again, "now try again. *Properly*. Don't mess it up."

"Yes, boss." I loop the string, hyper-aware of her eyes on me.

From the corner of my eye, I glance toward Ellie. She's watching me now, lips curled into a quiet smile that hits me dead in the chest.

There's something in the way she looks at me, like I'm not just a guy sat on her rug being schooled by her daughter. Like I mean something.

I can't look away. She tilts her head, and that smile deepens. Soft, a little knowing.

I grin back, helpless.

"Erm, hello?" Mia waves a half-finished bracelet in front of my face. "You've been staring at her for five minutes and this bracelet still needs more beads."

"I wasn't…" I clear my throat. "I was concentrating."

Mia sighs like I've failed her. "You're such a love-struck fool."

"Love-struck fool," Theo repeats without even looking. "It's embarrassing."

"Just snog already and save us all the tension," Ryder mutters from the floor.

Ellie flushes, burying her face into her cardigan with a muttered, "You're all insufferable."

But she's smiling. Properly smiling. And I swear, I'd live in this moment forever if I could.

Ellie checks the clock, then glances at Mia, still cross-legged on the rug, cheeks pink from hot chocolate and laughter. "Alright, bug," she says, nudging Mia's ankle, "it's nearly eleven. Time to start winding down."

Mia groans and flops onto the rug like the weight of bedtime is too much to bear. "I'm not even tired."

"You just yawned into your hot chocolate," Ellie deadpans.

"That was a sympathy yawn," Mia says, pointing at Ryder. "He started it."

"I did not," Ryder protests, offended.

Mia looks at me. "Tell her I'm fine."

"Absolutely not," I say. "You're not getting me in the middle of this."

Ellie smirks. "Smart man."

Mia gives in and stands, stretching like she's just run a marathon.

Ellie grazes her hand across my shoulder as she walks past. It's barely a touch, but it's enough to leave my skin buzzing.

I watch them disappear down the hallway, something warm blooming low in my chest.

The others keep talking. Theo launching into a story about a stage dive gone wrong, Naomi already wheezing before he hits the punchline.

I grab the nearest popcorn bag and stand. "Alright, gremlins. I'm making a dent in this disaster zone."

"You're a good man, Hayes," Luca says, raising his beer like a toast.

"Not all heroes wear capes," Ryder adds from the floor, still tangled in the mat.

Naomi rolls her eyes. "If you find my will to live under the sofa cushions, let me know."

I grin, chucking a napkin at her on my way past.

The kitchen's quiet. Quieter than it's been all night. The hush that settles after the laughter fades—after the games end, and the chaos thins into leftover crumbs and sticky fingerprints on the worktop.

I grab a bin bag from under the sink and start gathering the wreckage. Empty plates. Napkins scrunched into balls. Popcorn kernels are in the weirdest places.

Someone abandoned a juice box behind the kettle.

There's a spoon stuck to the countertop with what might once have been Nutella, and one of the bead trays is wedged between the toaster and the bread bin like it's hiding from the war.

Honestly? I don't even mind.

This place, Ellie's place, it doesn't feel hollow like it did this afternoon. It doesn't feel like a house that's been paused. It's alive.

The fridge hums. The boiler kicks in. Voices filter from the living room. Every bit of mess I clean feels like proof she's getting her home back, one thread at a time.

I finish tying off the bin bag and sling it over my shoulder like some sort of domestic Santa. "Be back in a sec!" I call, though I doubt anyone's listening.

Outside, the air is frosty. The kind that bites a little, but not enough to hurt. The patio's slick from the evening rain, and the bins are tucked along the side of the fence.

I toss the bag in, sort the recycling like a functioning adult, and lean back for a moment. Hands on my hips, breath fogging the air.

There's something about the night that makes everything feel clearer. As if the world has been stripped down to its bones.

That's when I hear it. "Come here often?"

I turn, already smiling.

Ellie's standing in the doorway, arms folded, leaning against the frame like it's a stage cue she's hit a thousand times. Her cardigan's wrapped tight around her, the porch light soft on her face, picking up the curve of her smile.

"Only on bin duty," I say, walking toward her. "Romantic strolls under the moonlight. Very exclusive."

"High standards," she muses, stepping down onto the path. "Rubbish bags and a cold patio. Can't believe I didn't fall for you sooner."

She's teasing, but there's something beneath it—something quieter.

Softer.

"You're kind of irresistible right now," she adds, voice lower now.

I stop in front of her. Just enough to see the flutter of her lashes, the wind catching her hair. "Yeah?" I murmur.

She nods, a breath of laughter caught in her throat. "Very rugged. Very domestic. It's a strong look for you."

For a second, we just look. No rush. No noise.

Just us.

Her eyes meet mine, steady, and I swear the rest of the world just falls away. "You didn't have to clean," she says, voice even softer now. "You've already done so much."

"I know." I shrug. "I just... wanted to."

Ellie watches me like she's turning that over in her head. Stepping closer, she tucks her hands in to her sleeves. "I never said sorry," she says.

That throws me. I frown. "For what?"

"Leaving the way I did. Back then." Her eyes drop to the ground. "Just—disappearing."

I exhale. "Ellie, it's okay—"

"Not at the time it wasn't," she cuts in, lifting her gaze to meet mine. "It wasn't fair. You didn't deserve that. I should've said something. Anything. But I didn't. I just... left."

I reach out before I even realise I'm moving. My hands find her face, fingers brushing her jaw, her cheeks, her temples. Her skin is cool from the night air, but soft beneath my touch. "It was a long time ago," I say quietly. "And we're here now."

She leans into the touch, the slightest tilt of her head in to my palm, like she's been holding her breath for days and is letting some of it go.

There's something raw about the way she does it.

Like this moment, this one right here means more than either of us can say.

And then she's closer.

I don't know who moves first. Maybe we meet somewhere in the middle, both of us aching in the same direction.

Her lips brush mine softly, and my breath catches so sharply it feels like I've been punched. It's barely a kiss. Just the suggestion of one. But every cell in my body answers to it like it's gospel.

She exhales against my mouth, soft and shaky, and the sound alone just about wrecks me. She tastes of red wine and something sweeter, and the world narrows to nothing but the shape of her mouth and the press of her body.

I pause, just enough to pull back a fraction.

My forehead rests against hers, both of us breathing hard, the space between us charged like a fuse waiting for a spark.

"Baby," I murmur, my voice rough with want. "Are you sure?"

She doesn't even blink. Just looks up at me, wide-eyed and steady, and nods. "Kieran, I can't think of anything I want more right now."

And that's it. The match is struck.

I kiss her, *really* kiss her, like I've been holding back for years and my body's finally allowed to feel it.

There's no hesitation now. No gentleness. Just heat and hunger and every feeling I've buried rising to the surface all at once.

Her hands fist into the front of my hoodie, dragging me closer, and when her mouth parts beneath mine, I swear to God, I lose it. Her lips are soft and yielding, her tongue sliding against mine with a confidence that sends heat pouring through me.

It's not just want. It's need. Molten and unstoppable.

She makes this sound. A low, breathy hum that vibrates right through my chest, and then she's pressing harder, her body flush against mine, every curve fitting like we were made to line up like this.

We pull back, only for a moment, only by an inch. But it feels like a chasm.

And then I see her.

The porch light hits her face just right. Cheeks flushed, lips swollen from the kiss. Her cardigan hangs loose off one shoulder, clinging to her arms, her chest rising and falling like she's trying to catch her breath but doesn't want to.

She looks undone in the most beautiful way. Like this moment is all she's thinking about.

And something in me snaps.

Fuck it.

I lift her. It's instinct. No hesitation. My hands slide to her waist, and she lets out the softest gasp as I hoist her up onto the edge of the garden wall.

Her legs wrap around my hips, her arms looping around my neck like she's been waiting for this all night.

She looks at me like she feels it too, that crackling, no-turning-back energy.

And Christ, she's never looked more irresistible.

That cardigan slips further, revealing the slinky little number she must've changed into after Mia went to bed. It clings to her like liquid, the kind of fabric that makes you want to touch just to see how it feels under your hands.

And *Jesus*. It's not just thin. It's *sheer*.

The light behind her silhouettes everything, and when I glance down, I can see the gentle curve of her breasts, the outline of her nipples pebbled through the fabric. Whether from the cold or from me, I don't know.

But I don't care.

I swallow hard, heart hammering so loud it's all I can hear. "You did this on purpose," I murmur, dragging my hands up the backs of her thighs, fingers catching on the hem of her dress.

Her breath hitches, but her smile is wicked. "Maybe."

My hands slide higher, skimming the smooth line of her hips, her ribs. Every inch of her I've only imagined touching until now. "You're breathtaking, Ellie."

She shifts against me, pulling me tighter between her legs, and her mouth finds mine again. Hungrier this time.

No softness. No hesitation. Just fire.

I groan into the kiss, hands fisting in the fabric of her dress as her teeth graze my lower lip, tugging lightly.

The way she's clinging to me, grinding against me. It's everything, too much, and not enough all at once.

Her dress rides higher as she moves, the silky fabric slipping up her thighs, exposing smooth, bare skin to the cool night air.

I press closer, desperate for more friction, more heat, running both palms up the sides of her legs and gripping her ass like she might slip through my fingers if I don't hold her there.

I trail kisses down her neck, tasting her, and the way her pulse jumps beneath my mouth threatens to unravel me.

She tips her head back, giving me more, always giving me more, and I take it, mouth hot on her collarbone, tongue skimming the dip where her heartbeat pounds hard and fast.

"Fuck, Ellie," I whisper against her skin, voice wrecked. "You're gonna kill me."

She laughs. A low, breathless sound that sends another bolt of heat surging through me.

I press my forehead to hers. We're both breathless now, still moving, still clinging to each other like letting go might break the spell — or burn us both to ash.

"I want you," she whispers, voice raw and unguarded. And the way she says it, like a confession, undoes me completely. "I want this — with you."

"Me too. *Christ*." My hands tighten around her hips. I lean in, brushing my mouth against hers, grinning now. "But I'm not taking you on a garden wall, baby."

She laughs at that, ducking her head and burying it in my shoulder, warmth blooming between us. I hook a finger beneath her chin, coaxing her face back to mine.

And then I kiss her again. Slower this time. Deeper.

I try to memorise it all — the quiet sigh she breathes into my mouth, the way her body shifts closer, like instinct.

My hands cradle her face, thumbs skimming along her jaw. Her cheeks are flushed, her skin hot with want, and I swear I could spend forever right here. Learning her by heart.

We're moving without thinking now. Her legs tightening around my waist, her hips rolling against me, seeking friction, chasing something we're both aching for.

It's messy and clumsy, and perfect. Every gasp from her, every groan from me, feels like it leaves a mark.

Her fingers tangle in my hair, tugging just enough to make me growl into her mouth. And when she rocks against me again, harder this time, a sharp, helpless noise escapes my throat before I can swallow it down.

I kiss her like I'm starved, like she's the only thing that's ever tasted real.

Her hands are everywhere. Gripping my shoulders, sliding under my hoodie, fingernails grazing my skin. And I can feel the fine tremble in her body that matches my own.

God, I want her. Here. Now. Against the wall, under the stars, with nothing between us but heat and need.

I slide my hands up the backs of her thighs again, higher this time, dragging her closer, feeling the sheer heat of her pressed against me.

I want to tear this fucking dress off her. I want to lay her back and find every inch of her. I want to hear the sounds she makes when it's my mouth, my hands, my body driving her over the edge.

I want it all. But even through the haze of lust, something in me pulls the reins tight. Not like this. Not rushed. Not out here in the cold, with the house full of people.

She deserves better than that. She deserves everything.

I pull back. Just enough to rest my forehead against hers again, forcing myself to breathe, to think.

My chest heaves. Her chest heaves. We're both trembling with the effort it takes not to just lose it right here.

"Baby," I rasp, barely getting the words out. "Not like this."

She blinks, dazed and beautiful and wrecked, her hands still curled in the front of my hoodie like she never wants to let go.

"We'll get there," I promise her, brushing a kiss to her temple, slow and reverent. "I swear to God, we will. But not here. Not like this."

Her forehead drops to my shoulder with a soft, wrecked laugh, and I hold her there, breathing her in, feeling the fine, shaking tension still thrumming between us.

I kiss her temple again. Her hair. Anywhere I can reach without taking it further.

"I want to take my time with you," I whisper. "All of you. No rushing. Just... us. And I swear to you, Ellie. It will be worth the wait."

She lifts her head after a moment, and the look in her eyes guts me. Soft, brave, full of something I can't even name but feel down to the bone.

"So, what now?" she breathes.

I smile, trace the line of her jaw with my thumb. "Now," I murmur, voice rough and full of every feeling I can't say out loud yet, "I walk you inside."

She doesn't move right away. Just stays wrapped around me.

I can still feel the flutter of her heartbeat beneath my hands, the way her dress clings to her in the chill, her skin flushed and electric.

And then she nods.

I shift her more securely in my arms, lifting her as I cross the garden, still peppering kisses to her neck.

The back porch light catches in her hair, soft and golden, and she tucks her face into the crook of my shoulder like she's grounding herself there. Like I'm the safest place she knows. And fuck, I never want to put her down.

But we're not alone tonight. The house is still full of people—*our people*. And as much as I want to steal her upstairs and finish what we started, this isn't that moment.

So instead, I carry her to the back door, nudging it open with my foot, and step back into the warmth of the kitchen that's still dimly lit. Still scattered with the aftermath of the evening.

And of course, because the universe has a twisted sense of humour, standing right there by the fridge, beer in one hand and a leftover breadstick in the other, is Luca.

He glances up, clocks us instantly.

Ellie wrapped around me. My hands gripping the backs of her thighs like I've forgotten how to stand without her.

His brow arches.. His mouth quirks. And then he says, deadpan. "Well. That escalated."

Ellie groans against my neck, burying her face there with a muffled laugh.

I glance at Luca. "Don't start."

"I'm not saying anything," he says, way too casually, taking a sip of his beer. "But if you're planning on defiling the kitchen table, can you at least move the bead kits first? Pretty sure Mia's making me a bracelet."

Ellie laughs against my skin, the sound vibrating straight through me, and I feel her shift, cheeks flushed as she unwinds herself from me and slides down to the floor.

"I hate all of you," she mutters, tugging her cardigan back up around her shoulders like it might shield her.

Luca lifts his bottle in salute. "And yet, we're the ones who bring snacks and emotional stability. You're welcome."

Ellie rolls her eyes and flicks a bead at his chest. He doesn't even flinch.

"I see the foreplay's over, then. I'll be in the living room. If you hear moaning, it's just Ryder losing at Uno."

As he saunters off, I glance at Ellie, who's still pink-cheeked and breathless beside me.

Her eyes meet mine and we both break, laughing.

God, I love this madness. And her? I'm done pretending I don't.

But that's what terrifies me, too.

I exhale slowly, watching the way she tucks a strand of hair behind her ear, the way her fingers linger near mine like she doesn't want to let go.

I don't either.

"Hey," I say softly.

She turns to me, brows lifting. "Yeah?"

I hesitate. My tongue feels heavy in my mouth, like the words are stuck there, like if I say them out loud it'll make them real.

But if I don't say it now, I'll spiral with it later. "What if I mess this up?" I ask, voice barely above a whisper.

Her expression shifts, brows pulling together, not confused, just, soft. Like she hears what I'm not saying. "Mess what up?" she asks.

"This." I motion between us. "You. Me. All of it."

I look at her and I see everything I've been chasing without knowing it. Not the noise, not the crowds, not the rush of being on stage. Just this, quiet and real and terrifying.

Because if it's real... it can be lost.

"I haven't felt like this in a long time," I say, voice rough around the edges. "And even then... not like this. This feels like it matters."

"It does," she says softly.

I nod, eyes dropping to the floor between us where her knee rests so close to mine I can feel the heat of her. "And I've been the guy who leaves," I admit. "Or the one who stays half-in, one foot out the door. And I told myself that's just who I was. Like if I didn't give too much, I couldn't lose too much either."

I shake my head, the old self-loathing rising, thick and familiar. "But you're here. And you're you. And I just keep thinking... what if I don't know how to do this? What if trying isn't enough?"

The words catch in my throat. I force them out anyway.

"I'm trying to be so strong for you, Ellie. But I'm scared. Scared I'll fall short. Scared I'll let you down. Scared I'll end up being someone else you regret. And I don't want that. You mean too much to me."

She doesn't flinch. Doesn't pull away. Instead, she shifts closer until her knee brushes mine, her hand sliding into mine like it's the most natural thing in the world.

Maybe it is. Maybe this is what it feels like when you stop running.

"You won't be," she says, voice steady, anchoring me. "And you don't have to have all the answers right now. Fuck, I don't either. And my life's a sodding mess."

She lets out a small, self-deprecating laugh, but there's no bite to it. Just truth. "I'm figuring things out one step at a time, barely keeping my head above water most days. But that doesn't mean this…" she squeezes my hand. "Isn't real. Or that it doesn't matter."

I nod slowly, the knot in my chest tightening and loosening all at once. "Still scared I'll mess it up anyway."

She squeezes my hand again, firmer. "Then let's not think about messing it up. Let's not think ten steps ahead at all."

Her eyes meet mine. Clear, unwavering, and so sure it undoes me.

"Everything's still messy," she says. "For me, for you. There's so much I haven't figured out yet, and the last thing I want is to try and shove this into some neat little box it doesn't belong in. We don't need to label anything. We don't need to rush."

I stay quiet, letting her words settle deep.

She takes a breath. "Whatever this is, it's special. It was back then. It still is now. But it doesn't have to be perfect or make sense overnight. We can just... see where it goes. One day at a time."

My throat feels tight.

But for the first time, it's not fear choking me.

It's hope.

I nod again, slower this time. "Okay."

Her thumb brushes across the back of my hand. "Okay."

And somehow, just like that, I believe her.

CHAPTER 33

spoil sport

ELLIE

THE KETTLE CLICKS OFF JUST as I realise I've been staring through the kitchen window without really seeing anything.

In the daylight, the garden looks smaller than I remember. A little unkempt. A little forgotten. Mia's old skipping rope is wrapped around the fence post like ivy, and one of her socks clings to the washing line like it got left behind on purpose.

For a second, it almost makes me laugh.

But the memory of last night is still there, painted into the corners of the garden like a secret. The way he kissed me like he meant every second. Like he wasn't asking for permission. Because he already knew I'd given it.

And I had.

I pour the water into my mug and wrap my hands around the ceramic like it might steady me. My fingers are stiff, but the heat sinks in fast, chasing out the chill.

I stir sugar into the tea with slow, absent motions, letting the steam curl into the air. Letting the weight of last night settle into my bones like something warm. Something real.

The truth is. I would've let him keep going. Every inch of me had said yes. My body. My mouth. Even my silence.

But Kieran... he'd stopped. Not because he didn't want me. He'd made that clear.

He stopped because he wanted more than a moment in the dark. More than something hurried, half-finished, pressed between shadows and reckless hands. He wanted more than just the right now. He wanted me. *All of me.*

And he was willing to wait for it.

No one's ever done that before.

Not really.

And that's what scares me the most. Not the wanting. The being wanted back.

Because this isn't crashing in like a tidal wave. It's creeping up in quieter ways. Slipping beneath my skin, finding all the broken, quiet places I thought I'd buried for good.

It's the way he makes me feel seen without having to perform for it. The way he makes it easier to just be. No masks, no shrinking, no pretending I'm okay when I'm not.

Around him, I don't have to edit myself down to something manageable. I can be messy. I can be honest. I can be me.

And maybe that's the thing. It's not just about last night. It's about the five months before it. Since he walked back into my life. Five months of memories clawing their way to the surface. Five months of new moments folding in with the old ones.

All of it leading here.

To this. To the space he's held for me without asking for anything in return.

It's only been three weeks since I packed Mia into the car and drove through the dark, looking for something—*someone*—safe. But I think I'd been switched off from David for so much longer than that.

I just didn't realise it. Not fully. Something in me had let go a long time ago, long before I even had the words for it.

I think about what Kieran said last night. His voice low, almost breaking.

What if I mess this up?

And honestly? I'm scared too. Scared of how easy it is to want this. Scared of how much it *already* matters.

In some ways, it feels like everything is moving too fast, faster than I know how to keep up with. But in others, it feels like it's been building for years. Like we've been orbiting this without even realising it. Like all the mess and hurt and wrong turns were always leading here.

To this exact moment.

It doesn't feel wrong. It doesn't even feel reckless. It feels like exhaling after holding my breath for too long.

I look out at the garden again, thinking about the person I used to be. The girl who spent years twisting herself into someone smaller, more convenient, more tolerable.

The girl who thought surviving was the same thing as living. And now? I don't recognise that girl anymore.

Or maybe I do. Maybe I finally see her clearly. The way she tried so hard, carried so much, folded herself into corners just to keep the peace.

And now, for the first time, I'm ready to choose differently.

Because with Kieran, it doesn't feel like just surviving. It feels like *everything*.

I'm not naïve. I know life doesn't click into place in a single kiss. It might be messy, uncertain, and rough around the edges.

But it also feels like it could be right.

Every instinct that once told me to run is quiet now. Not silenced by desperation or fear. Just soothed by something steadier.

Something truer.

I don't know what's ahead. I don't even know if we'll get it perfectly right. But for once, I'm not bracing for it to fall apart before it even begins.

Mia's voice cuts across the quiet, pulling me back into the morning. "Mum! Do we have any more of those chocolate bars? The ones with the caramel?"

"In the cupboard next to the toaster," I call. "But that doesn't count as breakfast."

"I already had toast," she shouts back. "This is second breakfast."

I huff a quiet laugh, grab my tea, and head for the living room. "Alright, *Frodo*," I mutter under my breath.

She doesn't respond, just lets out a sigh from the sofa like I'm ruining her hobbit lifestyle.

When I step into the living room, she's already curled up under the throw blanket, hair still wild from sleep, a bar of chocolate now balanced on her lap as she flicks through the documentary channel. I set my tea down on the side table and drop onto the sofa beside her.

She barely glances at me as she breaks off a square. "You're being weird."

I blink. "Weird?"

"You keep smiling at nothing," she says, eyes still glued to the TV.

I raise an eyebrow, but the corner of my mouth betrays me. It lifts. Just slightly. "Maybe I'm just having a good morning."

Mia shrugs, popping another square of chocolate into her mouth. "I mean, it was pretty cute last night. You and Kieran pretending you're not in love."

I choke on my tea.

She looks at me then, but her face is smug and unbothered.

I wipe my mouth with the sleeve of my jumper, glaring at her over the rim of my mug. "You're impossible."

Mia shrugs. "You're the one that was making googly eyes all night."

I snort. "I was *not* making googly eyes."

She breaks off a square of chocolate, pops it into her mouth, and mumbles, "Please. You're one rom-com away from doodling his name in a notebook."

I gasp. "Rude."

She grins around a mouthful of caramel. "Just saying."

I reach over and ruffle her hair, making her squeal and bat me away half-heartedly.

"Brat."

"Lovesick," she sings under her breath.

She flashes me a grin and turns back to the TV, utterly victorious.

I open my mouth to argue, but stop. What's the point? She's not wrong. I just don't have the right words for it yet.

By mid-morning, she disappears upstairs with her snack stash and her headphones, officially dismissing me from her realm until at least lunchtime.

The house falls quiet again. Still a little echoey without David's things in it, but it doesn't feel like a space I need to fill.

I clear the mugs, rinse out the cereal bowl, and set up at the kitchen table with my laptop and a fresh cup of tea.

The light through the window hits the floor in a way that makes the laminate glow, and for a moment, it almost feels like I'm in someone else's house. Someone else's life.

But the tea is mine. The chair beneath me is mine. The silence is mine.

I open my emails, and my inbox is a mess. Unread bills. Appointment reminders. Spam from places I haven't visited since 2016.

I start clearing, replying, and flagging anything that needs attention. It's almost satisfying. Like sorting through a box of tangled threads and finally finding the ends.

Then something catches my eye.

Subject: Graduation - Guest Confirmation

I blink, click.

My breath hitches halfway through the message as it loads.

Graduation. I'd almost forgotten. Everything that happened over the last few weeks—David, the house, Kieran. It blurred the edges of my calendar.

How is it almost November already? But it's there, clear as anything. A date. A milestone. Something that once felt unreachable.

I scroll to the bottom and hover over the reply button.

I used to know who the tickets were for. Mia, of course. David. My mum and dad. Brenda.

But now?

Subject: RE: Graduation – Guest Confirmation

Hi, thank you so much for your email regarding graduation. Please find below my guest list confirmation:

1: Mia Carter

2: *Brenda Collins*
Kindest regards,
Eleanor Carter

I hit send before I can hesitate.

There's an ache in my chest as the message disappears. Bittersweet. Like I'm grieving something and claiming something else in the same breath.

I glance at my phone, thumb tapping open the last text I sent to Mum.

> Just wanted to let you know David and I have separated. I'm home if you want to talk. I'd like to talk.

It's been days.

Read. No reply.

I told myself it was enough just to say it. To put the ball in her court. To leave the door open.

But silence has a way of answering for people, doesn't it?

I lock the screen and set the phone down, forcing the ache back behind the quiet resolve I've been learning to live inside.

I think about Kieran. About his hand in mine last night. The way he looked at me like I was something bright.

I think about how safe I feel when he's around. How full the house sounds when he and the boys are here. How easy it is to smile without checking who's watching.

But I don't add his name. Not yet. Not because I don't want him there. But because I don't want to put pressure on it.

I close the inbox and breathe a long, slow exhale. The kind that doesn't feel forced anymore.

But then, as I'm scrolling, something else catches my eye.

Subject: Accident & Emergency | Staff Nurse | South Havens Trauma Hospital

I sit up straighter and every nerve flickers awake.

What is happening right now?
It's not just the hospital. It's the contact name beneath it.

Linda Browne: Senior Sister, Accident & Emergency.

I haven't seen Linda since my last placement—the same placement where I crossed paths with Kieran again, after all those years—but her voice rings sharp and clear in my head. She once told me I was built for it. That I stayed calm in the pressure that made other people bolt. She was the first person who made me feel like I could be more than capable. I could be needed.

I click the job posting. Read it once. Then again. My fingers hover over the mouse like it might disappear if I blink. It's fast-paced. High-pressure. Everything I've been training for. Everything I've missed.

Without thinking too hard, I grab my phone.

> You're not gonna believe this.
>
> South Havens Trauma just posted a new position. A&E. Guess who the contact is?
>
> Linda!!

The reply is immediate.

> NAOMI [11:34]
>
> SHUT THE FRONT DOOR
>
> Ellie, that's fate. Apply. Right now. Do not pass go. Do not make tea. Just APPLY.
>
> (also tell Linda she still owes me prosecco)

I smile. Can't help it. It stretches across my face before I can fight it.

> Already drafting the email.

And I am.

It's not a job offer. Not yet. It's just an opening. A flicker of a door. But it's mine to knock on. Mine to walk through.

And right now, that's everything.

The light outside has shifted now. It's that late-afternoon blue that softens everything. I let it wash through the kitchen window as I move through the house in quiet, steady motions.

I open the drawer by the front door, the one David always claimed as his, and start sorting through it like I'm excavating a life I didn't realise had been layered over mine.

Receipts. Keys I can't identify. A pen I'm pretty sure he never once used. A tangle of headphone cords and charger cables that don't fit any device we still own.

I don't linger. I don't dig. I just clear. There's something cathartic about it. No sadness. No dramatics. Just... sorting. Deciding what gets to stay and what doesn't. What's mine and what never really was.

It's like turning the page on something that needed to end a long time ago.

Later, I lace up my trainers, Kieran's hoodie already pulled over my head. The same one I never gave back. The one that still smells like him.

I tell myself it's just because it's comfortable. But I know better. I don't intend on returning it anytime soon.

I head to the bottom of the stairs and call up, "Mia? I'm going for a run. I won't be long!"

A muffled "'Kay!" floats down from her room, followed by the distinct thump of music through her headphones.

"Don't open the door to anyone, alright?" I add, louder this time.

There's a pause, then another muffled, "Got it!"

I don't make a plan. I just step outside, feel the cold air nip at my cheeks, and start moving. I walk first. Then jog. My feet hit the pavement in a rhythm that feels instinctive.

My breath clouds the air. My heart settles into a steady beat. And the rest of the world fades. I don't take headphones. I don't need music. The sound of my footsteps is enough.

It's grounding. Real. Mine.

By the time I get back, the sun has slipped behind the rooftops, casting long shadows over the street. The air carries that crisp, early-evening bite that can only mean autumn is in full swing, my favourite time of year. When the nights stretch longer, the evenings grow softer, and everything feels like it's winding down into something slower.

I peel off the hoodie and step into the bathroom, shedding layers until I'm under the shower, letting the water hit my skin in a warm, endless stream.

I stand there longer than I need to, head tilted back, fingers combing through my hair. It feels like a ritual. A washing away of everything I don't want to carry anymore.

When the water runs lukewarm, I step out, wrap myself in a towel, and pad barefoot to my room.

Not the one I shared with David. I haven't stepped foot in there since I got the house back, and I'm not sure when I will.

I sleep in the guest room now. The room that's warm and still, where the streetlamp outside spills soft amber through the curtains and paints gentle lines across the walls. I've added a blanket I love, a potted plant on the dresser, and a candle that smells like vanilla and clean laundry. The bed is always made. The sheets are fresh. It's quiet here, and calm.

It doesn't carry ghosts.

This space is mine. And it feels like safety.

I pull on my favourite fleece pyjamas and pull the duvet around me like armour.

The house is calm. The laundry's done. The dishes are dry. Mia is tucked up in her room, watching something on her iPad with one earbud hanging out like always.

It feels… still—it feels real.

And just as my eyes flutter shut, my phone buzzes against the bedside table.

> KIERAN [23:46]
>
> Can't sleep. Blaming that dress you had on last night. Criminal.

                                        You mean my cardigan? 😊

KIERAN [23:47]

No, Ellie. That slinky little number you had on under it.

                                        Ohhh, that old thing?

KIERAN [23:48]

Mmmm. And those thighs. 😏

                                        This is dangerously close to sexting, Hayes.

KIERAN [23:49]

I haven't even started yet, Carter. Want me to? 😉

                                        Goodnight, Kieran 🙈

KIERAN [23:50]

Spoil sport.

Night, Ellie 🖤

I set my phone down with a smile tugging at my lips. There's a heat in my cheeks I don't try to smother. A thrum under my skin that hasn't gone away since last night.

And underneath it all, something steadier.

I'm not rushing this. I'm not losing myself in someone else. I'm walking toward something, something that feels honest. Slow. True.

Today wasn't dramatic. It wasn't perfect. But it was mine.

Every damn second of it.

CHAPTER 34

under my skin

KIERAN

THE APARTMENT'S QUIET, SAVE FOR the high-pitched whine of MotoGP through the speakers. On-screen, bikes lean into corners like they're defying gravity, tyres skimming asphalt, sparks flying as footpegs kiss the tarmac. The race commentator drones in the background, half-cut by static and adrenaline.

Theo's sprawled next to me on the sofa, one leg thrown carelessly over the armrest, the other resting on the coffee table—like a human pretzel. He's shirtless, naturally, a half-empty bag of Wotsits tucked against his side, orange dust staining his fingers.

Luca's locked away editing in his room. Ryder disappeared hours ago with a shrug and no explanation—standard. And I'm here, watching the world blur past in high definition, but barely registering any of it.

I've barely taken in ten minutes of the race. Not because it's dull —it's chaos in high definition. But because my head's somewhere else entirely.

She's under my skin.

Has been for days now. Midnight texts that grow flirtier with each passing night, phone calls stretching long beyond reason, conversations about everything and nothing at all. Sometimes we just sit in silence, listening to each other breathe, like being in the same moment is enough.

And somehow, it is.

But it's becoming more real with each passing second, pushing me closer to something that feels dangerous and thrilling and terrifying all at once.

And that voice in the back of my head, the one that's always been good at fucking things up, starts whispering again.

What if this doesn't last?

What if you're not enough?

What if you let her down?

I've only had glimpses of what Ellie and I could really be. A few fleeting, stolen moments. But it's already enough to ruin me for anything less. I want all of her. Not just the good moments, not just memories I'll carry like trophies.

I'd spend forever learning her silences, reading the secrets she carries but never shares. I'd show up for every messy, complicated moment, even when she insists she can handle it all alone.

I want her storms as much as her softness. Her laughter mid-sentence, the apologies she doesn't need to make, the way she looks away when something truly matters. All of it.

But now, with all that want, comes something to lose.

Ellie was always just out of reach. Close enough to ache for, never close enough to hold. But now she's here. In my world. In every thought that threads through the quiet. And suddenly, it's not just about wanting her. It's about keeping her.

That's what rattles me, the weight of it all, the chance I'll mess it up. And the fear? It's never been louder.

A sudden roar from the TV—someone overtaking on a tight corner—snaps me out of my head. I glance down and realise I've been squeezing a bottle cap so tight it's left a deep red indent in my palm.

"You good, mate?" Theo asks, flicking his gaze toward me, clearly sensing my spiralling thoughts.

His voice is casual, but when I glance over, he's watching me.

That quiet knowing in his eyes. The one he gets when he's clocked I'm not really here.

"Yeah," I reply automatically. Then pause, sighing. "No."

Theo doesn't press. Just leans forward slightly, reaches for his beer, and mutters the word that carries more weight than it should. "*Talk.*"

I roll my eyes, because of course. That one word, no judgement, no bullshit. All cards are on the table.

He shifts, facing me properly now with that calm patience. "Ellie?"

"Who else?" I scrub a hand over my face.

He tosses a Wotsit into his mouth, crunching thoughtfully. "Figured. You've had that lovesick puppy look for weeks."

I give a dry laugh, stealing a Wotsit from his bowl. "Mate, it's bad. She's constantly in my head."

"That's supposed to be a good thing," Theo says lightly, offering the bowl between us like a peace offering. "You deserve something good."

"Yeah. I know…" I trail off, frowning at the bottle in my hands. "But what if I screw it up?"

"You're not going to."

"You don't know that."

Theo leans forward, elbows braced on his knees, expression sobering. "Is this about Ellie, or are we talking about Freya?"

I pause. Hearing her name spoken aloud after all this time still stings more than I expected. "Bit of both," I admit softly, glancing down at my beer. "I fucked things up royally back then."

The TV hums with the distant roar of engines, the commentator's voice rising with tension—but it all blurs into background noise. We sit in the stillness of that name for a second.

"You remember how it ended," I say. "We barely made it to a year."

"You were twenty-two, mate," Theo says gently. "You barely knew how to tie your shoes, let alone hold down a serious relationship. None of us did."

I let out a low breath. "I was selfish. She needed someone who was... there. Not just showing up between rehearsals and last-minute shows and all-night writing sessions. I wanted to be that for her, but I was always chasing the next thing. And eventually, she got tired of waiting."

Theo nods but doesn't interrupt.

"And when it all fell apart, I told myself it was because love didn't fit in this kind of life. That I couldn't have both. Not properly."

"But you're not that guy anymore."

"I know," I say, but it comes out flat. "At least, I want to believe that."

"You think Ellie makes you feel like that guy again?"

"No!" I say quickly. "God no, it's not her. It's me. It's the old stuff. The pressure. The fear. The way I start thinking too far ahead and suddenly I'm convinced I'll mess it all up before it even starts."

Theo tilts his head, watching me. "So don't think too far ahead."

I raise an eyebrow.

"I'm serious. You get in your head when you're ten steps down a road that doesn't even exist yet. What does Ellie need right now?"

I hesitate. "Someone present. Someone who listens."

"Exactly." Theo sits back with a satisfied nod. "Right now, you're giving her exactly that. The future stuff? Deal with it when you get there. You're inventing hurdles that aren't there."

"But that's the problem," I mutter. "What if I can't give her what she needs long-term? Right now, I'm here. I can show up. But what happens when we're back on the road? When we're halfway across the country and she needs more than late-night calls and half-written songs?"

"You're assuming she'll need something you can't give," he says. "But maybe what she needs is what you're already doing. Being there. Being honest. Showing up now, instead of making promises you don't understand yet."

I look over at him. "When did you become all wise and philosophical?"

"Somewhere between your third existential crisis and my weekly therapy appointments," he smirks, cracking his knuckles. "Seriously, man, Ellie grounds you. Anyone can see it. You're steadier, happier. Even Ryder noticed, and he barely looks up from his phone."

"I know that," I say quietly. "It's just... hard to trust that I won't become the version of me I used to be. I don't want to be a disappointment."

"You won't be," he says simply. "Not unless you let fear call the shots."

That line hits hard. Solid and sharp.

Then, more gently: "You're in love with her."

I let out a breath, heavier than I mean to. "I think I could be." I run a hand through my hair, exhale again. "Is that crazy?"

Theo takes a long sip of his beer, then tips his head like he's really thinking it through. "No," he says. "It's not crazy. It's honest. Maybe stop worrying about screwing up and just enjoy being here for once."

"That easy, huh?"

He shrugs casually, smirking. "Never said it was easy, mate, but it sure beats overthinking yourself into misery. You deserve something real."

He picks up the remote and hits pause, catching a bike mid-turn at the apex — rider crouched low, knee grazing the red-and-white curb, caught in perfect, perilous balance. The room stills with it.

"Kieran," he says, voice steady, "stop worrying about fucking it up, and just be in it. One step at a time."

I stare at the blank space between us.

Then nod.

He's right. I know he's right. And still, somewhere deep in my chest, that fear lingers. But it's quieter now. Smaller. Manageable.

"Well, that's enough deep shit for one night," Theo says, stretching with a groan. "You want another beer?"

I huff a laugh—the tension bleeding out of my shoulders. "Yeah. Think I've earned one."

"Damn right you have. Talking about feelings and shit. Very brave."

He's already halfway to the kitchen when I flip him off behind his back, grinning.

He tosses me a beer across the counter. I catch it and pop the cap. Theo cracks his open and sinks back onto the sofa beside me.

The screen flickers back to life. Engines scream. Tyres bite into the track. Another rider dives inside, desperate for position.

"You know — I really do like her," he says.

"Yeah?"

He nods. "She's cool. Real. Got that no-bullshit thing going on, but she's warm with it. You don't get that combo often." He pauses. "And she makes you less... guarded. Like your shoulders drop two inches when she's in the room."

I stare at the bottle in my hand, rolling it between my palms.

I smile into my beer. "Yeah. She's kind of everything."

"Then hold onto it. Trust yourself this time."

I let the words settle. They don't scare me the way they did before. They feel... earned. Like they belong to a part of me I haven't had access to in years. A part that wants more than just noise and distraction and keeping things safe.

I stare at the ceiling like it might hold the answer. "She was a moment back then. One I didn't think I'd get back." I glance over at him. "And now she's here again... I can't let her go."

Theo doesn't respond right away. Just nods slowly, then says, "Well. You're definitely in it."

I let out a breath. "Yeah. I think I've been in it for a while."

He nudges my foot with his. "Then hold on to it. I've known you since we were kids, man. You don't talk like this unless it's real. And I've seen how you are with her. Hell, even when she's not around, you're steadier. Like you're finally anchored."

I don't reply for a moment. Just sit in it. Let the truth of it settle in my chest. Let it land somewhere deep.

"She makes me want to show up," I say eventually. "Not just for the big stuff. For the in-between. The normal. Even the boring. I never wanted that before."

Theo smiles, small and steady. "That's how you know it's real."

I clink my bottle against his. "To not fucking it up."

"To not fucking it up," he echoes.

We fall into a comfortable silence, one of those rare moments where everything feels suspended. Just two friends, a sofa, and a truth that finally doesn't feel too big to carry.

Theo kicks his feet up again, glances sideways. "You're allowed to be happy, you know. You don't have to brace for impact every time something feels good."

I nod. Not just because I agree, but because I want to believe it.

Maybe this thing with Ellie doesn't need a warning label. It just needs to be lived.

I lean back, let the cushion catch me, and let myself believe, for just a moment, that this could actually work.

Theo heads to bed not long after the race ends, muttering something about needing to sleep off the emotional whiplash I just put him through.

I chuckle, low and quiet, and toss a cushion that he doesn't even try to dodge.

The apartment sinks into silence once he's gone, save for the soft creak of the old pipes that run through the building.

I stay on the sofa for a minute, just letting the stillness settle.

My beer's long gone—the bottle warm in my hand.

I set it on the table, stretch, and let the thoughts still rattling around my head lead me to the corner of the room where my notebook's sitting, half-buried under a hoodie.

I flip it open and sit cross-legged on the rug, fingers trailing over pages already filled with half-thoughts and abandoned verses. The pen feels good in my hand. Familiar.

I don't plan what I write. I just… let it happen. A few words, then more. Fragments. Glimpses. Whatever I can catch before they slip.

The curve of her mouth when she smiled at me. Her breath against mine when she whispered that she wanted me. The way she looked in the porch light, her cardigan slipping off one shoulder like the night was trying to undress her too.

The melody's already forming in the back of my head as the lines start to spill. Nothing fancy, just a steady pulse, something gentle but sure.

I pause, mouth curling into a grin.

My legs stretch out in front of me, spine cracking as I lean back against the edge of the sofa. The page in front of me is looking like something whole. Still messy, but alive.

I glance toward the corner of the room, where my acoustic rests against the wall beside the amp. I hesitate for half a second, then reach for it, fingers curling around the neck like it's instinct.

I don't even bother plugging in. I want it raw. Real. Just wood and wire and breath.

The strings are cool beneath my fingertips, but they warm fast. I strum once, softly, letting the sound bloom through the stillness. A low, open chord. A starting place.

The rhythm comes first, lazy and swaying. Something you'd hum without even realising. Something that settles in your chest before it ever hits your ears.

I let it guide me, let it pull me along as my fingers slide into the shape of the next chord, then the next.

It doesn't sound like us onstage. It doesn't sound like a show. It sounds like Ellie.

The way she talks when her guard's down and her hair's a mess and she's wearing one of those ridiculous oversized cardigans that make her look like she's been living inside a cup of tea.

It sounds like her laugh when she's not trying to be polite. Like the softness she gives to Mia when she thinks no one's looking. Like the version of her that only comes out when she's not afraid to take up space.

The hours slip past like they always do when I get in this zone.

At some point, Luca yells through the wall, asking if I'm writing another heartbreak banger or if I've finally grown a soul.

I ignore him.

I glance at the time. Past midnight now.

The world's gone quiet. And I should probably crash. But I don't.

I set the guitar down gently, scribble a few more lines in the corner of the page, then reach for my phone.

Thinking about you.

ELLS [00:15]

😇Thinking how?

> Loaded question.

ELLS [00:15]

Waiting, Hayes.

> That little noise you made when I kissed your neck.

ELLS [00:16]

You should've heard the noises I'd have made if you didn't stop.

> Jesus, Ellie. You trying to kill me?

ELLS [00:17]

You started it 😌

> I should've kept going. Don't think I haven't replayed the way your thighs gripped me.

> The sound you made when I pressed against you.

ELLS [00:18]

Kieran. You're making it very hard to sleep right now.

> If I were there, sleep wouldn't even be on the table.

ELLS [00:19]

What would be? 😌

> You. Definitely you.

ELLS [00:19]

Fuck. This is a dangerous game.

> Baby, I'm just getting started.

My pulse quickens, grin widening. The world narrows to just me, her, and the promise hanging between our words.

Tonight, there's no fear.
Just her.

CHAPTER 35

the ones who show up

ELLIE

THE SMELL OF BURNT TOAST and hairspray fills the air.

Naomi's got one hand wrapped around a coffee mug and the other wielding a curling iron like a weapon, standing in front of the hallway mirror with total concentration. Her hair's half done. Wild curls pinned in sections, steam hissing as she twirls another strand around the barrel. I'm leaning against the doorframe with my dress zipped only halfway up, a mascara wand clamped between my teeth like a rogue makeup artist in crisis.

"This is surreal," she says around a mouthful of coffee. "We did it."

I grunt in agreement, lips stretched wide around the wand, then give up and yank it out. "I know. Like, this is happening. Today."

"Our names on certificates. Official and everything."

"Actual adults."

Naomi snorts without looking away from the mirror. "Don't push it."

Mia drifts past the bathroom like she's already got somewhere better to be. She's dressed in a collared shirt and blazer combo that looks like one of Naomi's old school dance outfits, toast in her hand and a smirk on her face.

"You two are so dramatic," she says, and disappears down the hallway before we can answer.

I catch Naomi's grin in the mirror. "Wait 'til the ceremony, kid. You'll be crying into your programme."

"I'll be yawning into it," Mia calls back, voice light and teasing.

I step into the bedroom and pause in front of the full-length mirror. My dress, which felt like a fun splurge when I bought it weeks ago, looks… grown-up. Like something someone else might wear. Navy satin, soft and weightless, with spaghetti straps and a low, scooped back. Paired with matching stilettos and a clutch that holds approximately three items, I almost look like someone who has her life together.

Almost.

Naomi appears in the doorway, her eyes trailing over me from head to toe before she lets out a low whistle. "Okay. Yeah. If we don't get handed awards today just based on hotness alone, I'm calling the Dean."

I roll my eyes, but there's heat in my cheeks. "Do I look alright?"

She doesn't miss a beat. "You look *unreal*."

I reach up to adjust a loose curl near my temple, fingers shaking. My hair's pinned up in soft waves. The kind that took three attempts, too much hairspray, and several creative swears. But now that it's done—I look like me. Just a version of me that's made it through.

I lift the straps of my dress higher, trying to settle the nerves, and Naomi steps in behind me to zip me up. We catch each other's reflections in the mirror. For a moment, everything stills. The clothes, the makeup, the effort. It's not just dressing up. It's marking something. A threshold. A line in the sand between who we were and who we're becoming.

"Proud of you," Naomi says, her hand resting against my shoulder.

My throat tightens. I bump into her hip. "Right back at you."

She smirks and spins, pointing to her back. "Now zip me up before one of my boobs tries to make a break for it."

I laugh and do as I'm told, dragging the zipper up her dress. It's black velvet and unapologetically bold. Off-the-shoulder with a sweetheart neckline and a fit so snug it looks painted on. Her curls are half-finished but already dramatic, and with her heels and that dark red lipstick she only wears when she wants to feel invincible, she looks like she could storm a runway and burn it down after.

"You look like vengeance," I say, stepping back.

She turns, pleased. "That's the goal."

Mia appears again in the hallway, still holding her toast like a prop, eyeing us both with a dramatic sigh. "Seriously, you two look like you're going to the Oscars."

Naomi tosses her dark curls. "As we should."

"Ugh," Mia groans, reaching for the umbrella. "I'm pretending I don't know you."

Naomi links her arm through mine as we follow Mia down the stairs and into the hallway, the last echoes of burnt toast and perfume trailing behind us.

"Best morning ever," she declares.

And she's not wrong.

The taxi ride is quieter than I expected.

Naomi's scrolling through her phone, probably checking the post she just uploaded of us all glammed up in the hallway mirror. Her lips curl in amusement every so often, the screen lighting up her face in soft flashes. Mia's got one earbud in, eyes trained out the window, fingers tapping against her knee to whatever beat she's listening to. Her dress is neat, her hair brushed and tucked behind her ears, but the slight smudge of chocolate on her lip betrays the caramel bar she snuck earlier.

As we head closer to the city, I watch it slip past the window. Bathed in grey light and softened by drizzle, the weather that usually feels like a warning. But today, it doesn't weigh me down. If anything, it makes everything feel gentler, quieter.

Red brake lights blur on the glass, flickering like a pulse. The buildings roll by, some old and familiar, others newer, but they all look a little softer today. Maybe it's the weather. Maybe it's just me.

Because for once, my thoughts aren't spiralling. Not full of dread, not of doubt, just still. Settled.

But, of course, graduation had to be in November. Nothing

screams celebration like damp tights and numb fingers. And the British weather never misses its cue. Waits until everyone's done their hair, pinned their hats, buttoned up their best coats, and then swoops in right on time.

My curls don't stand a chance. The minute I step out of the taxi, they're going to frizz like I've just licked a socket.

But still. It's surreal.

It's graduation day.

The words settle in my chest, weighty in a way that feels good. Like something earned. Like something that's mine.

There were so many nights I didn't think I'd get here, nights spent trying to be everything at once. A mum. A partner. A student.

Nights where I studied with Mia asleep beside me, a highlighter in one hand and a grocery list in the other. Mornings I walked into lectures already hollow from a night shift. Afternoons I pretended I wasn't running on caffeine and sheer willpower.

Even now, the memory of all those days I white-knuckled my way through still lingers like a bruise just beneath the surface.

But I made it.

We made it.

The taxi slows as we pull up outside the hall, and the buzz hits instantly.

Umbrellas bloom like flowers over the crowd, some barely holding up against the drizzle. People spill across the pavement in caps and gowns, clustered around parents, friends, whoever scored a ticket. There are camera flashes, last-minute hair fixes, the occasional panicked shout about forgetting something. It's chaotic. Joyful. Loud in the best way.

I spot her before she sees me.

Brenda.

She's by the entrance, coat already dotted with rain, holding an umbrella that's far too big for her and looking like she wouldn't have missed this for the world.

I don't hesitate. I shuffle over, heels clicking against wet pavement, heart full before she even says a word. "You made it!" I say.

"Of course I bloody did," she huffs, pulling me into a hug that squeezes all the air out of me. "Look at you, my girl."

She pulls back and does that thing she always does. Gives me the once-over, like she's checking for damage, but only the kind that matters. Her eyes shine.

"You look like a movie star."

I flush, still not used to this kind of praise. "Thanks, Bren."

She tucks a loose strand of hair behind my ear, eyes soft. "Go make us proud."

Inside the hall, the chaos only grows.

Graduates stream in from all sides. A sea of black gowns and flapping sleeves. The building smells like old books and floor polish, echoing with the sounds of clattering heels and nervous laughter. Staff bustle around with clipboards, calling names and pointing people toward roped-off areas. Naomi and I are ushered toward the gown collection, where a frazzled woman hands us robes that smell of starch and pressure.

We step into a side room to don our gowns, and there's something sacred about it, like a rite of passage.

Naomi's adjusting the pleats of her gown in the mirror while muttering about boob sweat. I'm trying to figure out if my hood is supposed to sit this high on my neck or if I'm being strangled by academic tradition.

"You know where you're sitting?" An usher asks as we're handed a seating plan.

"Third row, left side," Naomi says, scanning the paper.

I take a deep breath and glance around. So many faces I barely recognise. So many others I've known for years, some who nearly quit, some who made it look effortless. We're all stitched together now by the same thread.

The ceremony hall is grander than I expected. All vaulted ceilings, stained glass windows glowing in the rain-dimmed light, and long rows of chairs creaking beneath the shuffle of bodies. The space hums with nerves. We take our places—robed and sweating—the buzz in the room vibrating like a tuning fork under my skin.

Naomi leans in. "I swear, if I trip walking across that stage, you better pretend you don't know me."

I laugh, but it's breathless. "*Please*. I'm wearing stilettos. If anyone's going down, it's me."

"You could've worn flats."

"I wanted to feel put together for once."

"You're gonna feel put together when you stack it face-first into the podium."

"Thanks for that."

"Anytime." She quips.

We share a grin then, but beneath it, the tension sits heavy. This is it. The culmination of all those nights on Naomi's living room floor with textbooks open and wine in hand, making promises we weren't sure we could keep.

And now we're here.

The ushers move. We rise with the row ahead of us, edging toward the stage, gowns swishing against our legs, nerves twisting tight in our chests.

Naomi turns and gives me one last wink. "See you on the other side."

"Don't fall," I whisper.

"Wouldn't dare."

I fall quiet, letting my eyes scan the room. Grads fidget in their gowns, laughter bubbling between nerves, names echoing one by one as they cross the stage to polite applause and camera flashes. There's something tender about it all. This messy, beautiful ritual of endings and beginnings. I watch from the sidelines, not quite in it, not quite outside of it either. I feel a swell of something I can't quite name. Pride, maybe. Relief. A flicker of disbelief that I made it here at all.

And then…

"Naomi Clarke."

She walks up like she owns the place. Poised, powerful, head high and stride flawless. My chest swells as she takes her scroll, the overwhelming surge of emotion that's been building all morning, and it's only then I realise my hands are cold. My legs are shaking. My heart is a drumbeat in my ears.

Then it comes…

"Eleanor Carter."

Shit the fucking bed.

I step forward.

The lights hit first. Warm, bright, and almost blinding. The hush in the room wraps around me like a second gown. I take the stairs, each one deliberate. No wobble. No stumble. The weight of the moment presses against my shoulders, but I carry it.

I walk to the centre of the stage and glance toward the crowd.

Brenda's beaming, hands clasped to her chest like she might burst. And God Mia, she's cheering, *actually* cheering. Her blazer sleeves pushed up to her elbows, eyes wide with pride.

I used to picture this moment. Standing on this stage, looking out at a sea of faces, searching for familiar ones. I imagined my parents sitting there, straight-backed and serious. I imagined David clapping dutifully, one hand on Mia's shoulder.

But they're not here. And somehow… I don't want them to be.

Because in their place are the two people who matter most. Brenda, who never stopped believing in me, and Mia, who's been my reason every step of the way.

They're here. Fully, unapologetically here. And that's enough. That's everything.

Just when the emotion rises hot behind my eyes…

"WOOOOO! GO ON, ELLIE!"

The shout ricochets through the hall like a firework. I turn — *stunned* — and there they are. Near the back. Kieran, Luca, Ryder, and Theo, crammed together like a pack of overgrown teenagers, whooping like they're front row at a concert. Kieran's cupping his hands around his mouth, grinning like he's been waiting for this exact moment. Ryder's waving his baseball cap like a man possessed.

I laugh, and the dean chuckles as he hands me the scroll, like he's seen a hundred graduations but never a moment quite like this.

My fingers wrap around the certificate. My cheeks are flushed. The world feels large and close all at once.

I shake the dean's hand, scroll firm in my grasp, heart hammering against my ribs.

And as I walk off stage, cheeks warm and vision blurred, I know, without question…

This moment? It's mine.

And God, it's never felt better.

***

The crowd spills out of the hall like champagne. Bubbly, chaotic, and fizzing with adrenaline. Umbrellas pop open as the drizzle turns heavier, gowns flapping in the wind, families calling out names across the steps. Laughter echoes off the stone. Everyone is hugging everyone. Cameras flash. Someone's baby is crying. The scent of wet leaves and hairspray clings to everything.

I don't know where to look first.

Naomi's beside me, arm looped through mine, velvet soaked at the hem already, curls half-loose from all the hugging. She's buzzing. Absolutely glowing. Her cheeks are pink, eyes wide, already waving at someone across the street.

I love her like this.

But it's not her I'm scanning the crowd for.

It's him.

And then I hear it. Laughter, low and unmistakable. It cuts through the noise like a melody I know by heart. I turn, and there they are, moving toward us like they own the pavement. A band reunion disguised as a graduation crash. Underdressed in the most on-brand way. Leather jackets, untucked shirts, trainers soaked through. They're grinning like they've just got away with something illegal.

Kieran slows as he gets closer, and it hits me like a tidal wave. That look. The one that always finds me first. His eyes sweep the gown, the curls pinned at the nape of my neck, the navy satin dress he's only seen in photos until now.

And I swear, I see it land on him.

Like this moment, this one right here is getting folded up and tucked somewhere beneath his ribs.

He stops right in front of me, rain dripping from his hair and catching in his lashes. His white shirt clings to him, sleeves rolled to his elbows, almost translucent from the drizzle. Like the weather's determined to torture me even more. His jeans are soaked at the hems, and his hands stay buried deep in his pockets, like if he reaches for me now, he might not stop.

"Hey, you."

My cheeks flush. "Hey."

"How the hell did you lot even get in?" I arch a brow.

He grins, soft and mischievous. "We have our ways."

Of course they do.

He takes a step closer, eyes locked on mine like I'm the only thing left worth noticing. "You were incredible up there."

I huff a quiet laugh. "Thanks to you lot shouting like I just won the lottery."

"You did," he says, voice low, meant only for me. "You just don't know it yet."

Before I can respond, Luca swoops in behind him.

"Well, if it isn't our two favourite brain boxes," he says, flashing a grin. "Officially clever and officially fit. Dangerous combo."

Naomi snorts. "You're such a menace."

"You're welcome," he replies, and pulls her into a hug anyway.

Theo appears next, somehow producing two crushed bouquets out of nowhere. He hands one to me, one to Naomi, like a magician revealing his last trick. "For academic excellence and general hotness," he declares. "Accept these humble offerings."

Naomi raises a brow. "Are these from a garage?"

"No!" he says, wounded. "Tesco. The expensive aisle. I had to fight someone for that one."

Ryder just grins, hands in his pockets as usual, eyes warm and proud. "Congrats, both of you," he says. "We're proud as hell."

It's ridiculous. It's perfect. All of them talking over each other, teasing, hugging, completely themselves. My people. The family I found when I didn't even know I was still looking. And they showed up.

Of course they did.

"Radiant, you were," Brenda says, suddenly beside me, her hand smoothing down my arm. "You've come through fire for this, Ellie. And you did it with grace."

That gets me. A lump rises in my throat, fast and hot. All I can manage is a small, wobbly smile. The kind that says more than words ever could.

"Thank you for inviting me, love," she says, pulling me into a hug that smells like lavender and lemon drops. "I'm so incredibly proud of you. And your parents would've been too."

My throat tightens. I nod against her shoulder. "I'm so glad you came."

We pull apart, and I glance out at the crowd. Families still mingling and taking photos, mums crying into tissues, dads clapping each other on the back. For a moment, something aches deep in my chest.

"I thought about asking them," I murmur, half to myself. "I kept going back and forth about it. And then I just… didn't. I wasn't ready to make it their day too."

Brenda doesn't flinch. Just nods, steady. "You've been through enough, love. You needed this one for you."

"I still feel a bit guilty," I admit. "Like maybe they should've been here."

"They're your parents," she says, looping her arm through mine. "They love you. And things will work themselves out. There's still time for that."

I exhale slowly, grateful for her steadiness. "I hope so."

She squeezes my hand. "I know so."

Brenda cups my cheek, brushing a thumb across it like she used to when I was small. "Go and celebrate properly, yeah? You deserve to feel it. And don't worry about Mia, she's coming home with me tonight. Already sorted."

Before I can say a word, Mia appears at my side, practically bouncing.

"Brenda says she's got popcorn and a film marathon ready," she announces, eyes wide. "And I get to stay up as late as I want."

Brenda lifts a brow. "Within reason."

Mia grins and slips her hand into mine. "Seriously, Mum. Go have fun. You looked so happy on that stage. This is your night. You deserve it."

God, this kid. My heart squeezes as I pull her into a hug, pressing a kiss to the top of her head and passing her my flowers. "Thanks, bug. You behave, alright?"

She pulls back with a dramatic scoff. "I'm an angel."

Brenda snorts. "That's one way to put it."

I laugh—heart full in a way I didn't realise it had space to be. I watch them walk toward the car park. Mia chatting animatedly, Brenda nodding along, umbrella bobbing in rhythm. My little girl and the woman who stepped up when no one else did.

And that's when Naomi appears at my side again.

"Okay, hear me out. Cocktails, rooftop bar, and someone better be taking photos because I didn't wear this dress to be ignored."

She does a little spin—the velvet catching the light—and I swear half the crowd turns. She's electric. Flushed cheeks, pinned curls, eyes alive with that post-triumph glow.

Ryder gives her a look I can't quite place. "Yeah, that's not a dress you ignore."

Naomi smirks. "I know."

He leans in, voice low. "Keep wearing things like that and I might start writing you poetry."

"Please don't," Theo groans, already fumbling for his phone.

Naomi just winks, looping her arm through mine. "You coming, graduate?"

But my eyes are already drifting elsewhere. Back to Kieran.

Still standing a few feet away, hands in his pockets, looking at me like I'm the only person in the world. His grin is soft, a little crooked, and my heart does that stupid somersault again. It's not flashy. It's not showy. It's quiet and steady and clear.

And suddenly, rooftop bars and cocktails feel distant. Not wrong —just not mine. Not tonight.

"I think I've got other plans," I say softly.

Naomi follows my gaze and smirks. No teasing this time. Just that look. The one that says *finally*.

She leans in, voice pitched just for me. "Go get your own rooftop moment, babe. You earned it."

And then she's gone. Heels clicking, curls bouncing, dragging the chaos along with her. Ryder calls after her, "You're buying the first round!" and she flips him off over her shoulder like a queen.

Theo whistles, clearly impressed by the velvet and the audacity. Luca grins at me and calls, "Wear protection, kids!" just loud enough to turn heads.

"It's like watching the prom queen sneak off with the rockstar." Theo laughs.

"You're all absolute children," I mutter, laughing despite myself.

Kieran lifts his hands in mock surrender. "Just a heads up, our place is off-limits for the next twenty-four hours. Enter at your own risk."

"Oh my God," I mumble under my breath, face heating. But I'm smiling so hard my cheeks hurt.

And then his fingers brush mine. Just lightly. Just enough.

I look up.

He's closer now, his hand warm as it wraps around mine. Solid and sure. The crowd fades. The voices, the drizzle, the background noise of a hundred different reunions… it all softens into something hazy. Distant.

It's just us.

And Kieran's gaze is locked on mine, like he's trying to memorise me from the inside out. There's no mask in it. No charm, no teasing. Just fire. Want. Something deeper than either of us have dared to name. And in that breathless, perfect quiet, I know I could fall into this, *into him*, and never look back. Because whatever this is between us, it isn't fleeting.

It's already rooted. Deep, steady, and impossible to dig out.

CHAPTER 36
it's always been her
KIERAN

THE CROWD IS FADING BEHIND us, swallowed up by the hum of traffic and the golden blur of streetlights. Ellie's hand is tucked into mine—warm and sure—her thumb brushing absently over my knuckles like she doesn't even realise she's doing it.

We're not saying much. Don't need to. The air between us is thick with something electric, something inevitable. Her heels click softly against the pavement as we walk, her laugh from moments ago still echoing somewhere in the back of my mind.

Theo's ridiculous commentary. Luca's parting shout. My warning to the others not to come anywhere near the apartment. It was all noise. Loud, chaotic, stupidly perfect noise. But now, it's just us.

I glance at her out of the corner of my eye.

She's radiant. And not in the cliché sense people throw around like confetti. She's the kind of radiant that lives in the way her shoulders are finally relaxed, in the way she walks like she's not bracing for something anymore. Her dress clings to her like a secret, her hair slightly damp from the rain, and there's a faint flush on her cheeks that's got nothing to do with champagne.

She looks over at me, eyes sharp and amused. "What's the plan, rockstar?"

I can't help the smile that tugs at my mouth. "The plan?"

"Yeah," she says, tilting her head, her voice lilting with playfulness. "You've got this look, like you've got something up your sleeve."

I stop walking just long enough to turn to her fully, fingers tightening slightly around hers. "There's only one plan, Ellie."

"Oh yeah?"

My response is nothing more than a low, rough, "Mmhmm."

And then I lean in.

Her breath catches just before my mouth finds hers. Slow, and deliberate, with the pressure that promises more. Her lips part on instinct, soft, warm, and slightly sweet from the champagne. I deepen it just enough to feel her sway closer. Her hand curls lightly into the front of my shirt, her fingers brushing over the buttons like she's already imagining undoing them.

When we finally break apart, she's breathless. Glowing.

Her voice is low, but laced with intent. "Wave down a taxi, Hayes. *Now*."

And fuck if I don't move like it's the most urgent thing I've ever been told to do.

We pile into the back of the taxi like it's an escape car.

Ellie's pressed up against me, her leg brushing mine, the heat of her body sinking into my skin through the damp fabric of her dress. And Christ, that slit, every time she shifts, the fabric parts just enough to flash smooth skin and the promise of more, and it's doing unspeakable things to my self-control.

The driver mumbles something about the rain, about the roads being slick, but I don't hear it. I can't think about anything except the way her fingers curl around my thigh like she owns it. Like she's been waiting all night to touch me.

She doesn't say a word. Just rests her hand there, her thumb stroking idle, dangerous little circles against my jeans. I swear I feel every pass of her touch like a lightning strike straight through the centre of me. My body's already on high alert, heart racing like I've run a marathon instead of sitting completely still.

I glance at her. She's looking out the window, all casual elegance, like she's not setting my entire nervous system on fire. Her lips are curved in the faintest smirk.

"I can feel you staring," she says softly.

"Not even gonna pretend I'm not," I murmur.

She finally turns to me then, her eyes catching mine, low and molten. "You planning on doing something about it?"

"Soon as we get through that door," I say, voice rough with everything I'm holding back.

Her fingers flex slightly on my thigh, and I feel it like a pulse.

The taxi turns the last corner and I reach over, brushing a damp curl away from her cheek. She leans into my touch, just slightly, her eyes on mine like they've got nowhere else to be. Then, as we pull up outside the apartment, I toss the driver a few notes without even checking the total, already reaching for the door.

Ellie takes my hand, fingers tight in mine, heels clicking as we half-run, half-laugh toward the building entrance. Her dress clings to her legs, satin dark with rain, and her laugh floats through the air like it belongs to another world. Something wild and free and impossibly real.

By the time we're inside, wet and breathless, I know one thing for sure.

I'm not letting her out of my arms tonight.

The ride up feels longer than it is. The elevator glides slowly, the floor numbers blinking overhead, and Ellie leans back against the mirrored wall like she's posing for a magazine shoot and has no idea. Except she does. *She definitely does.*

The slit of her dress parts again, revealing more of that endless leg, and I swear I nearly groan out loud. Her skin's still damp from the rain, glistening faintly in the low light. A curl sticks to her collarbone. Her lips are parted just slightly, chest rising and falling like she's barely keeping herself together.

And *fuck*—same.

She catches me looking. Smirks. Lifts an eyebrow like she's daring me to say something.

I don't. I step in close and her breath catches.

She tips her chin up just enough to meet my gaze, and I watch the heat flicker in her eyes, something alive and hungry and entirely mine.

"Come here often?" She murmurs, voice all velvet and challenge.

I don't answer. I just look at her. Because there's no witty comeback left in me. No smart remark. Just want. Thick and hot and curling low in my gut.

The space between us vibrates with tension, like a wire stretched to its limit, ready to snap.

Her fingers find my wrist. Not pulling. Not guiding. Just touching.

And it's enough to unravel me.

I shift closer, one hand braced beside her head, the other skimming the bare curve of her hip where the dress parts, sliding just high enough to make her eyes flutter.

"Kieran…"

My name on her lips is barely a breath. Barely a sound.

But it wrecks me.

I lean in and our mouths crash together like they've been waiting for this all night. She gasps into the kiss, and I drink it in, taking my time, letting my tongue slide against hers—deep and slow.

She moans softly, hips tilting just enough to make me groan into her mouth. My hand slides down her back, fingers splaying at the base of her bare spine where the fabric dips low. Anchoring her to me as my other hand slips just beneath the edge of her dress. Enough to feel silk, skin and temptation.

Then, the elevator dings and the doors slide open, shattering the moment.

It takes everything in me to pull away, to grab her hand instead of backing her into the mirrored wall and forgetting the rest of the night exists.

"Come," I rasp, guiding her out like I've still got my shit together.

She follows, quiet and breathless, heels clicking against the marble floor as we make our way down the hall. Until her voice cuts through the tension, low and dry behind me.

"Don't threaten me with a good time, Hayes."

I glance back, and she's smirking. Just barely. But it's there, and it hits me harder than it should.

"Careful," I say, voice still thick. "I might take that as encouragement."

"Please do."

Jesus.

This woman.

The key slips into the lock with a quiet click.

Behind me, Ellie's close. So close I can feel the heat of her breath against the back of my neck. Her silence is louder than anything. Thick, expectant, and laced with want.

The door creaks open, and I hold it for her. She brushes past, her hand trailing across my chest as she steps inside. Nothing more than fingertips, but it leaves a fire in its wake. The door clicks shut behind us with a finality that feels a lot like fate.

She's already halfway into the apartment by the time I turn, like she owns the place, like she owns me. The hem of that navy dress flutters around her ankles as she turns back to face me, framed by the city lights behind her. Her skin glows gold in the room's warmth, and her hair's still a little damp from the rain, strands curling wildly around her face.

I drink her in.

Every curve, every detail, every inch of exposed skin I haven't touched yet.

Then my eyes drop.

"That slit," I mutter. "Should be illegal."

Then she grins. Like she knows. Like she planned it that way.

I back her toward the sofa, hands at her hips, walking slowly— like I'm dragging out every second. The dress shifts with every step. Satin brushing against her skin, that slit teasing more and more. And I swear it's the only thing keeping me from dropping to my knees right here.

She hits the edge of the sofa and doesn't stop, just sinks into the cushions. Legs folding with effortless grace, hair tumbling around her shoulders like something out of a dream I've had far too many times.

I reach out slowly as I gaze down at her. My fingers trace along her jaw, feather-light, then down her cheeks. She leans into the touch like it steadies her. I tuck a loose strand of hair behind her ear, watching her breath catch.

"Ellie," I murmur, voice thick. "You're so beautiful."

I kneel in front of her, and as she parts her thighs to let me in, the fabric of her dress falls away completely, baring the smooth length of her thigh. My breath leaves me in a rush.

I rest my hands just above her knees, gliding upward.

"Jesus," I whisper. "You're gonna kill me."

She smiles, fingers combing through my hair, light and teasing.

"You complaining?"

"Not even close."

I press a kiss to the inside of her knee, slow and reverent, then another a little higher. Her breath hitches, the smallest sound, but it lands like thunder in my chest. I drag my lips up her thigh, tasting salt and heat and the faint trace of her perfume.

When I reach the point where the dress still covers her, I pause and look up.

Her eyes are locked on mine. Full of fire.

"Take it off," I say, low, almost a growl.

She doesn't ask which part.

She just reaches for the thin straps and slides them off her shoulders with slow, devastating grace. The satin pools at her waist, leaving her bare from the chest up.

My eyes drag over her curves, her skin—all flushed and perfect. Her nipples are tight from the chill and the heat between us. Her chest rises with every breath, hands still curled around the dress like she's holding on just enough to stay grounded.

"You, are perfect."

She reaches for me, and I move. Mouth on hers, hungry and reckless, like the kiss is the only thing tethering me to the earth.

It's messy. Desperate. Teeth and tongue and soft moans swallowed between us. Her hands are under my shirt, over my chest, tugging at the waistband of my jeans like she's just as gone as I am.

Then she shifts, pulling me forward, pulling me over her.

Her legs cradle my hips as her fingers fist the back of my shirt, dragging me down until I'm covering her completely.

My weight settles on top of her, hips aligned, chest to chest, and everything inside me short-circuits.

I cup her full breast, fingers spreading to take in every inch. She gasps, quiet and breathless, and arches into me like she's chasing the contact. I roll my thumb over her nipple—feel it pebble under my touch. She whimpers, hips shifting beneath me, and the sound goes straight to my cock.

"Fuck, Ellie," I breathe, dragging my lips down her jaw, her throat, over the spot where her pulse races. "You're unbelievable."

She doesn't answer, just lets out a needy, broken moan. Her nails skim down my back. Her thighs lock tighter.

I trail my hand lower, down her ribs, over her stomach. Slow. Deliberate. I want her aching for it. I want her shaking.

When I reach the hem of her dress, I tug gently, letting the fabric inch up her thighs. She lifts her hips to help, eyes locked on mine.

"Off," I murmur, rough with restraint. "I want it all off."

She nods, breathless, arms raised. I shift back, pulling the navy satin up and over her.

Then it's gone, crumpled on the floor like it never mattered.

She's left in nothing but a scrap of navy lace and the flicker of city lights dancing over her skin.

Jesus fucking Christ.

I sit back on my heels, just looking. She's stretched out and undone. Entirely mine. Her chest rises and falls in shallow, unsteady breaths, and her legs shift, inviting me in.

"I made a promise," I whisper, "that I'd make you feel everything."

Then I reach for her again. "This is me keeping that promise."

My fingers trail along the edge of the lace, and her breath stutters, hips jolting.

"Is this what you wore under that dress all night?" I murmur, my mouth against her collarbone as my hand slips beneath the fabric, finally touching her.

She gasps, body arching. "Fuck," she breathes. "Yes, Kieran."

I press a slow, steady circle against her clit. She arches—mouth open with a sound that wrecks me.

"Ellie," I groan, sucking gently at the spot just below her ear. "You have no idea what you do to me."

She lifts her hips again. Shameless and begging. "Then show me."

And fuck me, I do.

I slide my hand further under the fabric of her thong, my fingers wet from how ready she is, how much she wants this. I drag my touch through her, slowly at first. Just enough to tease.

Then I sink two fingers inside her, deep and purposeful.

She gasps, her whole body jolting under the sudden stretch, her head falling back into the cushions, eyes rolling back.

I find a rhythm, firm and steady, and curve my fingers just right, brushing that sweet spot over and over.

She cries out, hips jerking, her thighs trembling on either side of me. "Oh my god. Kieran…"

Her hands are in my hair now, gripping tight, trying to anchor herself as I work her open. I press in deep, then draw back slowly, dragging against every nerve-ending until her mouth falls open on a strangled moan.

"You were made for me, Ellie." I murmur, voice hot against her throat.

She whimpers, writhing, chasing the rhythm with every roll of her hips.

I press my palm snug against her, grinding against her clit in time with each thrust, and she's almost there. I can feel it.

I pull out of her and rise slowly, meeting her eyes. Her chest is rising and falling like she's just run a marathon. Then I scoop her up into my arms, because there's more. So much more.

"Bedroom," I whisper against her mouth.

She nods, her voice gone, her fingers digging into my shoulders as I carry her across the apartment and into the bedroom—but I don't lay her down.

Not yet.

Instead, I lower her slowly to her feet at the foot of the bed, her body close to mine, her breath warm against my neck. She steadies herself with a hand on my chest, and then she looks up at me, something dark and determined gleaming in her eyes.

She undoes my shirt slowly, fingers brushing just under the collar. She kisses her way across my jaw, down my throat, lips dragging against stubble. Her hands slide over my skin as she spreads my shirt open, her mouth mapping the path downward.

She unbuttons my jeans.

My breath hitches as she works them open, her fingers brushing the hard line of me. Then she frees me, one hand wrapping around me without hesitation.

A low, broken sound leaves my throat.

She looks up, grip steady, eyes blazing.

"You're unravelling me," I manage.

She just smiles, wicked and soft.

"That's the idea."

And then I'm kissing her again, rough and urgent. My hands in her hair, hers dragging down my back now.

I kick out of my jeans, blind with need.

Then I lift her. She wraps around me effortlessly, and I carry her to the bed, kneeling onto the edge and lowering her slowly, gently.

Her back hits the sheets, her hair spreads like a halo, and her legs part for me without hesitation.

And I still can't believe she's here. That she's mine.

I kiss her harder. Tongue sliding against hers as my hand trails down her side, memorising her all over again.

"Hands," I whisper against her neck. "Put them above your head."

She obeys, fingers curling around the headboard.

"Don't let go."

I trail my mouth down her chest, taking my time. I suck one nipple into my mouth, then the other, lavishing her with attention until she's writhing, arching, gasping beneath me.

I drag my tongue over her stomach, kiss along her hips. She opens for me without a word.

I hook my thumbs into her thong, sliding it down slowly.

"Kieran," she moans.

I grin.

"Still gripping that headboard?"

She nods.

"Good girl."

Then I press my mouth to her—and she *shatters*.

She gasps my name, hips jolting, trying to chase it. But I hold her down. I lick, suck, tease. Slow, deliberate, and devastating. I keep her on the edge until she's trembling. Until her voice breaks.

And just when she's about to come. I stop.

"Kieran," she begs, eyes wild.

"Not yet," I murmur. "We'll get there, baby. Just trust me."

I crawl up her body, hard and aching, cock pressing against her stomach. She wraps her hand around me and strokes once.

I groan, my head dropping to her shoulder.

"I need you," she whispers. "*Now*."

I reach for the drawer, tear open the foil, and hand her the condom. She rolls it on with shaking hands. And fuck, it's the sexiest thing I've ever seen.

I hook her legs around my waist and slide into her in one smooth thrust.

Fuuuck!

She gasps, clinging to me, and I am still just for a second.

"You feel," I rasp, "so fucking good."

She nods, barely breathing, her lips parted like the air's caught somewhere in her throat. Her eyes lock on mine and I can feel the tremble in her legs where they're wrapped around me. I move, slow and deliberate, dragging every inch, every heartbeat, letting her feel the weight of it. Her breath stutters, her fingers tighten against my back, and all I can do is hold her gaze and give her everything I've been holding back.

"Harder, Kieran," she whispers.

And my control snaps.

I pull out almost completely, the loss of contact making her gasp. And then I drive back in, hard and deep. My hands lock around her hips, fingers digging in, grounding me as I thrust into her like I'm trying to etch myself into her skin.

She cries out, arms flying up around my shoulders. Her heels dig into my back, pulling me closer, deeper, like she can't get enough. Like she doesn't want space between us. She's taking all of it. Every inch. Every thrust. Every broken breath that cracks the silence between us.

And I want to give her more.

Not just pleasure, but all of it. The kind that stays in her bones. The kind that ruins her for anything that isn't this. Isn't *us*.

I shift my weight, never breaking rhythm, and reach up to grab a pillow from the top of the bed. Sliding it beneath the curve of her lower back, I lift her hips just enough to tilt her to me. Her gasp catches in her throat as the new angle hits and her nails sink into my shoulders, leaving hot, stinging trails in their wake.

"Oh my God," she whimpers, arching her body and tipping her head back. "That feels so… fuck!"

I lose myself in the sound, in the feel of her wrapped around me, taking everything I give and silently begging for more.

I brace one hand beneath the pillow to keep her steady, the other gripping a firm handful of her ass, fingers digging deep as I pull her into each thrust.

"You take it so good, Ellie," I growl, voice rough with everything I'm holding back.

Her body trembles beneath me, every wrecked moan ripped from her throat.

I drive into her again and again, burying myself to the hilt, the sound of skin meeting skin sharp and relentless, mixing with the broken rhythm of her breathing. Her hands claw at me. My hair, my back, anything she can grab, like she's trying to anchor herself to this moment, to us.

She's close. I can feel it in the way her legs shake, in the stuttering gasps that spill from her lips, in the desperate tension pulling tight between us.

She's right on the edge. And I'm not stopping until I see her fall.

So, I slow. Deliberate and controlled. Drawing it out just long enough to make it unforgettable.

"Look at me, baby." I murmur, voice rough but tender, thumb brushing along her bottom lip.

Her lashes flutter, then lift. And when her eyes find mine, wide, glassy, and brimming with something fragile, it feels like the entire world stops for a moment to breathe with us.

And in that breath, when her eyes find mine, everything stills.

She lifts a hand and cups my face, her touch feather-light but desperate, like she's grounding herself in something real. Then, a single tear spills down her cheek, trailing across her skin.

"Baby," I breathe, the word catching somewhere in my chest. I lift a hand to catch the tear with my thumb, my other cradling the back of her neck. "Are you okay?"

She doesn't answer right away. Her mouth opens, closes. Her throat works through the silence, and I wait.

"I don't—I've never..." Her voice is quiet, barely a whisper. "I have never had this before. No one has ever made me feel like—"

"Like you're everything?" I finish for her, voice low. "Because you are, Ellie. Everything and more."

She blinks hard. More tears. No retreat. Just raw, unfiltered truth.

I run both my hands to the sides of her neck. Keeping her anchored as I press my forehead to hers. "I promised you," I say, "you will *always* feel everything with me."

Her lips part, and she presses a gentle kiss to my lips.

"God, Ells," I whisper, heart thudding, "I think I—"

"Shhh."

Her fingers curl around the back of my neck, pulling me closer. "I know," she says, voice shaking but sure. "I feel it."

I let out a breath I didn't know I was holding, something like relief breaking across my chest. Then, I kiss her. Slowly. Completely. Like every second of this has been waiting for us to arrive here.

I move slowly, deliberately, letting the rhythm build between us. There's no rush, no need for more that this. Just the steady grind of my hips against hers, our bodies aligning perfectly, as if made to fit together exactly this way.

Her hands slide over my back, nails grazing lightly, anchoring. Her breath stutters, like she wasn't expecting it to feel like this.

Our eyes stay locked the entire time. She doesn't look away, not even when her mouth falls open, not when her thighs tighten around my waist, pulling me deeper, harder.

I move with her, each thrust a promise. Each breath a confession.

And then she shatters.

I feel it first, the way her body tenses, trembling under me. The way her breath catches and a soft, broken moan tears from her throat. Her legs lock around me, holding me like I'm the only steady thing she has.

She comes undone with her eyes still on mine. Not hidden. Not ashamed. Just open. Honest and bare.

And fuck, in this moment, she is the most beautiful thing I have ever seen.

The way she opens for me. Gives in to it.

And that's all it takes.

I groan against her skin, burying my face in the crook of her neck as release rushes through me, hot and blinding, a full-body tremor that drags me under right along with her. My hips slow, easing us through it, deeper and deeper until we're both spent.

Until there's nothing left but the sound of our breathing. The echo of our heartbeats tangled together in the quiet.

She cups my face, her touch light and grounding. Her thumb brushes just beneath my cheekbone, a wordless comfort. And I lift my head, eyes meeting hers.

She's soft now. Glowing. Flushed and radiant and entirely real.

I lean in and kiss her, not frantic or hungry, but full of everything I still don't know how to say.

She exhales into it like a sigh of relief, like she's been waiting for this exact softness. My arms slide around her, holding her close as I deepen the kiss. Her hands come up to cradle my jaw, her fingers brushing behind my ear, anchoring us there, in that breath, in that kiss.

When we finally part, neither of us moves.

I wrap her in my arms fully, gathering her against me as we shift onto our sides. The sheets are tangled around our legs, the quiet glow of the bedside lamp casting a warm hush over the room. Her cheek rests against my chest, one hand splayed gently over my heart, the other still curled near her mouth like she's holding something sacred between her fingers.

My thumb traces slow circles over her bare shoulder, brushing the curve of her skin again and again like I can't stop touching her. Like I don't want to.

Because this wasn't just sex—not even close.

It's her.

It's always been her.

CHAPTER 37

everything and then nothing

ELLIE

THE FIRST THING I FEEL is his arm. Warm and heavy, slung across my waist like it belongs there.

The second is the soft ache in my legs, a delicious hum lingering deep in my muscles, a secret only I get to keep.

And the third is him. Kieran. Pressed up behind me, his chest rising and falling against my back in slow, even breaths. One hand curls loosely at my stomach. Not gripping, just resting. As if even in sleep, he can't let go.

The room is cloaked in grey-blue shadows, that in-between hour when the city hasn't quite woken up. Golden streaks of early sunlight slip around the edges of the blinds, painting soft patterns across the bedsheets. I don't move. Not yet. I stay still, tucked into the shape of him, wrapped in warmth and something dangerously close to peace.

Last night replays in vivid flashes. His mouth, his hands, the way he looked at me like I was something sacred. How he said my name, as though it wasn't just a word but a vow.

He told me he wanted me to feel everything.

And *God*... I did.

It was like he reached inside and rewrote every part of me that had been quiet for too long.

He made me feel beautiful. *Worshipped*. Real.

I shift slightly, just enough to glimpse his face soft in sleep, lips parted, one arm tucked close, the other still resting on my waist. His hair is tousled, stubble shadowing his jaw, making him unfairly gorgeous even now.

And he's *mine*.

Maybe not officially, maybe not in the ways people label.

But in all the ways that matter?

Yeah. He's mine.

I press a soft kiss to the inside of his wrist, just above where his fingers rest on my skin. He stirs, groaning quietly.

"Careful, Carter," he mumbles, voice thick with sleep and the gravelly rasp that never fails to wreck me. "Kiss me like that and I'm never letting you leave."

I smile against his skin. "Is that supposed to be a threat?"

He shifts closer, burying his face in the crook of my neck. "It's a promise."

"You're clingy in the mornings," I tease, tracing circles on his forearm.

"You weren't complaining last night when I was clinging to you."

I laugh softly. "That was different. That was… enthusiastic."

He chuckles, rough and smug. "Enthusiastic? Ellie, I made you forget your own name."

I roll onto my side, grinning. "Cocky this early, huh?"

He lifts one eye open just enough to smirk. "You bring it out in me."

"I was perfectly well-behaved."

His smirk deepens. "You literally climbed on top of me and…"

I slap a hand over his mouth, laughing. "Okay, okay! Let's not relive the highlights."

He nips playfully at my palm, then twines our fingers together, kissing the back of my hand. "Highlight reels on a loop in my head, just so you know."

"You're impossible."

"And yet…" He lifts my hand to his chest as if it's proof. "You stayed."

That gets me. Because yeah. I did. It wasn't just about last night. It was about choosing him. Choosing us, even if I don't yet have the full picture.

I soften my voice. "You hungry?"

"Starving," he says. "I make a mean coffee and can burn toast like a pro."

"Be still, my beating heart."

He kisses my knuckles again, grinning.

I roll my eyes, but I'm smiling as I lean in to kiss him. It starts gently, but the moment I slip my fingers into his hair, it deepens. His breath hitches, grip tightening.

Then he rolls me onto my back, slow and sure, the sheet sliding between us. He braces over me, one arm at my waist, the other brushing my cheek. His gaze moves over my face as if memorising me all over again.

"You're okay?" he asks quietly.

I nod, not trusting my voice, pulling him down to kiss me again. This time, it's fire.

"Still hungry?" he murmurs against my skin, voice rough and teasing.

I drag my nails lightly along his shoulder, biting my lip to hide a smile.

"Starving," I whisper. "But I think breakfast can wait."

He's already tugging the duvet aside when I grab his hand, breathless from how he looks at me. He wraps me in a sheet, and we pad barefoot down the hallway. He nudges the bathroom door open with his shoulder, flicking on the warm, muted light. His movements are unhurried, like he knows exactly what we need.

The glass shower is faintly fogged, lingering warmth curling around us. He turns the tap with practised precision, testing the temperature, then glances back at me and crooks a finger. "Come here," he murmurs.

I drop the sheet and step into the space between us without hesitation, his arm sliding around my waist, pulling me flush against him. He presses a gentle kiss to my shoulder, just enough to make my heart stutter.

Steam rises, enveloping us in a quiet cocoon.

When he guides me beneath the spray, everything else falls away.

I rest a hand on his chest, feeling his steady heartbeat, and lean in to brush a kiss over his collarbone. He groans softly—the sound punched from his chest.

As my fingertips drift slowly across his skin, my eyes catch again on that tattoo. It's small and intricate, tucked just to the left of his heart. A delicate tangle of lines I glimpsed once before, that morning in Rosemere, but couldn't quite make out then. And last night, in the heat and darkness, I somehow missed it entirely. But now, in the soft morning light, I see it clearly.

Gently, I trace its edges, following the lines until the shape reveals itself.

"When did you get this?" I ask softly, curiosity colouring my voice.

His breath catches slightly as my fingertips linger. He glances down, eyes softening as he realises what I'm asking. "After that week," he murmurs, voice quiet, vulnerable.

My heart skips. I lean closer, looking again, and I see it perfectly.

A Ferris wheel.

Simple and subtle, but unmistakable. A memory etched permanently into his skin, into his story. Our story.

Emotion wells thick in my throat. "You…kept it with you, all this time?"

He meets my eyes, his gaze warm and full of quiet certainty. "I think part of me always knew our story wasn't finished, Ells."

My chest tightens, something beautiful and fragile swelling between us. I open my mouth, but words escape me.

Kieran gently cups my face in his hands, thumbs brushing lightly over my cheekbones. His voice drops, achingly tender, filled with the raw truth he's held for years.

"It's always been you, Ellie." He pauses, eyes holding mine steady, voice barely more than breath. "I love you."

My heart stumbles.

The words hit like a wave. My pulse kicks hard beneath my skin, and that rogue butterfly I thought had quieted flutters violently to life, its wings beating against the walls of my chest like it's trying to escape. My whole body feels suspended in that moment, caught between breath and heartbeat.

I open my mouth to speak, to say something, anything, but nothing comes out.

Not because I don't feel it. God, I do. It's all I've been feeling. It's threaded through every breath, every look, every time I reach for him without thinking. But the words catch somewhere in my throat, thick and too heavy with everything they mean.

Kieran's thumbs brush lightly along my cheekbones, grounding me.

"Hey — baby, look at me." he says gently, lifting my chin to meet his gaze. "You don't have to say it back. Not yet."

My eyes sting. I shake my head, helpless.

"I know," he murmurs. "I know you feel it. I see it every time you look at me."

I swallow hard, eyes locked on his.

"I just... I had to say it, Ellie. I need you to know that this..." he glances down briefly, his hand moving to rest over his heart, over the tattoo I'm still tracing, "It's real for me. *You're* real for me."

And somehow, that undoes me more than anything else could. Because he's not asking for reassurance. He's just giving me truth.

And in the silence that follows, I let it settle between us like something sacred. Something I'll carry with me until I'm ready to speak the words myself.

But he knows. And that, for now, is everything.

I press my hand to his chest, feeling the steady thump of his heart, and lean in to kiss the place where the tattoo rests on his skin. He exhales and dips his head to press a kiss to the crown of my head. It's feather-light, achingly tender.

Then, without a word, he reaches past me, grabs the shampoo bottle, and lathers a small pool in to his hands.

I reach for it too, but he gently nudges me back under the spray, fingers sliding into my hair with ease. He massages slow, deliberate circles into my scalp until my knees threaten to give out beneath me.

I melt into him completely, eyes drifting shut, the water coursing over my shoulders while his touch quiets everything else.

This tenderness I didn't know I could have.

I repay the favour, lathering his hair, running fingers along his scalp. He exhales, like I've taken the weight from his shoulders. My touches trail lower, slow, purposeful, tightening his jaw, darkening his eyes.

We don't rush.

We kiss beneath the spray, pressing open-mouthed kisses along throats, collarbones, the corners of mouths. My fingers draw patterns across his ribs; his thumb strokes my jaw, holding me close.

Then he shifts.

His body presses me gently against the tile, hand braced beside my head, fingertips skimming my waist.

"Still with me, Carter?" he murmurs against my throat.

I can't speak. I only nod, dazed and desperate.

His mouth trails heat along my throat as his hand glides down my side, slow and sure. Then his knee nudges between mine, parting my thighs as he presses me back against the tile. The contrast of the cool against my hot skin makes me shiver.

My breath catches, sharp and wanting.

And then his fingers slip between my legs, sliding through the slick ache he's already coaxed from me. I gasp as his touch finds the spot that undoes me entirely.

He moves with devastating precision. Each stroke is slow and deliberate, like he's mapping me with intention, like he knows exactly what I need and isn't in any rush to give it all at once. His body cages mine, one arm braced beside my head, the other slipping between us, fingers seeking, sliding, curling. Every movement is pure purpose.

My head falls back, eyes squeezed shut, mouth parted on a sound I barely register. His fingers sink into me, hitting just right, and my pulse hammers in my ears, in my chest, between my legs.

He murmurs something, my name I think, but it's wrecked and low. Full of heat and restraint, like it's costing him to keep from breaking apart right along with me.

The tension builds fast and my leg locks around his hip, holding him there, grounding myself against the sheer force of what's coming. My nails rake across his shoulder, digging deep, and then I shatter.

Pleasure explodes inside me, white-hot and all-consuming, the climax crashing through me in wave after wave. I cry out, not caring how loud, not caring about anything except this. Him. The way he keeps his fingers moving, coaxing me through it, relentless and tender all at once.

Every nerve burns. Every breath is his.

And I come undone, completely and entirely, with nothing left to hide.

And then it's just us. His chest pressed to mine, steam curling around us, the only sound our ragged breathing and the quiet rush of water.

Forehead pressed to his shoulder, breathing ragged, we stand quietly, wrapped in steam and each other.

When we finally step out, limbs heavy and fingers like prunes, we're slow. Grinning, sleepy, and completely wrapped in each other.

I pull on one of his oversized t-shirts, breathing him in and he gives me that look, the one promising he's seconds from hauling me back to bed.

Instead, he grins, damp hair tousled. "Stay put. I'll make something."

"Something edible or coffee and leftover cereal?"

He points. "One, rude. Two, underestimating my culinary skills is offensive."

I arch a brow. "Right, because toast is gourmet."

"Gourmet is subjective," he calls back, heading for the kitchen. "Also, I make phenomenal toast. Even if it's dark around the edges."

I laugh softly, padding after him. The apartment filled with the faint warmth of last night, windows fogged from morning drizzle. He fills the kettle, movements casual, domestic.

This quiet side of him is addictive in a way I didn't expect.

When he sees me, something soft flickers in his expression.

"You okay?" he asks, voice low, gentle.

I nod, moving closer. "Yeah. Just… happy."

His smile is slow, tender. "Me too."

I slide onto one of the barstools, watching him rummage through the cupboards for coffee and something vaguely breakfast-adjacent. He's humming under his breath, and I let it wash over me like sunlight.

This is the version of him I never really got before. And it's addictive in a way I didn't expect.

He sets two mugs on the counter and spoons in the coffee. "Milk and sugar, right?"

I blink. "You remember that?"

His smile curves at the corner. "Course I do. You glared at me for ten straight minutes that time I brought it black."

"Because it tasted like regret."

He snorts. "Fair."

The kettle clicks off. He pours, passes me a mug with one hand while grabbing the bread with the other.

I take a sip and hum appreciatively. "Okay, I take it back. You might actually have some domestic skills."

"Don't let the lads hear you say that," he says, popping slices into the toaster. "It'll ruin my reputation."

I rest my chin in my hand, just… watching him. The way he moves around the kitchen like he's done this a hundred times. The way his hair falls into his eyes when he leans forward. The little frown he gets when he concentrates on something as simple as buttering toast.

He feels like peace.

Kieran hands me a plate with two golden slices. Miraculously not burned.

"I'm officially impressed," I murmur, taking a bite. "Didn't think you had it in you."

He leans on the counter opposite, sipping his coffee. "Just wait till I make you scrambled eggs sometime. That's where the real romance happens."

"Oh wow," I say, deadpan. "How will I ever recover?"

He flashes a grin. "You won't."

The toast disappears faster than I'd like to admit, mostly because Kieran keeps watching me over his mug like he's already planning our next round in bed. His smile is lazy, satisfied, and a little smug. But there's warmth behind it, too.

"Don't look at me like that," I murmur, licking butter off my thumb.

"Like what?" he asks, setting his mug down.

"Like you're trying to decide if I'm breakfast or dessert."

He shrugs, utterly unrepentant. "Bit of both, probably."

I roll my eyes, but my cheeks flush. Heat curls low in my stomach again. "You're impossible."

"And you're stunning. Especially in my t-shirt."

"Charmer."

Kieran steps around the counter, arms sliding around my waist, chin resting on my shoulder. "You say that like I'm not completely and hopelessly into you."

I lean back into his chest, our coffee mugs forgotten on the counter, the hum of the city filtering in through fogged-up windows like background music. His heartbeat is steady against my back.

I could stay like this. I want to.

But eventually, reality calls.

"I should get going," I murmur, glancing at the clock. "Mia will be up soon. And Brenda's no doubt already fed her enough sugar to fuel a small army."

Kieran sighs against my shoulder. "Right. Responsible parenting. Got it."

I laugh under my breath, then kiss him softly. Like a promise.

"I'll see you soon, yeah?" I whisper.

"You'd better."

He kisses me again like we're trying to etch this moment into something permanent.

And maybe we are. Maybe we already have.

I pull back slightly, just enough to see him properly. His eyes are soft, full of open affection and quiet heat, and I swear I could fall into them if I wasn't already halfway there.

"This..." I say, brushing my fingers along his jaw. "Was everything."

His brows lift, like he wasn't expecting that.

I smile. "Everything and more. I didn't even know I could feel like this again."

He swallows, the words hitting somewhere deep.

"And I know we've still got things to figure out. Life stuff. Complicated stuff. But last night... and this morning..." I pause, then say it. "I'll hold onto it. No matter what happens next."

Kieran doesn't speak right away. His thumb just strokes slow, steady circles against my hip.

Then, quietly, he says. "You've got all of me, Ellie. You always will."

My breath catches as I look at him. "Always, huh?"

"Since the second you gave me five minutes," he says softly. "To the last breath I've got to give."

My thumb grazes his cheek. "You only needed five minutes," she murmurs. "But I think I'll give you forever."

Kieran exhales like she's just knocked the wind out of him. His voice is rough when he speaks. "Then I'll spend forever making it worth it."

No smirk this time. No tease. Just truth.

He pulls me in, and I go without hesitation, burying my face into his shoulder, the beat of his heart loud against my cheek.

I laugh under my breath, blinking back the sting in my eyes. "God, I'm so glad you were an idiot with that beer bottle."

He grins. "The most productive injury of my life."

I release myself from his embrace and grab my bag, take a deep breath, and head for the door. But before I step out, I glance back one last time.

He smirks. "You going home in my t-shirt, Carter?"

I raise a brow. "Well, you didn't exactly hand me back my dress after you peeled it off."

He grins. "Guess that means it's mine now."

"Possession is nine-tenths of the law," I say, backing toward the door with a smug little shrug.

His eyes darken just a shade. "So's temptation."

My stomach flips.

And as I turn and slip out the door, the grin still playing on his mouth stays with me, along with the quiet heat of his gaze, and the feel of his t-shirt brushing my thighs like a promise I'll be wearing all the way home.

The taxi ride to Brenda's is quiet. Not the heavy kind, just soft. Easy. My head's full of last night, my fingers still curled into the hem of Kieran's t-shirt like it might slip away if I don't hold on tight. I can still feel his breath on the back of my neck, his mouth on my shoulder. Still hear the low rasp of his voice when he whispered *"look at me, baby"* like I was something sacred.

It almost doesn't feel real.

But the ache in my legs says otherwise.

We pull up outside Brenda's, and Mia's already on the driveway, standing with a bag of popcorn in one hand and a sparkly cardigan slipping off one shoulder like she's just walked out of a tween magazine shoot. She spots me through the window and lights up.

I barely get the door open before she launches herself into a hug.

"You smell weird," she mumbles into my coat. "Like shampoo. And perfume. And…" she leans back, nose scrunching. "Is that boy?"

Brenda laughs from the porch, arms folded and clearly enjoying herself. "Told you she'd say something."

Mia grins. "I've been dying to ask since I woke up."

"Rude," I mutter, hugging her tighter. "Absolutely correct. But rude."

Mia skips off toward the taxi like it's a red-carpet moment, and Brenda steps in to give me a proper squeeze, the kind that says *I've got you* with no need to spell it out.

"You alright, love?" she murmurs near my ear.

I nod. "More than alright."

Brenda pulls back just enough to give me a once-over. "That shirt's not yours."

I smirk. "Nope."

"And you're glowing."

I snort. "Shut up."

She winks. "Good. It's about bloody time."

The drive home is short. Mia hums softly beside me, tapping something out on her phone, her glittery cardigan sliding halfway off her shoulder. She looks relaxed. Happy. Like a girl who's had popcorn and fizzy drinks and permission to stay up too late.

"Brenda gave me waffles for dinner," she says as we turn onto our street. "With ice cream."

I glance at her through the mirror. "Rebel."

Then I glance again at her profile this time, and my heart stretches in that strange, achy way it always does when I'm not expecting it. This ease, this safety, it's all I've ever wanted for her. For us.

Mia bolts up the path with the key already in hand. She lets us in with a satisfied little click, kicks off her shoes in the hallway, and heads straight upstairs to her bedroom, already on the phone with Claire.

I lean down to gather the stack of post that's been shoved halfway through the letterbox. Most of it's boring. Flyers, something from the GP surgery, a letter from the council. I scoop it up as I walk toward the hallway, sorting with one hand while reaching for my bag with the other.

Then my eyes catch on an envelope.

Plain. White. Heavier than the rest. My name and David's printed in neat, generic type through a plastic window. No logo. No frills. No colour.

My stomach tightens.

The paper crackles slightly as I turn it over and slip my finger under the flap. The edges are crisp beneath my nails. I'm still standing in the middle of the hallway, bag sliding off my shoulder, when the words land.

I read it once. Then again. And again.

Then everything inside me stills.

Repossession.

The word punches through me like a fist. Every syllable, loud and cruel and final. Missed payments. Multiple attempts to contact us. Formal proceedings are already in motion.

I blink.

It doesn't make sense.

My grip tightens around the paper. My eyes track the dates again. And again. And again.

My knees buckle.

I slide down the wall, the letter still clutched in my hand, an icy dread blooming in my chest. I don't cry. I don't even make a sound. I just sit there and let it take me. Let the weight of it press down in waves. Tight and suffocating. One breath at a time. One second after the next.

Behind me, Mia's voice drifts in from the kitchen. How did she even get there?

"Mum? We're out of digestives, can I have toast?"

I can't answer. I can't move.

This can't be happening.

It's a mistake.

It has to be.

I press the letter to my chest, trying to breathe through the crushing tightness. It feels like drowning in shallow water, like I'm gasping just beneath the surface, and the surface keeps rising.

I thought I was finally getting a grip on my life. Thought I was healing.

But it turns out I've been living in a house already half in ruin.

And the cracks I couldn't see?

They're about to split everything wide open.

But even now. When everything's shifting, when the cracks are showing, and when the future feels like a question I can't yet answer...

Somehow, it's still you.

END OF BOOK ONE : Ellie + Kieran's story will continue in Book 2: "Still It's You"

acknowledgments

This story has my heart.

It's the most personal thing I've ever written, because at its core, it's stitched with pieces of me. Writing this book meant revisiting the hardest, softest, rawest parts of myself. It meant healing wounds I didn't know still needed tending. And for that reason, I want to start by thanking Ellie.

Ellie, my girl, thank you. For letting me tell my story through yours. For carrying the weight of my memories and the ache of what-ifs. You're fictional, yes, but you are so real to me. You were brave when I couldn't be, and gentle when I didn't know how to be. I hope readers find pieces of themselves in you, and I hope those pieces feel seen and held.

To my mum and dad. While Ellie didn't have the most supportive parents, I was lucky enough to have the exact opposite. Mum, you were my rock through teen pregnancy, and I truly don't know how I would've made it through without you. You didn't just support me, you carried me. You never made me feel like I'd failed, even when I felt like the world was watching and waiting for me to. Dad, thank you for being steady and sure, for being proud of me even when I wasn't proud of myself. I'm endlessly grateful that I got to write a story where I could imagine the opposite. Because I know how lucky I was to have you both.

To my husband. My best friend, my anchor, my forever person. You taught me that I was enough exactly as I am. You made me believe I was worthy of love, of softness, of safety. Thank you for loving me through the chaos of first drafts and deadline panic, for bringing me cups of tea when I was too deep in a scene to move, and for not mentioning the growing laundry pile. Thank you for making me laugh, and for giving me space to dream. This book exists because you let me chase it.

To Jennie, my soul sister and hype woman. You read every chapter as I wrote it, squealed over scenes like they were gossip, and loved Ellie and Kieran with a passion that matched mine. Thank you for the playlists, the TikToks, the late-night voice notes, and the way you always seemed to know exactly what I needed to hear. I'd be lost without your friendship—and this book would've been a lonelier process without you beside me.

To my beta readers and street team, thank you for jumping into this world with both feet. Your early reads, your thoughtful feedback, your enthusiasm and kindness. I genuinely don't have the words to express what it meant to me. You helped shape this story into something better than I could've created alone, and I'll never forget it.

To Laura, thank you for answering all my questions and giving me endless amounts of advice and feedback. I felt like I was winging it the whole way (ok, I was winging it the whole way), but you made everything feel a bit more possible.

And finally, to you, the reader. Thank you for choosing this book. For choosing Ellie. For giving your time, your energy, and your heart to something I poured mine into. I hope this story leaves you breathless. I hope it gives you hope. I hope it reminds you that love is worth the risk, even after the fall. And that sometimes, the best kind of love is the one that finds you when you least expect it, but need it most.

about the author

Samantha is a full-time NHS nurse, a proud Yorkshire lass, wife to her soulmate, and mum to a teenager who keeps her on her toes. She's been a lifelong bookworm with a not-so-secret dream of writing a novel. Though, by her own admission, she never quite believed she'd actually do it. And yet, here she is, doing the damn thing.

Romance is where her heart truly lives. Samantha writes slow-burn, emotional love stories layered with angst, warmth, and the kind of characters who feel like they could walk straight off the page and into your life. Her debut novel, Somehow Still You, is the first in the Reverie Boys series, a project that's been nothing short of a labour of love. She's poured her heart, soul, and probably a fair amount of Yorkshire tea into these characters.

Her greatest hope? That readers fall for them just as hard as she has. If you're up for a chat, a behind-the-scenes look at her writing life, or a solid bookish ramble, you'll find her hanging out on Instagram. She'd absolutely love to say hi.

instagram.com/samanthaannewrites
tiktok.com/@samanthaannewrites
threads.com/@samanthaannewrites

Printed in Dunstable, United Kingdom

77849058R00255